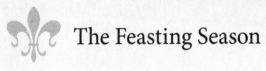 The Feasting Season

The Feasting Season

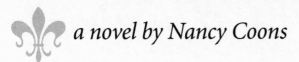 *a novel by Nancy Coons*

Algonquin Books of Chapel Hill | 2007

Published by
ALGONQUIN BOOKS OF CHAPEL HILL
Post Office Box 2225
Chapel Hill, North Carolina 27515-2225

a division of
Workman Publishing
225 Varick Street
New York, New York 10014

Design by April Leidig-Higgins

"J'ai mordu dans le fruit," words and music by Charles Trenet, © 1955, Éditions Raoul Breton. *Antigone,* by Jean Anouilh, © Éditions de la Table Ronde, 1946. *The Letters of Vincent Van Gogh,* translation Constable & Robinson Ltd., © 1926–1929.

This is a work of fiction. While, as in all fiction, the literary perceptions and insights are based on experience, all names, characters, places, and incidents either are products of the author's imagination or are used fictitiously.

Library of Congress Cataloging-in-Publication Data
  Coons, Nancy.
    The feasting season : a novel / by Nancy Coons. — 1st. ed.
      p. cm.
    ISBN-13: 978-1-56512-519-3
    1. Women authors — Fiction.   2. France — Fiction.   I. Title.
    PS3603.O5817F43 2007
    813'.6 — dc22   2006028420

10 9 8 7 6 5 4 3 2 1
First Edition

Acknowledgments

Warm thanks to Christine Engelberg for listening and believing; Chris and La Vigar for providing inspiring refuge and rugby tips; Barbara Hall, Jacqueline Fleming, and Kris Landsverk for early feedback; Philippa Seymour for horsey stuff; Jerome Calandre for wine details; Anne-Claire Katgely for tweaking Meg's French and Graeme Curry for tweaking Nigel's English; and most of all to Mark, Elodie, and Alice, for whom these imaginary characters have become part of our family.

Special thanks to my agent, Wendy Weil, for championing this book and to Andra Olenik at Algonquin for getting it.

Despite its setting in contemporary France, which I have covered for years as a food and travel writer, this is a work of fiction. It is neither a guidebook nor a reportage, and above all it is not a roman à clef. It is simply an *histoire*, a story, in which only *la belle France* plays herself, a country so *folklorique*, so *romanesque*, that she needs no embellishment.

—NC

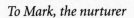

To Mark, the nurturer

Thus do I pine and surfeit day by day,
Or gluttoning on all, or all away.

—William Shakespeare, Sonnet 75

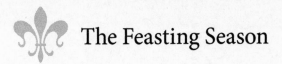 The Feasting Season

Ma LA VIE EN FRANCE

1 🏵 The War Room

à: meg.parker@francetel.fr
de: nikos.petras@nytravpub.net

hey meg—Publisher launching new travel series. upscale, hardcover,
four-color photography. adventure angle. suggested you for France (of
course). interested?
—nikos
p.s. need page proofs ASAP

Friday, February 7, 5 AM: There are page proofs stuck to my cheek. My
neck is cramped and I can hardly lift my head. Oh god. Fell asleep at the
desk again. The screen of my computer glows blue. Sleep mode. I sit up
and rub my face with both hands. The lights in my bunker are still on.
It's chilly down here. The electric heater soughs quietly at my feet but it
doesn't make a dent in two-hundred-year-old damp.

A fruit cellar is a funny place for a home office. The cross-vaults peel
with greying plaster, the flagstones gleam with condensation. Only the
walls feel welcoming. They are covered, every inch of them, with the history of France. Prints and etchings and old photographs. De Gaulle in a
képi. Napoleon on horseback. Vercingétorix, mustachioed and raising a
shield before the armies of Caesar. My grandfather in his Seventh Army
uniform, captain's bars on his shoulders.

I pull that same jacket around my shoulders and shiver. It was the
Lapeyres' rooster that woke me up. French roosters don't sleep any later
than American ones.

I roll back the chair and head for the metal ladder that leads up into
the barn and my home, where my family lies sleeping.

Then I stop. Right. That's why I snuck down here last night in my nightgown. Page proofs for Nikos. Captions to write. Another bread-and-butter guidebook. Then another textbook to finish—*La Vie en France, Level Two.*

I turn back, tap a key, and the screen awakens. Nikos' e-mail. I sigh and hit Print.

The printer whirs and chatters and spits paper onto my lap. My equipment doesn't quite fit down here. Phone. Fax. The floor is a snake pit of twisting cables that lead up the wall and out the ventilation slat. Strange that we have cable internet here in Dampierre-lès-Vaucouleurs. We don't even have sewers yet. A caged work light hangs from a rusted meathook. There are no windows, of course. The laptop is my window on the world.

I open the file I was working on. Oh god. Still have to dig up these statistics.

> *La Vie en France, Level Two*
> *The French place greater emphasis on good food than any culture in the world, investing xx euros per capita every year in ingredients and xx hours per week on the preparation and enjoyment of meals. Expectations of quality are high, even in daily life.*

I sigh and type the new section.

DIALOGUE

Practice this with the cassette, taking care to distinguish between your u's and ou's.
Pierre: Qu'est-ce qu'on mange aujourd'hui, Maman?
 What's for dinner today, Mom?
Francine: Il y a du pâté de lapin aux pruneaux.
 There's rabbit pâté with prunes.
Pierre: J'adore le pâté de lapin aux pruneaux.
 I love rabbit pâté with prunes.
Francine: Ensuite il y a des moules marinière.
 Then there are mussels in white wine.
Pierre: J'aime moins les moules marinière.
 I don't like mussels in white wine as much.

Gibbon it's not. This is all I write these days. The bookcases are thick with dust. They sag with Froissart, Diderot, Castelot, Durant, Caesar's *Gallic Wars*. They're propped up with my brass artillery shells from Verdun and chunks of shrapnel from the Libération when Patton's Third Army rolled through my garden. There's a pith helmet next to the Foreign Legion képi, a tasseled fez, a thick-embroidered chasuble. The history books—287 of them, if Lytton Strachey counts—are just a collection, really. Only the dictionaries get much use these days.

I tap Save, push back my chair again, and head for the ladder, running my fingers over my diploma as I pass. The tips come up grey. Notre Dame, Indiana. Certificates from Trinity College, Cambridge, and the Sorbonne. They're carefully and expensively framed, a youthful pat on my own back. Not that anyone's seen them in ten years but me. Nigel never ventures down here. I hang the army jacket on its hook, next to a tangle of barbed wire I clipped in a forest on the Maginot Line. Then I climb the ladder and push up the trap door.

It is raining, as usual, in Lorraine. The barn, cathedral-vast, echoes with the pounding of water on the roof. I push on into the house and creak up the stairs. A soft, inhabited silence permeates the bedrooms—the regular breathing of the children, the muffled snores of Nigel, the ticking of four alarm clocks. I hear a thumping sound in our room. Gerald, our Irish setter, is thwacking his tail on the four-poster bed from his spot—my spot—beside Nigel. I lift the down quilt and shove him gently to the foot of the bed. He settles happily, licking his lips, sighs, and goes back to sleep. Nigel's long body, swaddled in flannel, is warm. I put my cold feet against his legs. He turns over onto his back and looses a wrenching snore.

I sink into my groove in the mattress. The tail is thumping again. Now why? I peek out from under the quilt. In the growing twilight I can just make out a form. It is Cloey, looming in half sleep by the bedstand, his Lucky Luke pajamas buttoned up wrong. I raise the quilt and he tunnels under, nuzzling my breasts, even at three the old nursing reflex half-remembered in a dream. I turn him gently and spoon him against my belly, breathing in his sourdough scent. His pajamas feel strangely hot against me, then strangely cool. I lift the quilt again and feel clammy wetness spread across the mattress.

Oh god. I will not be going back to sleep this morning. I extricate myself from the tangle of limbs and scramble to my feet. A rag. A rag. Tiptoeing through the bedroom door I collide with Kate. She is barefoot, her too-small nightie gapping above gangly wrists and pony legs. They grow so fast when they're five.

"*Maman?*" she whispers. "I had a bad dream. *Je peux dormir avec toi?*"

I kiss her damp forehead and brush sticky straggles of hair from her eyes. "No, honey, get back into your own bed. It's almost time to get up anyway."

I guide her across the hall to her room, where the nightlight casts bizarre shadows across a minefield of toys and books. She is asleep again before I can kiss her cheek.

Then I duck into the bathroom, pull open the casement windows, push open the shutters and lean out over the back orchard. I want to breathe deep. Rain drops a solid wall between me and the pewter sky.

I strip off my ammoniac nightgown. Nikos' e-mail flutters to the floor.

travel
adventure
interested?

I climb into the shower and turn the water on hard.

8 AM: Nigel is sitting at the breakfast table reading yesterday's *Telegraph;* he will bring home this morning's edition, imported from England, tonight. Without looking he lifts his tea to his lips and sips from time to time. Her Royal Highness (or is it "Her Majesty"?) smiles coyly from the mug his brother Colin gave him on Boxing Day last year. Colin was joking. With Nigel you never can tell.

"Smarmy git," he mutters.

I look up from the other side of the table, where I'm helping Cloey mix cocoa powder into his bowl of milk. I don't think he's referring to the Queen. Nigel doesn't explain. When he turns the page and folds it back I see the face of the prime minister. Oh. That smarmy git.

Kate is dipping Nutella-smeared bread in her bowl of hot chocolate. "What is a git, Papa?"

"Anyone thick enough to believe 'Labour' could be 'New.'" His eyes never leave the page.

"Nigel..."

He lowers his paper. His orange hair is combed straight back and ironclad with gel. The shade of it—brows and lashes, too—is an exact match to Kate's and Cloey's. So is his translucent white skin. Their opaline pallor surrounds me, ghostly and pure and somehow vulnerable, as if the light over the table could sear through their skin.

"Sorry, love. A git is an ass. A fool. A nitwit. Three letters. G-I-T. Good word, really."

"Nigel." I can't catch his eye.

Kate regards him with his own ice-blue eyes, then ducks her face toward her bowl. Her English is already weak. Nigel isn't helping.

He turns the page and folds back the crossword. "Seven letters. 'Juggernaut, avatar.'" He studies the ceiling beams, abstracted. Then he brightens. Too bright. "Am-er-i-ca! Bugger. Starts with 'k.'"

I hide my face in my bowl of coffee.

Cloey does the same, gripping with two plump hands, but goes too far and the bowl spills over him, crashing to the slate-flagged floor.

"Clovis!"

"Oh-oh."

There follows a familiar ballet. Nigel leaps up to protect his trousers, knocking down the ladder-back chair; Gerald rockets from his bed by the Aga, shoving Kate aside; her Nutella tartine frisbees through the air and lands face down; Cloey rises and stands on his chair; Kate dissolves in silent tears.

I am on my feet too. A rag. A rag.

But I don't need one. Gerald has hoovered down the tartine and is lapping up the cocoa with his tongue.

"That's it, that's it! Katharine honey, you're fine. Everybody upstairs. Shoes! School bags! Snacks! Hup, two! March!"

Nigel reaches across Gerald for his mug of tea and stands, crossword in hand. "'Krish-na.'"

"Nigel."

"Hmm?"

"Oh, never mind." I stoop and gather up the pieces of broken crockery myself.

8:30 AM: I have cleaned and changed Cloey, bundled him into anorak and sock-monkey backpack, and trundled him onto the school bus. At the age of three and a half he has already commuted to the local public nursery school for a year and he climbs onto the high bus step with barely a backward glance. I have braided Kate's ponytail and zipped her into her Tintin jacket and pried her pink plastic ponies from her fingers. I buckle her into the back seat of Nigel's Rover and kiss her cheek.

I huddle against the rain beside Nigel's door. Driver's seat on the right, a point of defiant pride. He rolls down the window and busses my cheek with bowed lips.

"Bye, love." He pats my shoulder. A woolen scarf perches over his collar and I finger it gently. It is, I know, his nod to the Continent, a dash of Latin derring-do. After ten years in France he still dresses in head-to-toe caricature of the British Middle Class, from his leather-buttoned waistcoat down to the lead-weight brown Churches. I reach to stroke his hair but stop myself; I might crack it.

"I'll ring you at lunchtime, darling." He starts the engine.

"Don't forget tomorrow night. Dinner. The Chevalots. The Heritiers."

"And Andrew and Brenda?"

"Right. Of course." As always.

He throws the Rover into reverse. I waggle fingers and wrinkle my nose at Kate as the windshield blanks over with the reflected sky.

9 AM: Alone at last.

I walk straight past the kitchen mess and climb down to the bunker. I slip on my grandfather's moth-eaten jacket. I open Nikos' e-mail.

adventure angle
photography
france
interested?

My fingers hover over the keyboard. Interested. But I sigh and pull out the page proofs to *Hit the Road with Roadies*.

> *This delightful little country inn outside the village center offers cozy rooms neatly furnished in charming Louis XVI reproductions.*

I erase.

> *This charming little country inn outside the village center offers delightful rooms cozily furnished in neat Louis XVI reproductions.*

Or is it Louis XV? Must look up.

Napoleon glowers at me.

4 PM: I'm back on *La Vie en France, Level Two.*

> *France has one of the most advanced early education systems in the world, providing full-time schooling, nine to five, for children from the age of two years. The only requirement is that they be toilet trained.*

DIALOGUE

> *Francine: Lève toi, mon chéri. Tu vas encore rater le bus.*
>
> Get up, honey. You'll miss the bus again.
>
> *Pierre: Mais Maman, laisse moi dormir.*
>
> But Mama, let me sleep.
>
> *Francine: Tu dois aller à l'école.*
>
> You have to go to school.
>
> *Pierre: Je veux jouer.*
>
> I want to play.
>
> *Francine: Tu veux rester bête toute ta vie? Il faut y aller!*
>
> Do you want to grow up stupid? Get going!

The phone rings and I start.

"Megs darling? Just got back from lunch with Andrew. He's working on the drawings now. Needs the dimensions. I don't suppose you could nip out and . . . ?"

"Nigel, I'm in the middle of work right now."

"Right. Of course. 'Work.' "

"Can't we do it over the weekend?"

"Right then."

The conservatory. Another British import, copied eagerly from the back pages of *Country Living* and *Hill and Dale*. Nigel is obsessed with the idea of glass-encased hothouses soaking in soft light overlooking the Sussex Downs. It's just that this isn't Sussex. Here in Lorraine a glass-bubble sunporch will splatter with clay and draw hailstones instead of sun. I've tried to talk him out of it but he and Andrew just keep moving ahead.

I reach for my coffee mug and swallow cold dregs.

5:20 PM: I am reading proofs when the doorbell rings over my head. I look at my watch. Not again. I forgot to meet the school bus. I clamber up the ladder and open the front door. Fabienne Lapeyre, our neighbor, is standing on the welcome mat, Cloey drooping on her hip, Kate clinging to her left hand.

"Busy, are we?"

She takes me in head to toe. She is wearing spotless white with gold stiletto sandals despite the February drizzle. I am wearing sweatpants and a paint-stained t-shirt under the army jacket. There is a pen jammed through my twisted hair and I am wearing no makeup. Have I brushed my teeth today?

"*Salut!*" I peck her on both cheeks, holding my breath in case I'm right about not brushing. I smile and shrug. "Just another deadline!" I reach my arms out for Cloey, who turns his head into Fabienne's neck. Kate regards me. I kneel and push her matted hair off her face, tucking it behind her ear.

I glance up at Fabienne. "Time for a quick cup of coffee?"

Oh god. The kitchen.

Fabienne, like most of the women in this blue-collar farm village, is perfect. She works as a cashier in the nearest Hyper-Shoppe, has four kids, and helps run the family farm up the road. Before I've made the breakfast coffee her clothesline flaps with freshly washed laundry, windows flung wide for the daily cleaning. Every morning she parades her troupe of immaculate goslings to the bus stop. Every noon she roars back home from work and the odors of a hot, meaty dinner float from the roof fan.

"*Non, merci!*"

I breathe. "Well, thanks for bailing me out with the kids—again."

She pours Cloey into my arms and minces down the muddy cobblestones. "That's okay. They're used to it."

I search out Kate's hand and draw my children into the house. It is very dark. I really meant to tidy up, throw some logs in the kitchen fireplace, have cocoa standing by. I trot around, turning on lights. This morning's breakfast dishes are still on the table. I was so anxious to get to my bunker.

Gerald materializes outside the kitchen door, grinning ingratiatingly, tongue dragging long over black lips. His auburn fur is plastered with mud, his ears are matted with burrs. I reach for a rag, put out a defensive hand, and pull the handle. He barrels across the floor and tackles Cloey, who screams in delight. Kate falls on top of them. It feels good to laugh.

I tie on my apron, its pockets still encrusted from last week's breadbaking binge, pour hot milk and cocoa into a saucepan, and take on the mess.

7 PM: Oak logs flare and crackle in the fireplace. Herbs from the garden lie on the chopping board. A garlicky chicken sputters in the Aga, where Gerald's wet rags steam on the chrome rail. I lean into the cream-enameled warmth and smile. The four-oven Aga is one of Nigel's British imports that I actually love.

I look around. That's better. I have showered, brushed my teeth, and dressed for the day—well, for the evening—in my favorite fifties bowling shirt. So far, so good.

Cloey sits on the kitchen potty, his overalls around his ankles, studying Tintin *Le Temple du Soleil*. Gerald lies in his tartan-cushioned basket by the stove, legs spiking over the basket edge. His tail lifts.

Cloey beams. "Poot poot camembert!"

"Ooh Gerald you are *dégueulasse*, DISGUSTING!" Kate runs to throw her arms around his neck.

By the time I get back from the potty cleanup, Cloey has crawled into Gerald's basket and is snoozing happily. Kate has taken over the Tintin and leans against them both.

Rain machine-guns against the windows. It is dead black out and the wind is howling. I pull the curtains and turn my back on the darkness. Here, inside, the kitchen glows. The chicken crackles. I crouch by the basket and study my family in the chiaroscuro. They give off the scent of buttered toast. I close my eyes and breathe it deep. Kate reaches up absently and strokes my cheek, her thumb in her mouth.

I'm almost looking forward to Nigel's coming home.

The phone rings. I pick up and quickly hold it away from my ear. It's the roar of Le Lévrier, the city of Nancy's sports bar, dubbed The Hare and Hound by the ex-pats who have made it colonial headquarters.

"Megs darling?"

"Hi, Nigel."

"Just having a quick one with Simon and Andrew. Won't be long. Looking at sketches."

"But I've got a chicken in the . . ."

His hand is over the mouthpiece. He comes back. "Andrew sends his love."

I sigh. My mouth thins. "Do you know what time—"

There is a roar of male voices. The television volume goes up in the bar. "Sorry, darling. Home in a bit! Pass it! *Pass it out.* Bloody hell, Woodruff couldn't catch a—" There's a click.

Doesn't sound like they're looking at architectural drawings to me. I walk to the Aga and open the oven door. The chicken sputters angrily.

I rouse Cloey from the dog bed. Might as well eat. "Come on, sweetie. Garlic chicken tonight!" I lift it out of the oven and carve it for three.

Kate settles into her chair. Cloey kneels in his. I lay a leg on each of their plates and heap on a pile of roasted garlic pods. "*Ouay!*" Kate cries. "I love *l'ail.*"

I help Cloey squeeze the skin, smearing the paste on a chunk of bread, almond-smooth. Kate follows suit.

I smear a chunk for myself and pop it in my mouth. "Mmm," I murmur.

"Mmm," she murmurs. I close my eyes. They close their eyes, too.

"Food tastes better with your eyes closed," Kate pronounces.

"Mm. Absolutely." I smear another chunk. "With your eyes closed you really taste it. No distractions. All mouth."

"All mouth." Cloey wipes his lips.

We eat in happy silence.

"You cook different from Papa." Kate pops a snow pea into her mouth and closes her eyes.

"I do."

9 PM: The children are asleep. I have poured myself a glass of wine and curled up on the daybed, shoving the heap of *Hill and Dale*s aside. Gerald's narrow head lies on my lap and when I stroke it he sighs with wheezy contentment. I stare into the fire.

Damned conservatory. Glass bubble. It's Nigel who lives in a glass bubble. Ten years in France and he spends every day of his life in Britain, reading British papers, working with British colleagues, drinking British ale and tea. The Sky satellite dish protects him from foreign news. The wine cellar is stacked with third- and fourth-growth Bordeaux but he still calls them "claret." We've yet to have a dinner party where the conversation stays in French, though he speaks it fluently. His mind ticks away in English, cracking crossword clues, playing the Shakespeare game.

I smile just a little. That's how he got to me, back in Cambridge. I was twenty. I had barely made my way off the plane from O'Hare and was sitting in a pub on Bridge Street, trying to look like a native. I wasn't doing a very good job. I sat at a sticky plank table, alone, trying to catch the bartender's eye with my best midwestern smile. After half an hour I was still drinkless. A very tall form in tweed detached itself from a darts game and came over to me.

"They won't come to you, my dear, you have to go to them."

"Oh." I blushed. "Thanks." I took in his pallor, orange hair that flopped into his eyes. Older. Thirty at least. His voice was gentle. His accent was to die for.

"What are you drinking?" He studied me down his nose, tossing his hair aside.

"Oh. Um, a pint of—of—" I peer desperately at the arsenal of taps bristling over the bar.

"Want to taste the ale? Real ale. Make it here. Rather nice. A sight better than your Budweiser."

Was it really that obvious? I hadn't even spoken a full sentence yet.

"Yes. Please. Thank you."

He came back from the bar, two slope-sided pints of amber in his hands, and cocked his head at the seat across from me, eyebrows questioning.

"Yes! Sure! Please! Thank you!"

He folded his long form into the spindle-back chair. "Nigel Thorpe, by the way."

"Meg Parker!" I sat up and thrust out a chilly hand. It took him by surprise. He received it with a light shake and a curious smile. I pulled it back and gripped the glass with two hands.

"Well. Cheers!" I took a deep swig. The ale was warm as spit and flat as a week-old Coke, with mangy flecks of foam on top where the head should be. I winced despite myself.

He had drained his by a third already. "Would you rather have something else? A cider perhaps?"

"No. No. This is good. Good."

His smile gave me the lie. "You're here to study?"

"At Trinity. A scholarship."

He nodded his homage. "Well done, you."

"Thanks!" I beamed, then blushed and buried my face in the pint. It tasted better this time.

"Subject? Speciality?"

"History. French history. And French of course. And Latin."

"Alors, vous êtes connaisseur des langues."

My head snapped up. Connais-*seuse*, I thought. I smiled. *"Un peu. Vous aussi?"*

" 'I shall never move thee in French unless it be to laugh at me.' "

I shake my head, puzzled.

"Henry the Fifth. Summer Shakespeare at John's."

"Who's John?"

"St. John's College. Amateur stuff. Been doing it for years. It's good fun. This one's been in rehearsal since June. As a matter of fact, I've got one in half an hour. Couldn't convince you to come have a listen, could I? There are French bits. You might have suggestions." His chair was sliding back. "How in god's name did you learn French in . . . ?"

"Indiana. My grandmother was French. She wouldn't speak English with me." I was following him out the door.

I saw him almost daily for a month. He took me to the right bookshops. He met me outside Judge's, the business school where he was "brushing up for Barclays," he said. He took me out for curries and shepherd's pie. He led me up the ladders and stairs to the roof of the Wren Library and we looked out over the Backs, the Cam sparkling in the September moonlight. He poled a rented punt under bridges, past Gothic tracery and Jacobean chimneys and Norman stone. He never touched me except to guide my elbow around darting bicycles, ease me out of the path of double-decker buses hurtling up the wrong side of the street.

Then came the performance of *Henry V.* I sat in the boxwood-lined gardens of St. John's, bundled in wool, a plaid blanket over my lap. He was in makeup with a hammered-tin crown and steam came off him in the spotlights. When he acted his body was stiff but his voice rang true, relishing the words, savoring them, making them his own.

> *If thou would have such a one, take me;*
> *and take me, take a soldier;*
> *take a soldier, take a king.*

When he kissed Fair Katharine, I felt a pang. I needn't have.

At the cast party he was more loose-limbed and exuberant than on stage, shirt open, his neck still smeared with greasepaint. His hair flopped wet into his eyes. He had already drunk a lot and when I threaded my way to him through a knot of actors—Gloucester, Exeter, Bedford, now in jeans—he swept me into his arms and gave me a very theatrical kiss.

His hands slid over my back, his mouth moved to my ear. " 'You have witchcraft in your lips, Kate.' "

10 PM: I pour myself another glass of wine. Gerald thumps his tail absently. His eyes open blearily, then roll shut. They are very close together, filling the space where his forehead should be. Where his brain should be, Nigel says.

When I graduated from Notre Dame, I didn't move to Cambridge, though Nigel had been "ringing me" and writing letters no boy in Indiana could touch. I went to Paris. Every summer break from college I'd made a Paris pilgrimage, sharing a crash pad with friends, marketing and cooking, tasting and eating, and, incidentally, doing summer coursework at the Sorbonne.

This time I rented alone. Nigel joined me weekends. I marketed. I cooked. Rabbit. Milk veal. Sweetbreads. Daubes. Anything I could manage on a two-burner hotplate. He ate, mouthfuls alternating with talk, talk of his successes, his new connections, his inroads at Barclays. We drank a lot of wine, after which he would start spouting *Henry V,* his hands sliding over me, me giggling against his chest.

It wasn't just me, the Shakespeare thing. It was a pub game he and Ian had devised as roommates, honing their wits after summer jaunts on the St. John's College stage.

"Loyalty."

Ian would throw the word down on the pub table like a gauntlet. Nigel would raise his glass to his lips, eyes probing the ceiling.

" 'To the last gasp with faith and loyalty.' "

" '*Truth* and loyalty.' "

"Right. 'Truth and loyalty.' "

"Fair enough. Dog, then."

I put down my cider. "That's easy. 'Let slip the dogs of war.' "

Nigel patted my shoulder. It's their game, not mine.

The Paris visits were more productive for Nigel than I realized. By the time I'd finished my summer courses, Nigel had been offered a transfer to France. He surprised me in the sublet that August, two years from the day we met, sweeping in the door with a bottle of Champagne in his hand and a wave of excitement around him.

"Paris! But that's—that's fantastic! You can—we can—" I looked around me at the chipped travertine. He was popping the cork and filling two jelly glasses.

"Yes. We can get better digs than this." He drained his glass. I did, too. He was smiling strangely at me. Suddenly his long form buckled and he was on one knee. " 'How answer you, la plus belle Marguerite de la Nouvelle Monde, mon très cher et devin déesse?' "

I laughed and laid my hand tenderly on his hair. He was wearing it gelled back hard by then. "*Du* Nouveau Monde. And your accent is terrible."

"Supposed to be. Henry's French *was* terrible."

"Yours isn't."

"Not as good as yours." He rose to his feet, rubbing his knee. "I need you here with me. We'll take France by *storm*. 'When France is mine and I am yours, then yours is France and you are mine.' "

I gave him my best midwestern smile. His cheeks were pink with triumph. I was conquered.

We took the Eurostar back to England and in the Cambridge Registry Office on Castle Hill he slipped the ring on my finger.

" 'Wilt thou have me?' "

We drove back with an Avis truck.

11 PM: I pour myself a third glass of wine. Gerald shifts, thumps his tail once.

Paris.

I look around me. This old farmhouse feels too big when the kids go to sleep. I think of the apartment Nigel and I rented together. Two rooms, one of them with a strip kitchen. Still, it had its charm. Black beams striping the sagging ceiling. Herringbone parquet hollowed from the weight of centuries of armoires. Two windows that opened over a carriage yard green with gingko and wisteria. Sirens, Klaxons, mobylettes blaring and buzzing beyond the gate.

"Bit on the pokey side but it'll have to do," Nigel said when he came up the stairs with a case of ale. "How they get away with eight hundred quid I don't know."

I loved it. I set up my new laptop on the dining table and resolved to write that book I'd been dreaming of. No more dry monographs on "Advancements in Archery Technology in the Hundred Years' War." I wanted to be Lytton Strachey. I wanted to tell the *story*. I had an outline, a title. *The Comeback Kid: Napoleon's Return from Elba.* My grandfather followed in his footsteps, landing at St-Raphaël in 1944 and pressing northward through the southern Alps. My grandfather. His French war bride. I wanted to weave the two tales together.

But I didn't. Nigel was transferred to set up a Nancy office in darkest Lorraine. I closed the lid on the laptop and followed. We bought the farmhouse. I had barely hung the wallpaper when Kate came along. Then freelance contracts came along, too. From publishers, not of monographs or history books, but scholastic textbooks. Guidebooks. Bread-and-butter work. We had a family to feed now.

That was when I claimed the fruit cellar, filling it with my history books and the military treasures that Nigel wouldn't allow upstairs. My bunker, he called it. I liked that.

Midnight: Nigel's headlights slash across the kitchen. I lay out a plate of chicken for him. The front door thuds and there is the clump of brogues. Gerald's tail thumps. I sit up on the daybed and smile.

"Hul-lo, what is that stench? Something Gerald dragged in?"

I stop smiling. "Sorry. It must be the garlic. I did garlic-roasted chicken, the one with the pods."

He makes his way to me for his evening kiss-and-pat, then veers away. "Good lord!"

"Sorry."

He fills a glass with ice.

"Aren't you hungry?" I hover my hand over my mouth.

"Had a bite."

"Oh. Okay." I clear up the dishes.

"D'you get those measurements for MacGregor?"

"No. I was working."

"Right. 'Working.'" He sips. He studies the ceiling beam. "'Work, work your thoughts and therein see a siege.'"

I clamp the lid down on the chicken and haul it to the fridge.

1 AM: I am shivering in my army jacket. Nikos' message glimmers on the screen.

> *interested?*

I tap Reply. I type:

> *Interested.*

I stare at the screen awhile, hands twisting in my lap. Then I hit Send.

2 ⚜ The Home Front

Saturday, February 8, 7 AM: I hate waiting for New York to wake up. Nikos won't come into the office for hours. He will eventually, though. He works on Saturdays. He works early, he works late. He's always working.

interested

I pace in my bunker, rubbing my arms. I study my walls. I dust off the faded color photo of my parents, with their overalls and matching ponytails. I blow grit off my nineteenth-century histories. The humidity isn't doing them any good, even with the silicone packs.

It isn't doing me any good either.

travel adventure france

8 AM: "Come on, sweetie, you'll miss the bus!" Kate has burrowed down under her duvet, ten blackened toes peeking out. There is a moan, then a waiting stillness.

"Three, two, one!" I grab the quilt and whisk it off. A wave of damp warmth rises and floats away, leaving Kate curled in the fetal position, her nightie around her waist, her bare legs bound to her chest.

"*Non!*" Her limbs spring out suddenly and she bolts for the bathroom.

Saturdays don't feel like Saturdays in France. There's something unnatural about hauling the children out of their warm nests and shoving them onto a school bus while the parents lounge around in their bathrobes. I have pulled on jeans and sweater but Nigel clearly has no intention of dressing. Or getting up.

"I thought the French adopted the word 'week-end,'" he grumbles from under the quilt.

10 AM: Nigel can stay in his British bubble. Today I am in France, and the farmers' market in Vaucouleurs is the highlight of my week. My Citroën DS is rolling down the *route départementale* on a cushion of air, past skeletal orchards, past rain ditches seething yellow, past pollard willows gnarled like fists. Lorraine may be bleak in February but this car makes my day. It's a 1972, one of the last, but its low-slung grace and cocktail-lounge comfort is pure fifties. Nigel bought it for me when we moved here. I still have the card in the glove compartment: *Une DS pour ma très chère déesse.* A Goddess for my very dear goddess. He regrets it now and winces when I roll up to his office in Nancy for a rare lunch in town. I don't care. Charles de Gaulle rode in one. What more could anyone ask for? Its bakelite knobs and *monobranche* steering wheel, its self-inflating suspension, its wide bucket seats, its sofa-scale banquette in back are the real thing. I slip a CD into the player I had installed—my only concession to modern times. Charles Trenet croons over the speakers.

J'ai mordu dans le fruit de la vie
Et depuis je suis mordu pour ça . . .

I've bitten into the fruit of life and now life's biting back. I smile.

The place du Marché is transformed, with trucks and trailers spanning over the square as far as I can see. I breathe deep. The scent of spit-roasting chicken fills my nostrils and my mouth waters. Eight for dinner! An excuse to buy a little of everything around me. And there is plenty. Card tables stacked with creamy cheeses, truck fronts hanging with dried pork sausages, terrines as big as baby tubs mounded with homemade pâté. Even in February there are vegetables on the farmers' tailgates—Brussels sprouts, beets, turnips, carrots, and cabbages blooming like great green flowers. It's okay to touch, to smell. I squeeze. I sniff. I taste and lick my fingers.

It's better than those summers in Paris. I have more people to cook for now. I think of my parents, raising their own organic vegetables on their back-to-the-earth farm in Indiana. I love the feel of raw materials, too . . . the heft of them, the scent of them, the *possibilities*. My basket is sagging already.

My favorite poultry farmer stands stamping in the cold and blowing on her hands behind a folding table. She beams at me with yellowed teeth.

"And what are you looking for today?"

"It depends." I smile. "What have you got?"

possibilities

She opens a plastic cooler under the table and fishes out a carcass. "Couple of guinea fowls, two good fat ones. Ducklings. And yesterday we killed the last *coq*." She heaves out a plucked rooster by its yellow claws, scarlet comb dangling toward the pavement.

I admire the limp body like a newborn grandchild. "How beautiful!" She clicks her tongue in admiration too.

Coq au vin. My French guests might be happily surprised. They seem to expect the worst when I cook—cheeseburgers? Hamburger Helper?—then flutter in shock at my simplest efforts. "*Quel Cordon Bleu!*" What a gourmet chef!

My menu falls into place. I ease the great brute into my basket and head for the fish truck for oysters, then to my favorite cheese lady. This morning's clouds have lifted. I am disproportionately happy.

12:30 PM: Not for long. Driving home down the poplar-lined highway, I tune into France Inter. A rich, reedy voice is pronouncing an opinion in portentous cadences.

"—typical self-regard parading as progressiveness. To impose untested agricultural technology on the world market is only the latest in a series of American slaps to the face of civilization . . ."

Oh god. The president does it again.

A second voice interrupts and the volume rises, each commentator cutting into the other's phrase. No matter. They couldn't agree more.

"—blindered to the increasing disdain of European peers—"

"—in the thrall of big business at the expense of the common good—"

Their eloquence knows no bounds.

1 PM: Nigel has microwaved fish fingers with ketchup, an effort that surpasses his usual cheese sandwiches, but not by much. Sometimes I think he does it on purpose, when I've been "off having adventures"—work, travel, the market, anything—and haven't served his lunch on time. I hoist my purchases onto the work island and kiss Cloey's head, Kate's cheek.

"Hullo, love," Nigel says. I present my lips to him for a peck. He veers away. "Potent stuff, garlic."

3 PM: The Le Creuset casserole sputters on the Aga, at its bottom a half-inch of goose fat rippling crystal-clear. I tie on an apron and swing the rooster onto the cutting board. I take careful aim. The cleaver sails through the air and chops off his head. *Whock!*

off having adventures

Whock! Off come the yellow feet.

smarmy git

I stretch the wings out and probe for the joint with a butcher knife. I twist the limbs off with a quick crunch of cartilage. My cleaver rises over my head and swings down like a guillotine. *Whock!*

"*Maman?*" Kate calls tentatively from upstairs. "What you doing?"

"Just chopping up the rooster for dinner, honey."

"Oh. Papa, she's just chopping up a rooster."

"Tell her to chop more quietly. She wakes up Cloey, we're buggered."

Gerald gives a low moan of longing from the iron-framed daybed. I pick up the ruby meat chunks one by one and lay them in the hot grease. Gerald's whine grows urgent. The fat hisses up furiously and spits at my arms. I pick up a thigh and aim for the last space in the pot.

Gerald, overcome, cannons off the daybed and tackles my leg in a frenzy of confused desires.

"No!" I scream and jerk away. My hand grasps wildly for support but finds the edge of the pot. A wave of hot grease washes over my hand.

For an instant I observe the sizzle from a curious distance, the same instant I have already snatched it away. Then I clutch my hand to my belly and double over. I peek at it. The pinkie and fourth finger are scarlet. A delicate cawl of white puffs over the knuckles. I feel blood pounding and flesh swelling and I reach for my wedding band and slide it off on a slick of goose grease. Not a moment too soon; the two fingers are fat and growing. They remind me of the fish fingers Nigel served us for lunch.

Gerald is wagging his tail and lapping up grease from the floor. The wedding band lies in my right palm and I study it briefly, detached. I have never taken it off before.

wilt thou have me?

I stuff it into the apron pocket and head for the sink.

6 PM: When I get back from Dr. Arnault's office, my left hand is mummified in gauze and pounding with pain. I open the oven with my right hand. The coq au vin simmers docilely in the cast-iron pot. Nigel had to heft it in for me. He stands hunched over the sink now, prodding a stubby knife into oyster joints, grimacing as the shell shatters.

"Bloody hell!" he sputters and turns the tap onto his palm, where a stigmata of blood has appeared. "Can't get the knife into the joint! How do you do it?"

"You have to cradle it in your palm. Cover your hand with a towel to protect it. Search for the muscle, it'll give!" I mime feeble knife twists in the air.

"Revolting things, oysters. Like something you'd find in a handkerchief. Can't we skip the starters?"

"You know we can't. They'll think I'm being—American!"

"You *are* American, darling. It's one of your more endearing charms. 'Tender, raw and young...'"

"But they expect me—they'd think I—" I glance around desperately. "Just leave them in the sink. I'll forget the gratin. We can eat them raw." Nigel winces. "Maybe Hervé can help."

He tosses the crumbling shell into the heap, wipes his hands on the apron. It is a Jackson Pollock of bread dough, rooster blood, and shattered oyster shell. I must remember to hide it before the guests come.

"Help me check the coq au vin?"

He opens the Aga and draws it out. It is melting into flavor. I fish the neckbone out of the wine-rich broth. The meat is falling off the vertebrae. I cradle it in my good hand, nibbling the bits of tender flesh, lapping up the drips, savoring the steam.

"Good lord. Are those *feet* in there?"

My eyes drift open. Yellow claws are floating in the juice. "Well. Yes. They help thicken the sauce."

Nigel shudders.

8 PM: The hooks and eyes on my vintage silk dress refuse to cooperate with one hand. I did manage to twist my limp hair up in a Deneuve *banane* but the pins slipped. I leave it down on my shoulders, stick in horn combs instead. I trace on red lipstick. Thirties, I think. Maginot. Charles Boyer. I check the mirror. The bandage spoils the effect but ... I shrug. I skip the perfume. The scent of garlic and wine sauce is floating up the stairs. That's all the smell I need.

The doorbell rings and Gerald looses a flak-attack of barks. Please don't wake Cloey, I pray silently. In high heels I ease my way down the stairs.

Nigel is guiding the guests into the open kitchen, dwarfed by a cellophane-swathed bouquet. There is a chorus of *"Saluts!"* I kiss cheeks right and left. Giselle pulls her mauve-lined lips carefully to the side. "We brought you something from the homeland!" She slips a bottle into my hands. It is Gallo Chardonnay. I swallow a sigh and smile bright thanks. Hervé kisses my cheeks in a cloud of cologne, then raises my bandaged hand in the air for all to see. "Did nobody tell you the war was over? You've already liberated us!"

Nadine and Thierry crowd around me for kisses. "A little something for you!" Thierry says and hands me a bottle of Southern Comfort.

I gasp weakly. "You shouldn't have!"

I feel Nigel towering behind me, the sweet scent of porto floating around fresh-shaved jowls. He is doing up the top hooks on my dress. "Looking very smart, darling," he whispers, lips so tight to my ear the hairs tickle inside. Oh dear, I think. I hope the others catch up on the aperitifs.

The door bursts open and Andrew and Brenda MacGregor bustle through. "Heard you laughing so we let ourselves in!" Brenda pulls off an Andes-Indian cap and shakes loose a limp cascade of grey hair. "Hullo there, Maggie dear, looking chilly tonight!" She scuffs firm hands up and down my bare arms and plants a whiskery kiss on my cheek. "Never mind. Whatever that *lovely* smell is coming from the cooker should warm us up soon enough!" She rubs her hands together. "Nigel, bit of something for after. Thought our Maggie might appreciate it. Andrew?" She jabs him with an elbow.

Andrew presses a bottle into my hands. "For our Yankee girl." He kisses my cheek. I glance down. Bourbon.

Andrew and Brenda turn to face the others, hands crossed over their bellies, pumping their shoulders up and down in anticipation of an introduction. The others smile stiffly, waiting for the conversation to return to French.

I take a deep breath. Another international soirée. Here goes nothing.

"Andrew is an architect," I launch in, in French. "He's planning a glass conservatory for our barn . . ."

10:30 PM: The oysters were a good thing after all. Thierry and Hervé roll up their sleeves and tackle the crateful and soon the sink is full of shells. We eat them standing, forking them out of the brine, laughing and washing them down with the Champagne Nigel pours with dedicated regularity.

"Eating American-style," Hervé winks. "Always on your feet!" Nadine and Giselle look longingly at the dinner table.

Andrew and Brenda drift off, waving away the oysters — "Never could abide the things!" — and forming an Anglophone knot by the fire. Nigel soon drifts after them. Around the sink, the French conversation stays neutral and light — school, taxes, the new sewage system coming in. But then we all move to the table.

I wave and point out a mixed seating plan, but Andrew and Brenda plant themselves at the far end and Nigel joins them. That leaves the French faction at the other end, with me holding forth at the head.

"Smells delicious. Where did you get this . . . unusual china?" Nadine asks. She cups her plate of coq au vin with long-nailed fingers.

I flush a little. I have unpacked my Lorraine faïence for the occasion, painted with the double-barred cross. "They're war memorials. A series they created just after the First World War."

"How interesting!" Giselle says. But she isn't really interested. "You *are* fascinated by old things, aren't you?"

"Well. Yes."

Hervé leans back in his chair and looks around the room. I try to see it through their eyes and wither inside just a little. Nigel doesn't like my collection but I have managed to slip a few favorites upstairs: my lead soldiers in Second Empire uniform, the etching of Diderot, the bayonets crossed over the mantel, the bleeding bowl from the Hospices de Beaune.

"It's like a museum here. You are an *amateur* of history."

I try not to flinch at the word. "Well, yes. I am . . . kind of."

Nigel tears himself away from Brenda's chatter and switches briefly to French. "Meg studied history at Cambridge University. That's where we met."

I look up at him gratefully, then wish I hadn't. He is looking down his nose with a smirk.

"Ah! An American historian. A strange concept for a country with so little history of its own." Thierry laughs and the others join him.

I take a deep swallow of Givry.

"Oxymoron, really. Like 'European Union.'" Nigel unfolds himself and rises, coming down to our end to refill glasses. Giselle and Nadine lay protective fingers over their goblets, fanning their faces in protest. He adds an extra inch to mine. I feel his hand on my shoulder. "My Yankee girl's quite the aficionado of French history. Just a sideline, really." I flush. His hand is patting me now.

"That would explain the DS in the driveway, then!" Hervé grins. "Just like de Gaulle's!"

"And that interesting dress." Nadine and Giselle are exchanging glances.

"*Maman?*"

It is Kate. I have never been more grateful for an interruption. Even if she did choose to wear the Mickey Mouse nightshirt I tried to throw away.

11 PM: At last I come back downstairs from tucking Kate in. It took some doing, after all the oysters I let her eat, holding her like a shield against me through the rest of the main course.

The guests are passing the cheese tray. Andrew has, at last, resorted to French. He has worked in Nancy for twenty years but remains perpetually baffled by the reluctance of the French to acquire his language.

"The . . . concept . . . *l'idée, c'est* to *ouvrez la maison à la lumière,* to open the house to light."

"A conservatory is a very English tradition, isn't it?" Giselle asks. "We're not so familiar with them here. You must wash the windows often, no?"

The phone is breeting. My office line. I push back my chair.

"Excuse me." I hurry to the barn, struggle down the ladder, taking care in my high heels. I dive for the phone.

"Meg? Nikos. Good time to talk?"

I sigh with relief. "Yes, actually." Andrew will go on for ages now that he's got a bottle of Givry under his belt.

"So this adventure series is good to go. Publisher's open to a pitch for France. You got any ideas?"

possibilities

"Adventure? What exactly does he have in mind?"

"We're talking mountain treks, boat trips, ballooning, spelunking . . ."

Spelunking? "Doesn't sound very *French* to me. The French do civilized sports. Skiing. Tennis. Promenades. Then they . . . eat."

Nikos chuckles. "Open to ideas. Pitch me something French, then."

"Well. Can you give me a framework?"

"About forty thousand words. Pub date this time next year. Sorry, I know it's crazy."

"You're talking about a lot of time on the road, aren't you?" I hesitate. "Um. There'll be some . . . juggling to do. I'll try to come up with some themes. Talk to Nigel."

"He wasn't too keen on your last project, was he? *Hit the Road.* Away from home a lot."

"No, he wasn't. But he knows I — "

"Meg? Gotta run. Another editorial group grope. Get back to me, okay?"

"Okay." I hang up the phone and sit a moment, looking at the pictures around me. Grandpa. De Gaulle.

pitch me something french
I brace myself and head up the ladder.

Midnight: The plates are heaped with cheese rinds. Nigel has opened yet another bottle. He's refilling Andrew's glass, and his own.

"Sorry. Work." I pull back my chair.

Thierry glances up in midbreath. "—Precisely what we were saying!" He spreads his hands in triumph. "America loves to work. Work, work, work. This is what they know. Work and money. Profit. The dollar. But it isn't just to get ahead. There is *fear*. There's no security. Every individual afraid of falling behind—"

"—because they know they could end up on the street," Hervé interjects.

"—fired in a second, cut off without pension, without protection."

I arrange my face in a neutral smile. Devil's advocate, again. "It's true there is a strong spirit of competition—"

"—of greed! Of self! Where is the great spirit of brotherhood? of humanity? of solidarity? of—"

I feel my heart sinking. Usually we make it to dessert before they start in.

Thierry notices my face. He raises his glass and spreads his arms gallantly. "But naturally we're not speaking of our lovely hostess but only of an abstraction. Meg is a European now!"

"But of course!" The women lean forward as one, Nadine pressing my arm with neat parallel fingers. "You are nothing like the Americans we know of!"

Nigel lifts his head suddenly, a dormouse rousing from a teapot of English chitchat. His nose and cheeks have a cheery glow. "Megs? She's my Yankee girl! Wouldn't change a thing!"

I rise. "Anyone for brandied plums? They're from our orchard. I canned them myself."

Nadine and Giselle raise their delicate hands in surprise. "*Quel Cordon Bleu!*"

1:30 AM: I sink against the front door and squeeze my eyes shut as tires crunch away across the gravel. My blood is singing with wine and fatigue. I feel as if I've been pummeled.

amateur

I peel out of my high heels and make my way barefoot back across cool flagstones. Nigel is clattering plates in the sink and filling a plastic tub with suds. His shirt hangs open, sleeves rolled up. His hair hangs into the steam. He has retrieved the crusty apron from the cupboard and tied it around his waist like a loincloth.

"I'll take care of the washing up!" he crows.

He really *has* had a lot to drink.

I walk around the table, tonging together wine goblets with my right hand. My left hand is pulsing with pain. I carry the glasses to the sink.

There is an oyster lying open on the counter in the last of the melting ice. I touch the undulation of translucent flesh. It recoils, expands. I lift the shell and tip it into my mouth. My eyes close. Oh god. Sweat and brine and something silver-sweet. I hold the flavor in my mouth and lay my forehead against Nigel's back, feeling warm damp wicking through cotton

"Oh, Nigel."

Nigel lowers the dish brush and turns.

I remember this chest. My cheek connects with flesh at the hollow between two soft square breasts. My hands snake around behind the swelling belly and grope for his backbone.

"Whatever is the matter with my Yankee girl?" he murmurs into my hair.

"Mmmph." I can't express it. I sigh.

" 'She speaks yet she says nothing: what of that?' "

I smile against his skin.

His hands slide down my back to my bottom and pat. I pull away just a little. My hand is throbbing.

He pulls me gently back. His hands are busy now and his gaze is focused on the ceiling, seeking the appropriate citation. I pull away. He pulls me gently back again.

" 'O, wilt thou leave me so unsatisfied?' "

I giggle just a little. Like in Cambridge, a long time ago.

His lips hover over the hollow of my ear. " 'Will you vouchsafe to teach a soldier terms such as will enter at a lady's ear—' "

I duck my head. There are goose bumps on my neck.

" — 'and plead his love-suit to her gentle heart?' "

He pulls the apron off with a flourish. My wedding ring sails out of the pocket and ping-pongs across the floor. He turns his loose gaze to follow its fall. Then he swivels that gaze back to me.

The daybed smells of dog hair and diapers and beer. We roll in clumsy cuddles. It feels good to be touched. Hands still flecked with soapsuds, he fumbles with the hooks and eyes, then reaches in and kneads. Studiously. Carefully. So familiar. So comfy. So sweet.

Gerald paces in the darkness outside, whining.

4 AM: The pounding pain in my hand wakes me up. Nigel is still collapsed on top of me, snoring, his trousers around his ankles. I am wearing only a bandage. I shift weakly and a trickle drains between my legs. A rag. A rag. I squeeze my knees together, waddle to the table, clutch an oystery tea towel from the sink and stem the flow. Gerald has slumped asleep against the glass door, his fur flattened into whorls on the pane. I swing it open with a rush of icy air and he skulks in, his tail whacking gratefully against my legs. He plunges his muzzle between my knees and whuffles. Sometimes I think he knows that musky mix of Nigel and me. I press his head away and he crawls into his basket.

I limp up the stairs and peek in on Cloey, a dark angel in the glow of the nightlight. I check on Kate, indistinguishable in a mountain of stuffed animals that rise and fall with her breathing.

I squat on the bidet and rinse, one-handed, in a flush of warm water. Nikos' e-mail still lies on the bathroom floor, the ink running.

travel adventure france

I turn the water off and sit for a while, straddling porcelain, lost in thought.

just a sideline

Then I wrap my old kimono around me and climb downstairs to my bunker. I pull my grandfather's jacket over the silk. General de Gaulle squints down his nose at me. And Captain Parker, too.

pitch me something french

I type.

> *Nikos—*
> *How about a history theme?*

3 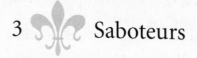 Saboteurs

Monday, February 10, 3 PM: The trapdoor of my bunker is closed. I have shut out my life upstairs. Only this counts. With eight fingers I am typing a pitch to Nikos as if my life depended on it.

Vive l'Histoire!
France Then and Now

Ten themes. Major historic events in French history, written as story capsules. Brought to life. You Are There. First person. Vivid text.

Vivid text. I sigh. Adjectives. Adverbs. What I wouldn't give . . .

Great battles. Turning points. Key moments. Heydays.

ex:
Agincourt
Storming of the Bastille
Norman conquest
D-Day
Aigues-Mortes Crusades
Napoleon's comeback from Elba
Joan of Arc lifts siege of Orléans

Not just military. Also art history, literature, archeology

Van Gogh
Géricault
Colette
Molière

> *Lascaux cave paintings*
> *Celtic standing stones*
>
> *To distribute geographically around France.*

I take a gulp of cold coffee.

> *Photographs to illustrate, evoke, reconstruct. Capture the feeling.*

I'm convincing myself as I go.

> *What I would bring to it: Advanced education in French, Latin, and history, especially French history. Read history at Cambridge, Sorbonne.*

Well, the names are impressive. And Nikos needs to know I'm qualified. I need to be taken seriously here. For a change.

> *Written several textbooks on French society/culture/history.*

Only for junior-high kids, but why quibble?

> *Nikos, I can do this. What do you think?*

I tap Send. The eyes of Napoleon and de Gaulle are on me. I lift my chin and smile back.

9 PM: Nigel has the conservatory plans spread across the dining table where a heap of glossy magazines lie open.

"You see, Megs? No visible damage to the façades. No buttresses. No ugly steel beams. This one's rather nice, I think. Have a look!"

He thrusts a thick issue of *Hill and Dale* toward me, turned to a two-page glossy spread of a Tudor manor, a faceted window box swelling out of a weathered brick wall like a great glass blister.

"It's not that I don't think they're pretty, Nigel," I lie. "It's just that—we've got an old farmhouse with a stone-framed barn door and a cone-shaped chimney and . . . Well, those are *local* things and these conservatories are . . . not. It's just not *French*. Couldn't we use the money for something more useful?" Like heat in my bunker.

"Megs, you're always on about how dark the house is."

"I know but you can't just knock a *hole* in it to let the light in."
He turns back to his crossword. "Just leave it to Andrew, love."

Midnight: It's so cold in my bunker I can hardly type, even with the electric heater against my feet. I don't care. I am smiling at Nikos' message:

> *Hey Meg. History, huh? could be interesting IF you keep it lively.*
> *you'll have to brief me on a couple of those Major Turning Points*
> *in european history. agincourt? aigue morte?? write me thumbnails.*
> *then we'll discuss and get something together to present to publisher.*
> *— nikos*

Now I type as fast as I can.

> **Agincourt: 1415.** *A key battle of the Hundred Years' War between*
> *Charles VI of France and Henry V of England. French outnumbered*
> *British at least 3 to 1 but English overwhelmed them. Thousands of*
> *French aristocracy slaughtered . . .*

I keep typing. I could do this all night.

Tuesday, 2 AM: I *am* doing this all night.

> **Bayeux: 1066. Normandy.** *William of Normandy launches fleet of oared*
> *ships from French coast across Channel to claim English crown . . .*

Must sleep. Must sleep.

3 AM: I'm still typing.

> **Aigues-Mortes: 1248. Provence.** *On coast of Camargue (where the*
> *Rhône river delta drains into the Mediterranean), King Louis IX (aka*
> *Saint Louis) launches 1500 ships toward Jerusalem . . .*

> **Cluny: 1230. Burgundy.** *Benedictine abbey dominates Europe*
> *through wealth and political influence. Romanesque abbey and church*
> *among wonders of the world . . .*

> **Arles: 1888. Provence.** *Vincent van Gogh invites Gauguin to Arles to*
> *paint, profit from famous light. Gauguin finds him too temperamental, leaves. Van Gogh cuts off ear . . .*

> *Omaha Beach: 1944. Normandy. First wave of Allied landings dis-*
> *embark all along the coast of Normandy in an attempt to liberate*
> *Nazi-occupied France . . .*

> *Route Napoléon: 1815. Côte d'Azur. Napoleon returns from exile*
> *on Elba to press northward through the Alps to Grenoble, retaking*
> *Paris. Could tie in Allied Seventh Army that followed same route in*
> *southern liberation, 1944 . . .*

Grandfather Parker's army. I hug his jacket around me and hit Send.

Tuesday, 8 PM: "Then after he marched over the pre-Alps he bivouacked in a hill village. And that's where your great-grandmother lived."
"France!"
I tuck the sheets over Kate's thin chest. "Well, yes. The Isère. She was very pretty, and Grandfather Parker must have been dashing in his uniform. You know, my special jacket."
"With the pokey metal things on the shoulders?"
"Bars. That's right. He was a captain."
"Then what happened?"
"You know the rest. He . . . liberated her. They fell in love."
"And lived happily ever after."
"They did. Now sleep."

9 PM: New York is awake at last. Yes! I am pacing around my desk. Nikos *gets* it. It's a beginning.

> *Okay. This is good. Will forward to publisher and get back to you.*
> *I got a good feeling about this. Start looking at calendar for travel*
> *dates.*
> *—nikos*

Libraries! Museums! Monuments! Battlefields!
travel
adventure
Nigel.
The kids.

10 PM: "But for that Road project you were gone for days at a time." Nigel is sitting at the dining table, an empty glass in his hand. He's barely touched the plate of sweetbreads I warmed for him, congealing now in buttery Sauternes. A little rich for a weeknight, maybe, but they were so fresh. Not anymore. He's been home late every night this week.

"I know, but that was only a few regions here and there. You were wonderful with the kids, and we found sitters."

"Sitters."

"And the children are older now."

"Cloey is two."

"Three and a half. Well, still. Nigel, this would mean a lot to me. Just think! History!"

He lifts his glass and finds it empty. He puts it down. "Yes. Your speciality." He heads for the freezer. "If you think it's really . . . necessary. I mean, things are going well enough for me at Barclays."

He heads for the liquor cabinet. I can see his mind ticking, probing. Please, not the Shakespeare game. Not now.

"'Unapt to toil and trouble in the world . . .'"

I hate it when he trots out *Taming of the Shrew*. My jaw squeezes shut. I push back my chair and head down the ladder.

11 PM: I am typing furiously.

DIALOGUE

Note: While *histoire* means both "history" and "story," it can also mean "bad feelings," "hassles," or "lies."

Francine: Tu es rentré à quelle heure hier soir?
　　　What time did you get in last night?
François: Putain! C'est quoi, cette histoire? Je ne sais pas.
　　　Bloody hell! What's the deal? I don't know.
Francine: Ne me raconte pas d'histoires. Je sais bien qu'il était deux
　　　heures du matin.
　　　Don't tell lies. I know. It was two o'clock in the morning.

François: Il faut toujours que tu fasses des histoires. Laisse moi tranquille.

You always have to hassle me. Leave me in peace.

Francine: Salaud! C'est toujours la même histoire.

Son of a bitch! It's always the same story.

Wednesday, 11 PM: Late for a phone call. It can only be Nikos.

"Hi, Nikos."

"Meg! Looks great. Let's move on it. I want to set you up with the photog."

"Photographs? Good! There's so much we can do! Van Gogh, Cluny Abbey, William the Conqueror. We'll need to talk about the story list!"

"Yeah. Your itinerary, too. You'll be traveling with the photographer."

Oh god.

"Traveling *with* a photographer? But I don't have to work *with* the photographer, do I? Can't he just—follow up after I turn in my stuff?"

"Better if you travel together. To be sure you're covering the same story."

My heart sinks. Just when things were starting to come together. I pull the khaki jacket around my shoulders. "Traveling on assignment with photographers can be *awful*, Nikos."

"Meg . . ."

"They're always pulling over to the side of the road to shoot something that has *nothing* to do with the story. They *always* try to get me to carry their equipment. They—"

"I know. I know. Still. Jean-Jacques Chabrol is interested. He's good; I think you'll like him. Into food and wine in a big way. Comes from an old Bordeaux family. Relatively easy to work with."

"Relatively? Nikos—"

"No. He's a nice guy."

"He'd better be. You're talking about a lot of road time."

Thursday, 6 PM: Kate stands beside me at the cutting board, pressing the onion-half down with stiff fingers, knife raised. *"Comme ça, Maman?"*

I cup my hand over hers. "Like that. Yes. Hold it firmly now . . . that's it, lead with your knuckles so you don't cut your fingers . . . and bring the blade down in rows."

She pushes the knife onto the onion. It slips out from under its top layer and shoots across the kitchen. Cloey dives for it and carries it back. "Got dog hair on it!"

"It's okay, honey. The knife's a little dull." I rinse it off. "Try again."

Kate lowers the blade, tongue caught between her teeth. "But the knife worked for Papa when he was repairing the—Ah, *non!*" The onion flies across the room again.

9 PM: Worse and worse. Nikos is serious. I'll have to travel with a photographer. And a balky one at that.

> *Hey Meg—*
> *J-J Chabrol needs convincing. He has reservations about illustrating history theme. I'll put him in touch with you. Introduce yourselves. Try to think of concrete art proposals. You're going to have to work together on this.*
> *—nikos*

He's already being difficult and we haven't even talked yet.

"Convince" the photographer? Oh god.

photographs to illustrate, evoke, capture the feeling

Right.

Saturday, 6:45 AM: Can that be the doorbell? Gerald sets to with a fury, snarling and barking in great liquid gulps. I squint at the alarm clock in the dawn twilight. I grope for my kimono. Nigel lies undisturbed, whistling snores.

unapt to toil and trouble in the world

The doorbell rings again. I hear Gerald hurling himself against the oak door. I hurry down the stairs, haul him back by his collar with one hand, and swing open the door. A very small man is standing there. A bush of dusty black hair juts out from under an absurdly small white cotton cap. He drops his cigarette into my boxwood and extends a bristly arm.

"Madame Thorpe? Raimondo. MacGregor sent me. To see the wall.

For the conservatory." He smiles from ear to ear, showing three dark brown teeth on a row of yellow. His hand is as hard as tree bark, his French lilted with Latin.

I wrap my kimono around my waist and shiver. "Come in. Did my husband know you were coming?"

"Monsieur Thorpe fixed it with MacGregor. Today I will see the wall. Then MacGregor will give you the estimate."

"Monsieur Thorpe . . . arranged this?"

I lead Raimondo into the barn, past my iron ladder. Gerald circles around his dusty feet, ducking and panting and wagging wildly, spattering the cobblestones with tiny ribbons of urine. A broad stone wall looms fortress-thick in the half-light. Leaning against it are fifty years' accumulated barn clutter—old shutters, broken windows, toothless rakes. They are draped with dusty cobwebs and stuck thick with straw.

"That is it? The wall?" Raimondo stands very still, as if waiting. "It must be clear if I am to measure it." He smiles and shrugs.

"Oh. Of course. Sorry!" I set to work, scuttling away rakes, planks, shutters, clutching the windows against my kimono and dragging them to the side. My bandage is unraveling. I haul. I heave.

Raimondo squints into space, lost in thought. When I have finished clearing the space, he shifts his weight. He gazes at the wall, Leonardo assessing a potential fresco.

"Can't be done," he pronounces.

"I'm sorry?" I am panting cold steam.

"The wall. It is supporting the crossbeam." He tosses his head upward toward the massive oak timber that spans the width of the barn. From it radiates the haphazard structure of beams, logs, and planks that holds up our two-hundred-year-old roof.

I stand, my arms wrapped around my robe. "But isn't it . . . ? I mean, the beam could be supported during the works and the hole . . . the opening . . . could be reinforced. Of course it could be reinforced. Couldn't it?"

Raimondo turns his brown gaze on me. His eyes slide over my kimono. He shakes his head slowly.

"Madame, when can I talk with your husband? Is Monsieur at home?"

I feel my spine stiffening. It's hard to feel broad-shouldered when you're not wearing underpants. "You can speak with me."

He screws up his mouth and looks at the mud-slicked floor as if longing to spit. But he paints on a Latin-charmer smile. "Madame. I can do anything you pay me to do. But these walls . . ." His gaze pans the barn full-circle. He glances up at the beam. Then he shrugs, hitches his measuring tape off his low-slung belt, and starts to measure.

11 AM: "But Nigel. If you'd seen the way he looked at me. And I . . . I can't take this on right now. I have a *book* to write."

He glances up from the sports page. "Of course you have. Your 'book.' Needn't worry. I'll see to everything."

Monday, 2 PM: At last there is an e-mail from the photographer. I brace myself. It's in English. Sort of.

> *Madame Parker.*
> *Here is Jean-Jacques Chabrol. We work on the new project together perhaps. You will discuss with me? I call you tonight if it convenience you.*
> *—jjchabrol*

Neutral enough. Wonder why he said "perhaps." A little patronizing, maybe? He assumes I only speak English. "Needs convincing." Okay. I reply in my creamiest French:

> *Monsieur Chabrol,*
> *I will indeed be in this evening. You may call anytime. I am looking forward to working with you on Vive l'Histoire. Nikos asked me to introduce myself. I am a freelance writer and a historian . . .*

Maybe a wee bit exaggerated. Still, I have to establish credibility.

> *. . . having studied history, Latin, and French at Cambridge and the Sorbonne.*

I leave out Notre Dame. Not to slight it. He just probably hasn't heard of it, and the French name confuses things.

History, especially French history, is my specialty. I think you will find the subjects I've proposed interesting. I hope you will enjoy the challenge of photographing them to illustrate my text.

Let's stay in touch. As soon as Nikos provides contracts and we finalize the story list, I will give you my suggestions for appropriate art.

Cordially, M. Parker

There. That should strike the right tone of professionalism. Authority. Confidence. If Nigel doesn't take my work seriously, I do. So will this J-J Chabrol. I copy it to Nikos and turn back to *La Vie en France*.

Wednesday, 3 PM: It's been two days and I haven't heard back from Chabrol. He never did phone. Nikos has come through with a budget—pathetically small but viable if I'm careful—and the book looks like a sure thing. *Vive l'Histoire!* I can hardly contain my excitement. Apparently Chabrol can.

I write another e-mail.

Monsieur Chabrol,
Though you haven't replied to my e-mail I presume you are considering the proposed stories and how you might illustrate my text. I have many ideas on this subject and would be happy to discuss them with you. Also, I think it's important that we address the shooting schedule, given the tight deadlines the publisher has imposed. Please contact me at your earliest convenience.
M. Parker
p.s. I attach the current story list, again.

Thursday, 10 AM: "She's a sweet girl. Solid. Kate and Cloey will love her." Mathilde Leblanc—everyone calls her the Mémé Mathilde—is hanging a rabbit from a hook in the barn shed. Its eyes are glazed, its feet still twitching. With gnarled fingers she slips a knife around its neck skin and yanks. The skin strips off in one piece, leaving a neat pink carcass behind. She wipes her hands on a blue flowered apron. "Her grandfather went to primary school with me, a *petit-cousin*. She's a farm girl. Grew up in the old house. A good girl."

Sophie Leblanc. Good farm stock. Wholesome. Just what I need for a babysitter. A nanny, really. And she lives just across the creek.

"Well, good. I'm glad. I really need someone I can count on, that the kids can count on."

Mémé Mathilde smiles with bright store-bought teeth. "You can count on a Leblanc."

5:30 PM: I cross my fingers when the doorbell rings and shoot a quick prayer up to the nanny gods. I open the door.

Oh dear.

Claws of jet-black hair grip kohl-smeared eyes. Pant cuffs trail raggedly over unlaced sneakers. A mound of pale belly gaps under a cropped Lycra top. A spike-studded belt hangs precariously just above the mons. There is a marijuana-leaf tattoo below her navel. There is a tarnished silver hoop stapled through the bristly mound where her left eyebrow used to be.

"*Bonjour, Madame,*" she says softly. Her silver-blue lips break into a shy grin. "I believe we have an appointment."

Under the costume I can just discern a round-cheeked girl of about twenty. "Yes. And you must be . . . ?"

"I'm Sophie Leblanc. Am I inconveniencing you, madame?" She searches my face and holds out her hand, nails fish-belly silver. I shake it. She cranes to see over my shoulder and beams.

"*C'est bien toi, Clovis?*" Cloey's face splits into a wary grin and Kate inches forward, encouraged. "And this is Katharine, no?" Kate ducks her head and smiles. "*T'es trop chou, quoi!*" Cute as a cabbage. She kisses them each on the cheeks, twice.

We sit at the dining table. Suddenly I feel a little bit embarrassed. It's a strange job I'm hiring for. "It's not really full time, you see. It's—now and then—full time sometimes, then not. I mean, I'll go away for a week or a weekend and then come back for a while. Then I go away again. You would have to be very flexible. Do you have another job?"

"No, I could be available to you when you need. Maybe next year I'll be accepted for a teaching job in the city. I have a diploma in *maternelle* education."

My mouth pops open. She looks at me earnestly, a little nervous. She wants this job. I want this nanny.

I offer her a cup of coffee and she asks for hot chocolate instead. Then she takes Cloey into her lap and shares it with him.

9 PM: I have a nanny. I don't have a photographer. Still no reply from Chabrol. There is a note from Nikos, though:

> *Chabrol more skeptical than ever. Have you talked yet? What's up? Need you two to agree on stories.*

More skeptical than ever? Oh god. What if he's another prima donna like the one who shot *Hit the Road*? Maybe I should do this alone after all. I write again.

> *Monsieur Chabrol,*
> *It might be best for me to work alone. I'm sure we can find a way for you to follow up on my research after the text has been written.*
> *—M. Parker*

I know Nikos said he didn't want it to work like that, but I don't want to tackle another road project with an uncooperative *artiste* tagging along.

Midnight: History books are heaped high on my desk, fringed with colored sticky notes.

A message flashes on the screen. Chabrol. At last. In French.

> *Madame Parker,*
> *I too would prefer to work separately. But I just spoke with Nikos. He insists we work together.*
> *—jjchabrol*

I sigh. I can tell this is going to be an uphill climb. Then another message flashes on. Chabrol again. He's a night owl, too.

> *Madame Parker,*
> *Nikos mentioned Bayeux. I will be shooting there at La Normande for Goût du Nord over weekend. If you come there we can talk.*
> *—jjchabrol*

Come there? He's summoning me to Bayeux while he shoots food? It's halfway across northern France for me. He can't be serious. I type:

> *Monsieur Chabrol,*
> *It is out of the question that I . . .*

But I stop and think. Bayeux. Maybe we could get started on the Norman Conquest story. And check out the D-Day beaches. I look longingly at my book pile. Churchill is flagged in neon.

Maybe once we got started on site, Chabrol would get into the spirit.

But this weekend?

Bayeux. Omaha Beach.

Nigel *could* take care of the kids.

Nigel. I lean back in my chair and rub my eyes. Nanny. Photographer. Mason. Kids. Husband. Hurdles to jump.

Friday, 7:30 AM: "This weekend? *Tomorrow?*" Nigel has lifted his face from his *Telegraph*. I have been making a show of reading the *Républicain Lorrain* while working up the courage to broach the subject.

"Well, yes. The photographer is being difficult and Nikos thinks we should meet to talk through the history stories in person."

"Bit late notice, isn't it?"

"Yes. I know. But he doesn't answer my e-mails. You know. Photographers. Not big on words."

Nigel sips his tea. "And the children?"

"Well, you'll be here."

"Right." I can hear the kitchen clock ticking. "What about the new girl, Sylvie?"

"Sophie."

"Sophie, then."

"But Nigel, *you'll* be here."

"Right."

10 AM: I'm writing to Chabrol.

> *Monsieur Chabrol,*
> *If I come all that distance I hope we can get started on the Norman Conquest and D-Day themes. Will you be booking a hotel? If so,*

do look into a room for me. It is, after all, very short notice. Please confirm.

      —*M. Parker*

The reply comes almost immediately, as if he was typing very fast.

Yes, Madame Parker, of course I will book your room for you. As a matter of fact the host has invited us as guests.

I write back:

Can you pick me up at the gare?

He has answered before my hands leave the keyboard.

The hotel is near the gare you can walk i will meet you for dinner at 8 after i finish shooting

A real charmer, this Chabrol.

Saturday, 8 AM: Cloey is dipping Nutella toast in a bowl. Kate is carrying spoonfuls of hot chocolate to her pink pony's plastic lips, then dabbing away the goo. Nigel is still in his bathrobe. Saturday morning. He'll have to dress to walk the kids to the bus. I pet the hair back from his eyes.

"I'm off. I'll give you a call later. Don't forget to meet the kids at the bus stop at noon."

"Where is it you're off to again?"

"Bayeux. Norman conquest, remember?"

"I remember." He lifts his tea mug. Ticking. Abstracted. I wait for the coming citation. It comes.

" 'Are all thy conquests, glories, triumphs, spoils, shrunk to this little measure?' "

I sigh and kiss his brow.

"Well. Bye then."

"Bye, love."

I waver by the children. It's only three days. And they've got Nigel, right? Still, my heart is twisting oddly.

They barely notice the lingering kiss I plant on their cheeks or the final sniff of baby-neck I steal before backing out the door.

5 PM: The local train between Caen and Bayeux takes forever. I boot up the laptop on the fold-down table and scroll through the story list.

> **Carnac: 3800 BC? Bretagne.** *The standing stones of Carnac are France's best known relics of the era of Celtic dominance . . .*

> **Vallée des Merveilles: 1800 BC. Provence Alps.** *Valley of Marvels contains some 30,000 prehistoric carvings . . .*

> **Orléans: 1429. Loire Valley.** *Hundred Years' War. Joan of Arc raises mounted troops and marches to Orléans, besieged by the English . . .*

I am giving myself goose bumps.

I'm glad I sent an updated list to Chabrol before I left. There are a lot of stories here. Tonight we'll talk, tomorrow we'll shoot. By this time tomorrow *Vive l'Histoire* should be well under way. Balky photographer or not.

7 PM: It was a seven-block walk from the station to the Hôtel La Normande. I had to juggle the laptop and suitcase, my bandage fluttering helplessly at my side. French chivalry died at Agincourt.

Still, the hotel room is downright sumptuous. I have been standing here, wrapped in a thick white towel for twenty minutes, deciding what to wear. The vintage silk dress I brought—it is a two-star restaurant, after all—seems too soft. I need to be taken seriously. I opt for the blazer, square in the shoulders, with the antique brass buttons I found at a flea market.

I dress carefully, enjoying the luxury of the room and—even more luxurious—privacy. At home there is always someone in the bathroom with me. I study myself in the soft-lit mirror, an indulgence I rarely permit myself. Thirty-two's okay, I think. Old enough to hold my own. I hate my mouth: fat, crooked. Hair's okay, dishwater blonde but shiny. I tie it up in a twist. The bandage is grimy from struggling with luggage through four *gares*. Nothing I can do about it here. I flex the fingers. They are healing. The itch under the layers tells me so.

I check my watch. There's time to call home before I go downstairs. I punch the number into the cell phone. The faint toot of our home line repeats four, then five times. Then someone picks up with a clatter. Cacophony. Pans crashing, meat sizzling, hood fan roaring, bottles tinkling. Gerald is barking sporadically. Cloey is barking back.

"Hello! Hello! Who's there? Honey, is that you?"

"*Maman?*" A tiny voice. Kate always sounds three years younger on the phone. She can barely make herself heard but there is just enough connection for her to broadcast a martyrly sigh. "When are you coming back?" I don't need a videophone to see her expression: I know. Her eyes are round and moist and tragic as a Greek mask.

I take a breath and smile firmly into the phone. "Honey, I only left this morning. I just got here!"

There is a long interval of clanging pans. I hear Nigel swear. "Bugger!"

A luxurious, wet breath gushes into the mouthpiece at Kate's end. "I . . . don't . . . feel . . . good."

My stomach tightens. "What is it, sweetie? Where do you hurt?"

She pauses and reflects. A glass crashes. Kate raises her voice. "My sroat hurts."

Oh god. My molecules regroup into motherhood, the usual mix of emotions washing over me. Skepticism. Guilt at feeling skeptical. Worry. And irritation that Nigel isn't taking care of it.

"I'm sorry you feel bad. Let me blow you a kiss. There! Can I talk to Papa?"

But the phone has already clunked down on the dining table, lying like a beetle on its back. I wait to see if Nigel picks up. There's a rhythmic chopping sound. Then, "*Bugger!*" Then the sound of clomping brogues. Water gushing.

I sigh and press the red button. "'Night, Nigel," I think. "*Bon appétit.*"

I check my watch, glance in the mirror one last time and button up with brass. I take a deep breath. Time to face the photographer. I heft the laptop in my good hand and head for the stairs.

8 PM: When I step into the dim-lit dining room there's no mistaking which is my table. There are three tripod spotlights aimed at it and a

thin man standing on a Louis XV chair pointing a camera lens straight down into a plate of sculptured food. Three waiters and a maître d'hôtel flutter nervously around him, weaving cables under chair legs and smiling reassurance at a roomful of diners, who squint into the halo of light, their own food growing cold before them.

"That's it. Good. *Voilà.*" The camera clicks and winds, clicks and winds. Then Chabrol steps down from the chair and strips off his cameras. His thin form is swaddled in a bulky sweater and his neck is wound around several times with an enormous Arabic scarf, a black-and-white kaffiyeh, the kind Nigel calls a Gaza tea towel. A matted mass of salt-and-pepper hair hangs over his face and shoulders and he drags it back and twists it at his neck. He is squinting to see beyond the lights.

Why are photographers always so scraggly? He looks like some Latin-Quarter student. And he's lighting a cigarette. Of course.

"Madame Parker?" Every head in the house swivels from him to me. I raise a hand to shield my eyes from the light and my face from the stares. I see his silhouette drop to a crouch and pull the light plugs from the extension socket. The halogen bulbs fade to darkness and my pupils expand again in the soft candlelight. His face takes form, sharp-boned, beak-nosed, haggard, and unshaven. He's older than I thought.

He steps toward me, biting the cigarette. He looks at me warily, then he extends a hand.

I give it a firm shake. "Pleased to meet you, Monsieur Chabrol."

He nods. There is a cell-phone trill. "Sorry." He doesn't look it. He turns away and gropes in the hip pocket of his sagging jeans. I look around me. The diners look back at their plates. I pick my way over the cables and sink into my place.

8:15 PM: He is still muttering softly into the phone, pacing the dining room, a hand covering his free ear. The maître d'hôtel does not look pleased. The waiters circumvent the light trees, looking as if they'd like to chainsaw them down. Chabrol shrugs apology to them and, one-handed, starts to gather up cable.

"*Bon, benh, alors, écoute.* I'll call you back," he says finally. "Maybe tomorrow's good, *d'accord?*"

He pockets the phone. "Sorry." He begins to take down the lights, piling them into metal trunks by the bar. He works silently, methodically, folding, wrapping. His back is to me. He's in no hurry. He works until every cable and tree are disposed of. He closes the trunks.

Then he comes to his chair and sets himself carefully down. The wary look is back. He reaches for a cigarette and puts it between his lips.

"Do you mind?" Why does my voice sound small?

He lights it anyway. He drags deep. He looks at me.

"So," he says. That's all. He smokes. My shoulders feel very thin under the blazer. "You don't look like you sound. In your e-mails, I mean."

I smile uncomfortably. "What do you mean? What do I 'sound' like?"

"Older." He smokes and looks around the room. I don't know how to take that. I take a deep breath and decide to take it as a compliment. Keep the ball in your court, Meg. This is your book. I make an effort to think about *Vive l'Histoire*. Good thoughts. I take another breath. I give a midwestern smile.

"So," I say. "Are you hungry?" I look at the plate of seafood and foam and drizzles of coral coulis.

"Yes. That's just for the photographs." He looks around and catches the eye of the maître-d', who is instantly beside Chabrol's chair, looking much happier now that the shooting is done.

"Yes, Monsieur Chabrol?"

He lays a hand on his shoulder. "Maybe go through the whole thing again? In order this time? If that's all right with Jules."

The maître d' nods. "That's precisely what Jules said. Excellent. And the wine?"

"Fernand will know. I place myself in his hands."

I slump back in my chair. He's placing *me* in Fernand's hands, too. I don't even get to look at the menu, let alone the wine list.

9 PM: The waiter brings a tiny hors d'oeuvre, a single scallop seared with cilantro. I lift my silverware and push it onto the tines of my tiny fork. *"Bon appétit!"* I say.

He looks at my bandage. "Your hand?"

"A grease burn. Coq au vin. Goose fat. Sorry it's so dirty. I had a time getting my things here from the *gare*."

For a moment he looks uncomfortable.

Good.

I slip the scallop into my mouth.

10 PM: We have been eating for more than an hour and have barely said a word. He is so intently involved with his food and his wine he seems to have forgotten my presence. Only when Fernand comes, he rises and puts a hand on his shoulder, studying the label, discussing. He insists Fernand taste with him. They stand, swirling. I sit, waiting.

I can't get too upset. The food is too wonderful. At first I shower each dish with superlatives. "Incredible! Magnificent!" Then I don't bother. He is only eating.

We have been presented with a parade of some of the most delicious dishes I've tasted since Paris. Simple. Instinctive. Oyster foam with urchin coulis. Rouget on a checkerboard of pungent black radish. Scallops tartared with tamarind. Pigeon in black blood sauce scented with cocoa. The fork tines slide through my lips. I catalog the ingredients. Nutmeg. I think I can fake this one at home.

"I think I can fake this at home," I venture out loud. I try a smile. He looks up from his plate. His expression is hard to read. Skepticism? Contempt? I flush. I don't speak again.

The wine is extraordinary. Our glasses are filled and refilled. I feel my cheeks growing pink. With increasing effort I remain silent, but when I lift a sip of old Sauternes to my lips a soft moan escapes. He looks up for the second time of the evening. His face doesn't look so wary now.

When the espresso cups are empty and the last petits fours swept away, I speak.

"That was incredible. The chef . . ."

"Jules would be better if he didn't fuss so much about the looks."

"That's a funny thing for a food photographer to say."

He shrugs and looks around the room.

I straighten my shoulders. "So. Have you thought about the story list?"

His face closes like a book. He reaches for a cigarette.

"I haven't had time to study it."

"You haven't had *time?*" It slips out like that. My spine stiffens. He's had two weeks.

He blows out a thick stream of smoke.

I bend over my briefcase. His eyes glance around the room. Exasperation? Nothing to mine. I fish out a copy and push it across the table to him.

"I brought you a copy. Just in case you forgot yours."

He leans forward and drags it toward him. He doesn't pick it up. "Vive l'Histoire!" he says. It doesn't sound nice when he says it. "And you'll be advising me on how to illustrate your book?"

For some reason this makes me blush. "Well. Nikos said you might need . . ."

"Need . . . ?"

". . . input."

"Ah. Yes. It can be difficult, photographing historic events. Especially when they happened a thousand years ago. Not every photographer can do it."

The food is going sour in my stomach.

"There are things . . . there are places . . . there are people . . ."

"Dead people?" His face is carefully neutral.

I feel adrenalin rising. "I've studied French history for years. I know these subjects *well*. There are so many possibilities for illustration if you'll just let me guide you."

"*Guide* me?" He looks like he is going to laugh but his mouth won't let him. He passes his hand across it.

Oh god. This can't be happening. "But I've done so much research."

My cell phone trills in my bag.

"Excuse me," I say with exaggerated courtesy. I pick up the phone and make a show of slipping discreetly out of the dining room so as not to disturb the other guests. When I glance back he is blowing out a column of smoke and stubbing out the butt.

"Hello?"

"Megs?"

"Hi, Nigel. What's up?"

"Sorry to be a bother. It's just that Kate—"

"What's wrong? Is she sick after all?"

"Well, she says her throat hurts. And she is a bit warm. The baby thermometer—"

"It's on the top shelf of the bathroom cabinet." As always.

"I know, I know, love, but . . . I feel a complete prat asking but . . . you know the end of the thermometer? The tip is round and I wondered if it's meant . . ."

I bury my eyes in my bandaged hand. "No, Nigel, it's an oral thermometer. You put it under her tongue."

There is a pause. "Right then. Of course. I'll—I'll keep you posted. Nothing too serious, I expect."

When I come back to the table we are no longer alone. Fernand has pulled a chair up to the table and is opening another bottle. The chef— "Jules Debaur" embroidered on his unbuttoned white tunic— stands over us, wiping his red face with a tea towel. Fernard is gesturing with both hands, summoning two men in half-lenses and ascots from a neighboring table.

"Come on, join us, Georges, Frédéric. I want J-J to taste this. You, too."

I look around me, aghast. I thought we were discussing the story list.

Chabrol sits with his back to me. He is muttering to the chef, shaking his head, holding long fingers in the air, pinching the tips together. Men do that a lot in France. I think it has something to do with testicles or . . . or . . . close calls . . . Fear? Pressure? Glad I missed *that* joke. When he spots me, he fishes quickly for a cigarette.

"Madame Parker, Jules Debaur." He introduces me around the table with a neutral expression. He avoids my eyes, though I'm flaring them at him desperately. I give a forced smile and sink back into my chair.

Midnight: There are four empty bottles on the table. My head is fuzzy with wine and my lungs are full of smoke.

Chabrol is telling a story. He speaks very softly with his eyes down, a smile playing around his mouth. Everyone leans forward, heads bobbing in anticipation. ". . . So he's soaked, okay, head to toe in Latour, right, hair dripping red, sticky, and the gendarme is just standing there, looking him up and down." He glances up. The table chuckles all around, waiting. "And the gendarme says 'Is this the '82 or the '83?'" The group explodes. Chabrol leans back and lets fly with a ringing laugh. It startles me. It's as if it escapes from somewhere bottled up inside him.

"*Quelle histoire!*" Jules is wiping his eyes. "Can't believe it. The baron himself. That's one for the history books!"

Chabrol leans back and looks at me. He pulls on his cigarette. There's something I don't like about the way his mouth is set. "Perhaps we could put that in *your* book, no?"

I keep my mouth shut. He's still using the formal *vous* with me while intimate *tu*'s are flying all around the table. Have they known each other all their lives?

Fernand leans over and holds the bottle to my glass. I cover it with my fingers. "Have to work tomorrow. Thanks!" I glance pointedly at Chabrol.

Fernand shakes his head. "You Americans aren't accustomed to real wines. This is not your Pink Zinfandel!"

"It's not that . . ." but I know it's not worth trying. I look at Chabrol. He is letting his glass be refilled for the umpteenth time. His bony nose dips in deep and sniffs.

"The '71," he says. "I remember that one."

"I used to open that for your father. How is your mother these days? Now that the old bastard's gone."

Chabrol bends over the ashtray and taps his cigarette. He takes a drag and squints. He doesn't answer.

"Things still that bad? After all these years?"

I look blankly from face to face.

"Forget it," Chabrol says. He leans back for a while, eyes down. He seems to be studying his shoes. "I drink Burgundy these days."

Furtive glances dart around the table. Then everyone laughs far too heartily.

1:30 AM: The carpeted stairs sink like escalator steps beneath my feet and I have trouble getting the key in the lock. There were seven empty bottles on the table by the time I pushed my chair back and aimed for the lobby. Too late to phone Nigel. No message. I grip the cell phone carefully in my bandaged hand and tap out a text message to Nikos.

You mus talk to Chabrol. Balkin at histry theme. Help!

I punch Yes and collapse in a fluff of white linens, my cheek on the good-night chocolate.

Sunday, 8:30 AM: I crawl carefully out of bed and into the marble-lined shower. I emerge red and human again. Then I wrap myself in the thick monogrammed bathrobe and dial home.

"Nigel?"

"Hello." I hear a newspaper rustle.

"How's Kate?"

"No fever. Still says her throat's sore. She went off to see the Mémé Mathilde."

At eight thirty in the morning? With a sore throat? "Um. Okay. Hope you dressed her warmly. I'll be home tomorrow by noon and we'll see."

I boot up the laptop. There is an e-mail from Nikos:

> *Not to worry. I'll deal with him. You have to get his attention first. It's true he's not keen on the history concept but he'll come around. He signed his contract. Fedexed yours yesterday.*
> *—Nikos*

Get his attention. It was hard enough to get his attention last night. When I detached myself from the "party" he barely looked up. I pointed at my watch and said "Nine tomorrow?" He shrugged.

It's going to be a long day. I won't let him spoil my fun, though. *Vive l'Histoire* at last!

I dry my hair, dress, and climb down the stairs to meet Chabrol for breakfast, briefcase in hand.

10 AM: The thermos of coffee stands empty. I have finished its entire contents and another thermos of hot milk. I have also drunk a pitcher of orange juice, eaten two croissants, half a baguette, a cinnamon bun, a yogurt, and three tiny jars of blackberry jam. No sign of Chabrol. I have read *Le Monde* and started on *Le Figaro*. I have reread my notes on William the Conqueror and studied the map until it blurs.

If we don't get started we won't be able to see the Bayeux Tapestry before noon. I wanted to get to the D-Day beaches and hunt up the departure point for the Norman launching. Dives-sur-Mer is a long way east. It gets dark early. I drum caffeinated fingers on the table.

Well. That *was* a lot of wine he put away last night. I rise to ring his room, heading for the front desk.

"Yes, Madame Parker. There is a message for you."

She passes me a folded piece of La Normande stationery. There is fluid fountain-pen script in neat blue rows.

> *Madame Parker,*
> *Sorry but I had to catch an early train. Will talk with Nikos.*
> *Cordially, Jean-Jacques Chabrol*

7 PM: The train connections were terrible; I had to change three times. By the time I roll my suitcase in the front door, I am sweating, my bandage is undone, and my teeth are sore from clenching my jaw.

There's a FedEx on the dining table. The contract. I will not sign it until Nikos gets another photographer, I swear.

Kate gallops down the stairs and swings into my arms. I gasp and laugh.

"Sweetheart! You don't look sick to me!" I lay my hand on her forehead. Cool. A little sticky. I kiss it, wipe Nutella from my lips, and smile.

"I am much better now!" She hangs around my neck. "You took pictures? Like you said?"

I shake my head. "No pictures this time, honey. Not for my book, anyway."

"Then why did you go?"

Good question.

8 PM: Nigel sets a toasted-cheese sandwich before me. I wave it away. "Thanks honey. I ate enough last night to last the week."

He sinks into the chair across from me. His hair has detached from its neat helmet and is falling into his eyes. He has poured himself a two-inch whiskey.

"Next time let's call Sylvie."

"Sophie. Nigel, I was only gone a day and a half."

He drinks deep.

Monday, 11 PM: The e-mail drums have been beating all day. I wrote to Nikos first.

> *Nikos. I'm not signing a contract if Chabrol's the photog. Isn't there someone out there with a sense of something besides food?*

Nikos wrote back.

> *Talked with JJ. Maybe if you lighten up a little.*

What does he mean by that? I am bristling again. I have been bristling all day.

> *Nikos, this book is important to me. I am qualified for it. Chabrol is not. He clearly has no sense of his own heritage.*

His reply comes quickly.

> *He's one of the best. you just have to get him on board. talk through the stories with him. you're off to a bad start is all.*

I fire back:

> *HE's off to a bad start, you mean.*

An hour goes by. Then another. Then Nikos replies.

> *Look. I can't play nursemaid on this one you two have to work it out.*

Nursemaid. Worse and worse. Now *Nikos* is talking down to me.

Tuesday, 8 AM: "Kate honey. Finish your tartine. It's time for school!"

She's hunched over a book, her bowl of milk untouched. I brush her hair aside and peek.

"Cookbook?"

"I can make crêpes. We made crêpes in the *maternelle*. There are no onions to cut in crêpes."

I sigh. "Onions aren't so hard to work with once you get the knack. You just have to . . . hold it firmly."

10 AM: I slump listlessly, leaning my cheek on my hand, my elbow on the desk top, and scroll through *La Vie en France*. I should be cleaning up breakfast. I should be spading the roses. I should be making crêpe batter so Kate can cook after school.

But I scroll down. Work.

Nearly 40 percent of the French population smokes, consuming twenty billion cigarettes every year. New laws banning smoking in public spaces are weakly enforced. Cigarette packages feature dire warnings of lung cancer, heart disease, even impotence, but France continues to light up. More than sixty thousand deaths annually are attributed to tobacco in France . . .

DIALOGUE

François: *Tu peux me donner une clope? Je n'en ai plus depuis ce matin.*
Can you give me a cigarette? I haven't had any since this morning.

Laurent: *Mais tu m'en as déjà piqué deux depuis midi.*
But you already took two from me since lunch.

François: *C'est vrai? C'est dingue. J'ai l'impression de ne pas en avoir fumé depuis des heures.*
Is that right? It's crazy. I feel like I haven't smoked one in hours.

I lean back and sigh. I click on incoming e-mail. I sit up suddenly. There is a new message from Nikos—a forward of a message from Chabrol, in English.

Nik—I will do this. Work is work. I leave to Parker to lead. I will follow.
JJ

Well! That's more like it. But I look again. There is a trail of carets below, then the text of Nikos' message that Chabrol was replying to. I scroll down:

> >
> >

> *JJ— I still think the concept is good. Give Meg time; she can loosen up when she gets off her high horse. Follow her lead. Do what you can. I trust your taste. A contract is a contract and work is work.*
> *—Nikos*

I don't think I was supposed to see that. Below another string of carets, there is more. This is from early Sunday morning—just when I was showering for our breakfast meeting.

> >
> >

> *Nik—Me too I am upset. This is a bad idea. I photographe the life. This history idea, it is impossible. Don't make me do this book old friend. Parker is very rigid she is academic. a schoolmarm a casse-couille chiante a pain I should have not signe the contract. jj*

I feel a hot prickle on the back of my neck. He must have dug out his French-to-English dictionary for that. I don't need mine. *Casse-couille.* Ball-buster. My face is burning. I scroll through carets to the earliest message, almost against my will.

> >
> >

> *Hi J-J—*
> *Meg wrote, she's pretty upset. She's really into this concept. Be honest. Is the history theme do-able?*
> *Nikos*

I was definitely not supposed to read this. Nikos drank one too many lattes and punched Forward too soon. Schoolmarm. Ball-buster. I stare at the screen. Chabrol is the one who's . . . who's . . .

chiante a pain

I'm tempted to get out my *Dictionary of Modern French Idioms* and fire back a retort. Does *jerk* work in French?

But I sink down low in my chair.

They're not convinced, either one of them, that my history concept will work.

5:20 PM: I am pounding chicken breasts with a cleated hammer. I am pounding so hard I don't hear the doorbell. Fabienne has to tap on the kitchen window with lacquered nails.

Cloey and Kate hang in her arms.

Forgot to meet the bus again.

Wednesday, 10 AM: I am working on *La Vie en France, Level Two*. The *Vive l'Histoire* contract lies in the corner.

> While 80 percent of women in France work outside the home, domestic responsibilities—cooking, cleaning and childcare—traditionally fall into women's domain. Women continue to tackle 80 percent of home chores...

DIALOGUE

Francine: Chéri! Tu peux sortir la lessive du lave-linge avant qu'elle ne se froisse?
Honey! Could you get the laundry out of the machine before it wrinkles?

François: Mais je viens de rentrer du travail. Laisse moi tranquille.
But I just got home from work. Leave me alone.

Francine: Moi aussi, je viens de rentrer du travail. Tu crois que tout ça se fait tout seul?
Me too, I just got home from work. You think all this does itself?

François: Mais le match de foot commence dans dix minutes.
But the soccer match starts in ten minutes.

Francine: Je m'en fous de ton match de foot. Je dois faire à manger pour les gosses!
I don't give a damn about your soccer match. I have to make dinner for the kids.

François: Qu'est-ce qu'on mange ce soir . . . ?
What's for dinner tonight . . . ?

6 PM: I have browned the pigeons until their breasts are pink, then tonged them aside. I am reducing the juice, slowly, surely. I grate in nutmeg. I whisk in bitter cocoa. I stir in the blood and it thickens, emulsifies. Got it. I taste, my eyes drifting.

Thursday, 2 PM: The contract lies untouched. I am *still* working on *La Vie en France, Level Two.*

> *The toilet-training of children is a serious business in France and begins at an earlier age than in other European countries . . .*

DIALOGUE

Francine: Attends, Hugo, je vais te chercher le pot-pot!
Wait, Hugo, I'll go get you the potty!
Hugo: Po-po!
Potty!
Francine: Attends, attends, Hugo . . . ! Hop-là, trop tard . . .
Wait, wait, Hugo . . . ! Whoops, too late . . .

Friday, 10 AM: I have wiped the dust off my képi. The frayed leather bindings on my history books gleam.
The contract lies unsigned.

6 PM: Kate lowers the knife blade and the onion skids across the butcher block to the floor.
"*Merde!*"
"Kate! Honey! You don't say that. If you have to, you say 'Mince!' "
"*Mince, alors!* Can we not just *buy* us a *tarte à l'oignon?*"

9 PM: I am slumped over *La Vie en France, Level Two.*

> *Village life in France continues to die by attrition. Farmers' markets, small-scale butchers and bakers are being rendered obsolete by supermarkets that feature mass-produced international goods . . .*

DIALOGUE

François: Il est où le pain?
  Where's the bread?
*Francine: Il n'y en a plus. Je n'avais pas le temps d'aller au centre
  commercial.*
  There isn't any more. I didn't have time to go to the mall . . .

2 AM: I lie in the four-poster staring at the ceiling gloom. Nigel snores beside me.

There have been no more messages. The contract lies untouched.

The year stretches ahead of me. The years. More page proofs. More textbooks. La Vie en France, Level Three. Level Four. Level Five.

qu'est-ce qu'on mange aujourd'hui maman?

I pull on my kimono and climb down the ladder.

My bunker looks good. My grandfather glares encouragement over his clipped mustache.

ball-buster

academic

One photographer stands between me and the history book I've always wanted to write. And he has signed a contract.

I'm stuck with him.

I pull Captain Parker's jacket tight. Jean-Jacques Chabrol *will* follow my lead. I slip the contract out of the FedEx pack. I reach for a fountain pen. Vive l'histoire, I think.

I sit in my oak chair and sign.

4 ❧ Coup de Grâce

Thursday, March 13, 11 AM: Back in my bunker, I am sending yet another e-mail to Chabrol. He has remained silent since I signed the contract, two weeks ago. I'm getting restless. I need a confirmed story list. I need a schedule. I need *something.*

> *Monsieur Chabrol,*
> *I would be grateful if you would review the story list and cooperate with me in scheduling our research travel and "shoots." It would be a waste of time for me to propose dates without feedback from you, given your busy freelance life. Please contact me at your earliest convenience.*
> *—M. Parker*

Ball-buster? More like begging at this point.

There is, once again, no reply.

Friday, 8 AM: I have packed up my laptop and am heading out to the Toul library again. Sophie has been easing her way into the household, taking on longer and longer hours as I slip off to copy notes from *The Letters of Vincent van Gogh.*

The doorbell rings. *"Salut les jeunes!"* Sophie strides in on heavy platform soles, the cuffs of faded cargo pants dragging like a train behind her. She is wearing a ten-inch kilt as a kind of hip-belt, a cropped fishnet blouse, and gloves with the fingers cut off. Her eyelids are glittering red.

Cloey screams, "Sophie!" and sends his Choco-Puffs flying. Gerald is beside himself, lunging back and forth between the spilled milk and

Sophie's blue-nailed fingers. She swings Cloey onto one hip, swoops up the cereal bowl, and carries both to the sink, singing, "'Allooo, Kate!" over her shoulder.

Kate slides off her chair and runs to her. "Halloooo, Sophie!" She studies Sophie's ensemble and switches to French. "Why do you wear a skirt *and* pants?"

Sophie wriggles her eyebrow stubble. "Keeps my *fesses* warm, that's why!" She has already wiped up the milk. She dries her hands and extends one to me. "*Bonjour, Madame!* Is your hand feeling better?" I hold up the clean, pink-scarred fingers and nod.

"*Bonjour, Monsieur.*" She gives Nigel's hand a firm pump. He looks up from his *Telegraph.*

"*Bonjour.*" He eyes her skirt. "Royal Stewart, you know. The red ground means Royal Stewart."

Sophie holds her face in a firm, uncomprehending smile.

"*C'est un écossais . . .* Oh never mind."

I slip out the door, smiling.

11 AM: Silence. Concentration. The library desk lamp shines down on the pages of Van Gogh's letters to his brother Theo. My hand rests on my chin. He loved Arles. He found the colors beautiful, the houses, the cafés, even the shade of the women's skin. He begged his brother to send him more paints to capture them.

October 1888

My dear Theo,

I won't write a long letter because tomorrow early I am going to start work in the cool morning light to finish my canvas . . .

The wood of the bed and chairs is the yellow of fresh butter, the sheet and pillows very light lemon-green . . . The shadows are subdued . . . a contrast with the night café . . .

The night café. *Terrasse du café le soir.* The Maison Jaune. His yellow house on the place Lamartine. The famous bedroom.

I ease the glossy art book open and page through to *La chambre à Arles.* Caned chairs. Lumpy bed. I turn to the night café, glowing amber under a wedge of cerulean sky.

I scan copies of the artworks to send to Chabrol.

Saturday, March 29, 11 AM: I am ready to get going on Arles, but there's no news from Chabrol. He never acknowledged the paintings I e-mailed.

Still, it's spring. I come back from the market, my basket heavy with the first asparagus, thick yellow-white stalks bulging with sinew and juice. I can already taste them. I'll make a hollandaise with the eggs the widow Mathilde gave me. She's better than a market, with her eggs and sprouting lettuce shoots and the spring peas she sends home with the children. The kids love her like a grandmother.

I have just enough time to duck down the ladder before they get home. I grab a mug of coffee and climb down to my office.

There is, at last, a message from Jean-Jacques Chabrol.

> *Madame Parker,*
> *You mentioned Arles. This is a good time. I am there tomorrow. Meet me for shoot?*
> *jjchabrol*

Tomorrow? I flop back in my chair and stare at the screen. *Tomorrow?*

Who does he think he is? I have obligations! I have children! And *I* am supposed to arrange the itineraries, aren't I? After Bayeux, he has the nerve . . .

I won't do it. I won't.

But I sit a moment and drift. Van Gogh. The Maison Jaune. The caned chair.

The night train.

I could be there for breakfast. I dig out my calendar and shuffle through the pages. Sophie was coming for library time anyway.

I type back:

> *Great! I'm eager to get*

No. I erase. He's supposed to be following *my* lead. I type:

> *Monsieur Chabrol,*
> *Meet me for breakfast Sunday at Café Vincent (place du Forum) and I'll try to arrange access to the landmarks. Given the short notice this will be difficult but we can improvise on site. Please confirm.*
> *—M. Parker*

I Send and sit staring at the screen, as if willing it to reply. The phone rings instead.

"Madame Parker?" I haven't heard his voice since Bayeux. Wary. Soft.

"Yes. Monsieur Chabrol?"

"Yes. I'm in Marseille for a bouillabaisse story. You can come to Arles tomorrow? Good. I'll stay at the Hôtel des Romains tonight and meet you. It's just across the way."

The Romains. On *Vive l'Histoire*'s paltry budget? "Good. There's a train in from Avignon at nine-thirty. I'll meet you. And Monsieur Chabrol?"

"Yes?"

"Please bring your story list and agenda so we can work out our travel schedule." I swallow and straighten my shoulders. "I'll need more notice next time."

"Of course." I hear the click of a lighter. "I am at your disposal. I am to . . . follow your lead."

I hope so. I swallow. "Good. So I'll see you in the morning? And we can start shooting the—"

The dull warble of a phone rings somewhere. "I'll call you back."

I sit, listening to the dial tone. I hang up and wait some more. He doesn't call back.

I climb up the ladder to look for Nigel.

10:45 PM: Southbound. The night train rolls into Nancy and wheezes to a stop. I heave my laptop and bag up into the sleeper car and stumble into the cabin just as the train lurches ahead.

"*Ssshh!*" hisses a voice from an upper berth.

"*Désolé,*" I whisper.

The *couchettes* are stacked like bunk beds, three along each wall. There is only one left, at the top. I grope for the ladder and haul up my bag and laptop. I unfurl the quilted sheet-bag onto the slippery mattress. I snake my way into it and try to settle.

The train is rolling well now, jostling rhythmically through the darkness. A woman below me has a thick smoker's cough and bubbles and hacks in spasms. Every time she coughs a woman across from me murmurs *"Oh la la"* and turns away.

I shimmy into something like a sleep position and stare up at the padded ceiling just above my eyes.

Kate. Cloey.

It was easy getting away this time. Kate only mentioned her "sore sroat" once and Cloey barely looked up when I left, so absorbed was he in the card tower Sophie was building on the kitchen table. Nigel asked her to come even though it's the weekend. As I headed out the door with my bags I heard him muttering into the phone. ". . . just a quick one, then? Sevenish? Match starts at nine . . ."

I have to sleep. I imagine Cloey's fat, moist cheeks and try to deconstruct the smell of them: Choco-Puffs, ammonia, bread dough, soap. I think about Kate's hair and catalog its colors: red and copper and butterscotch, streaked hair by hair in a blend any salon would kill to reproduce. It is Cloey's hair, and Nigel's too. I make an effort to relax, to let myself rock with the train. The northern soil is rumbling away beneath me as I barrel headlong toward something new.

Sunday, March 30, 8 AM: I nearly slept through the Avignon stop and stand blinking, furry-mouthed, on the quai. The air is strangely warm and dry. Resinous, clean. Southern. By the time the connecting train to Arles rolls up I'm feeling fresh and alert. Provence!

As the local train to Arles snakes down the Rhône Valley, the light burns with a soft intensity. It focuses the dappling bark of the passing lime trees, the strobing rows of melon fields, with a clarity no camera could capture. To my left, the rock bluffs of the Alpilles flash white above the silvery brushstrokes of olive trees. Farmhouses, tiled in terracotta and stuccoed in ochre, strew across the fields, flanked by spears of cypress. The vineyards stretch to the horizon, pale spring green misting over them as the first shoots force through black bark. Van Gogh could have painted it.

I fold open *Le Provençal* and skim the international page. *L'Amérique proposes 'high-tech' meat to world market,* the headline shouts.

I scan down.

America's latest scheme to dominate the international meat market drew boos from Brussels yesterday. "We see it as a way to feed the world," a U.S. spokesman said. "And to line America's fat pockets," one shocked witness added to the post-forum buzz.

My newspaper crumples into my lap.

10 AM: The little Mercedes taxi winds along the Rhône riverbank then darts suddenly inland into a tightening labyrinth of alleys and squares. I do love Arles. We reel past the place de la République and the Église St-Trophime, its façade a beige rainbow of arcing statuary. I resolve to steal a moment to get back there. I hope I can sneak away from an intense shooting schedule, at least for a few quiet minutes.

We creep down back streets, the houses blocking out the sun above us. There are shutters everywhere, tall and louvred and painted in buttermint hues, like icing on old quarried stone. I roll down the car window. We're getting close to the place du Forum now. Cafés. A statue of Frédéric Mistral. The tableau of southern tranquility I know so well.

The taxi skids to stop. "Sorry, madame. Can't go any farther. Want help with your bags?"

The Mercedes trunk springs open as if of its own will. I lift out my bags and the taxi spurts hastily away. Then I turn the corner and step into pandemonium.

The place du Forum has exploded into a Felliniesque festival, with tables, umbrellas, tents, and cookstands squeezed onto every surface but the statue of Frédéric Mistral. The turgid chromatics of flamenco guitars blast from loudspeakers suspended in the trees. There are fat yellow lightbulbs swagged between them and clouds of steam rising from iron pans, sizzling with saffron paella. Waiters snake between the long tables and bottle after bottle of rosé passes down the rows. The party seems to have been going on for hours.

This is a good time to come to Arles, he said. Right.

For a moment I stand, disoriented by the fracas around me. Then I get my bearings and begin to quarterback through the mob toward the Café Vincent.

I cross its famous terrace, jammed with iron chairs and tables and drunks. With this mob it's hard to picture the gas-lit masterpiece that immortalized it. I push open the door and roll my bag into the bar.

A wall of smoke blinds me and I cower at the din. A hundred customers are wedged into a space where twenty should be. Every surface is littered with coffee cups and wineglasses and ceramic ashtrays heaped with stubs. The roar of hoarse laughter thunders off the hammered-tin ceiling. There are workers and bikers, grandmothers and teenage boys. Everyone, everywhere, seems to have a red Camargue scarf knotted at the throat.

Except one. Arabic cotton, black and white, a straggling matt of grey-streaked hair. He is sprawled backward in a bentwood chair, one hand in his limp jeans pocket, the other pinching a cigarette, gesturing. His face is pasty-pale and unshaven, his hair unwashed. Three men with high-polish tans crowd his table. They wear linen jackets over their shoulders and they're tipping sherry glasses to their lips, laughing. Is he never alone?

Chabrol looks over and spots me. His eyes drop briefly, as if he were bracing himself. His companions turn to look.

I am aware that I haven't changed the clothes I slept in on the train. I take a breath and smile brightly.

Chabrol rocks forward and rises to his feet. "Madame Parker."

I roll my bag, suddenly enormous, across the tile floor.

"Here's the reason I've come to Arles," he says lightly to his friends. "Madame Parker and I are tracing the steps of Vincent van Gogh." His hand passes over his lips.

The group focuses suddenly on crushing out cigarettes. Then the tannest of them leaps to his feet and the others follow, shaking my hand all around. Chabrol bites his filter and gives my hand a cursory squeeze. "Baptiste, Jean-Loup, Olivier."

"Please!" Baptiste gestures to his chair. *"Bienvenue à la Féria."* His accent has a nasal southern ring and his words have twice as many syllables as usual; it sounds like "Bieng-eh-ven-oo-eh!"

"Féria?" I blink. I drop into the proffered chair.

"What you see all around you, Madame Parker. *This* is the féria!" He sweeps an arm at the crowd in the bar, on the square outside.

"Baptiste is the head of the tourist committee in Arles," Chabrol explains.

"And we're delighted you're here!" Baptiste gives me his most professional smile. Chabrol looks elsewhere.

"You're lucky," Baptiste presses on. "You're seeing our small town at its liveliest. It'll make a very good story for your readers."

"But—" I shoot a glance at Chabrol, who has lit another cigarette and stretches his arms as he exhales. "We're here to cover the sites Van Gogh—"

"You see," Baptiste continues smoothly, "every spring for one weekend Arles becomes more Spanish than the Spanish. We celebrate our roots in Spanish culture, our roots in the marshlands of the Camargue. We feast, we dance, we have bullfights . . ."

Bullfights? I try to remain polite. "Ah. I didn't realize Arles was under Spanish rule at one time."

The men exchange looks and shrug. "She wasn't. But we feel that culture very strongly. Our Roman arena is suited to Spanish-style bullfights. As well as our own simple Camargue *courses*."

"In fact . . ." Chabrol looks at his watch.

"Ah yes, we have to hurry. Please forgive us for not offering you a drink, Madame Parker. You'll accompany us of course?"

"To?"

"To the bullfights!"

10:30 AM: The crowd pulses through the streets, flowing toward the Arènes. We flow with them. There are drummers and dancers, a band lurching rhythmically, trumpets wobbling out of tune. Women sway their hips in bright East-Indian cotton prints, hanging on the arms of men in black velour vests.

Chabrol slips through the crowd, festooned with cameras and lenses. He swivels back and shoots into faces before they have time to freeze, then just as quickly slips away. I trot after him, jostled left and right, gripping my laptop shoulder bag. Chabrol entrusted my suitcase to the Vincent bartender. Now I wish I'd let him take the laptop, too. He copes well, Chabrol. I have to grant him that.

The crowd carries us through the arched gateway into the Roman arena. I have never seen it like this. Its great stone arches buttress concentric rings of bleachers that now fill slowly with fans, twenty thousand strong. Some scan programs that size up the competition, some scan the crowds with binoculars. The band pumps away, trumpets blatting, drums thumping.

Chabrol catches my eye. "Over here, this way," he says. I follow and we thread our way sideways up the risers. The companions from the café hail us. They seem to be seated in some sort of VIP box, swagged in red and perched directly above the ring.

I gasp. "You certainly have the right kind of friends!" Then I regret it. Take the lead, Meg. "Listen, Monsieur Chabrol. How long is this going to last? When are we going to . . . ?" But he has already swung away and is trotting down the risers two steps at a time.

The companions jump to their feet, beaming, and part to create a seat for me. "You've been to a bullfight before?" asks Baptiste.

I take my eyes off Chabrol's retreating back and take a deep breath. "Not really, no. Just a little amateur event in Mexico years ago. It was awfully—"

"We will guide you. It's a glorious tradition, very ancient, and there are nuances that are not immediately apparent to the uninitiated."

The din is growing all around us, but Baptiste leans into my ear and launches into a detailed summary of the principles of the Spanish corrida. Jean-Loup leans into my other ear and contradicts him, cutting off each phrase with *"Mais non!"* and *"En fait c'est justement le contraire!"* Neither finishes a complete sentence and I divide my attention as best I can. Part for my neighbors. Part for practicing the piece of my mind I'll give to Chabrol when this bullfight is over.

11:30 AM: The third bull of the morning has just crumpled onto its knees, slobbering blood into the sand. I thought it would never die. Now its carcass is being towed away on a sledge to wild cheers and a shower of red carnations. I am pressing a tissue hard against my lips. The matador strides toward our box, shoulders thrown back in his jeweled vest, feet turning out like a dancer's, and bows from the waist. Then he lifts something to the sky. Baptiste applauds violently.

"What's that?" I ask.

"It is the ear," Baptiste explains. "He was awarded the bull's ear for his expert performance!"

Jean-Loup slouches back and shakes his head in disgust.

"A very poor performance. Clumsy. A brute. He missed his coup de grâce by a meter, stabbed wide of the spinal nerve. That's why the bull took so long to die."

I wet my lips. "Is it finished?"

"No, no!" Baptiste is still pounding together his hands. "There are three more bulls before noon. The next matador is a favorite—a girl from our own Camargue."

I try to show my delight. Chabrol climbs down the risers to our box. He has been all over the arena. He is slightly out of breath and he's grinning.

"So, Madame Parker. What do you think? It's beautiful, isn't it?" I blink weakly. He sizes me up and wipes away the smile. "Come with me, I'll take you below. You can see the inner workings."

He has already taken off down the steps at a trot. I pick my way carefully after him.

We plunge down dark stone stairs to a lower level, under the boxes, cramped and catacomb-dim. We seem to be below the level of the playing field; my eyes are even with the legs of the arena crew, who are raking over the bloody sand. All around the rim there are photographers, dozens of them, shoulder to shoulder, straddling tripods, long lenses aimed onto the field. Some are lounging now between the fights, smoking and exchanging friendly obscenities. One spots Chabrol.

"*Putain!* If it isn't Daddy's boy wonder!" He claps Chabrol on the shoulder.

He winces, though I'm not sure whether from the blow or the taunt. "*Salut,* Armand."

A small knot of colleagues gathers. "J-J! Thought I saw you skulking around up there."

"Another of your gastronomic dream assignments, *salaud!*"

They light up. I hang back in the shadows and look at my watch, taking care that Chabrol notices. If we're done by noon, I calculate, we can do the Maison Jaune and the Hôtel-Dieu before nightfall. I press my hands to my stomach. Might as well relax and go with it, I think. It's not every day you see a bullfight. And Van Gogh went to bullfights. Maybe I can work it into the tourist info in the back of the book.

There's a roar from the arena and the photographers swing back their lenses. Chabrol heads for an obscure doorway marked "Access forbidden." Then he hesitates and turns to me.

"Come on." He cracks open the door and slips in. I look around me and hover for an instant. Then I hike up my laptop and follow.

We are climbing a spiral stone staircase into one of the medieval towers and it is pitch dark. The air is close and dank and I can't see my feet. I drop to all fours and clamber up, laptop bouncing on my back. I can make out a wedge of light above and see a floor and then a cracked door.

"Monsieur Chabrol?" I whisper, brushing my hands off and squinting into the sun. I step through the door. We are on a rooftop towering over the stands, the whole of the arena encircled at our feet. Chabrol is photographing, knees bent, swinging the whirring camera left to right, clicking. His camera bag dangles from a sawhorse painted in large red letters: ACCÈS STRICTEMENT INTERDIT.

I look nervously around. "Monsieur Chabrol, we're not supposed to be up here."

For some reason Chabrol turns to me and smiles.

1 PM: We ride the wave of people out the entrance gate and pull over into an alley, where Chabrol's VIP clique regroups. "All that sand makes you thirsty, no?" says Jean-Loup, rubbing his hands together. "A little pastis, Madame Parker?"

I search frantically around for Chabrol. He is checking his messages, his phone clapped to one ear, a hand over the other, squinting through smoke. I lean into him and raise my voice.

"Excuse me? We'll still have enough light to do the Maison Jaune and the Hôtel-Dieu this afternoon, won't we?"

He nods, then his eyes go abstract again, listening.

"Shall we?" Baptiste offers an intervening arm. "Even hard-working writers need nourishment, no? A glass of something and then—paella!"

3 PM: The restaurant of the Romains is packed with sleek urbanites spurning the mobs on the *place* outside. Baptiste whispers a few words to the hostess who suddenly turns the full force of her welcome smile on me. "We have a couple of small rooms in reserve for our friends. We would be honored!" Our meal seems to materialize from nowhere as soon as we slide into our chairs. My suitcase reappears and is spirited upstairs. Friends in high places, I think.

I can't help but relax when the paella is served—studded with shell-fish and langoustines, perfumed with saffron. "Is this what they're eating out there on the *place,* too?" I ask Jean-Loup.

He smiles and, with poised knife and fork, pushes a deftly dissected shrimp skin onto the rim of his plate. "Gérard makes a better version for his guests."

I taste. The langoustines are fresh and tender. I peel another one and pop it into my mouth, briny, almond-sweet. I lick my fingers and close my eyes. When I open them Chabrol is photographing my plate.

Now Gérard, white jacket unbuttoned at the end of the shift, has swept us into the bar to join him for one last *digestif.* I stick to amontillado sherry while the others move on to harder stuff. I glance at my watch again. I know Chabrol sees me do it—I make sure he does—but he is absorbed in the stuffed bull head mounted over my head. He slides suddenly off his chair and drops to a crouch, photographing the broad black head through the crystal glasses. He lifts my hand absently out of the picture and rearranges the stems. Then he shoots some more.

I am beginning to feel the weight of a sleepless night train and too much pastis. I try to keep alert, waiting, hoping to catch Chabrol's eye. At last, the men lean back in their chairs in a pleasant stupor that even a third espresso can't overcome.

I sit forward expectantly. "Maybe now would be a good time to visit the Maison Jaune? Where Van Gogh lived with Gauguin? Where his famous room was, in the painting with the bed, the caned chair . . . ?"

". . . and maybe the famous ear?"

Who said that? My head swings toward Chabrol. He is intent on lighting a cigarette. Jean-Loup and Baptiste are exchanging looks. Chabrol hides his expression behind his camera, photographing the empty tapas plate before him. He adjusts the tiny fork carefully and shoots again.

I take a quick breath. "Let's go to the place Lamartine. His neighborhood. The Maison Jaune neighborhood. Please?"

Chabrol glances at his watch and suddenly concurs. *"D'accord!"*

At last.

4 PM: Chabrol's back retreats before me, cameras bouncing at his ribs, and I trot behind.

We move through a labyrinth of cobbled streets, pressed in by high stucco walls, rows of pastel shutters framing ironwork filigree. Lace curtains pull aside and pale elderly faces peer through. Unlike the *quartier* around the place du Forum and the Arena, there are no souvenir shops here, no deluxe Provençal fabric stores, no arts-and-crafts boutiques. There are greengrocers and bakeries and hardware stores, their windows crammed with dusty pots and pails.

We turn a corner and I almost trip over something black and bulky. On the sidewalk in front of a small butcher shop, six severed bull heads stand in a row, round eyes glazed, a trickle of blood trailing onto the newspapers beneath. I recoil. Chabrol lifts his camera and fires furiously.

"Are those from this morning?" I ask as we jog ahead.

"Their meat's highly prized," Chabrol explains over his shoulder. There is a trace of long-suffering in his tone. "They don't die in vain, you know."

The sidewalk seems to be narrowing as more and more people crowd past us, all flowing in the same direction. "Where are we going?" I pant. "Where are all these people going?"

Chabrol walks ahead. "Maybe they're looking for traces of Van Gogh, too."

I study his shoulder blades and the set of his head, which remains neutral. I bite my tongue and trot ahead.

i am to follow your lead

The street empties suddenly into a square, really a hub of several streets and alleys. Chabrol stops abruptly and gestures. *"Voilà* your place Lamartine."

A cluster of concrete-slab cubes skew sloppily over a broad open space, treeless and fluttering with laundry. But the pavement seethes with people, pressing against metal barricades and craning their necks. A small *camionnette* rolls slowly through the parting crowd, a loudspeaker blaring.

"Mesdames et messieurs, keep yourselves securely behind the barricades. Do not enter the street. Anyone passing the barriers does so at his own risk."

I catch up with Chabrol, searching his face.

With his chin he gestures toward the far end of a broad alley. "The *lâcher des taureaux.* The running of the bulls."

There is a deep vibration under my feet. I swing on him. "You— We're—Van Gogh—"

A thundering roar drowns out my accusations. The crowd's whoops and whistles crescendo into a wall of sound.

Oh god. "But we were going to—You said—You did this on *purpose*— You—"

Chabrol has swung himself up onto an ancient horse hitch and wrapped an arm around a drainpipe, his lens pointed hard down the alley. I follow his focal point. A row of teenage boys in white shirts and red scarves is sprinting down the street, chests thrust out, chins thrust up, eyes bulging. Just behind them I see why. A slim-hipped Camargue bull is galloping down the cobblestones after them, horns swinging to the right, to the left, bucking, snorting on its way.

I shrink back against the wall, the crowd pressing back with me. A cry, then a cheer, ripples down the length of the mob, a mix of French and Spanish too raw to separate.

"Olé! Olé!"

"Allez! Allez!"

The boys bound past me, so close I smell their thrill, and the bull sweeps after them, his horns grazing their sagging cargo pants. One black-haired teen catches the bull's eye and he lowers for the charge. I watch the boy's face transform from cocky taunting to pale terror, from fight to flight. He plasters himself against the stucco as the bull hurtles toward him and plunges a curving lance into the wall, just between his legs. My hands pile over my mouth. The boy freezes. The bull pulls back, looks around himself, disoriented, drained, and trots sheepishly down the street. The boy slides down the wall to a fetal crouch, a child again.

I see Chabrol dropping off his perch and I push toward him.

"Did you see that? Did you get that? Did you see that boy's face?"

"Hold this." He thrusts his tripod into my hands and jogs down the street after the bull.

6 PM: By the time I extricate myself from the crowds and make my way back to the Hôtel-Dieu, its iron gates are closed. Chabrol has long since disappeared into the seething flux of revelers and I don't have a clue where he is. The tripod hangs heavy in my hand. I lean my forehead against the bars and gaze balefully into the garden, where the miniature hedges are dark slashes in the fading light. You just have to get his attention, Nikos said.

My phone buzzes in my pocket and I palm it to my ear, my head still resting against the bars.

"Mm?"

"Meg darling?"

The kids. They've been spending a quiet Sunday *en famille*, while I trot around after a wayward photographer all day.

"Hi, Nigel."

"Just checking in. Everything humming along there?"

I smile bitterly. "Fine. A little crazy. There's a festival going on."

"Splendid, add a bit of color to your 'story,' won't it?"

I pass my hand over my eyes. "Lots of color. Has Kate been complaining about her throat?"

"She hasn't mentioned it and I haven't asked. Cloey's been a bloody nuisance though. Put Kate's Barbie—its head rather—down the loo and I've been all day digging it out. Had to use the fire tongs."

I sigh. "How is she?"

"Barbie? Disaster. Never get her hair set to rights again."

I smile into the phone. "I mean Kate. Is she upset?"

"Oh. Well, she's been at the neighbor's all afternoon."

I frown. "Mémé Mathilde's? But—" I stop myself. "Um. What's Cloey up to?"

"Since the Barbie incident? Knackered. Asleep in front of the box, I think."

I think?

"Sorry, love, there's the doorbell. Bye for now. Have fun. 'Work, work, work!'"

I lean back on the gate. Work, work, work.

I trudge back through town and cross the place du Forum. Under the vaults of the Hôtel des Romains lobby, Chabrol is talking on his phone. He raises a hand in greeting. I lift mine but before it's halfway up he turns his back. My hand drops.

"But I shipped them yesterday by Chronopost. You'll have them tomorrow morning, first thing. Yes. Yes. For Thursday, the others. Yes. Good. Ciao. Madame Parker."

I am facing the desk. I thank the clerk cordially for my key. I take my time. Then I turn.

"Madame Parker. Sorry, the crowds . . ." He crosses the lobby and pulls the tripod from under my arm. I drop it like a lead weight into his hand.

I look at him. "The Van Gogh story?"

He shrugs and points toward the lobby windows, opaque against the darkness outside. "I'm afraid the light—"

"No more light. Yes. I am aware of that." I stand very straight. My face is as still as I can force it to be. "Monsieur Chabrol, we need to talk about this story. We need to talk about this book. I did not come here to . . ." I try to keep my voice even. "Go to bullfights."

"Of course, of course." He looks at his watch. He casts desperately around the lobby as if searching for some new deus ex machina to rescue him from me—a phone call, a FedEx, a running bull. "Listen, I have some things to do, but—" he hesitates, takes a deep breath, and passes his hand over his eyes, as if he wanted to blot out the sight of me. "Will you have dinner with me later? We can talk." His hands are on his hips now. He is focused on his shoes. He looks like a man facing a firing squad.

I'm not hungry. All I can think of is a hot bath and a bed. I sigh. "All right. Later. We'll talk. What time?"

"Nine perhaps?" He looks up.

"Nine. I'll bring the story list."

He catches a breath. He holds my gaze with effort. "The story list. Of course. *Alors,* until nine. See you then."

"See you then."

8 PM: Silence. I am up to my ears in bubbles in the antique copper bathtub that sits smack in the middle of my hotel room, the rich red-ochre walls closing around me like a womb. I sigh and sink deeper, the smell of the night train and paella and ten thousand cigarettes floating off my skin. The natural sponge propped behind my neck soaks up hot water and soothes my aching head. I massage my feet with a tiny lavender-scented soap.

Friends in high places. Maybe that will help get us into the sites we need to photograph. I didn't exactly have time to set up the contacts.

I slide deep under the foam.

9:30 PM: I've been sitting in the lobby since nine, thumbing through decor magazines and checking my watch. The mellow goodwill the bath soaked into me is gradually steaming away. My mind flashes to break-fast in Bayeux but I brush the thought aside. He wouldn't bolt this time. He couldn't. He's signed a contract, Nikos said he had.

chiante a pain

I wonder.

The double glass doors fly open with a gust and Chabrol bursts in, red-cheeked and out of breath, his ponytail half undone.

"Madame Parker. I'm sorry. The time got away from me. And I had phone calls to make, and the noise was too bad on the *place* so I . . ."

"That's okay, Monsieur Chabrol." He has a strange look around his mouth. Guilt? Hard to read. I wonder if he was hiding. "Where shall we eat?"

"I've booked a restaurant I know, L'Arlésienne. You don't mind? They're old friends."

"Seems like everyone is your old friend."

"Yes. Well." He looks at his shoes for a moment. Then he rubs his hands together and says *"Bon!* I'm so hungry I could eat with my bare hands." He heads toward the door and out into the féria, then hesitates, turns back, and holds the door for me. I follow.

If the *place* was festive at lunch, it is transformed now into a riot of reckless celebration. The music pounds so powerfully I cup my hands over my ears and trail in Chabrol's wake as he jostles through the crowd. We slip down a series of back streets, leaving the mob behind, and reach a discreet oak door in the center of a shuttered façade. Chabrol presses it open and steps back to let me in.

The restaurant dining room glows, rows of iron candelabras casting striped shadows on golden-ochre walls. Beams, black with age and curved with their own weight, rib the plank ceiling, and a steep oak stair flanks a wall of quarried stone. The tables are full of diners talking quietly, tête-à-tête. What a contrast from the place du Forum tonight, I think.

"J-J!" The host spreads wide his arms and wraps Chabrol in an embrace, kissing him soundly on both cheeks. "It's been years. I was so glad to see your name on the book tonight. And this is the lovely Madame Chab—?"

"Madame *Parker,* Marius. She's writing a travel book for American readers. I'm taking photos—for her. We've been working all day . . ."

I glance at him.

". . . and are very tired."

"And very hungry, I hope! A pleasure to make your acquaintance, Madame Parker. Does it please you, our little féria?"

"Very much." I follow him toward the stairs. "Even though it was a bit of a surprise."

Chabrol glances at me, passes a hand over his lips and says nothing.

We climb the steps and emerge in a small dining area framed in wood and glimmering with candlelight. Only two other couples murmur over their meals.

"Please!" says Marius, pulling out a caned chair.

I brighten a little. "It's the same chair Van Gogh painted in his Arles bedroom!"

"Madame is very observant. We had them made by a local artisan."

"We're here in Arles to write about—" I catch Chabrol's eye "—and photograph, of course—Van Gogh's traces."

The host shoots a look at Chabrol, too, then recovers his smile. "Will you drink something? A pastis?"

Chabrol nods and smokes. I sit.

Marius returns with three glasses, a bottle, and a pitcher of water. "May I?" he asks and pulls out a chair for himself.

"Van Gogh. We were talking about Van Gogh."

He pours an inch of amber pastis over the ice cubes in each glass, then fills them slowly with water, the liquid clouding yellow-white. "It's not a story we're proud of. I am surprised you—*Alors*. To your health!" He raises his glass. "To old times!" We drink. "And to eat tonight? You won't be disappointed by the lamb."

The subject of food takes over. Chabrol and Marius huddle and consult, Chabrol's hand on his shoulder. No one asks my opinion. "The asparagus? Impeccable. The rack of lamb? Cooked pink? Of course. And I'll bring you the cheese. You'll see what I mean about the Banon . . ." He isn't taking notes. This is personal; he is feeding a friend.

"*Bon!* What are you drinking? No ordinary wine for you, J-J." He lays his palms on the tabletop and leans into Chabrol's ear. "You know I still have a bottle of the '82 downstairs. Amazing stuff. Spectacular. What a—"

Chabrol taps his cigarette hard over the ashtray. "Just a bottle of Palette, Marius. And water, please."

The host studies his face for an instant then shakes his head. "As you wish. It's a pity. After all these years . . ."

11 PM: We sit. He smokes. His phone buzzes in his jeans pocket periodically but he swats it off when it rings. I smile my gratitude but he doesn't look up.

The entrée is asparagus, bulging white stalks wrapped in salt-cured ham. I can't help but laugh. "They look just like the asparagus I bought at the market yesterday. I was going to do a hollandaise. Until you called."

He doesn't seem to hear. He is leaning back, digging out his digital, and photographing the plate. Here we go again. But he pockets it immediately.

"*Bon appétit.*" He sounds almost pleasant.

He reaches for his silverware. I reach for the asparagus stem and lift it to my mouth. He looks up. I smile a little self-consciously. "It's okay, my husband says in England they're allowed to eat asparagus with their fingers." I do. I'm aware, under his curious gaze, of how messy a job it is. Still, it's delicious. He looks back at his plate and takes up his knife and fork. Are his ears pink? The French are so formal. Though he doesn't seem the formal type.

"Your husband is British, then?"

A first attempt at personal conversation. I stop in midbite, swallow, set down the stalk. This is new territory.

"Yes. We met at Cambridge."

"Ah. Yes. Cambridge."

He goes back to his asparagus. I go back to mine. This time I use my knife and fork.

Midnight: It's easier when we eat. The silence is filled by the sound of chewing, carving, chewing, sipping. It is hard to stay angry when your mouth is full of lamb. We eat until it hurts, but I can't stop. I didn't get to look at the menu, but Marius and Chabrol have not failed me. The lamb is so savory with thyme, the roasted potatoes so sweet, the greens so subtle, the cheese satiny-ripe.

Only over the cheese does he relax, just a little, into ordinary talk. It feels strange at first. He seems almost human.

". . . So it was in Syria I shot my first story for them. Eleven pages. It wasn't very good. Bad light. Cropped to pieces. But they chose seven of them with, well, food. Crockery dishes full of meats. Baskets full of spices. I began to get calls from the food magazines then. I don't know." He lifts his glass a little. "I guess it's in my blood."

"Food and wine?"

He shrugs as if to change the subject and looks around the room. I lay my cheese knife across my plate and lean forward. "Monsieur Chabrol."

Is that a flinch? It reminds me of Gerald's face when he knows I'm going to throw him out in the rain. "Yes. The book. I know." He takes a deep breath and braces his hands on the tablecloth. "I'm not sure . . . I'm not sure the history angle will work visually."

I don't know what to do with myself. Laugh? Cry? I control my face. Diplomatic. "Um. So I gathered."

He glances up, encouraged by the tone. "There's so much we could do with this book."

"Not if you don't take the pictures." Do I sound stern enough? My glass is lifting to my lips again and the rosé smells good. "I should be furious. I *am* furious. Tomorrow we have to work *hard*. All day."

"I mean the history stuff. You don't really believe—"

I feel my stomach tightening. "I do believe. I do. The publisher is enthusiastic. And I certainly have the credentials, the qualifications to . . ."

His look stops me. It's less pleasant than before.

academic

chiante

I lower my eyes. I roll my napkin in a ball.

He shakes his head and blows out hard. A sigh? "Listen, Madame Parker. France is alive. This history stuff is . . . well, dead."

Oh god, I think. Are we back to square one?

He takes a swallow of rosé and goes on. "There are *living* traditions, you know. Bullfights. Festivals. Why do we have to chase after dead guys? Ghosts."

"Ghosts? *Ghosts?*" I force myself to take a breath. And a swallow of rosé. Keep calm, Meg. "I *feel* those ghosts. I'm aware of them wherever I go in France. I think I'm not the only . . . I *feel* the history. I see it in my mind's eye."

"And me? I'm supposed to photograph . . . what?"

"Well, if you'd get into the spirit of it, you could easily *evoke*—"

"*Evoke?*" He leans back, his jaw set. For a moment I think he's going to get up and leave. I hold my breath. Then he pats for a cigarette. He lights up and blows out. He puts his hands up. Truce.

"Look, Madame Parker, we . . . May I call you . . . ?"

I let my breath out. "Meg. Please call me Meg."

"Mayg. It's Jean-Jacques. Or J-J. It's a nickname. I can't get rid of it."

"Okay . . . Jean-Jacques." I can feel the knot in my stomach loosening. "You were saying?"

He reaches for the wine bottle and refills my glass, then his. "We have to work together a lot this year. We have to try to—"

"J-J!" There is a jubilant shout from the top of the stairs. It's Baptiste and Olivier, fresh from the féria and radiating boozy cheer. "Madame Parker! Here you are hiding when *le tout* Arles is dancing in the streets!"

I look up at Jean-Jacques. He's looking at me. Chagrin? He spreads his hands helplessly. "How did you find—?"

"Marius, the old fox, tipped us off you'd booked. But you can't stay in this stuffy little attic all evening."

There's nothing I'd like more right now, I think. We were finally getting somewhere. A sigh swells in my chest. I stifle it.

Marius trundles up the stairs. "I'll bring glasses. We will drink a glass together."

Jean-Jacques looks at me.

"Why not?" I shrug. "It's the féria!"

I excuse my way to the bathroom to collect my thoughts. Maybe this trip won't be wasted after all.

When I return, Marius has laid the table with enormous crystal balloon glasses. He carries a bottle to the table reverently, its body wrapped in a white linen towel. Jean-Jacques slumps back in his chair and fishes yet again for his cigarettes, his face suddenly neutral.

"*Et voilà!*" cries Marius and flips the towel away like a magician. "Château Brissac-Chabrol 1982! I saved it for just such a gathering!" He tugs a corkscrew from his hip pocket.

I hunch forward to study the label. "Haut-Médoc. Pauillac. Brissac-Chabrol?" I sound out the faded letters. "Chabrol?" I look up.

"J-J hasn't told you? He's the son of a great wine family, one of the oldest of the Bordelais. He was born to the grape. Just like his father, eh J-J?"

Jean-Jacques scrapes back his chair and heads for the men's room.

1 AM: All the crystal glasses are empty but mine. Jean-Jacques' is bone-dry; he wouldn't accept a drop. The bottle lies in a basket, dregs clinging to the green glass. Baptiste is talking about Van Gogh. I am trying to listen but I have my glass to my nose and I am breathing and tasting and savoring. Château Brissac-Chabrol. I have never tasted a wine like this. This dense. This complex. This subtle.

Jean-Jacques slouches back in his chair. He is smoking. Sometimes he looks at me. Is he angry? About the wine? About the book?

"I mean simply this," Baptiste continues, "that Vincent van Gogh was on the edge of madness when he lived here, a drunkard, perhaps crazed by absinthe. He fought. He whored. He didn't pay his debts. And the people of his neighborhood passed around a petition to have him removed."

Jean-Jacques is smoking. I don't think he's listening.

"He was enraged, grieving, angry with his neighbors, his brother, his friend Gauguin, who abandoned him. When he cut his ear he was re-moved to St-Rémy, the mental hospital."

I digest this. "I knew all that. I knew he had trouble with his brother and Gauguin but I didn't know the townspeople—"

Marius interrupts. "Ah yes. He wasn't respected when he was here. He was not appreciated. And so nothing of his was preserved. Nothing at all."

My head snaps up. Nothing at all? I look up at Marius, then at Baptiste, then at Jean-Jacques. I feel blood rising. "But . . ."

Baptiste leans forward and presses his hands together, prayerlike. "Madame Parker," he says softly. I know that tone. It's the voice I use when I talk to Kate. "Madame Parker, the Maison Jaune itself no lon-ger exists. It was demolished in the war. We have many fine galleries, however."

No Maison Jaune. No Maison Jaune? I turn, wide-eyed, to Jean-Jacques. "*Art* galleries? But we are looking for historic traces." My face is burning. "I *know* the Hôtel-Dieu is . . . I was there, *today* . . ."

My voice trails away. For once, no one interrupts me. Jean-Jacques is studying the ash on his cigarette. Baptiste smiles gallantly. "Of course, the Hôtel-Dieu gardens are beautiful and they have been restored to look exactly like the painting by Van Gogh. But the building itself is private these days."

I look around the table. Jean-Jacques sucks in, blows out smoke. I turn to Baptiste, lay a hand on his arm, a little desperate. "What about the drawbridge, from *Le pont de Langlois?*"

He brightens politely. "Ah, yes. There is a reproduction constructed just outside of town. Modern, of course. But I am sure it could support your story very effectively!"

I sink back into my chair. All that library work. This is what I get for making an impulse trip without making contacts in advance. Or talking the story through with the photographer. I aim a resentful glance at Jean-Jacques. He is squinting at me through a searing cloud of smoke. I drop my eyes.

"*Bon. Écoutez,*" Baptiste pushes back his chair and opens his hands. "What are we sitting here talking about paintings for? There's a féria outside! Come on, Madame Parker, I'll show you that sometimes Arles knows what she's doing!"

2 AM: We have rejoined the revelers on the streets and flow with them toward the place de la République. The Gallo-Roman obelisk at its center has been strung with lights and hung with flowers, and the vast open square has transformed itself into an impromptu dance floor. Speakers have been propped at the obelisk base and Spanish guitar music — assertive, sensual, compellingly rhythmic — drives the masses to movement.

Baptiste is beside himself. He has clearly not stopped drinking since breakfast. He flings an arm over my shoulder and drags me forward. Oh god.

"Madame Parker!" he shouts over the music. "This is how we celebrate here in stodgy old Arles!" He clamps a hand behind my waist, pulls me to him, and begins to swirl me around the *place*. My protests are drowned in an explosion of "Olés!"

His feet fly in and out, back and forth, in tight, neat jerks, and his heels hammer out the rhythm. He's really very good. I shuffle my feet, frantic to keep up. I stumble slightly and he catches me and takes me off on a spin. All I need is a rose in my teeth, I think. I wrench myself away and double over, trying to slow the revolving cobblestones.

"Please. I can't do this."

Baptiste laughs. "You're inexperienced, Madame Parker. You have to get used to Spanish dancing."

I raise my head and search the square with rolling eyes. Jean-Jacques is there, in the midst of the fray, but he isn't dancing. He's shooting as fast as he can.

3 AM: I have shaken hands and kissed strangers' cheeks all around the place de la République and now, at last, stumble back to the hotel. Jean-Jacques is nowhere to be seen.

We haven't photographed a single Van Gogh landmark. What there is to photograph.

I lower myself into the deep leather armchair in my room and ease my boots off my swollen feet. Bed. Bed. I gaze longingly at the wrought-iron baldaquin in the corner, but I'm too tired to get up and go to it. Blessed silence rings in my ears.

There is a soft rap at my door.

"Madame Parker?" It can't be. I hope Baptiste didn't follow me. He was kissing my hand by the time I made my escape. A one-man welcome committee. I haul myself with difficulty out of the chair and limp in my stocking feet to the door. Jean-Jacques is standing there.

"Madame Parker — euh, Mayg. Sorry to disturb you."

I smile wanly. "Jean-Jacques, I am very tired."

"I'm sorry, but . . . Just come see this."

By the time I pull my boots back on he has already turned and headed down the hall. The crowds on the place du Forum have thinned to a few weary diehards and the music has mercifully stopped. I slog across the littered square to its far end, where Jean-Jacques halts and turns to me.

"You see?"

"See what?" I am pulling at the boot zipper and peering in the vague direction of his pointing finger.

I straighten. I see what he sees. The terrace of the Café Vincent, where we met seventeen hours ago, lies bathed in yellow light. The golden sweep of its awning blots out the chimney-crowned houses that loom black behind. Above, I can just make out a wedge of cerulean star-spangled sky.

It is Van Gogh's painting in three dimensions.

I look at him and smile. He's looking at me. I can't see his face very well. I think he's smiling back.

He takes the tripod from his shoulder and extends the legs.

Monday, 8 AM: I am waiting in the breakfast room watching the door for Jean-Jacques. He agreed to get up early so we could make the most of the Van Gogh landmarks. Reconstruct them. Evoke them. Last night it seemed like he was almost on my side.

But my coffeepot is empty and the milk pitcher, too. I look at my watch. He wouldn't. Would he?

"Mayg?"

Jean-Jacques comes into the room and pulls back the other chair at my table. His hair is still unwashed and he is scratching his unshaven chin. "Sorry. My phone alarm didn't go off." He's bound that Arabic scarf around his neck and its black-and-white graphics seem to draw the color from his face.

"I'm afraid I've drunk the coffee." I look around for the waitress.

"It's okay." He reaches for a cigarette and I suppress a sigh. The waitress comes up. "Just an espresso, please."

He drags on the cigarette. When the coffee finally comes, he drinks it in one swallow.

"So."

"So!" I try to keep my tone bright. "That was a good start last night with the Café Vincent! I'm . . . I'm glad you came to get me."

"We'll see what comes out. There was a lot of stuff in the way."

My heart sinks a little.

He is smoking and looking around the room, rubbing his eyes. Elsewhere. I straighten my shoulders. Right. Clearly I need to call the shots here. Literally. This trip can still be saved.

"So, why don't we start at the Alyscamps? It's open, I checked, a hike but it's worth it. There are funeral monuments scattered around, just the way Van Gogh painted them, and—"

"Funeral monuments." He is rubbing his forehead as if it hurts.

"Well, yes. Don't worry, I know the paintings well. I can help you frame the shots."

"You can . . . help me." His hand hovers over his eyes. He pulls deep on the cigarette.

"Yes! I've always been very strong in art history. It's one of my specialties. I did a paper at Cambridge on . . ."

But he takes his hand away and looks at me. I stop.

"Well. Shall we?" I slide back my chair.

He pushes back his.

10 AM: We are walking down a long pathway, shaded by cypress and lined with broken rock, old stones carved with letters and tooled with bas-reliefs.

". . . And the *stelae*—that's Latin for funeral stones—were lying at a three-quarter angle with a foreground of poplars. Like that, over there . . ."

Jean-Jacques' camera hangs over his chest. I look back at him and point at the scene. He steps forward obediently, a dark look on his face, and raises the camera.

"Do you mind if I . . . ?" I gesture toward the camera and raise my hands. "I know the composition so well I just . . ."

He threads the camera from off his neck and holds it up for me. I look through the viewfinder. "That's it. Try that!"

He takes the camera back. He aims and shoots. The camera hangs back on his chest. His hands hang back at his sides. "Then what?"

"That was good, don't you think? I mean there were several shots—I mean *paintings*—here in the Alyscamps actually. Gauguin did one, too. This is where they buried their dead, the Romans. The Gallo-Romains. Did you know that?" I try a smile. If he would only lighten up.

"No." He looks at his watch.

I don't care if he looks at his watch. I was the one looking at my watch all day yesterday. Today, I am calling the shots.

11 AM: We have taken a taxi out to the drawbridge. It's a carefully built wooden structure outside town and set in a backlot of an industrial

field. I admit there's not much to it. At least I admit it to myself. To Jean-Jacques I say "This is it! See? Just like the painting!"

"Ah. Just like the painting."

He hands me the camera without my asking and lights a cigarette.

12 PM: The garden of the Hôtel-Dieu is in full sunlight when we arrive. "Sun's overhead. No good." He doesn't look sorry.

"But . . ."

"Unless you want me to . . ."

"Well. You could try."

"Okay. I will *try*." He raises the camera and walks up and down the hedge-lined paths. He clicks. He lowers the camera and shrugs. "Okay?"

"Well, actually, the painting was from *this* angle. If you stood over here . . ."

He paces over to me. He doesn't hurry. He steps precisely into the spot I cede to him. He aims.

"May I?"

He hands the camera to me.

"That's it! Great!"

He takes it back. He aims and clicks.

"Okay?"

"Okay. Now what? How about the place Lamartine, without the crowds?"

"How about lunch."

1:30 PM: He has brightened considerably over the cold buffet at L'Écurie. Just the sight of his face relaxing makes me relax, too. My stomach loosens its nervous knot and growls loudly. I blush, hoping he didn't notice. Or that he has the good grace to pretend.

But he actually laughs, that ringing laugh that swivels heads around the room. "See? Even historians get hungry."

It is the first time he's smiled all day. He hands me a terra-cotta plate. "Try these chickpeas."

We taste as we fill our plates. "Mm. Cumin."

"And lemon?"

"Lime, I think."

"Mm. You're right." He looks at me. He heaps a scoop onto my plate. There is roasted eggplant with garlic and red peppers in oil, anchovies and aïoli and sausage-stuffed zucchini. He saws slices of cold red lamb and lays one on my plate, one on his own. We head for a table and dig in. I slip a whole strip of red pepper into my mouth and lick away the olive oil. God, that's good.

By the time he has poured the last of the rosé into my glass, his cheeks have taken on some color and his face has softened. He photographs the food, of course, but I don't mind. It's cold anyway. I'm just grateful to see him smile.

3 PM: We have walked up and down the back streets of Arles. Jean-Jacques is shooting right and left, people, shop displays, street vendors. Now he's not stingy with the film. Must be for stock. Photo agencies. There is a spring in his step now that wasn't there this morning.

At a butcher shop he leads the *boucher* to the front door and asks him to hold up a string of sausages. The butcher smiles from ear to ear and Jean-Jacques snaps. At a pastry shop laden with sweets he gestures to the server through the plate-glass window and catches her startled smile.

He saunters back to me. Now he is feeling magnanimous. "So, another masterpiece to capture?"

"Well, there's the Roman theater. Near the Arena."

"Near the Arena?" He looks at his watch. "Okay."

This time when I point out the scene Van Gogh painted, he steps carefully over the stone seats of the amphitheater and crouches to frame. I make an effort, too. I hold my hands behind my back.

"This about right?"

"Yes. Just a little to the—no. Really, that's fine. That's good."

"Good." He shoots for a while and stands. He looks at his watch again. "Does that take care of Vincent van Gogh?"

I look carefully at him but his face is straight. "Yes, I guess so. Except maybe the place Lamartine. Or if you wanted to redo the Hôtel-Dieu in better light . . ."

"When's your train?"

"Not till late. I'm taking the night train north."

"*D'accord.* Listen. There are more bullfights at four o'clock if you'd like to —"

"Oh god, no more bullfights."

"No. These are *courses camarguaises*. The traditional bull 'races' from the Camargue region." He looks at my face. "No, these are interesting. They're . . . gentle. No swords. No blood. Just some guys trying to catch the cockade from the bull's horn."

I look at him warily. "Can we shoot the place Lamartine afterward?"

He sets his jaw slightly. "Sure, whatever. Come on. You'll like it. It's traditional. It's . . . historic."

Now he is smirking, but only a little.

5 PM: He's right. I do like it. It's just a game, team sports, twenty men in tennis whites and sneakers bouncing around the arena waving their arms at a bucking bull, snatching at his horns. The bull joins in as if he actually enjoys it, lowering his head and chasing the players, who leap agilely over the barricade in the nick of time. The bull trots out of the ring alive and to wild applause. An announcer rattles off bids from local businesses who raise the ante with every round. It feels like a high-school tennis match in Indiana. Or a 4-H fair. I find myself cheering and clapping with the rest of the crowd.

The kids would love this. The kids. They should be home by now. Has it been a whole day since I called? I dial hastily and Kate picks up.

"Kate? Honey? I'm at a bullfight. Listen!" I hold the phone up to catch the whoops of the crowd. "Did you hear that? A real bullfight! Only nobody kills the bull!"

"When are you coming home, *Maman?*"

"Um. Tonight. Tomorrow."

"*D'accord.*" Dial tone.

I sigh and scan the arena. Jean-Jacques is threading his way through the stands, leaning over the rail and shooting with his long lens. When a player slips the ribbon off the horn, he lowers his camera and laughs. I can hear it from the other end of the arena.

7 PM: He's disappeared again. I leave the arena alone and wander over to the place Lamartine, hoping to find him shooting, but he isn't there. It's dark anyway.

I go back to the hotel to get my things. There's no message. He's never even given me his cell phone number. Only for the privileged few, I think. I check out and head for the *gare*.

As I lie in my *couchette* rolling northward, my phone beeps a text message. I grope for it, hissing apologies to my roommates. The tiny screen blinks on.

> *sorry. ran into friends. will send arles shoot this week. too bad we didn't find the ear. jj*

I hope he typed that with a smile.

5 ⚜ Negotiations

Thursday, April 3, Midnight: Deep in my bunker, the heater glowing against my feet, army jacket draped over my shoulders, I raise a fourth glass of Southern Comfort (somebody had to drink it) and savor the moment. This is going to be good. *Vive l'Histoire* will have it all—drama, local color, a sense of place in time and region. I'll weave in the tourist information, too. And the first-person format will really bring it to life. No more dry academic prose! Who cares if there was no Maison Jaune? I'll make them see it in their mind's eye.

I take a swig and attack the keyboard.

AGONY, ECSTASY, AN EAR FOR ART:
Vincent van Gogh bleeds for beauty
Arles, 1888

> *I care no more for life or art. Joy abandoned me along with Gauguin and the people of Arles have betrayed me. The whore Art has rolled me and left me destitute.*

Nikos is going to love this. Jean-Jacques will finally get it, too. I blow on chilly fingers and reach for my glass. Nikos wants me to keep it lively. I hammer on.

> *Aïe! how it pains me to wander Arles' gas-lit streets. Absinthe skews my thoughts. I cannot paint.*

I lean back. Good start. The drama's there. I take another swallow and go in for the kill.

> *As Arles and Paul have wounded me so will I wound myself. The razor! My ear will be a gift to the whore.*

But Nikos wanted it to be lively *and* informative. It's supposed to be a travel guide, too. I try again.

> *I care no more for life or art. Joy abandoned me along with my friend the Impressionist painter Paul Gauguin, and the people of Arles, this quaint Provençal town on the edge of the Camargue delta—to me a hellhole—have betrayed me. The whore Art has rolled me and left me destitute.*
>
> *As Arles and Paul have wounded me so will I wound myself. The razor! My ear will be a gift to the whore, like the ear of the bull presented to the victorious matador at Arles' traditional bullfights, part of its colorful annual féria.*

Jean-Jacques will appreciate that last part. I knew I could work it in somehow!

Jean-Jacques. I empty my glass of the last sugary dribble. Sometimes he seems almost like a nice guy. Then he gets that look. And just when I think he's on board, he bolts.

Still. When he sees the text and when Nikos gets the two together it will all make sense. Then we can get to work.

I can't wait to see the results of the shoot. I check tonight's e-mail for the fourth time. Nothing.

Friday, 9 AM. Oh god. My head is pounding and the cursor blinks violently before my swollen eyes. Maybe this Van Gogh text needs reworking before I send it to Nikos. He said he wanted it colorful, but maybe I'd had one Southern Comfort too many. Still, it's the *spirit* of the book, isn't it? I'll let him read it over and then we'll discuss.

I click Send.

5 PM: Emerging in the barn, I fill the willow basket with firewood. The wall looms vaguely before me. There are chalk marks tracing a square the size of a barn door. The "conservatory." That will be some hole. I head indoors and trip over a carton of empty bottles. Imported ales. Gin. The bourbon Andrew gave us. A lot of glass for the two days I was gone.

The dining table was a mass of architectural plans, magazines, and masons' estimates when I came home Tuesday morning. I wonder if

Raimondo has sent a bid. Evidently, Nigel is going ahead with this. Without me, of course. He's been close-mouthed about it all week.

As if he can tell time, Gerald hurls himself against the front door. I throw on a jacket and head for the bus stop to meet the kids.

6 PM: Kate is bubbling about her day.

"And we made letter songs. And we made letter games."

"You sang songs? You played games?" I am her only source of English grammar, but I try to slip it in gently, separating the tangled threads of two tongues. Since Sophie's been coming, it seems to be getting worse.

"Yes, and then we ate our *goûter* and then we *travail*'d our *chiffres.*"

"You ate your snack and worked on numbers?"

"Yes and then, and then—I need me a *tablier!*"

"You need an apron? What happened to the green one I bought you last fall?"

She turns her pale gaze on me and lowers her brows dramatically. "It is *disparu*'d!"

I laugh and brush her hair out of her eyes. "Disappeared! Well, I'll have to talk to the teacher about that. It must be somewhere!"

I cook, Gerald sprawled longingly at my feet. Kate and Cloey eat their gratin with earnest concentration. Then they play in their bath without splashing—miraculous!—and crawl into their beds without protest.

It's as if they're both watching me carefully.

Cloey clings to my neck a moment and drops off to sleep. Kate clings to my neck a moment longer and whispers in my ear.

"Are you staying now?"

My heart squeezes. It's starting already, and I've only gone away twice. "Yes, I'm staying. I will go away from time to time but I always come right back, just like this week. Papa's here. And Sophie."

"I love Sophie."

Why does my heart clench again? "I'm glad, sweetheart. We're very lucky we found her." I wrap myself around her until her breathing grows even and soft.

Monday, 10 AM: At last! There is a string of messages from Jean-Jacques. They are addressed to Nikos and copied to me and all carry attachments marked in priority-red. There is "Arles I," "Arles II," "Arles III," "Arles IV."

I smile with relief. Looks like he sent me the whole shoot. Maybe he *has* come around.

I click on "Arles I." But . . . this is a group of images of bullfights. The first fills my screen with a tight close-up of a matador's face, his cheeks beaded with sweat, his jaw smeared with blood. The next, a bull twisting through a cloud of sand, a mass of muscle and sinew. I scroll quickly. Men in velvet jackets leaping out of their seats, fists in the air. A man in sneakers and tennis whites laughing and vaulting over the rail, ribbon in hand.

I flop back into my chair, perplexed. It's beautiful stuff. It's nice of Jean-Jacques to send me copies. But where's the shoot for the book?

I open Arles II. It is the place du Forum at dusk, a blurred swirl of churning conviviality. Then the place de la République whirling with dancers. A white platter heaped with langoustine shells and scatterings of saffron rice. Then sherry glasses gleaming through with amber light. Gnarled fingers raising a plastic glass of black-red wine. A close-up of black shoes tangled in a sensual dance. And there is the boy, spread-eagled against the wall, his face a mix of terror and thrill, a horn between his thighs.

I sit very still. Then I raise one finger and click on Arles III. It is a small file. There is a wide shot of the courtyard of the Hôtel Dieu, grey-white, flat, and stark. There is the drawbridge; simply a drawbridge. There are scattered stones along the shaded gravel path of the Alyscamps. They are faithful replicas of the Van Gogh paintings. They are empty and still and cold.

academic

"Arles IV." I click. It is a single photograph. The Café Vincent. The painting is there. A wedge of indigo sky peppered with stars. The yellow glow under a sweep of awning. Scattered chairs, a few couples drinking. But the foreground, exaggerated by the wide angle, is a field of bald blacktop, interrupted by rows of parking barriers.

I remain erect in my chair for a long time, staring. Oh god. I don't know whether I'm angry or . . .

3 PM: I am angry. The more I think about it, the madder I get. I pace back and forth in my bunker, talking to Nikos. Or, rather, talking to myself, practicing what I will say to Nikos when he finally gets into the office in New York. It's 9 AM there. Only a few minutes before I can let fly.

This has gone far enough. If Nikos can't get Jean-Jacques on board for this history series, he'll have to get a new photographer. Or a new writer.

4 PM: "Petras here."

"Nikos?"

"Yep."

"It's me, Meg."

"Meg! How are you? What's up?"

"I'm calling about the art. About Chabrol's Arles shoot."

"Oh. Right." There is a pause. "Yeah, I got it last night."

"And?"

There is another pause. I hear the clicking of keys. "He does beautiful work."

"Beautiful work? Sure, beautiful work. For somebody else's book."

"Well, I do know J-J has reservations about the history theme."

"I thought we'd cleared that up." I pause. I try to phrase carefully, diplomatically. "He's supposed to follow my lead. You told him to follow my lead."

"It's not that he's uncooperative. I think he has trouble illustrating your themes. I mean, the story list has some pretty obscure — "

"Story list? Where was he when I made up the story list? Does he think he can sabotage all my research, all my planning? All my — Does he think he can just toss off whatever he thinks is . . . is *pretty* and — "

"Hang on. Hang on, Meg." Do I hear *chuckling?* "I told you you had to get his attention. Now you have it. He turned in great stuff, terrific stuff. Vital, gutsy, alive. But you have to admit the Van Gogh theme is pretty hard to shoot. If you want to illustrate your history theme, you've got to come up with something sexier than a drawbridge and a graveyard."

"What about my text?"

Nikos hesitates for an uncomfortably long time. "Sometimes you have to feel your way with a new project, Meg. Listen, I've got a meeting in five. I'll talk to J-J. Let's—"

"But we—"

"Let's all try to be flexible, okay? It's going to be a great book."

6 PM: I am chopping, chopping away at the veal on the butcher block, mincing it with a will. Vital. Gutsy. Alive. I push my hair out of my eyes with my forearm. Feel your way. Right. I whittle pork lard into a bowl, then butter, with flour. My fingers work fast and hard, intent, blending and feathering into fine crumbs. The dough comes together and forms a ball. Synthesis.

9 PM: Nigel eases a cork out of a bottle of Pauillac and carries two goblets to the table.

"Have a drink. You'll feel better."

His nose and cheeks are brushed with pink already. Quick pub stop with chaps from work, he said. Ian in town from the London office. At least it gave me time to feed the kids and soothe them to sleep before sliding the veal tourte into the Aga. We are actually going to eat a meal together.

Nigel pushes the glass toward me. "So this photographer's being a bother, then?"

"You can say that again. He's off on his own track. He's never read the story list. It's like he's never even read my e-mails. He doesn't really want to do this book . . ." My voice trails off. I take the glass and raise it to my lips. Pauillac. Like Chabrol's family. A rich, round cloud of scent—black currant, leather—fills my nostrils. I sigh despite myself. "Thanks for this, honey. Cheers." We drink, staring off into space. I roll the flavors over my tongue.

"You're looking a bit rough around the edges. What's that you're wearing? From Patton's last stand?"

I glance absently at my khaki-covered arms. "My grandfather's. Remember? From the war. Keeps me warm down there."

"Right. It would do." He looks around the dining room, the kitchen. They are, admittedly, in chaos. "Do you good to get above ground from time to time."

I try not to bristle. I smile instead and raise my glass. "You can lure me out with a good Pauillac anytime. I tasted an incredible one last week in Arles. It was from Château Brissac-Chabrol, do you know it? The photographer is from an old wine family."

But he is stifling a yawn and his eyes stray longingly across the table to today's *Telegraph,* open to the crossword.

Midnight: Nigel has collapsed in front of the Sky News, snoring so contentedly I pull off his Churches and tuck a throw over him. He missed the prime minister's comments on the world meat trade. Just as well. He'd probably have started in on New Labour again.

I pour the last of the Pauillac into my glass and descend the iron ladder.

I stare at Jean-Jacques' photographs for a while. They are so alive, they surge out of the screen. I can smell the matador's sweat. I can taste the langoustines. I can feel the boy's terror as the bull pins him to the wall.

I open the Van Gogh landmarks. They *are* very accurately framed. But the Alyscamps are bleak without the raw-daubed texture of the painting. The drawbridge is a drawbridge. The light is strong enough. The colors are bright enough. But they are lifeless.

I slump, leaning my cheek on my hand.

A new message comes in. I sit up suddenly.

It's from Jean-Jacques, not copied to Nikos.

Nikos said he'd talk to him. Oh god. Is he backing out after all?

I click. And stare.

It is a single photograph, no message. A full-length image of me, dancing with Baptiste. We are frozen in a swirl on the place de la République, his hand spread over the small of my back. I am bent over backward, hair flying, eyes rolling wild. And I am laughing.

Tuesday, 2 PM: I have to stop staring at the photographs. I have to keep hacking away at *La Vie en France.*

> *In French the word* you *can take two forms, either the formal* vous *or the intimate* tu. *This is a complex social issue to be studied carefully. The* vous *form addresses business and new acquaintances. Family and friends are called* tu. *When in doubt it is best to stick with the*

formal vous *though in some situations it is appropriate to ask permission for clarity.*

DIALOGUE

Francine: Tu as lu le texte que je t'ai envoyé?
Have you *(intimate)* read the text I sent you?
Pascal: Vous ne pouvez pas me laisser le temps de le lire? Écoutez . . .
You *(formal)* couldn't give me time to read it? Listen . . .
Francine: On doit travailler ensemble. On peut se tutoyer . . . ?
We have to work together. Might we address each other in the intimate form . . . ?
Pascal: Vous m'excuserez. Mon téléphone sonne . . .
You *(formal)* will excuse me. My telephone is ringing . . .

Thursday, 10 AM: The Van Gogh story had problems, I admit it. Imitating paintings may not be the best idea for a travel book. I was a little off-base on the research, too much background, not enough "liveliness." And my text. I read it over. Maybe it was a little *too* vivid.

The next story will be different. I'll approach this one without the Southern Comfort. I'll "lead" without pushing; the story is so compelling it will carry the job itself. And this time I will be prepared. Research! My forte. Just like back in college.

I heft down *Cluny Abbey: The Glory Days*. One of the richest moments in French history. Even Jean-Jacques will have to relate to this one. It's his culture, his roots.

His roots. De Brissac-Chabrol. An old family. The hyphen, the aristocratic "de." He doesn't use that part. And that wine, the wine he refused to drink. Marius couldn't get him to take a sip.

He's certainly hard to maneuver.

I keep studying his photographs. The bullfight material is so intense and sensual it's almost disturbing. And the image of me dancing with Baptiste . . . I've never seen what I look like, laughing like that. I don't look like a schoolmarm there.

Or a historian. Work, Meg. I open *Cluny: The Light of the Christian West*.

There is a grinding roar in the driveway overhead and the screech of brakes. Men are shouting in some Latin tongue, flinging heavy metal onto the ground with a clatter that shakes my ventilation slat. I hear a pounding and the hammering of metal directly over my head.

Damn. I strike Save and head up the iron ladder.

Outside my front door, an army of masons has arrived.

3 PM: We are standing in a semicircle facing the back barn wall. I am shivering in my army jacket, partly from the dank chill, partly from nerves. The chalk outline of the opening-to-be has been spray-painted in orange.

The hammer swings forward, arcing through the air and connecting with ancient stone.

BAM!

The noise is huge. The wall seems to shudder with the blow.

BAM! The hammer strikes again. A chunk of fieldstone pivots in place. Two men jump forward and wrest it from the wall, then jump back.

BAM! The hammer swings and strikes. Stones are spilling away now from the growing gap. The wall is several layers thick at the base, built like a pyramid. The men grip and pull away the stones as if rescuing miners from a crumbled shaft.

BAM! A shaft of yellow light slashes into the barn, three-dimensional in the swirling dust.

"*Ouah!*" the men shout. "Got it!"

They double their efforts, swinging, clawing, tearing out chunks of rock. The hole grows.

Raimondo grabs a worker's shoulder. "Go get the jackhammer. It will go faster."

My mouth is dry. I edge over to Raimondo, eyes still on the hole. "Aren't you going to brace the crossbeam?"

Raimondo turns to me, throwing a glowing cigarette butt into the straw at our feet. "What?" he shrugs, pointing at his ear.

BAM!

"*Aren't you going to brace the crossbeam?*"

The hammer falls still. The men turn. They are not looking at me. They are looking at Raimondo.

"Brace the crossbeam?" He looks at me. He looks at his boots. Then he looks up with his version of a winning smile. "Madame Thorpe. These walls have held for two hundred years. They are not going to fall now."

"But you said—"

"Madame, I know my métier. Trust me."

"But you said—"

I stop. The workers exchange glances. Then they lean back on their tools and grope for cigarettes.

I swallow. "You said the crossbeam was dangerous. Can't you shore it up with *something?*"

Raimondo pinches the skin between his generous eyebrows, shaking his head. Then he looks deep into my eyes with a sudden gentleness. He speaks very slowly, as if explaining to Cloey the wonders of the toilet.

"Madame Thorpe, to brace the beam four meters above the ground, it would be a lot of work. And that . . ." He pauses for effect. He rubs the tips of his fingers in the air. "That's going to cost you dear, madame."

I straighten my shoulders. "I don't care. It will cost me a lot more if the roof falls in." My hands are on my hips. I hope I look authoritative.

Within five minutes the entire team has melted into thin air and all I hear is the truck lumbering away down the highway.

6 PM: We stand in the barn and stare, Nigel holding Cloey, Kate wrapped around my knees. Gerald trots anxiously around, sniffing tools and nibbling cigarette butts. He eyes the hole suspiciously then lifts his leg on its base. If it weren't a meter above the ground it would be big enough to drive a car through.

Cloey's lips are trembling. "It's broke."

The wind picks up a swirl of rock dust and flings it in our faces. The barn door flaps on its hand-wrought hinges, confused by the new air currents invading its ancient domain. The beams protest. There is the groan of heavy wood shifting.

"Right. Girls? Shall we go in? Bit draughty. Come on, Cloey. There's a good lad. In we go then." Nigel hastily opens the door and presses us deep into the far end of the house. He opens the cupboard and pours himself a shot of whiskey and drinks it down. Then he notices me.

I am standing in the middle of the kitchen, looking at him. I turn to the children and smile brightly.

"Kate, love. Would you mind taking Cloey up for his bath? Just draw the water, honey. I'll be up in a sec."

Nigel pours himself another glass and cocks the bottle toward me.

"No thanks. Nigel?"

He is edging casually toward the television room.

"Nigel, are these masons legitimate, or are they one of MacGregor's moonlighting teams?"

Nigel's face arranges itself into a more familiar form. "Megs darling. They're *professionals*. Some of the laborers might be a bit dodgy, but Raimondo knows what he's doing. MacGregor works with him all the time. Saw him last week at the Hare and Hound."

"While I was in Arles?" Don't, Meg. Keep to the subject.

"Well, yes."

"Sophie was here."

"I expect she was. Yes, I believe so."

Lips sealed, I launch myself upstairs to bathe Cloey.

1 AM: Lying beside Nigel, I stare at the beams over my head. Did I hear a creaking noise? The wind howls outside and a low moan rises, like the sound of breath hooting over a mighty bottle.

"Mama!"

I creep across the hall. Cloey is lying in his crib, his eyes enormous in the nightlight's glow.

"*Maman!*" Kate appears beside me. "*C'est quoi ça?* What makes that terrible noise?" Her fingers snake around my hips and she presses against me.

"It's okay, guys. It's just the hole in the barn wall. The wind is playing it like a flute." Some flute, I think. I gather them in my arms and haul them off to my bed. If the roof goes, this solid-oak four-poster might save our lives.

We snuggle together and drowse warily, Nigel's snores playing counterpoint to the moaning of the wind.

Friday, 9 AM: I creep down the ladder. De Gaulle lies shattered, face down on the flagstones. The coronation of Charlemagne leans against the baseboard. Yesterday's vibrations wreaked havoc on my office wall.

I dial Andrew MacGregor. I have to listen, pacing, to Greensleeves for a while before his secretary connects me through.

"Meg? Lovely to hear from you. Haven't seen you for donkey's years. Actually, Brenda's been talking of having you round."

"Andrew, there's a hole in my house."

Silence at the other end of the line. "Yes. Well, Raimondo said he might pop by this week and have a look."

"Pop by? He ran a battering ram through my barn wall and left. There's not even a tarp over it. And Andrew, he didn't brace the roof."

Another silence.

"Andrew, are these guys insured? Is this one of your under-the-table tax-free on-the-side deals?"

"Meg. Listen, dear girl, Raimondo is one of the best builders in the Meuse and he knows what—"

"Is he insured? Because if my house falls down—"

"It won't fall down, Meg. Tell you what. I'll give him a ring and we'll talk about the crossbeam."

"You *know* about the crossbeam?"

"Well, yes, Nigel did mention it last week."

"I think the crossbeam should be braced."

"Of course, Meg dear. I'll look into it." There is a pinched tone to his voice, as if he were swallowing something bitter. "And I'll have Brenda ring you up. We'll have you round for a proper meal and a chat."

I sigh. "Okay. Yes, that would be lovely. That would be great."

"Good-oh. Right, then. Be in touch. Hugs to the kiddies."

I hang up the phone and look around my office.

If a sledgehammer did this, what will a jackhammer do?

Tuesday, April 22, 4 PM: It is quiet upstairs, too quiet. It's been more than a week since I called MacGregor but Raimondo never appeared.

I manage to work days, but I keep glancing overhead as if the ceiling might collapse on me.

I have been digging through reference books for information on Cluny, the great Benedictine abbey.

> *Reigning over a thousand monasteries, Cluny commanded vast wealth and answered only to the Pope. Urban II called it "the light of the world."*

This story will go together much more smoothly than Arles, I'm confident. Everything's set. In two weeks I'm meeting Jean-Jacques in Mâcon. He sent one short message:

> *It will be a busy holiday weekend in Cluny so I booked rooms.*

Another busy holiday weekend. At least he warned me this time.

I haven't had a response to my e-mails to the abbey, asking for access permission. I send another. Probably they aren't too fussy about the press. Modern-day monasteries open their doors to tourists a lot for spiritual retreats. They might even make beer, like the Trappists in Belgium. That would be 'visual.' Not very French, though.

I file my history books back on the fruit shelves. I must have covered seven hundred years of Cluny history. The more I dig, the farther back I go.

> *The great basilica was begun in 1088 . . . among the largest structures on earth . . .*

Medieval history. This time I'm on solid ground.

If only the home front was on as solid ground. Sophie seemed hesitant when I called. "Yes, Madame, I can come, of course. And I appreciate the printed itinerary you give me each time. But Monsieur Thorpe, he . . ."

Uh oh. I waited for her to continue. "Yes?"

"*Benh,* Monsieur Thorpe sometimes comes home later than he says. And last time he asked me to come only five minutes before he was leaving. And then he didn't come back until three in the morning."

Oh god. "I'm sorry, Sophie. He shouldn't take advantage of you like that. I'll talk to him. We want to keep you happy. The children are very fond of you and I appreciate your help very much."

The children are more than fond of her. They adore her. They can count on her more than their own father.

And me?

As I climb the ladder to find lunch, I glance toward the hole in the wall. From its jagged edge there is a crack radiating up to the crossbeam, thick as a lightning bolt.

Sunday, May 4, 11 AM: My Cluny notes are only half organized and I still haven't confirmed access rights. I'll pick up documentation there and we'll talk our way in. Cloey's school fair has taken us over. The Light of the World will have to wait.

I have been drafted to sell crêpes in the pastry stand. Kate's primary class helped hang decorations. Cloey has been rehearsing since January. When the fathers mounted the tent frames for the stands, Nigel remained glued in front of the Saturday match.

I pleaded. "Come on, Nigel. It'll do you good to mix a little with the natives. Help them put up the tents."

"Never was much of a Scout." His eyes drifted back to the screen.

This morning Cloey was so excited he wet the bed. He stood beside the four-poster in the predawn darkness, shivering. "The *Fête* today!" he whispered. "My costume!" I looked at the clock. Five AM.

The main street of Dampierre-lès-Vaucouleurs has been barricaded off and the gate of the nursery school has been swagged with red, white, and blue garlands. Up and down the cobbled *place*, tents shelter penny-carnival games, tombola, sausage and wine stands. I take my place at the pastry booth, kissing cheeks right and left. Nigel heads for the beer stand, where he's already spotted Henry, Paul's English father. His mother, Nicole, gives me a nudge and rolls her eyes. *"Tu vois!"* she laughs. "You see? They always find each other, *les Anglais*. They're like flies drawn to cow pies!"

3 PM: I've been flipping crêpes for four hours, smearing them with Nutella and passing them into grasping hands. Community life, I remind myself. I smile at the customers. Another hour and I can get back to Cluny.

"Bonjour, Madame Thorpe!" Sophie waves half-gloved fingers at me

and tows a boy up to the stand, a tall boy, mouth-breathing, pimple-scarred, and wrapped in studded leather. "This is Ahmad. He's my neighbor. He's your neighbor, too, no?" she laughs. "From the Thibault farm across the stream?"

I shake Ahmad's hand and study his face. Behind the gelled black hair-horns I can just make out the little boy who used to rake our leaves. The name Ahmad doesn't ring a bell.

"He used to be named Paul-Marie." She glances at his reddening face. "Until he accepted the faith of Muhammad."

"Well . . . Ahmad! I hope you enjoy the show!"

The beat of a pop song blares over the speakers.

Nigel? Where is Nigel? I spot his back at the beer stand, still with Henry. They are buying another round.

Onto the stage pours a stream of children—improbably tiny, nothing but pudge and eyes—and I spot Cloey, plucking at his crêpe-paper cowboy costume. His eyes are locked on the teacher. She raises her arms and sways. The children raise their arms and sway. The teacher turns around. They turn around.

Then Cloey spots me and freezes. His lips begin to work.

"Go on, honey!" I stage-whisper. "You're okay!"

He gropes for his zipper.

Oh god. Not here.

A jostling in the crowd and Sophie appears. "*Salut, bonhomme!*" she cries. Cloey's head swivels and his face gaps into a smile. "*Vas-y! Danse, toi, danse!*"

Cloey bobs his knees and turns with the others, grinning from ear to ear.

6 PM: I am sprawled on the daybed, Kate under one arm, Cloey under the other. My swollen feet rest on Gerald, who bathes them over his shoulder with a warm, wet tongue. Nigel has retreated to the back room to rewind the video of the missed match.

"Honey you were terrific. How come you got scared?"

Cloey picks at my bra strap and slides his thumb into his mouth.

"You were just fine once Sophie came up."

He takes his thumb out. "I love Sophie."

11 PM: I'm finally printing out my Cluny notes when an e-mail from Jean-Jacques comes in. I blink. Now what?

> *Re Cluny: Change of plans. Last minute food shoot in Geneva. Coming through Dijon on TGV Thurs, do you mind coming a day early? First night a friend can put us up. Can you handle car rental?*
> *jjc*

A day early? I shake my head and smile a little. Still, he actually asked if I mind.

Seems a pity to rent a car. Dijon's only two hours south of here. It will do the Citroën good to run some high-speed distances.

I type back:

> *I'll drive down in my car. Let me know train arrival time. I'm sure you'll find the Cluny story much more visually interesting. It's especially significant for its . . .*

I stop typing. Keep it light, schoolmarm. I erase. I rewrite:

> *It's one of the most glorious periods in European . . .*

I erase. I rewrite:

> *I'll drive down in my car. Let me know arrival time. Looking forward to this. Next stop Cluny Abbey!*
> *Meg*

Wednesday, 10 PM: When I come up the ladder with my laptop for tomorrow, Nigel is talking on the telephone.

"Weekend's all clear, nanny on call. Wondered if you'd fancy a curry at L'Étoile d'Asie Saturday night? Maybe ring up John and Nick? And there's the match Sunday of course. Simon's already planning to . . ." He spots me and pivots away. "Right then, listen, I'll be in touch about . . . Good. Good. Talk tomorrow. No, can't . . . Right. You've got it. Yes. Bye then."

He hastily hangs up the phone and turns to me with a strangely chipper grin. "All packed are we?"

I stand there, holding the laptop. "Nigel, Sophie told me you've been making plans while I'm gone. Last-minute plans. I thought we'd agreed that when I travel you'd spend time with the kids."

"Well now, just keeping in touch with a few blokes at work. Passes the time. Children do love Sophie, don't they? Terrific girl."

"But—"

He lays his hands on my shoulders and pats. "Now, now. With you dashing about always 'work, work, working,' a fellow can get lonely." Then his face shifts slightly and his hands slide down my back. Now they are patting my bottom.

Oh dear.

He moves closer. "Been working an awful lot lately, haven't you? 'Why are our bodies soft and weak and smooth . . .'"

"Nigel . . ."

"'Unapt to toil and trouble in the world . . .'"

I giggle a little despite myself. "Nigel, I have to pack . . ."

His hands are as busy as his memory, fiddling with my buttons, his eyes searching the ceiling for text. "'Such duty as the subject owes the prince . . .'" Now he is leading me up the stairs.

"I have to *pack*."

"'. . . Even such a woman oweth to her husband.'"

I dutifully submit. Then I start packing.

Thursday, 4 PM: I don't know when I'll be back, Sunday or even Monday if the weather is iffy. But I am looking forward to this.

I check my mental list: The freezer is stocked. The floors are swept. Nigel's at work. Gerald's in the garden. The kids won't be back until five. Sophie will meet them and let herself in. She has her own key now.

There's a squeeze in my chest. It's ridiculous to be jealous, I tell myself. It's wonderful the kids have bonded with Sophie. Isn't it?

I roll my bag out the front door and lift it into the trunk. I unbuckle Cloey's car seat, dump the petit-beurre crumbs onto the hedge, and stand it by the front door. There's nobody to kiss good-bye. I rev the Citroën engine with a hollow roar and back it down the driveway.

5:30 PM: The windshield wipers swipe through pounding rain and my tires hiss down the blacktop, cutting a slash across anonymous countryside. The French *autoroutes* are so seamless and slick you can't tell if you're in Provence or Normandy. A Belgian truck driver honks and flashes, waving with admiration as I pass. People love this car. I slip a CD into the player and the throaty snarl of Jacques Brel pours out.

My headlights slice through a wall of water. By the time I exit the A31 and pull into the Dijon train station, Jean-Jacques' train is due. As if on cue, the wide entrance doors slide apart and disgorge a dark-clad mass of urbanites. The mob melts into taxis and buses and idling cars.

I peer through the windshield and spot Jean-Jacques hanging back well behind the crowd. He's bundled in a lumpy knit cardigan, vaguely ethnic in grey and white, and the Arabic scarf is bound high around his neck and ears. I'd mistake him for a hitchhiking college kid if his hair weren't halfway grey. Why do photographers cultivate that bohemian look? They make a lot more than writers. A *lot*.

He peers up and down the parking area, and when I flash my lights he squints and smiles. Then his eyes sweep over the Citroën and his face hardens. Is he shaking his head? He sludges through the puddles, hauls open the back door, heaves in his gear, and climbs in beside me.

"*Bonjour,* Jean-Jacques." I swallow.

"*Bonjour,* Mayg." He extends a wet hand, squeezes mine lightly, then wipes his palms over his dripping face and hair. "So where did you get this beast?"

I can't contain a proud smile. "It's a 1972 DS."

He scans the dashboard, his mouth strangely grim. "I know." He digs for cigarettes in his baggy pants. "Historic."

Oh god. Is he going to be sullen again? He was just sounding nicer in his e-mails. But he cocks the cigarette pack toward me with a conciliatory air, as if to say, "Peace."

"No. Thanks." He's forgotten I don't smoke? I palm the gearshift and turn the key. The Citroën suspension rises on a cushion of air. Jean-Jacques is shaking his head again. Well, *I* love this car. I pull into the exit lane. "You haven't told me where we're going tonight. Where does your friend live? I hope he's expecting me, too."

"Of course. Just head south on the *route nationale* and I'll tell you where to turn. Very old friend of the family."

I raise my eyebrows and wait, but there are no details forthcoming. We dive down the tunnel of rain in silence. He punches in the lighter on the dashboard as if he'd been doing it for years, waits until it springs out, lights the cigarette, and exhales heavily. I disguise my discomfort by clicking the CD changer. Edith Piaf moans darkly.

Jean-Jacques listens a while, staring at his cigarette. Then he cracks the window with a sucking, wet roar and tosses out the stub.

"Do you have any other music?"

I look at him, startled, and lower the volume.

"I love old music. And she's amazing."

"Do you mind?" He leans forward and turns it off. Silence. Then he slumps down on the leather seat and begins tapping messages into his phone.

7:30 PM: "Turn up here," Jean-Jacques says suddenly, and points to the right. I brake and veer off the broad commercial truck route and press uphill.

"Now left."

It is dead dark now but I recall this road. It is the D122, a tiny intervillage one-lane that weaves through a series of stellar vineyards, the Côte de Nuits, the high end of Burgundy's Côte d'Or. I did this once in college, four girls driving a rusty Deux Chevaux. I couldn't afford to buy any wine then and I can't afford it now.

I can barely see through the rain. Stone pillars loom into view and flash past, their enameled signs reflecting famous names: Fixin, Gevrey-Chambertin, Morey-St-Denis, Chambolle-Musigny. The road is anything but direct, the villages labyrinthine. I roll past tight-squeezed stone houses and snaking low stone walls. We break into open vineyards and the world goes black. I follow the pavement on blind faith. Jean-Jacques is peering through the steamy glass now, craning to see. "Here. Turn right."

I see nothing. I slow and brake. Two reflectors mark a turnoff, little more than a tractor trail. I steer the Citroën up a steep, rutted path, tethered vines strobing past like ranks of soldiers. Shifting down into second, we climb, the car dragging back as if it would skid straight down into the Clos de Vougeot. I lean forward, weighing it ahead by sheer will.

"Are you sure?"

"Here. In here."

The vines give way to boxwood. Two pillars topped with weathered sandstone globes mark a driveway that leads deep into a gully, hidden in the folding undulations of this precious hillside. The wheels crunch onto gravel. One yellow lamp flares faintly through a twist of ivy.

"*Voilà.*" Jean-Jacques unfastens his seatbelt. I gape in the darkness. This has got to be one of the most valuable pieces of real estate in France. I didn't even know there were houses on this land. I step out of the car into pelting rain.

"J-J?" A gleaming oak door cracks wide, sending a wedge of warm light across my feet. A woman appears and, stepping gingerly into the downpour, wraps Jean-Jacques in her arms. He stands there, dripping.

"*Pauvre bête!* Get inside, hurry!"

Only now does she turn to me. "Please forgive me, come in, come in!"

We press through the door and stand on time-hollowed stone, blinking in the golden glow. The woman makes a pretty show of shaking raindrops from her fingertips. "You must be very tired and cold." She turns a sculptured face to me. Jean-Jacques is swabbing his hair with his scarf. He stops in midswipe and gestures toward me.

"Mayg Parker, this is Renée . . . euh . . . Bouvier. She used to be my wife." He glances sideways at my face. "But that's ancient history."

He buries his expression in his scarf.

10:30 PM: I am dwarfed by a massive armchair and sit awkwardly, my bottom sliding forward on polished leather. My cheeks are glowing with wine. Everything in this room glows—the fire, the heavy silver knives, the massive crystal glasses, the soft brass lamps that illuminate each painting, the Limoges cluttered with our cheese rinds and the last of the jellied ham. Even Renée glows, blond in ivory silk. I tip my snifter carefully and wait for the wine to descend. The rim of the glass hits my forehead and I splash deep-red liquid down my front.

Oh god.

"*Aïe!*" Renée says softly. Everything she says, she says softly. She untucks her stocking feet and leans across the coffee table. "Here, let's rub some salt in it. That should draw it out."

She rises and administers to me like a geisha, the scent of something expensive rising out of her blouse. I am suddenly acutely aware of the moth holes in my grandmother's cashmere twin set.

Jean-Jacques studies us from the love seat where he slouches, smoking, feet propped on the coffee table, one toe poking through a sock.

"So, you're looking very prosperous." He blows out a stream of smoke. "How's the *remplaçant?*"

Renée shoots him an arch look. "Your replacement? Robbie is fine. Just fine."

"Apparently." Jean-Jacques gazes around him at the walls heavy with art treasures. Then he leans forward to take the bottle from its silver coaster and pours a roping carnelian stream into my glass. "Robert usually only unpacks the goldfish bowls for Japanese clients. Me, I prefer my Romanée in a jelly glass."

I look up. This isn't the way he talked before.

Renée shoots a look at him then lifts one delicate shoulder and pouts. "Oh J-J, you're such a snob." She presses fingertips on my forearm. "I just wanted to make our American guest feel welcome. Do you know our little wines, Meg?"

I sit up and clear my throat. "Actually, I've been here a couple of times, visiting vineyards when I was in college. And I've come with my husband to taste. We always use Hugh Becker to—"

"*Tiens!* Hugh Becker! He's very well respected in the States, no? With many followers. Almost a cult. His readers come here with his recommendations in hand like grocery lists. Here in France we find his methods a little naïve, as if one could objectify the—"

"He panned your '99, didn't he? Mayg, would you like to see the *caves?*" Jean-Jacques' words swat Renée's aside like mosquitoes.

I turn to him gratefully. "Yes! I'd love to."

He glances at Renée and fishes for a cigarette. He studies it in his fingers. When he speaks again his voice is low. "*On peut se tutoyer?*"

May we use the intimate form? Is he talking to me? For some reason this makes my stomach twist in a funny way. "Well, yes, of course."

"Good. *Tu sais,* Mayg, we have a lot of research trips to do. We'll be traveling together a lot and . . ."

Renée is looking at him intently. He lays a cigarette on his lower lip and clicks the lighter.

There is a sudden blast of cold air. A pair of golden retrievers bound into the room, ricocheting off the chairs and leaping like spawning salmon toward Jean-Jacques, toward the cheese rinds, toward the silver basket of bread. One launches himself onto me, his tail beating so hard it swats my glass off the table. Romanée-Conti spatters like blood across the Tibetan silk rug.

"*Merde!*" Renée cries. "*Ils me font chier! Mon Baccarat—*"

"Lovely language for our guests to hear, *ma biche,*" booms a voice behind me. "Ah! J-J! I should have known, *putain!* She always reserves her choicest words for you!"

I pry the dog's paws from my chest and spring up. A broad-bellied man in a Barbour jacket stands dripping on the rug, beaming, his rubber boots caked with mud. "*Et alors . . . ?* You must be the reason Renée brought out her goldfish bowls!" He extends two callused hands and buries mine between them.

Jean-Jacques climbs out of his chair, sidestepping broken glass. "Robert, this is Mayg Parker. We're working on a book together. An American book. Euh . . . About history. France's living history." I glance at his face. It is carefully neutral.

Robert shoots bushy brows up. "Ah? Well, Madame Parker, you've come to the right place!"

Midnight: A circle of light from a single candle illuminates our faces. Robert, Jean-Jacques, and I tread quietly down an aisle, flanked on each side by bulging barrels, their oak planks stained deep purple with grape juice and age. On each lid, a casual scribble notes the year. The air is close and cool, thick with the scent of fermenting fruit, wet stone, and mold. A hollow dripping sound echoes our footfall. I can't help but tiptoe.

"The Cistercians planted grapevines here, over our heads," Robert intones as if he were telling a ghost story. "Over all the hillsides of the Côte de Nuits. They built this house for their sickly, to recover from illness above the river-valley damp. They were sober workers, ascetics, but they liked their wine. One half bottle per day, Saint Bernard allotted them. One glass for every meal."

We stop before an oak barrel and Robert grips the fat cork on its back and pulls. A sigh escapes. Robert gestures to me. "Smell," he commands. I lean over the tap hole and breathe in tar and vinegar. Oh dear. What do I say? This is supposed to be one of the world's great wines and all I can smell is sour grape juice.

He watches my face. "Eh? It's piss to you now, no? But just wait." He lowers a glass tube into the tap hole, then, stopping it with his thumb, draws it up. The tube comes out full of liquid, black until he holds it to the candle flame, then ruby red. Jean-Jacques leans in and examines it. With his left hand, Robert turns over three stubby glasses on a barrel head and lifts his thumb three times, releasing a spurt of liquid into each. They raise the glasses; I raise mine. They turn theirs thoughtfully against the flame, squinting. So do I. They tip their glasses and study the draping traces. I do the same. They lower noses into the glasses and sniff deep, then swirl them and sniff again. I follow. Then, as one, we lift our glasses to our lips and suck in a mouthful, swishing the wine over our tongues, cheeks, palate.

My eyes fill with tears. It is bitter and sour, nothing but grape juice with a thick gritty sting to it that roughens my tongue like a cat's. I look up. Robert and Jean-Jacques are staring into middle space, chewing the wine with fierce concentration. A stream of red spit sprays from their mouths into a bucket. They continue to chew the aftertaste and stare intently at each other, raising their eyebrows significantly.

I spit, too, my mouth puckering. I am baffled.

Robert remains silent. He screws the cork back into the barrel. It hisses, gases protesting against captivity. "You hear?" he whispers. "It's a living thing. Alive."

We approach an ancient iron gate, its bars enveloped in a blanket of cotton-candy mold. Robert solemnly passes me the candle and rifles through his pockets. He draws out a heavy key and holds it up to me.

"As old as the house!" He keeps his voice low, as if not to disturb the sleeping wine. He fits the key into the iron lock and its interlocking tumblers fall with a series of precise clicks. *"Vous voyez?"* he whispers. "They knew what they were doing in 1262." He pulls the door toward us. Jean-Jacques is studying his shoes. Robert cocks his head at what lies beyond and I step forward, bearing the candle before me.

The pale yellow light flickers down a tunnel of glass, row on row of the dimpled bottoms of a thousand, maybe thousands of, bottles. They are draped with swags of heavy mold. I move forward and my shoulder brushes the stone wall. It gives way, nothing but a blanket of fungus. I shudder.

"It's penicillin, this *champignon*," Robert says. "Not just any mush-room, not just any mold. This is what gives life to Romanée."

I move down an endless aisle. The smell of must is smothering. Bot-tles, years, bottles, years. It's like a library stack, the reserve section, leather tomes worn dark with handling, secreted away. On every shelf, tiny wood-framed blackboards dangle from nails, scrawled with dates. 1929. 1937. 1951. I can't suppress a gasp of awe. "It's incredible."

Robert watches my face. *"Eh? Tu vois?"* He switches to the intimate form. "These are my children. Every bottle is alive, seething with life. Growing. Changing. Some getting better, some getting worse." The can-dle gleams across his bushy eyebrows, casting wavering shadow-slashes over his forehead.

I turn to him, hypnotized. Over his shoulder I see Jean-Jacques, his hand half concealing his face.

"Do you want to taste?" Robert whispers, leaning into me. "Do you want me to uncork one of these? Smell the smell of . . . history?"

Jean-Jacques makes a strangled noise I can't interpret. I stare back at Robert.

"Yes." I am whispering, too. "Of course. I would be honored."

Robert glances up at Jean-Jacques. "Go ahead, J-J."

Jean-Jacques gropes the wall and throws a switch. The entire cave —shelves, barrels, vaulted stone ceiling, is suddenly bathed in the in-candescent glare of a dozen light bulbs. There is a broad plastic price list mounted on the wall.

Robert looses an exuberant laugh, then leans back, rocking content-edly on his heels. "Not bad, eh, J-J? It gets the tourists every time."

I stand stark, blinded, my mouth popping open and shut. It's a sales-room as much as a cave. Of course. Oh god.

Jean-Jacques wipes a hand over his mouth. "Better every time, Robert. 'These are my children!' 'The smell of history!' You've been handling a lot of American tours, no?"

Now my face is hot. He looks at me and seems to soften. "But listen, Mayg knows better."

I look daggers at him.

"No, she does. She likes to eat and drink. She's an enthusiast. I've seen her. Pretty good for an American. Come on, Mayg. Drink a glass with us."

I feel the heavy sleeve of Robert's Barbour on my shoulder. "Listen, Madame Parker, Meg, *écoute,* don't take it wrong. It's my little *pièce de théâtre.* And every word is true. You are a wonderful audience. Better than a busload." He grins at Jean-Jacques. "What do you say to a '71?"

Jean-Jacques looks at my face, then rubs his jaw. "How about a '61?"

2 AM: A '61 Romanée-Conti. My eyes are squeezed shut and I don't want to open them because if I do the taste will go away forever. Flavors and scents are vaulting over my palate, radiating over my tongue like subtly choreographed fireworks. I chew the wine, I fill my cheeks, I let it pour back over the base of my tongue. Then I swallow slowly, breathe rever-ently out through parted lips and open my eyes. Jean-Jacques is looking at me. He hasn't said anything for a while. Or at least I think he hasn't. My whole mind, my mouth, my tongue, have been elsewhere, in the world of this wine. I close my eyes again so no one can distract me. I raise the glass again and pull the liquid between my lips.

I hear a whirring click, then another. I open my eyes. Jean-Jacques holds a tiny digital camera before him, peering into the display screen. He is photographing the glasses on the barrel top, candlelight shining through. Does he never stop? He should be tasting this. Living this. I close my eyes again.

Robert is talking. He sits on a half-barrel, his hand propped on his thigh, waxing philosophical. I am only vaguely aware of his thesis. Berries and lavender and honey and hemp and musk and parchment and *history* roll over my tongue. I blink and try to look involved in Robert's monologue.

". . . like bulls in a china shop. They come here, so openhearted, so well-meaning, so full of good will, their wallets open, their minds closed, their asses farting dollars . . ."

I open my eyes and see Jean-Jacques give Robert a quick negative jerk of his head. Robert stops himself in midphrase, turns a visible mental pirouette, and looks at me as if he'd forgotten I was there.

It's okay. I am only half there. I am on the moon, alone with this wine.

Friday, 6 AM: There is the sound of hands clapping outside my bedroom door. "*Allez, allez!* Come on, come on! Let's go! You don't want to miss this."

I lie very still. There is darkness all around me. I roll over but only my body follows. My head stays heavy on the deep down pillow, still printing impressions of Art Deco lace into my skin.

"*Viens*, Meg! I have a big cup of coffee for you!"

Coffee. I find the will to lift my torso, then swing my legs over the side of the bed. I follow the sound to the door and grope for the knob.

"Halloo! *Bonjour!* Good morning!" It is Robert, his beaming face larger than life in the yellow light of the hallway. He thrusts a ceramic bowl of coffee into my hands. "A fishbowl of coffee for you. Enough for a carp. Drink. Get dressed. The light is coming and I'm going to make my rounds of the vines. You're coming, too."

"Um. Okay. Give me five minutes." When I open the door again, buttoning my jeans, he's still standing there, studying the hunting prints that line the corridor wall. "*Bon.* You'll need boots, of course. We'll find something."

I pad down the Persian runner behind him. "And Jean-Jacques?"

"Here." He slams a fist twice against a heavy plank door. "Haven't been able to rouse him." He pounds again. "J-J?"

Silence.

Has he bolted again? He certainly didn't seem very comfortable around Renée.

Robert flings the door open and bugles "J-J! We're losing the day!" I squint into the darkness, then look abruptly away. Jean-Jacques is sound asleep, sprawled facedown across the bed, his long hair strewn over his skin like the strings of a wet mop. Can't photographers afford pajamas?

"Photographers must profit from the light! *Alors?*" Robert throws the overhead switch.

6:30 AM: The front door swings open and the dogs jet out across the gravel drive, snuffling and grinning. We, too, step out into a new world. The sky has been scrubbed clean by the rain and it gleams like the cheeks of a baby just out of a bath. The house hunkers comfortably into a mass of honeysuckle, a broad linden tree sheltering the entrance. There is no lawn, only a minuscule meadow of close-cropped hay, sprouting with the last of the cowslips. Then the hill spills away in every direction, radiating as far as we can see in neat rows of grapevines. Mist billows over the ribboned land.

Robert strides forward and Jean-Jacques steps woodenly after him, his scarf wound high around his ears, his hands thrust deep in his pockets. The dogs lace around their feet, hanging back to lick my trailing hands and nudge me forward like a stray lamb. It's spectacularly beautiful, this scene, Robert setting forth into his vineyards. Maybe . . .

"Do you need your cameras?" I call, dangling my car keys in the air.

Jean-Jacques trudges ahead. "I have pictures of grapes. Lots of pictures of grapes."

For some reason, Robert throws an arm over his shoulders.

We tramp down the muddy rows, my feet slopping in hollow borrowed boots. There are swallows diving above us. Far below, miniature trucks crawl along the *route nationale,* another world.

Robert points his secateurs at the branches of a vine. "You see? I'm not greedy. I trim back to only ten buds. Ten clusters, ten *grappes.* That's not a lot of fruit for such a strong vine, but more tires them." He scans the hillside, hands on hips. "They fatigue if you exploit them, but their roots are strong. Their roots go deep, twenty, even thirty meters into the bedrock."

Oh dear. Is this more folklore for l'Américaine? But he isn't looking at me; he is looking at Jean-Jacques. "It's the roots that count. You can't tear them up so easily."

Jean-Jacques kicks a white chunk of marl.

8 AM: I push the trunk shut and turn to Robert. He and Jean-Jacques are kissing cheeks and clapping shoulders. Shutters fly wide with a clatter above us and Renée leans out. She is holding a silk dressing gown across her breasts but not very carefully; the lapels are slipping through slender fingers and gap open in the swelling light. "Sorry to see you go so soon!" she calls. Her fingers lose the battle. "Another time, perhaps. Good luck with Cluny!"

Jean-Jacques and Robert exchange glances. Then Jean-Jacques fishes for a cigarette and climbs into the car beside me.

9 AM: The Citroën rolls slowly over vineyard roads. There are signs to Aloxe-Corton, Savigny, the Hospices de Beaune. I can't help ogling. Pommard! Meursault! Puligny-Montrachet! Jean-Jacques keeps his eyes on his smoldering cigarette. At Chalon-sur-Saône I sigh and swing onto the *autoroute*. We skirt the Côte Chalonnaise in silence. When I cut west at Mâcon, I clear my throat.

"Been divorced long?"

"Not long enough."

I hold my tongue for a while. Then I try again. "You seem to get along, still."

He stares out the window at the vines flashing past. "She wanted to stay in the family business," he says. *"Moi, non."*

The Citroën lumbers around tight curves and down steep hills. "She seems to have done well for herself," I persist.

Jean-Jacques laughs a short bark. "She certainly has."

11 AM: "So the monasteries under the abbot had to pay incredible tithes to support these luxurious habits and the Cistercians, well *they* found the whole attitude of the Cluny order disgusting . . . corrupt . . . too voluptuous, indulgent . . . and the Citeaux Abbey—you know, the one that built Robert's house—well, *their* order was founded in direct defiance of Cluny, a real slap in the face—the Cistercians renounced all comforts, *everything,* restored the work ethic, the austerity the Benedictines had lost . . .'"

Jean-Jacques is leaning an elbow on the window letting the wind whip his face. His eyes are closed but at least he's smiling now. "You're driving very fast you know. History stimulates you."

I glance down at the speedometer—150 kph. I lift my foot and the Citroën drags back to a quieter 120. The temperature gauge is bobbing near red and wisps of steam feather from the hood.

I take a deep breath and slip a CD into the player. A wave of warm male voices pours forth, soothing, unguent.

Agnus Dei qui tollis peccata mundi

"'Who taketh away the sins of the world,'" I sing softly. "Gregorian chant. Plainsong."

"Very atmospheric. Are they monks from Cluny Abbey, these singers?" He is smiling oddly.

We roll along the A6, the music wafting through the car and streaming out the windows.

1:30 PM: Cluny seems very crowded today. It's Victory Day weekend and the streets outside the center are already lined with cars and campers. We round a curve and the famous bell tower of Cluny Abbey comes into view, its black slate cone pointing straight to heaven.

"There it is!" I grasp for his arm.

Jean-Jacques is looking the other way, at the crowds seething over the parkgrounds behind us.

"Jean-Jacques, this is it! The Cluny Abbey!"

"Yes. Good. Let's park and take a look around. Is the abbot expecting us?"

I shoot him a nervous glance but he looks pleasant enough. He almost seems to be looking forward to this.

We walk down the cobbled street, looking for signs to L'Abbaye de Cluny. Across the place de l'Abbaye, signs point to the *billetterie.* Ticket sales! I follow arrows to the Musée d'art et d'archéologie. Jean-Jacques walks quietly beside me, his hands in his pockets.

"Two, please," I ask the clerk. "We're here to photograph the abbey."

The clerk looks at me quizzically. "There's a tour group leaving at two o'clock."

I turn to Jean-Jacques. "Shall we take the guided tour first just for a *repérage?* To scout it out?"

"Why not?" Jean-Jacques nods with a carefully pleasant expression.

We follow the tour guide out the museum door and down slab steps to a broad plaza. I press in to hear.

"Today I am asking you to use your imagination. To look around you and see vast stone walls. To look above you and see elaborate stone tracery. To look before you and see an endless perspective of columns and arches and curving stone, nave by nave by nave. Because on this precise spot, you are standing in the spiritual heart of what was once the Light of the World."

I look around me. There are low stone walls below the parking area and a row of round sandstone benches some tourists are sitting on. I look closely at these benches. They're the sawed-off bases of enormous fluted columns. I feel a chill.

"It was, of course, destroyed," the guide continues.

Suddenly I feel rather than see Jean-Jacques looming behind me.

"Did the *sans-culottes* of the Revolution storm the abbey in rage? Yes. They sacked it, smashed the stained-glass windows, stripped the gilt, burned the furniture. But the building itself? No. The new Republican government simply declared it the property of the people. And they made the best use of it they could. They took it apart stone by stone and sold the building materials."

I feel my breath leaving me.

"And that is why I must ask you today to use your imagination. Imagine the magnificence that once was here."

I don't dare turn around.

I turn around.

Jean-Jacques has his head lowered. I can't see his expression.

"Imagine!" I hear him say. Then he begins to laugh.

Oh god. That laugh. It is an operatic baritone laugh that echoes off the stone and snaps the heads of tourists around.

If he had spit on me it could not have made me feel worse. For a moment I stand, blood flooding my face. Then I straighten my shoulders and climb the stone stairs, the tourists parting a wake for me as I go.

2:30 PM: I lean against the high column of a gate and bury my face in my hands. Jean-Jacques trots up and stands over me. I can't look at him. "I can't believe this. I can't believe this. I did so much research."

His face struggles but he pulls it into a mask of concern. Then it gives away again and he snorts. "I'm sorry. Sorry. But it's becoming a pattern, no? Van Gogh? The Maison Jaune?"

"But I researched this!"

"Just where exactly do you do all this 'research'?"

"I have a vast library of reference materials, very complete." I can't help the huffiness creeping into my tone.

"History books? Textbooks? I know, I know, you studied history at Cambridge. But you didn't happen, by chance, to look on the Internet?"

I jerk my chin defensively. "The Internet? Researching history on the *Internet?*"

"Not history, Mayg. Reality."

I duck my head.

He looks at me and relents slightly. "Come on, let's get something to eat. I'm hungry. I did do some looking on the Internet. I'll tell you about it over lunch."

3 PM: There is, of course, no restaurant in France open at this hour, so I'm drowning my sorrows in chocolate. The Confiserie Flagrant Délice has laid four plates of pastries on the marble-topped table between us and the waitress is bringing two more. Jean-Jacques is smoking and watching me eat.

"You sure you don't want some?" I mumble through a mocha *dacquoise.*

"The quiche was good. No more for me, thanks. We were lucky to find this place. Clearly it suits you."

I glance up at his face. That look. He sucks on his cigarette and blows to the side. I take a defiant bite of dark-chocolate mousse cake, ball up my napkin, and wipe my mouth. I slide another plate up. He watches me, a quizzical half-smile on his lips. Then he rubs his jaw. "So. You've been working very hard? Your writing? Your research?"

I look up from my fruit flan, surprised by his tone. "Actually, I have. I mean, I spent most of the month in my bunker poring over old books on Christian history, monastic orders. Richelieu himself was abbot here, did you know that?"

"Your bunker?" Jean-Jacques taps ashes into his quiche plate.

"Well, my office. I work in a fruit cellar under our barn. I can think there. I have all my college history textbooks and reference materials. I collect old history books. I have nearly three hundred. And my . . . stuff. Nigel calls it my Military Museum. I have a lot of paraphernalia from European wars, weapons, uniforms, shrapnel that—"

I stop. Jean-Jacques has leaned back in his chair. He is looking at me, blowing out smoke. He doesn't understand, either. I sigh.

I take a bite of hazelnut meringue and brace myself. "So, do you want to look around the remains of the abbey? I mean, see if there's anything. At all." I keep my eyes down. "The brochure talks about some Gothic ruins, an eighteenth-century reconstruction of the cloisters."

He puffs a pocket of air out his lips. It sounds a little like "Bof." I glance up. He studies the tip of his cigarette. "Mayg, *écoute,* I can't photograph ruins."

"Why not?"

"They don't show anything."

"But can't you somehow *evoke* something? You know, light and columns, the bell tower?"

"Evoke." He looks at his quiche plate.

I pick at my chocolate icing. "I *like* ruins."

He shrugs. "Sure. Okay. They can be beautiful."

"No. I mean, when I look at ruins I can see things. I can feel the past."

A short laugh. I wince, but it's over in one quick bark. "I'm not that interested in feeling the past."

He smokes a moment in silence. I stare hard into my cup.

"Listen." His tone softens. "We can go see if you like. But I do know of something livelier we can check out if you're willing to."

"Livelier?" Keep it lively. That's what Nikos said. "Okay."

He raises his hand for the bill.

We walk quietly down the main street lined with Renaissance houses and shops, all closed for the holiday weekend. This doesn't look too lively to me. I sigh and shake my head. So stupid. All that research, back into the Middle Ages. How could I be so careful, and so clueless? I didn't even look in a Michelin guide.

Jean-Jacques looks into my face and hesitates. "*Écoute,* Mayg." Then he shakes his head, takes a tissue from his pocket and dabs my cheek. "Chocolate mousse." Resting a hand on my shoulder, he leads me around a corner.

"Look, here." We are standing at the base of the great gate I climbed to earlier. There are two broad wrought-iron doors framed in quarried stone. He runs a hand over the weathered rock face.

"Here's your Basilique de Cluny," he says.

"What?"

"These stones. Napoléon had them taken from the abbey church to build these walls."

"Really?" I peer at the column. "You mean these are the stones the guide was talking about on the tour? That the *sans-culottes* took for themselves? That the people sold off?"

"That's right. He used the 'people's' stones to build his *haras*."

" 'Ara'? What's that? Is that where—" Then I stop. I rewind his words. I turn and look at his face. He looks back a little too innocently.

"Wait a minute! You *knew?*"

"I just . . ."

"*You knew there was no abbey left?*"

"Well, I . . ."

Adrenalin sweeps over me.

He regards me and shrugs. "I looked on the Internet."

The pastries churn in my stomach.

I stand and watch his face dissolve to a grin, then worse. He fights it but the laugh is there. He blots it away with his hand and pats intently for a cigarette.

I stand, stricken. Oh god. There are damp patches wicking under my arms.

"I'm sorry. I'm sorry." He gasps a little. "But after Arles . . ." He sees my expression and puts a hand on my shoulder. "Okay. I'm sorry, okay?" He peers apologetically into my face. "Come on, Madame l'Historienne. Let's go see the horses."

3:30 PM: We are strolling through the two-hundred-year-old barns of the Haras National de Cluny. Jean-Jacques seems to know his way around. He has his cameras around his neck now and they swing as he leads the way. I sneak a look at his face. He isn't smirking anymore. He's absorbed in the *haras*. I take a deep breath. I am, too, I guess. It *is* pretty interesting.

A breeding center for pureblood horses, still government-run. Very French concept, I think to myself. Great oak beams hold the long tile roofs and stall after stall stretches before us in the dim gold light. My nostrils are full of horse—sweat, manure, leather, and the nutty sweetness of fresh straw. I should bring Kate and Cloey here. A King Charles spaniel writhes around my ankles, his flat bug-eyed face turned adoringly to mine. I squat to pat his head and he leaps at my face, bathing my lips with his tongue. I laugh and swat him away.

"Still some mousse left?" Jean-Jacques says. No mockery, no malice. He leans into a stall, peering in the dim light. There is a keening whinny and a flurry of stomps. "This one's a beauty."

I come over and squint up at the card framed over the stall door. "Handmaiden. Pureblood. Born 1989. By Go-for-It (US) and Sheherazade (GB)." Through the iron grill I can just make out a fine-boned black mare, cheekbones round as platters, nostrils quivering. Her haunches skitter left and right and she bucks her head restlessly.

"In heat," Jean-Jacques says simply. "Timing's right."

I look at him, startled. "How do you know?"

He points at a blackboard on her wall where the word *ovulated* is scrawled in chalk. "That's why she's here. To be bred to one of the *haras* stallions. That's what *haras* means. In English I think it's 'stud.'"

I glance over, expecting him to leer. But he leans forward and reaches a hand between the bars. The mare extends her massive head and sniffs, then lowers her ears and nudges him. "You'll be okay, girl. Most natural thing in the world."

I lean forward, too, and reach a hand in. The mare jerks her head back, eyes rolling white, and snorts steamily. I jump back so quickly I scrape my arm on the iron grill. Jean-Jacques makes a squeaking noise with his lips and her head lowers again.

"How come you're so good with horses?" I rub my arm.

Jean-Jacques strides down the straw-strewn aisle. "My parents had stables. I used to ride."

"Really?" I trot beside him, alert. "So your parents . . ."

But Jean-Jacques has spotted a wooden ladder leading high into a loft, and he clambers up it, his cameras slapping his back. He aims a long lens down the aisle and his shutter whirs.

When he comes down we wander through another barn. Workers roll carts of feed, dumping food into troughs and lumbering on; great heads appear as they move down the line. They nuzzle Jean-Jacques' hand and blow softly. I hang back and admire from afar.

We cross a broad courtyard flanked by symmetrical stone barns, arched doors framed in brick and stone. They really are magnificent buildings. The stones of Cluny Abbey. I try to think of them as the stones of a great vaulted church but I can't get the feeling.

madame l'historienne

I feel blood in my cheeks again. Jean-Jacques is shooting and doesn't notice. He heads into another barn, where the stalls ring with earsplitting neighs. At the entrance, shining in the shaft of light that slants through the door, a white stallion bucks and churns circles. I edge forward to read his sign: Sheik, race: Arab, by Bel Espoir and Esmeralda. His hooves come down hard on the wooden manger and I jump back.

In the next stall a gigantic horse looms, stomping alternate hooves the size of anvils. The discs of his cheekbones are as big as wheels. His great round hips rise above my head, the muscles of his flanks so broad I can't see how the stall contains him.

"What is that? A Clydesdale?"

Jean-Jacques is framing a shot from a stool he dragged to the side. "That's a Percheron. Workhorses. Used to be war horses. We had an old one. They used to work the vineyards."

Château Brissac-Chabrol. I look at him. He's stroking the Percheron's massive muzzle as if he'd known him all his life.

At last we cross the grassy square toward the front gate. The air smells green. We pass under the iron grill, cross the road, and step into a campground. Or at least I think it is.

"Funny place for a campground, right in the center of town."

"People here for the competition tomorrow. They camp with their horses right here on the *haras* grounds."

"Competition?"

"The *concours complet d'équitation*. The horse trials."

I look up at him. "You knew about this, too, didn't you?"

He walks on, looking at his feet. There's a smile twitching around his lips. "It might be something for the book. Living horses. Instead of dead monks and ruins."

I narrow my eyes at him. " 'Busy holiday weekend,' you said."

He shrugs and walks on.

i am to follow your lead

Right.

We cross the grounds, transformed into a gypsy camp. There are tents and sleeping bags and gas burners glowing under bubbling teakettles. People in boots mingle and smoke, talking, hanging out horse blankets over their Land Rovers and vans, brushing down black-velvet jackets.

"Where are the horses?"

"They're in the boxes, here and over by the Hippodrome."

"You know your way around here, don't you?"

"I used to come here when I was little sometimes for competitions."

"You rode in competitions? Your family . . . ?"

But Jean-Jacques is panning the field, his digital camera extended away from his chest. He doesn't seem to hear.

5 PM: We're back by the museum and I'm looking longingly at the door.

"Come on," I plead. "You can't come here without trying."

"Mayg, *écoute*. A museum?" He looks back over his shoulder toward the *haras*. He reaches for his phone, then stops himself, sighs, and lets me lead him down the stairs.

There's a low-vaulted display room where carved stones gleam under halogen spots. "Look at this! It's incredible!" This is the Cluny I know, gargoyles and dragons and gape-mouth dogs, twisting and curving and woven in rhythms. I walk down a row of stone friezes, tracing their Celt-like carving with a finger. "See? It's not *all* destroyed forever." I glance up at him. At least he's not smirking. There's something else around his mouth, unreadable.

"Look! This is it! This is real! You can't tell me this is dead. Look at the faces, the jaws, so pure, so simple. But look at the *movement* of the lines and forms and . . ."

I glance up again. He was looking at me, not the art. Now he looks at his shoes.

7 PM: The Auberge des Cloîtres is packed but Jean-Jacques, thank god, reserved the last two rooms in time despite the horse show. We agree to meet for dinner at nine and he walks down the corridor, cell phone pressed to his ear. He hasn't been on the phone so much lately. He's been turning it to vibrate-only and even when it buzzes sometimes he slaps it away like a distracting fly.

He seems focused on what's happening here. So am I. So much so I nearly forgot to call home. I strip down and flop on the embroidered coverlet.

The phone rings four times before Sophie picks up.

"Yes, Madame Thorpe. The children are fine. I'm just cooking their pasta."

"Nigel—Monsieur Thorpe—was supposed to cook for them tonight."

"Monsieur Thorpe telephoned a moment ago. He is detained. He asked me to put them to bed." Her voice is strained. She sounds tired. I hear Cloey barking like a dog in the background.

"I'm sorry, Sophie."

"It's okay, Madame. But do you mind if Ahmad comes over to watch a film with me? We were planning to go to the cinema."

Oh god. "Of course, of course. Please feel free. I'll talk to my husband. Um, is Kate handy?"

"Just a moment. *Cloey, arrête de gueuler comme ça!* Stop that barking, will you? Kate?"

I hear the clicking of long fingernails, then the moist breath of Kate soughing into the mouthpiece.

"Kate honey? Hi, sweetie, it's Mama."

There is only moistness. Then *"Salut, Maman,"* and I hear the phone clunk down on the table, rocking on its back.

I dial Nigel's cell phone. He picks up after four rings. The sound of glasses clinking, male laughter, and televised sports roars into my ear.

"Nigel? Can you hear me?"

"Oh hello, darling," I hear him press his hand over the mouthpiece, muffling a comment to the side. He lifts his hand. "Everything all right? Researching away? Communing with monks?" Clearly he has an audience.

"Nigel, I just talked to Sophie. You said you'd cook for the kids tonight. She had plans."

"Sorry, darling, but she was quite happy to carry the ball." There are deep chuckles in the background. A muffled thunk. "She said she didn't mind a bit and since Geoffrey and Simon were heading out to the H and H I thought I'd give her a ring. How are the children?"

My mouth gaps open. "How are the children? Well, Sophie's cooking them pasta and Cloey's barking under the table and Kate wouldn't talk to me and . . ."

There is a roar and a deep cheer. Rugby.

"Listen, Megs darling, can I call you back? Bloody referee . . . wanker! . . . Sorry, love. Cheers."

The receiver leaves his ear and as he fumbles to hang up, I hear him mutter, "Biased colonial git . . ."

10 PM: The oak-paneled dining room is crowded with people in quilted equestrian jackets and Barbours. I am wearing the Hermès scarf Nigel gave me, emblazoned with the laureate palms of Napoleon. I spot Jean-Jacques, talking with the maitre-d'. He looks up at me. "Nice scarf. Research materials?"

I glance at him nervously. But he smiles and guides me to the table. We thread past diners speaking as much English as French. There are several teenage girls picking at their dinners, each with a much older man across the table lecturing them quietly.

"Aren't they a little . . . ?" I raise my eyebrows.

"No, it's not what you think. It's their trainer, their coach. They'll be competing tomorrow in the dressage and show jumping. They're pretty nervous, I think."

We study the small, handwritten menu. "*Bon.* We'll start with *oeufs en meurette.* Then andouillettes, no? And then . . ." Then he stops himself, with effort, and looks up at me. "What do you think? Do you like andouillettes? It's not for everyone."

Well, it's about time. I smile gratefully. "Yes, I know what andouillettes are. I may be American but I do know something about food."

"Like chocolate mousse gâteau." His mouth is doing that twist again.

"Not just chocolate mousse gâteau. Honestly, the French are always explaining food to me as if I'd landed from Mars. 'Here in France we have this thing called quiche!' Sometimes I think I could show them a thing or two. And they always order for me, as if they're afraid I'll ask for a hamburger."

"Okay." He lays the menu on the pink damask cloth. "You order."

"Okay." I nod my thanks. I study the menu intently. "I'll have . . . the eggs *en meurette.* And andouillettes."

"Good. Me, too."

We drink Petit Chablis from a pitcher, Jean-Jacques tearing chunks of bread off and stuffing them into his mouth with relish.

"Still, they don't have andouillettes in the States, do they? Where did you learn so much about French food in In-daho?"

"Indiana."

"In-dia-na."

"My grandmother was French, she's the one who taught me French. She used to let me help in the kitchen. My parents were farmers, organic farmers, and they both cooked. My grandfather did, too. Then I spent some summers in Paris while I was in college. I went to the markets. I cooked. I kind of fell in love."

Jean-Jacques takes a mouthful of bread and chews for a while. Then he swallows. "I cook, too," he says simply. His phone vibrates on the tabletop like an angry bumblebee. He picks it up and switches it off. Completely off.

I am honored. I take a swallow of wine and search around for something to say worthy of his undivided attention. "So is the chef going to bounce out and embrace you here tonight?" I spread my hands and mime it. " '*J-J! It's been ages!* ' "

He smiles and shakes his head. "No, I don't know this chef. I was pretty young when I used to come here."

"But you did use to come here. You seem to have been everywhere. You know all about wine. You know all about horses."

I stop. Jean-Jacques keeps his eyes down. Did I say something wrong? We eat our eggs quietly. I break a yolk, then dip a fat gold crouton in the wine-rich sauce and crunch. Pungent. Rich.

"Mm." I wipe my lips.

Jean-Jacques glances up. Then he concentrates on his plate.

When the andouillettes are served he brightens. "*Voilà*, you see how crisp they are? They know how to grill them in this kitchen."

He rises in his chair and digs out his digital, holding it out to his plate. I don't wait for the food to get cold. I bite into a forkful and it crackles in my mouth. When I open my eyes, Jean-Jacques averts his.

We eat quietly again, mutually intent on the food. But when the waiter brings our coffee I lean forward. "What did happen with your family, Jean-Jacques?"

He leans back, braces his hands on the tablecloth and glances at the phone, as if willing it to come to life and save him. Then he takes a deep breath.

"I broke with them. I went on my own."

I wait. I finally venture. "What happened?"

"My father and I disagreed. It happens sometimes."

"Do you ever—"

He stops me with a look, then reaches for a cigarette. He lights it and inhales. "What about *your* parents? In Inda . . . India-na?"

"They died when I was in college. Both of them, my father a year after my mother. Organic farming didn't do them any good. Cancer. Bad stuff."

"I'm sorry."

"It was a long time ago. I still miss them." I reflect for a minute and shrug. "I have my own family now. Maybe that's why I started a family so soon."

"Of course." Jean-Jacques focuses on his cigarette for a while. "King Clovis and Queen Catherine. Very historic." I look up. Is he mocking me again? There *is* a glint in his eye.

"You're not making fun of me again?" I bristle. " 'Madame l'Historienne'?"

"No. No, I'm sorry. And Mayg, *écoute,* listen, I'm sorry about the abbey, I should have told you. But you said you wanted to take the lead. I was instructed by my employer to follow, remember?"

I feel myself flushing. Schoolmarm. "Still, you could have—"

"I should have." His cigarette hovers. "I'm sorry. If I'd known . . . Well. I'm sorry."

If I'd known? I look at my coffee cup for a while. "Jean-Jacques." I take a breath. "Do you still . . . You called me a *casse-couille.* A ball-buster."

His head snaps up. "Nikos told you I—?"

"No." I am still looking at my cup. "It got forwarded accidentally."

He stubs out his cigarette. He leans back and looks around. He leans forward again. "*Putain,* I'm sorry." Then he reaches for another cigarette. And puts it back down.

I can't look up. "It's okay. I guess I kind of deserved it. I guess I was kind of coming on strong. Nikos said you needed convincing. That you were skeptical. And I want to do this book. I've always wanted to do this book. Even if we've . . . if I . . . got off to a bad start."

He picks up the cigarette and lights it. He smokes for a long time. I turn my coffee cup in its saucer. We sit in silence. He smokes it down to the filter, then he rubs it out.

Without looking up, he says, "Will you get up with me tomorrow, early? There's something you should see."

"What?" I ask. "For the book?" I can't read his face now.

"In a way. It's a kind of living history."

We pay the bill. He walks me to my room door.

"I'll come by at six-thirty," he says.

He hesitates. I can smell smoke rising off him. And something else, something nicer.

"'Night, Mayg." Then he puts his hands in his pockets and walks down the hall.

Saturday, 6:30 AM: I've been awake and dressed for an hour when Jean-Jacques knocks. I didn't sleep much. The coffee, I guess.

We step out of the auberge into a cool spring dawn, the scent of dewy grass and old stone and straw mingling in the mist. We walk quietly across the campground, where grooms sprawl in down cocoons across the lawn. A few people are up, heating coffee in Italian pots on gas flames, huddled in horse blankets against the chill.

Jean-Jacques leads me to a broad barn, where shouts of "Hyaw! Hyaw!" echo from within. I look questioningly at him. The door slides open and the angry white Arabian we saw yesterday bursts out on tight tethers to be led bucking and snorting away.

Inside, there stands a stuffed cloth dummy of a horse, headless on hydraulic pistons. It looks like a crude rocking horse. To the side, a row of windows reveals a laboratory where men in white coats count test tubes.

More earsplitting neighs come from the stallion barn. A Percheron, even bigger than the one we saw yesterday, pitches and rears against the guide ropes of two men, jockey-small, struggling against his mass.

Jean-Jacques presses me protectively back. When they lead the Percheron into the barn I see the men aren't so small; it is the horse that is gargantuan. He seems to calm at the sight of the dummy. The men attach a long hose under his belly, jump back and pull the ropes forward. He rears and mounts the decoy, ruts five frantic thrusts, and drops to the ground with a whinny, spent. The men scramble to detach the hose and carry their harvest into the lab.

My hand is over my mouth. But Jean-Jacques takes my elbow.

"Come see." He leads me up the steps into the shallow lab.

A technician is pouring a milky liquid into rows of test tubes, then sealing and labeling them: Homme de Fer, May 10. He sees me staring. "There are two hundred million sperm in that one dose," he smiles. "I distributed it into seventeen doses. But there was more left. I could have made eighty more."

I recover speech. "Doses?" I ask.

"For insemination." He reaches in his lab-coat pocket and pulls out a cigarette. "Pretty impressive, no? One stroke. A hundred heirs."

"Amazing," Jean-Jacques mutters. He is peering through the glass, where a grey pony is being fitted with the hose.

"Do they do this all day?" I blurt out.

The technician laughs. "No, just every morning. Then they're free to relax."

We watch another session, and another. Then we slip out of the booth and sidle carefully out of the barn, avoiding the tromping hooves of a pureblood.

"Um, that's not what I expected. I thought you were going to show me hurdle practice or something."

Jean-Jacques is lighting a cigarette. "I told you it was living history."

"Well, I know it's a tradition but . . . "

"Listen, I wasn't trying to . . . Don't you get it? Some of these horses are direct descendents of the war horses of Louis XIV, of Napoléon himself. Bloodlines, carrying on. You know. It's like the stones." He reaches long fingers down the back of my neck and pulls out a corner of my Hermès scarf. "Your very own Napoléon." He shakes the silk, searching my face.

I nod now. "I see. Yes. Louis XIV. A direct line." I stuff the scarf back down. For some reason the back of my neck tingles.

8 AM: We've shaken hands all around with a group of grooms and have shared a cup of coffee with them. Jean-Jacques seems so at ease here. He strokes the horses' flanks with an expert, gentle hand and asks all the right questions of the veterinarian. We watch a chestnut mare being inseminated with this morning's harvest, the vet armed with a shoulder-length rubber glove and a few hollow straws filled with sperm. I flinch. The mare skitters briefly in place, eyes rolling. Jean-Jacques holds her head and strokes her muzzle and she calms.

A family leads in another mare. It is the black beauty we saw in the barn last night. "Handmaiden," Jean-Jacques remembers.

But the groom is guiding her toward a back door. "*Génial*, great! This is it!" Jean-Jacques cocks his head questioningly at the vet. "May we?" The vet waves us after. Why is he grinning?

In a shed under a wood-beamed porch, the mare has been tied to a railing, her hind legs bound to prevent kicking. Her eyes swivel nervously. A groom twists her tail high over her back and wraps it in a plastic bag.

"Wait a minute. I don't think I want to see this." I make to leave the shed, suddenly flustered.

"It's the old-fashioned way. It's traditional. *La monte naturelle.* This is how they did it for centuries. You wait for the season. You choose the right bloodlines. My family always—"

"But I don't . . ."

It's too late. I am riveted to the floor. A dappled pureblood stallion is led, prancing and tossing its mane, into the shed. He nuzzles the mare's flank then, suddenly intent, draws back his head and snorts, eyes dim, transported. Suddenly he's all readiness. She is calm now.

The stallion rears, mounts, gives one shrill whinny and it's over. He hangs heavily on her back for a moment, suddenly benign.

Then *"Allez, hup!"* The groom leads him away.

The mare stands very still while they release her bindings and hose her hindquarters.

I stand very still, too. Then I feel my knees shaking.

Jean-Jacques is quiet for a moment. Finally he puts a hand on my shoulder.

"Mayg, I'm sorry. I didn't think . . ."

"The bastard," I say. I was trying to joke but it doesn't work. My voice sounds strange.

When I come out of the bathroom, my face and hands dripping, I find Jean-Jacques in the courtyard. He is staring abstractly at the cobblestones, a cigarette unlit between his lips, his hands in his pockets.

11 AM: High in the stands of the Hippodrome, I watch horses with braided manes go through their paces with neat feet and arched necks, riders erect in their saddles. They trot and turn, canter and stop on command. The riders are girls, mostly, nearly all of them blond, and their trainers stand on the sidelines pacing and smoking, arms folded.

A girl trots up to the stand, her dressage complete, and slips off the saddle, planting a kiss on the horse's nose. Her coach stalks up. I can hear him from here. "Your *fesses* were too high off the saddle again. Your back was rounded. Your . . ."

She wipes her eyes on her black velvet sleeve and dissolves into the crowd.

Jean-Jacques has been off shooting for two hours. I keep searching the mob for him.

There he is, off on the obstacle course. He is crouching beside a hurdle, shooting up under the horses as they gather their feet together and leap. His cameras hang low, swinging over the ground. His hair has slipped out of its ponytail and clumps down his back. He is wiping mud off his lens.

I watch him work. I can't seem to help it.

I shake my head. I look around myself. Horse trials. I can't believe I'm sitting here watching a horse show. I should be mortified. I should be back in the library, digging up . . . something. Or maybe I should just be back home.

Cluny. Cluny? I stare out over the grounds toward the steeple of the abbey. How can I tie these two stories into one?

I prop my chin dreamily in my hand, watching horses leap like dancers over the greens.

5 PM: My cheeks and shoulders are sunburned. I spent the entire afternoon on the field slipping under the barriers with my press card, asking questions of riders, trainers, fans. I can't help playing reporter, even if the real theme of the story is, well, medieval ecclesiastical power play.

It's cooling off now as the sun slants low in the sky. My sunburn is glowing hot and cold. My eyes are always probing the crowd. From time to time I see Jean-Jacques sprint past, trying to catch a galloping horse on his return circuit, or trotting backward, his lens pointed up into the face of an advancing rider. Then he melts into the mob.

At last the crowd mills toward the gates and the horses are led gently, weary, to their boxes. I walk past the Hippodrome sheds. There are saddles straddling fences, blankets pinned on improvised clotheslines, tall black boots airing in rows.

"*Salut!*" Jean-Jacques comes up behind me and I turn. He is spattered head to toe with mud, his hair matted, his scarf limp, his face smeared with the traces of blackened fingers where he wiped the sweat away. His nose took the brunt of the sun, glowing scarlet. He is grinning.

We walk together across the fields, following the crowd back into Cluny.

6 PM: Crossing through the temporary campground, a deep voice calls out.

"J-J? J-J . . . Chabrol?"

We both swing around and Jean-Jacques lifts a hand in greeting. A tall dark-haired Englishman in full equestrian kit—Barbour, calf-tight black boots, muddy jodhpurs—strides toward us.

"*Tu vois?* I remembered to leave out that nasty middle bit." He speaks literal British-French with a slightly tightened jaw. "Never touch the stuff, myself, these days. Strictly a Burgundy man."

The nasty middle part? De Brissac? Jean-Jacques changes the subject quickly. "Robin Kingsley-Wells, this is Mayg Parker. She's working on a book with me."

"*Enchanté.*" He nods my way. "What sort of book is it, then? Horsey stuff?"

I glance at Jean-Jacques. What sort of book is it, indeed?

"It's evolving, actually," I say. "History and . . . tradition."

"Well, plenty of that here. What, American, are you? Thought I heard a *petit accent.* Fraternizing with the enemy, eh, J-J?"

Jean-Jacques and I look at him blankly.

"Haven't been listening to the news these days? Quite the Franco-American contretemps. *Écoute, mon vieux,* why not come have a drink with us and we'll catch you up on current events? Sing around the campfire a bit? Simone will be delighted to see you, and the girls are here. Nathalie took her first blue ribbon today. We're all rather chuffed about it."

8:30 PM: Blackbirds sing flutey, throaty intervals over my head in the lime trees. The late spring light is changing blue to silver. I am sitting before flickering embers, a mug of wine in my hand. At my side a plate of pâté and cheese and bread lies half eaten.

I stare into the fire. All around me new friends and strangers mingle. I think I have met every horseman in Cluny tonight and every horse-woman, too. I have heard every misstep dissected, every good jump praised.

At supper, Nathalie, her nose pink from warm Champagne, acknowl-edged her first trophy shyly. "It's my first real grown-up trials," she said. "After I passed my Galop 8. I even beat Camille de Tournière, and she's much more experienced." She introduced me to Will-of-God before they led him away to the boxes. "Daddy bought him for me for my Bac," she confided. "He was very proud of my English results. Of course, he *taught* me English."

She tangled her fingers in the horse's mane. "You speak real French. But you're American?"

"I am." I caressed Will-of-God's muzzle with a cautious hand.

It was Robin who took pleasure in announcing the week's political crisis. France has banned all American meats from import, "high-tech" or not. America has retaliated by locking down imports on cheese. "Where's our honorable prime minister on all this?" he chortled. "Who can say? He'll do what the president tells him, won't he? Jump, boy, jump!"

I try not to listen, gazing down in my mug and conjuring instead the image of the horse trials and the sun and Jean-Jacques running back-ward. It makes me smile.

Now my mug is empty again and the fire is low. It's getting darker quickly. The group has thinned into small knots scattered over the grounds. I feel my sunburn stinging, a false chill prickling over a very real one. I shiver.

"Chilly? Splash of whiskey should set you to rights." It is Robin, strid-ing boldly through the campsite, scouting for empty cups. I sit passive while he pours two generous inches into my mug.

I am suddenly aware of Nathalie beside me, coltish legs folding under her as she settles.

"He's very nice, Jean-Jacques. He used to be my godfather."

"Used to be? How is that possible?" I take a sip of whiskey. It is very good whiskey but it burns.

"When he left Pauillac my parents had the papers changed."

"I didn't think you could do that."

"I am not sure you can." She looks at me with a conspiratorial smile. "Are you two . . . ?"

"He's very nice. We're working on a book together."

"Ah. I thought maybe . . . when he was looking at you earlier . . ." She gazes into the fire and pushes back a tangle of blond hair. "Yes. He's very nice."

She rises and melts into the darkness.

"Chilly?" It isn't Robin this time. It is Jean-Jacques, behind me.

"Mmm," I murmur. I feel a horse blanket settling gently over my shoulders under the weight of two warm hands. But the harsh wool digs into my sunburn and I cringe, recoiling against my will. The hands fly away.

"Sorry!"

"No. It's sunburn. I—I was out all afternoon."

"Ah. Sorry."

"No! Thank you!—"

But the voice and the hands are gone.

The next voices are Robin's and Simone's, blurred into one. "So your book, Meg, it's about the history of Cluny?"

I take another swallow of whiskey, then another. "Well, it's a book about all the regions of France, really. Historic places. Historic moments. I think."

"And you are in Cluny for . . . ?"

My tongue is loosening with every gulp. "The history of Cluny Abbey is incredible. Amazing." I take another. "Do you know that the Cardinal Richelieu was abbot under Louis XIV and he never set *toe* here? Just collected obscene quantities of tithes and taxes. And that the abbots hardly even answered to the pope? They set their own rules, the monks . . ."

I take a gulp and plunge on ". . . they lived indulgent lives, sensual, corrupt, beyond the laws of man and of God."

Am I quoting something or am I making this up? Beyond the laws of man and of God. That's pretty good.

This whiskey is pretty good. I focus with effort on the illuminated dome of the abbey. I hear more whiskey pouring into my cup. I swallow it. I fix with a will on Robin and Simone's firelit faces. They smile and fade.

"Mayg."

I listen. Jean-Jacques is behind me again. "Mayg, will you come?"

I struggle to my feet. Faces wheel around me. One is Jean-Jacques'. I smile in happy recognition. It's such a good face. Bony. Nose so big it looks like it ate his chin. Skin still smeared with dirt and sweat, hair matted every which way. I giggle. "You should wash, you know," I say earnestly. He smiles and reaches gently for my elbow.

He leads me away from the camp. The faces fade, the fires fade, a half moon takes hold, bathing me and Jean-Jacques and the empty end of the *haras* grounds in silver. I stumble and turn. He is holding both my elbows now and I am not swaying anymore. I am leaning toward him, my eyes closing.

My cell phone rings. I blink and turn my head. It rings and rings. I reach for it.

"Hello? Hello? Nigel? Is that you?"

I look up and Jean-Jacques is gone.

Sunday, 9 AM: I pick at my breakfast alone. Oh god. Has he bolted? I rub my aching head.

I'm loading my bags into the Citroën when Jean-Jacques appears, the scarf bound high around his neck. He glances up at me. "Morning, Mayg. Drop me at the *gare?*"

We roll in silence across the Mâconnais countryside, keeping our eyes on the road. My palms are slippery on the steering wheel. When we reach the *autoroute,* he takes a breath and tries a twisted smile. "So. What's our next rendezvous with history? Atlantis?" But he sees my face and the smile dissolves. "No. Sorry. *Sorry.*" He shakes his head. "Mayg, *écoute . . .*"

I drive in stricken silence. He doesn't try again.

At the Mâcon *gare,* I pull into the Europcar lot and set the parking brake. Jean-Jacques hesitates for a moment, his hands on his knees.

Then he releases his seatbelt and leans toward me.

I cower back a little. But he quickly grazes my cheeks, first one, then the other, with his lips. Before I can breathe again, he's heaved his bags onto his shoulder and is walking toward the station.

11 AM: I drive up the A31, my chest squeezing and expanding from moment to moment. The CD is still in the disk player. Random fragments weave through my consciousness.

lux aeterna

Light eternal. Light of the world.

qui tollis peccata mundi

Who taketh away the sins of the world.

I feel the prickling of his whiskers all the way home.

6 ❧ A Thousand Ships

Tuesday, May 13, 9 AM: The hole in the barn wall is still there. It howled last night in the windstorm, and I held Cloey and Kate in the four-poster again. It doesn't seem to worry Nigel. He slept like a baby. I wrapped myself around the kids like a quilt and watched the ceiling, warily, into the wee hours.

Today I pour them onto the bus, their eyes pink, their limbs rubbery, and watch the door fold shut. Then I walk home and put on my army jacket and descend to headquarters.

Cluny. Cluny. I don't know how to write this. I stare at the screen. I type:

Light of the world.

I erase it.

Sins of the world.

I erase it.

I drift. I see Jean-Jacques jogging backward across the obstacle course, his lens tracking a leaping stallion.

He laughed at me. I deserved it. Didn't I?

I leaned into him on the *haras* grounds. Did he lean back?

He ran away. My husband phoned. He ran away because my husband phoned. He ran away because I leaned into him.

It was only the whiskey talking. Wasn't it?

Oh god, what does he think?

Oh god, what was I thinking?

I rub my eyes. I try to type.

Beyond the laws of God and man

I stare.

11 AM: A shower of dust cascades down. I feel the staccato vibrations of something larger than a tank, more aggressive than a machine gun.

It is directly over my head. The jackhammer.

I pull myself up the iron rungs, hand over hand.

I emerge into the barn. Raimondo's men are wielding a pneumatic drill the size of an artillery cannon, but not aimed at the hole in the wall. They are pointing it straight into the ground. It roars and grinds, attacking the cobblestones and centuries of beaten earth beneath.

"*Bonjour,* Madame Thorpe."

It is Raimondo, smiling. He is wearing that absurd white mason's cap perched high on his mass of black hair, and there is a Gauloise threaded into the gap where his brown front teeth used to be. He pinches it out and grins guilelessly. "You see? MacGregor has found a solution."

I stare at the drill. "A hole in the floor?"

Raimondo's eyes narrow, the flicker of charm dimmed. "Madame Thorpe, you will see. You will see."

I stand and watch but no one speaks to me. The men close their circle around the great monster drill and I stare at their backs for a while, trying to resist plugging my ears. Then I back down my ladder and try to work.

The stones of God's own abbey torn asunder by man's angry hands . . .

Maybe I've got something here. But the horses?

Piled anew, four-square, foundations to a new world, a real world of straw and sweat and stallions who . . .

The jackhammer pounds overhead, dust sifting over the yoke of my chasuble, my pile of open books.

stallions who . . .

No. I can't write this.

Thursday, 9 AM: A subsonic shuddering rattles my fruit shelves. It grows heavier and spreads into an audible roar, then suddenly weakens and dies.

I scramble up the ladder two rungs at a time and leap to the front door. There is an eighteen-wheel truck backing up to the barn door, its vast bed bearing a single iron I-beam. There is a squeal and a hiss, and a hydraulic claw descends. It grips one end of the beam and lifts it, mass and weight denied as it dangles delicately in the air.

It is arcing toward my barn door and its two-hundred-year-old stone frame.

"No-o-oh!" I cry. "Look out for —"

But the driver twists the claw expertly and the beam clears the door. He lowers it onto the cobblestones and releases. There is another hiss, then silence.

I glance around desperately and catch Raimondo's eye. He sees me and looks at the ground as if to spit. Then he turns on a gummy smile.

"*Bonjour,* Madame Thorpe!"

I don't smile back. "What is this . . . this thing?"

Raimondo slumps slightly, discouraged. He shakes his head. Then he straightens again and smiles broadly. "This, Madame, is a beam. It will support your roof against the worst of dangers. Even the weakest of walls."

"But how —?"

"Madame Thorpe, you must trust Monsieur MacGregor. Monsieur MacGregor is a man who knows his work. You who cannot understand the complexities . . ."

He chooses, with visible effort at diplomacy, not to finish this sentence.

5:15 PM: Towing Cloey and Kate hand in hand behind me, we approach the barn in the softening light. The door gaps slightly open and we crane our necks to see inside.

Kate gasps.

Cloey pushes between us.

"What that? *C'est quoi?*" he sputters, mouth gaping.

The iron I-beam stands erect, its base hardening in a deep pool of concrete, its top towering above us, tightly bolted to the great oak cross-beam.

Kate recovers herself first and tugs my army-jacket hem.

"Are they building the Eiffel Tower in our barn?"

1 AM: Nigel is very late tonight and smells very beery. I coil myself around him, searching, not finding. The roof doesn't creak half so much.

Friday, 9 AM: I have drifted back to *La Vie en France*.

> *In France the practice of kissing cheeks is an ancient social form. While in formal situations one shakes the hand of an acquaintance or a work colleague, intimates kiss each other on both cheeks every time they meet and part. It is one of France's pleasanter customs and not to be misinterpreted.*

4 PM: Sophie taps lightly on the front door and lets herself in. I am in the kitchen straining veal stock, licking marrow out of the warm shank bones. I look up and pull up short. She is wearing no makeup and she looks pale, vulnerable. I wipe my lips on a tea towel and kiss her naked cheeks.

"Hello, Sophie. You look a little tired. You okay?"

She averts her eyes. "Yes, Madame." She takes a quick breath and plunges ahead. "Madame, Monsieur Thorpe has forgotten to pay me. I'm sorry to inconvenience you. I just wanted to go into Nancy this weekend."

I sigh. "Sophie, I am so sorry. He promised to take care of that Saturday."

She stands, studying her combat boots.

Oh dear. I rummage through my bag, find twenty euros and give it to her. "Here. I'll go to the bank this afternoon and get the rest."

She doesn't object. "Madame Parker, you'll be going away for long this time?"

Why do I feel a flutter at the thought? "Well, yes, I think we'll be working for four days this time. There is some ground to cover and it's a long way to the Camargue."

"Yes, of course." She hesitates. "Then, could you arrange a very clear schedule with Monsieur? So I can make plans with Ahmad? He wants to take me to the Arabic film festival."

"Of course. Of course." I fumble to reassure her. "I will make absolutely sure that Monsieur Thorpe understands this."

8 PM: When Nigel comes home he spots the fridge immediately. There is a printout in red and black hung from the freezer door. My itinerary for the Aigues-Mortes trip. The children's school hours, meal plans, bus departures, and bedtimes are highlighted in fluorescent yellow. Sophie's duties are marked in black. Nigel's are marked in red boldface type.

"New battle plan here?" Nigel glances over it and opens the freezer for the ice tray.

"Not really, it's the same as last time. But Sophie needs to be sure that . . ."

"Naturally. Goes without saying. Quite understandable."

"But she told me you haven't—"

"What, darling? Been caring for our mutual children?"

I stare at him.

He doesn't look at me, but ambles over to the liquor cabinet and pours himself an inch of whiskey. He's been doing that a lot. Then he opens yesterday's *Telegraph* and turns to the crossword. He sips and scans. I am standing by the refrigerator, looking at him.

"Here's one for you, Megs. Six letters. 'Hobby. Pastime.' He picks up his pen. "Perhaps, *Mo . . . ther?*"

My fists clench at my sides.

"No, I've got it." He takes a sip. He glances up at me, then studiously back at the page. "*Wri . . . ter.*"

My breath flies out of me. I head for my ladder.

La Vie en France, Level Two

Though France is a predominantly Catholic country, one out of two marriages ends in divorce. Laws are liberal and straightforward though time-consuming. Custody of children is traditionally granted to the mother.

DIALOGUE

Francine: Après neuf ans de mariage, tu me prends toujours pour un enfant!

After nine years of marriage, you still take me for a child!

François: Calme toi, chérie, tu n'as pas besoin de te comporter comme un enfant non plus. Je voulais seulement proposer . . .

Calm down, darling, there's no need to act like a child either. I was merely suggesting . . .

Francine: Arrête de me parler comme ça! Je ne suis pas ton animal de compagnie. Tu me traites toujours avec tellement de condescendance.

Stop talking to me like that! I'm not your housepet. You always patronize me so.

I rub my eyes.

11 PM: I sent the Cluny text to Nikos yesterday. I did hesitate for a moment, but I copied it to Jean-Jacques, too.

Now there's a message from Jean-Jacques with jpegs attached, copied to Nikos. It's the first I've heard from him since the *haras*.

Hello Nick—The story takes a new turn. What do you think of these? jj

There is no comment for me.

I scroll through. There is the black mare peeking, shy, impossibly fragile, between wrought-iron bars in a wash of yellow light. Beside her there's a column of time-mottled stone, the *H* insignia in gilt framed above. There are grooms leading a rearing stallion into the laboratory barn, his nostrils flared, his hooves pawing the air. And there are horses galloping like medieval chargers through the obstacle course.

The last one shows a fine-boned Arabian arcing overhead, its hooves and muscles blurred in a graceful sweep. The rider's face is in focus, her expression one of pure, radiant exuberance. Behind them, in sfumato tones, the steeple of Cluny Abbey dominates the horizon.

They are exquisite. So alive. I can see him, crouching in the field, shooting.

Dead monks, he said. Something livelier. I cup my chin and sigh, scrolling through the images again.

Another message blinks into the mailbox, also from Jean-Jacques. There is a jpeg attachment. It is not copied to Nikos.

I sit up. I click.

I see darkness, planes of red-gold against black. Robert's cave? I switch off my work lamp and my eyes adapt. It is a tight close-up of a woman's face, eyes closed, lips parted, lost in a glass of wine.

I feel blood creeping up my cheeks.

Is that woman me?

I stare at the image. My lips part a little at the memory.

Another message blinks into the mailbox, another jpeg, no cc to Nikos. It is as if Jean-Jacques were hovering online, considering, then tapping Send.

I hold my breath. I click.

It is of me again. This time I am sitting by the fire, holding the metal mug in laced fingers. My face is glowing in the firelight and I am gazing into the flames, hugging my knees. I am smiling as if I had a happy secret.

Sunday, 11 AM: "'. . . and when the ships set sail they nearly foundered with the weight of soldiers, arms and horses . . .'"

I sit under the apple tree reading aloud from a yellowed leather-bound copy of *The Crusades*. Kate is hanging upside down by her knees above me, her coppery hair brushing the pages.

". . . but how did King Louis get horses onto the ships? They are too—Cloey! Non! *Non!*"

"*Ouaah!*"

Drops of icy water spatter over me. I'm on my feet. "Cloey! No! Not the hose!"

Monday, 2 PM: *The Crusades* lies drying on my desk, its pages propped apart with silicone packs. I am poring over the Internet listings for Aigues-Mortes, on Google, on Yahoo, clicking every source I can find.

I will not get caught short this time. I don't want Jean-Jacques to laugh at me again.

not history meg reality

I confirm it, file by file, site by site.

> *Louis IX, known now as Saint Louis, launched his seventh crusade from the shores of Aigues-Mortes in 1248. There were no less than 1500 ships, some 35,000 men, all setting sail for Cyprus to engage the infidel on his stolen sacred soil.*

Yes! This will be good. The fortress still stands, a vast walled grid, massive quadrants of crenellated stone barely touched by the salt winds of the Mediterranean. Flags wave in the photographs. There are broad city gates and towers, thick ramparts.

I hope I can get him to catch the spirit this time. Work with me on this, I think. Work with me.

10 PM: Nigel is watching the Sky News. I lie with Cloey long after his thumb has slipped out. I stand in Kate's doorway and watch her breathe until my own breath aligns with hers.

Then I head out the kitchen door to the garden. I stand, hip-deep in the roses. They are heavy with buds. The dew is already rising. Gerald trails behind me, his tail beating the boxwood, sending up its rich, catty scent.

I crouch and put my arms around him.

Thursday, 11 PM: Flat in the *couchette,* my body is being transported southward, horizontal, passive. My arms still feel the cling of Cloey and Kate when I rolled the suitcase to the door. Cloey was in his Lucky Luke pajamas, the bottoms sagging low enough to expose a swell of tiny round bun. Kate's thumb was in her mouth. She stared into space.

"My sroat hurts."

By reflex my hand flew to her forehead but it was cool and dry. "I know honey. I'm sorry. It will feel better in the morning." She turned baleful eyes on me. I buried my face in her neck.

our mutual children

Nigel stood in the kitchen. I walked the distance between us and aimed a kiss up to his mouth. He didn't bend down to receive it. I tip-toed and kissed his jaw instead.

"Do keep to the schedule, honey," I said, trying to hold his gaze.

"Right. Absolutely. The battle plan. Have a lovely trip, darling. We'll be waiting for you. Won't we, children?"

The train carries me away through the night.

Friday, 6 AM: I crawl down the *couchette* to the window and lift the shade. The flats of the Herault stream past the window, stony-white, tiny villages bubbling out of the landscape in a skew of clay tiles. There are vineyards greening all around and neat groves of almond trees. I crack the window. The air smells dry and fresh. May in Provence. I love it.

Jean-Jacques is meeting me at the Montpellier *gare* with a rental car. I thread down the pitching corridor to the bathroom. With paper towels and cold pumped water I perform a hasty toilette. I brush my teeth. I brush my hair and tie it back. I peel off the jeans I traveled in and pull on a gauzy Indian-print skirt. I gaze into my own eyes for a minute. I reach for some spray cologne. Then I stop myself, put it back, and zip the makeup kit firmly shut.

7 AM: Stepping down at Montpellier, I look up and down the quai. No-body. I feel a squeeze of disappointment. I roll my bag through the station and head for the taxi ramp.

Jean-Jacques is standing beside the driver's door of a blue Clio, rest-ing his arms on the roof, smoking. He's wearing a limp grey t-shirt, no scarf. Under the tangle of hair, his neck and shoulders look thin and exposed, all Adam's apple. He doesn't see me yet. He stares into middle space, rubbing his forehead with his fingers. My heart is pumping oddly. I shouldn't have brought so much luggage. I raise my fingers and tenta-tively wave.

"Jean-Jacques? Hi!"

He looks up. He drops his cigarette. "Mayg." He smiles with apparent effort. "Hi."

I roll toward him but he doesn't move. I make for the trunk and he recovers himself. "Hi! Sorry!" He makes a sweep at my cheeks with his lips, so quick it scrapes me. Then he springs the trunk open and stands with his hands on his hips, smiling awkwardly. I start to lift my bag in and he fumbles for it. "Sorry! Let me." He holds it for a beat too long between us, then lowers it slowly into the car. "Did you have a good trip?" He swings the trunk shut and backs around the bumper to the driver's side.

I feel my mouth going dry. I did scare him in Cluny. "Fine," I say. I climb into the passenger side. I swallow. Conversation. "Um. How did you get the rental car so early?"

"They left me the keys at the ticket booth."

"Oh." I nod. "It's nice."

"Yes." He throws it into gear and pulls away. "Mayg. We have to talk."

I feel adrenalin stinging toward my fingertips. Oh god.

But we roll in silence through the urban tangle and clear the city. Jean-Jacques swerves the car onto a side road and suddenly the pavement breaks free of land, threading across a causeway over low churning waters. Then we turn just as suddenly onto a spit of sandy soil, the ribbon of blacktop flanked on one side by low marshy waters and on the other by cane-feathered dunes and the open sea.

I guess it's up to me. I clear my throat. "Thank you for the photographs. They're really beautiful. Um, Jean-Jacques, you mustn't think . . ."

"How's Nigel?" He is looking straight ahead, concentrating on the road.

I stop. I catch a breath. "He's fine, thank you."

"And Cloey? And Kate?"

I can't help but smile a little. He pronounces them "Cloh-EE" and "Kay-EET."

"They're fine, too. They were sad to see me go."

"C'est normal." He drives on.

We pass cancerous modern growth of resort architecture, blotting out all view of the marshlands and sea, then cross the flatlands leading to Aigues-Mortes. Jean-Jacques parks at the foot of high rampart walls and stops the engine.

"Have you had breakfast? We should get something before we go into the village. I want to talk to you. About the story."

About the story. Oh.

Suddenly I am nervous. He's not going to balk now, is he? This time the story is rock solid. He's got to know that.

I can feel my confidence seeping away again. "Yes. I'm starved. I wanted to take a moment to brief you anyway. Are you familiar with the history of Aigues-Mortes? Did you get the links I forwarded?"

"Mayg, I—"

"I did a lot of research on it. A lot of research. On the *Internet,* too." I look at him, hoping for a nod of encouragement. His face is still. "It's an incredible story, incredible. Louis IX—that's Saint Louis, the one with the fleurs-de-lys—used Aigues-Mortes as a launching point for two of his crusades to the Holy Land. You know this, right? He—"

"Mayg, I—" Jean-Jacques looks pained. We walk toward a café with tables out front.

"He had more than a thousand ships built, fifteen hundred I think, and brought in incredible numbers of men . . ."

Jean-Jacques looks around desperately. "I'll get coffee." He ducks into the bar and I fall silent. He seems so tense. Has he gone off the history theme again? Or altogether? He returns with a huge cup of milky coffee and a tiny espresso and sets down a basket of croissants. He sinks into the plastic chair. I plunge ahead.

"The ships. They were crammed with soldiers and weapons and . . ."

"Mayg, listen, maybe we should—"

"It must have looked spectacular." I gulp my coffee. "It was a regular armada, these great wooden sailing ships all heading out into the Mediterranean for God and King . . ."

Even when we push back our chairs and head toward the great fortress archway, I natter nervously on. "Jean-Jacques, you just have to imagine . . ."

A broad square flanked with vast grey-stone walls stretches ahead. We cross it. Jean-Jacques has fallen silent. He has his hands in his pockets, his cameras thumping at his side as he strides. I keep up.

"Please! Imagine thousands of white sails!"

"Mayg, I'm trying to—"

"Villagers standing on these ramparts waving scarves in the air to farewell the armies of God!"

"Mayg, *écoute*—"

"*What?*" I stop, desperate, exasperated. He crams clenched fists into his pockets. He walks on.

We reach the great back seawall and begin to climb the stairs. "From this very wall the citizens looked out over the waters, weeping and cheering and throwing flowers into the open surf . . ."

Jean-Jacques is shaking his head desperately. I am almost begging now. "Please! Try and imagine!" I say. He puts a hand on my arm to hold me back. I shake it off and run up the last steps onto the rampart walkway, waving my arm out over the open sea.

But there is no open sea. As far as I can see, there are salt flats, rustling with crisp dry reeds.

I blink. "Is it low tide?"

We stare out over the muddy flats.

"Mayg, I tried to tell you. I'm sorry. I tried to—"

Oh god.

"I've been trying to explain but—"

"You knew." Delayed horror rushes over me. "You knew?" He's done it again. I've done it again.

"Oh god! I did the research! I studied this! But I didn't just study the old books, though of course I did that, too. I researched this on the Internet. I *Googled* it!"

I turn to him, beseeching. "How did you know there was no sea here?"

Jean-Jacques looks embarrassed. He hesitates. Then, very gently, without a trace of a mocking smile, he says, "I looked at a map."

9:30 AM: It's got to be here somewhere. I am striding, straight and hard, toward the sea, slogging through reeds that slash at my bare legs. My sandals swamp with salty bilge. I stride on. My skirt drags at the wet grasses. I yank it up impatiently between my legs and tuck it into my waistband. I stride on. A few stunted trees block the horizon. I stride past them and see only the silos and smokestacks and towering cranes of salt refineries.

"Mayg?"

I stride on.

"Mayg, will you stop please? I'm sorry."

He's sorry. What's he sorry for? I am a fool, an idiot, clueless. Everybody treats me that way. Everybody's right.

"Mayg, listen to me."

I stride on.

"I should have told you. I tried to tell you. Listen, it's no big deal. We'll figure something out."

"No big deal? I came all the way down from Lorraine for this. I have a book to write."

"I guess I thought you would figure it out."

I turn on him. *"Figure it out?* You wanted to play a joke on me. Like with Robert. And at Cluny." I slog on. "You think this is all a big joke. You and probably Nikos, too."

"Mayg, that's ridiculous. Calm down."

"You wanted to laugh at me again. You and that . . . that *laugh* of yours. 'Madame l'Historienne'! 'L'Américaine'!"

He stops walking. I look back at him. His face has darkened. His hands are on his hips. "I thought you would figure out the Latin. You speak Latin, I recall."

"The Latin?"

"Aigues-Mortes comes from *aqua morta.* Dead waters. The Rhône delta filled these waters in ages ago."

I squeeze my eyes shut. Oh god.

I breathe in. Then I regird. "It's a-*quae* mor-*tae,* as a matter of fact. And yes, I did study Latin at Cambridge."

Jean-Jacques bows his head. His mouth is set and grim. "And French. And history. I am very aware of this. You remind me often. There is no need to patronize me."

I swing on him. My breath flies out of me as if I'd been punched. "Patronize you? *You* are calling *me* patronizing?" I feel a tidal wave roar through my veins. "Don't talk to me about patronizing! You and—and everybody—*everybody* patronizes me! You patronize me! Nikos patronizes me! Your friends patronize me! The whole of *putain de* France patronizes me! And England, too! My husband patronizes me! Even my mason patronizes me!"

We stand, facing off in the salt bog, my ankles closed round with saline slime. His baggy jeans are soaked to the knees. He looks at me pathetically. He shakes his head.

"Mayg, come back in."

I waver.

"*Écoute.* Come on. Let's go back in."

Mute, I turn and begin to slog back.

10:30 AM: On the place Saint-Louis, at the foot of the statue of Louis IX, we wash our feet in the fountain, spent. My skirt hem hangs heavy with mud. My sandals drip sludge and there are outlines of black silt between my toes. I dip and rub them in the water, stumbling. Jean-Jacques steadies my arm. He steps into the fountain fully shod, splashes around, sits on the stone edge, and pulls off his pouring shoes. Then he shrugs. Now what?

We settle on a park bench under the shade of a plane tree. It is strange to see him barefoot. His feet are bony and pale and misshapen and they bristle with hair. I look at mine, pink from scrubbing, dripping in the sun. They're no better. I tuck them under the bench.

We sit. Then I bury my face in my hands, shaking my head. "I guess I should take the night train back. What a waste of time."

Jean-Jacques rubs his jaw. "We could still do Aigues-Mortes."

I glance up at him. Scathing.

"Okay, I know, but I could shoot the flags, the ramparts. I don't know, clouds maybe. Do you think clouds could . . . *evoke* . . . a fleet of ships on the sea?"

He is not smirking. He is looking at his toes. He really *is* trying.

"It's okay, Jean-Jacques. It's okay. I . . . I blew it. There's no story. A fort on dry land launching a thousand ships? No."

He fishes for a cigarette and lights up.

My eyes are boring into the cobblestones. "Should I go home? Should I cancel the project? Admit it. Arles. Cluny. Now this."

I glance furtively up. He's staring at the cobblestones, too.

I don't want to go back just yet, either.

We sit. He smokes.

11 AM: I am searching my brain. "The Wars of Religion. There was a lot of fighting around here. Massacres. Maybe we could . . ."

I peek over at Jean-Jacques. He is keeping his face neutral.

"I know, I know. A massacre would be hard to photograph."

He keeps his eyes down and his face straight. He really is trying.

I cast around. "Maybe something with the Saintes Maries? The holy Marys that landed on the coast? I mean the *real* coast?"

He grunts but not unkindly. I look up to make sure.

"Do you know that story?"

"Only a little bit."

"It's amazing. A whole group of early Christians—we're talking 50 AD, not long after Christ died—they were rounded up and shipped off to die at sea. You know who was on that boat?—I mean this is legend, I know but—there was Mary Magdalene and Martha. And Mary Salome, or was it Mary Jacoby? And Lazarus. Not the one who rose from the dead, but the other one. Anyway, their boat floats across the Mediterranean and drifted ashore at Stes-Maries, just up the coast from here."

I am wriggling my toes, abstracted. I sense Jean-Jacques' eyes. I look up. He is watching me. I shrug. "Sorry."

There is that trace of something playing around his mouth. "So do you know the part about Sarah?"

"Sarah?"

"She was on the boat with them."

Oh god. "You knew."

"No." He stubs out his cigarette. "Okay, I knew a little. The name of the town. I didn't know all the details as you told them." The slightest, gentlest twist of his lips. "But I do know about Sarah. She was a servant girl who was set adrift with them, at least this is the story."

"I didn't know about her."

"She was dark-skinned. She was maybe Egyptian. And the Gypsies today, they've adopted her as a kind of patron saint."

"Gypsies?"

"Gypsies. They come to Stes-Maries around Pentecost every year to pay homage. She was buried here with the two Maries. They light candles in the crypt of the old church, and they carry her back to the sea."

"Her?"

"Well, the statue of her. They carry it from the church down the beach to the sea. It's a ritual."

"Wait a minute. Pentecost?" I search his face. "Are you telling me there just *happens* to be a gypsy festival in Stes-Maries this weekend? Did you know about this?"

"No. Euh . . . well, I did do a little looking on the Internet before I left. Just in case."

My face sinks into my hands again. He puts a hand on my shoulder and takes it quickly away. He reaches for another cigarette. He lights.

I look up at him and take a breath.

"Okay, Mr. Vibrant-Tradition. What have you got up your sleeve this time?"

11:30 AM: I am kneeling on the bench now, my feet tucked under me, facing him, imploring. "Why *not?*"

The cobblestones are littered with cigarette butts. "I don't think we should go there. It's not a good story for us. I looked into it."

"But Jean-Jacques . . . you said . . . I mean, Gypsies carrying a statue into the sea!"

"Look, I don't think it would work. It's a closed world. Private. It's not for outsiders."

"But maybe . . . why not? You're the one who believes in traditions, traditions still alive, active, *real.*"

"But not this one. I've been warned away from it by a friend."

"Warned away?"

"Well, some people don't like to be photographed. Some things—some traditions—are so personal they can't be printed in glossy books."

"Do you think we could go *see?*" I am sitting up eagerly.

He thinks for a while. "Well, my friend—the one who told me about this—lives in the Camargue. We could go talk to him. He has a farmhouse, a *mas.*"

He pauses and looks at me. "Unless you want to take the train home tonight."

I sit back on my heels. There's a funny pang in my chest. "Um, we could give it a try. I came all this way."

He's looking at me.

I hesitate. "Jean-Jacques, if you knew about Aigues-Mortes, why didn't you tell me? I wouldn't have come."

But he reaches for a cigarette and clicks the lighter. He inhales. Then he studies his naked toes.

My stomach growls.

He smiles and looks up.

"So. Are you ready for lunch?"

11:50 AM: I pick up some quiches at a pastry shop and a couple of bottles of juice while Jean-Jacques telephones from the sidewalk. When I come out of the shop he looks at my choices with a wan shrug.

"That's fine but you know . . ." His eyes are already searching up and down the street. "We're so close to Sète, the Bassin de Thau. Do you like—"

"Oysters? Yes. Bouzigue oysters are wonderful. Oh god, yes. Good idea. Where can we find some before the shops close?" We look up and down the street and, as one, break into a trot. Fishmonger, fishmonger.

We round a corner and come upon a *poissonnerie* just pulling its iron grill across the ice-filled sidewalk stands. "I'll get the oysters," he says. "You find bread!"

"Right!" I start to sprint down the street as the shutters clang around me. I duck under one and smile desperately. "Just a quick *pain de campagne*. Please?" The baker looks at me with disdain, but twists a brown baguette in a square of tissue and takes the coins from my hand. The shutter crashes down behind me.

I spot him down the street, carrying a net-bound crate, a bag, and a bottle of wine. I raise my baguette in triumph and we head for the car.

1 PM: Suddenly there's no hurry. We drive slowly across flat countryside, brushed in every variation of beige and gold and green, dry reeds and cattails waving in the salty breeze. Ponds melt in and out of the marsh-lands. Black-green parasol pines look like monstrous intruders against all this subtle nothingness.

" '*Ni arbre, ni ombre, ni âme,*'" I quote. "Neither tree nor shade nor soul. That's Frédéric Mistral. This is his country. His landscape. He wrote *Mireille* about this."

I think for a moment and make to toss an olive pit out the car window, then stop. "Hey! Maybe we could . . ."

"Isn't Mistral also . . . dead?" Jean-Jacques looks at the road.

I throw the pit at him instead.

We roll over the salt flats, birds fanning out of the reeds as we pass. At a grove of trees he turns off the road and stops the engine. "Do you mind eating on the ground? I mean, we could look for a picnic table somewhere near town but . . ."

"No. This is perfect." I open the car door and a wave of white egrets flutters up and out, wheeling over the wetlands.

We settle, cross-legged, on a high sandy spot at the base of a parasol pine. I pull my skirt down over my knees and it flutters as it dries, white salt painting new patterns over the batik. The sun is half-veiled and the breeze is cool.

A sudden silence passes over us.

Then Jean-Jacques sets to work on the wine cork and I tear off hasty chunks of bread.

"Cups?" I ask.

He reaches into a plastic bag and pulls out two. "Cups."

He fills them halfway and passes me one. He raises his.

"*Vive l'histoire.*" He says it gently.

I raise my glass, too, but with a doubtful shrug. We drink.

"*Alors.* The oysters." Jean-Jacques digs one out of the crate and cradles it in his palm. He sinks his penknife quickly into the joint and twists, tosses the top away and passes it to me. I take it and lift it to my mouth, my eyes closing in anticipation. It slides onto my tongue and I crunch once and swallow, an ocean of briny-sweet flavor bursting over my taste buds. I slurp the juice, laughing and wiping my lips with the back of my hand. Jean-Jacques looks. Then he looks quickly away.

I moan. "Oh god. There's nothing, *nothing,* like a bouzigue. I never get to eat these. Nigel hates oysters."

I freeze for a second. I don't know why. My hand still hovers across my lips.

Jean-Jacques hesitates, considering. Then he reaches for another.

4 PM: The light is already softening. The wine makes me sleepy and I lie back between the tree roots and doze. Jean-Jacques wanders away for a while with his cameras. When I open my eyes, the branches are waving darkly overhead.

"So, shall we head off?" He is standing over me with his hands in his jeans pockets.

"Oh. Right. I'm sorry. The night train, the wine . . ."

He said, "You mumble in your sleep."

"Really?" I feel suddenly flustered. "You were watching me?"

The tips of his ears flush. He reaches for a cigarette. Then he stops himself and looks at me. He takes a deep breath.

But all he says is, "We'd better get going."

8 PM: There is a fire crackling in the enormous stone fireplace in Didier's *mas* and he is hunched over it, poking up the flames. I am surrounded by old books and nature prints of water birds, tinted in soft hues over old etched ink. The shelves are scattered with shells and driftwood, pine cones and mottled eggs. There are binoculars dangling from the stair rail. A wind hums over the chimney hole. I have showered and changed and curled comfortably in a deep, soft armchair, feet tucked under me, cheek resting on my hand. My wet hair is steaming in the firelight.

Jean-Jacques has been gone for hours. He took his cameras.

"Thank you, Didier. It's wonderful here. I'm glad Jean-Jacques called. Have you known each other for a long time?"

Didier sits back on his haunches. He is only forty-something but he's wearing an old wool cardigan and slippers and he looks as comfortable as the chair I'm sitting in. "Our fathers have known each other since the war," he says.

I look up and wait but he watches the fire. "Jean-Jacques has had a hard time. He's made some tough decisions."

For some reason, I'm reluctant to press him further.

Jean-Jacques pushes the wide oak door open and a blast of sucking wind pulls him through. He dumps his camera bags and pushes his hair out of his face. He is still in his salt-stained pants. "Mistral whipping up out there! Incredible! *Putain,* what a force!"

I sit up. "Mistral?"

Didier points up the chimney. The hum has become a howl. "A mountain wind that comes down the Rhône valley. Very strong. When it cuts over the Camargue delta there's no stopping it."

"I know, but will that affect the festival tomorrow?" I ask nervously.

Jean-Jacques glances over at Didier. "We haven't talked about that yet."

Didier stands, brushing ashes off his knees. "You're not thinking of going into Stes-Maries tomorrow. Bad idea."

Jean-Jacques hesitates.

"Well, actually, that's why we came here," I venture. "I mean, Jean-Jacques seemed to think it was a bad idea, too. The festival. But it seems like — think of it! Gypsies carrying a shrine to the water!"

"Imagine," Jean-Jacques says. Is his mouth twitching?

I shoot him a look and sink back into my chair.

Didier frowns. "But — precisely. It all *sounds* very good, but when you find yourself in our tiny village in a mob of twenty thousand pilgrims, things aren't always so pretty. You would have to carry your gear in for miles and how close could you get? I don't know. And you won't necessarily be welcome."

"Mayg, it's a private ritual. It's not staged for tourists, you know."

"But isn't that the whole point? It's *living*. It's really happening now . . . for reasons that have existed for two thousand years. And . . . and . . ."

". . . And?" His hands are on his hips.

"Well. That's the whole point. It exists."

He looks at me. He wipes his jaw. "You mean not like Cluny Abbey and . . ."

". . . and the Maison Jaune."

Didier looks puzzled. Jean-Jacques is looking at me. His mouth softens a little. I test a small smile back.

Didier shrugs and rubs his hands together. "Coals are ready. Shall we eat?"

9 PM: Around the rough-hewn coffee table we're dipping carrots and crunchy green beans into a bowl of *anchoïade*, then carrying them dripping to our mouths. Jean-Jacques keeps his eyes averted.

Didier leans over the fire, turning sizzling slabs of meat over a grill. "Just about there," he says.

I crane to see. "What's that you're cooking? Steaks?"

"Yes. Bull."

"Bull steak? Are these from your own herd?"

"Of course. We like to keep it in the family."

The wind howls over the chimney and the flames flare and recede.

Jean-Jacques fills our glasses with something unlabeled and inky red. "This yours, too?"

"I have always kept my family's holdings."

I glance up but Jean-Jacques' nose is deep in his glass.

"Wonderful. Smells like Spain."

He swirls and sips the wine with prayerlike concentration. His lips purse.

I watch.

He looks up.

I look down.

The meat is delicious, purple-red and charred and sparkling with sea salt. There's red Camargue rice so nutty and sweet it sticks in my teeth, spicy baby greens so new they sting my tongue with flavor. Didier rolls them in olive oil, turning them in a crockery bowl and sprinkling on a handful of sea salt. The soft, goaty chèvre I spread on bread, tearing off bits with my teeth. The wine that smells like Spain washes it down, its round red aftereffects breathing across my tongue.

Jean-Jacques eats quietly, stopping now and then almost reverently to take pictures of the food. He smokes and talks with Didier of grapes and soil. I eat plump red strawberries one at a time. Delicious.

When I open my eyes he is looking at me.

Midnight: A silence has fallen. Jean-Jacques is smoking. The three of us stare into the fire as it leaps and crackles in the wind.

My phone beeps. A text message. Nigel.

I glance up at Jean-Jacques. He is staring into the fire.

I didn't call home all day.

I stand. "Good night Didier. Good night Jean-Jacques."

He isn't looking at me. He is staring into the fire.

I carry the phone up to my room.

1 AM: I lie in a low twin bed and listen to the wind shrieking through the window edges, shutters clattering and clapping in the dark. I turn on my stomach and pull the pillow over my ears. I feel the sheets on my skin. I smell Jean-Jacques' cigarette smoke trailing under the door.

Saturday, 5 AM: It is incredibly still. Uncannily silent. I wrap myself in the coverlet and tiptoe to the window to open the shutter. The whole of the Camargue reserve stretches before me in soft-focus grey. There is a horizon line so finely drawn it looks like India ink.

I lean out and breathe in. The air is cool and calm and fresh and new. It's as if the mistral had scoured it clean and carried all the residue out to sea. I cup my chin in my hands and watch the sky grow before me, lightening from grey to silver to rose, then gold, then blue.

Far down the shoreline I see a form. It is Jean-Jacques, walking. I duck back and reach for my jeans.

Then I stop myself. I sit down on the bed. With an effort I pick up the cell phone and thumb-type an answer to Nigel and the kids instead.

10 AM: We roll through the outskirts of Stes-Maries-de-la-Mer, a scattering of horse farms and *manades* crowded with tiny black bulls. Weary white horses hang their heads over fences, swaybacked from carrying tourists on *promenades à cheval*.

"The 'wild horses of the Camargue.' They don't look very wild, do they? I mean, you always see them in pictures galloping through the rushes."

"They used to be wild. I remember. They used to be beautiful."

There are a few gas stations and decaying *mas*. Then, closer in, the beach culture starts to take over and we enter a sprawl of cheap auberges and rental *résidences*. Already the sidewalks and gutters are crowded with cars. We park.

"So far it's not so charming, is it?" I concede. Jean-Jacques hauls his bags out of the trunk. I reach out and hike one over my shoulder.

"Thanks. We have a long way to walk."

I look at his face. "Um. Thank you for trying, Jean-Jacques. This will be wonderful, I'm sure."

He nods, neutral. "We'll see."

As we approach the village we see covered trucks and camper vans, entire fields packed solid with row on row of trailer-tents. There are towels and laundry fluttering from their tarp lines. Naked children potter around camp stoves. There are people everywhere, strangely dressed — ankle-length skirts in rich jewel-tone fabrics, head scarves, cinched vests. Their skin is dark, weathered by life on the road.

"You were right. This doesn't look very touristy."

We walk toward the town center and feel a flow walking with us. There are a lot of people here now, more and more. The sidewalks are crowded and we walk down the middle of the street, parting to let a few brave pickup trucks through.

There are children everywhere, butternut-skinned with heavy gold earrings hanging from tender lobes. They are dressed in white, extravagant flourishes of ruffles and poufs that drag on the sidewalk as they skip ahead of their families. Babies ride their father's shoulders, heads full of black curls bobbling as they walk.

"Where are they heading with all these children?" I ask.

"To the church. To be baptized."

We follow the flow. When we turn into the center I can't help but reel back. The streets are so densely crowded we can scarcely see the storefronts. Jean-Jacques raises his camera and shoots down the full perspective. Faces turn and glare. He slips it quietly back into his bag.

"I don't know, Mayg."

"Come on. Let's go to the church. The crypt. Sarah!"

He looks at me. There's something in his face I can't read. He smiles a little. "Okay."

We press on, clutching the camera bags. I try to make myself small and squeeze ahead. There are shouted greetings in a tongue I've never heard. Somewhere, down another street, someone is singing.

I cower as the mob intensifies. Jean-Jacques lays a hand on the small of my back. We press through the *place* and face the broad, crude Romanesque façade of the Église des Stes-Maries. I gasp. The entrance is seething with people. They are pressing into a wedge and pouring in the great church doors.

"Mayg, let's not."

But I want to see. I need to see. "This is *it*, Jean-Jacques. It's what we're here for." Breathless, I search his face. "Come on!" I grab his hand and shoulder ahead, Jean-Jacques threading after. There is music coming from the church, the deep droning of voices, ancient intervals, angular, austere. I am aware suddenly of his hand in mine. It tightens around my fingers, hard and warm. I drop it and push my hair out of my eyes.

We press together through the entrance and squint in the sudden darkness. There must be a thousand people in here. A mass is under way in the choir, a priest raising his hands over the head of a child. Families stand in tight knots, white-gowned children in their arms, on their shoulders. Their faces radiate intensity. Grown men are kneeling.

"*Putain,*" Jean-Jacques murmurs.

There are almost no windows in the broad single nave. The walls close in around the crowd, so densely covered with crude, hand-drawn ex-votos I can't see the stone. THANKS BE TO MARIE. THANKS BE TO SARAH. THANKS BE TO OUR LADY. There are scraps of hair tied with ribbon, bits of cloth, a baby slipper, a crutch, pinned to the panels, strung from the walls.

I look up at him. His face is drawn. He scans the crowd.

"Where is the crypt?" I ask him.

"The entrance is back there. But I don't think we should . . ."

My heart is racing. My mouth is dry. I look at him. "But . . ."

He looks at me. "*D'accord.* We can try."

I take his arm and pull, threading our way toward the crypt. The stairs are packed with people. We inch our way down sideways, me leading the way.

The ceiling is vaulted and low, but it's lighter here than upstairs.

Thousands and thousands of votive candles burn on tables, on shelves, on racks of spikes. The scent of paraffin and sweat and incense is overwhelming. At the center of the room, surrounded by a hundred bowing heads, I can just make out the statue.

It is a dark carved sculpture of a girl, her cheeks gilt, her eyes glazed madly white. She is dressed in a mass of fantastical dresses, one pulled over another, gold lamé and silver tulle and blue velvet overlapping. The crowd is pressing in on her, raising their children to her face to caress. Baby hands reach out and touch. Baby lips reach out and kiss. Parents close their eyes and murmur urgent prayers.

There is singing. And smell. And smoke. And there is no air.

I am gasping. I turn to Jean-Jacques. He is staring all around him. "Can you get this? Can you photograph this? It's incredible."

He shakes his head. "I don't dare." But his hands slip discreetly into his bag and he raises a lens. He holds it in above his shoulder and clicks.

Black heads snap around. He slips it into his bag. There are glowering faces. Someone swears filthily.

I look at Jean-Jacques in a flash of panic. "Okay. Let's go."

He doesn't say anything. He lays an arm across my shoulders and pushes back to the stairs.

We emerge on the swarming *place* panting, shielding our eyes against the sudden sun.

"Oh god. Incredible. I couldn't breathe. It's surreal."

Jean-Jacques is craning his neck, looking for a path of retreat through the throng. He pulls me around the back of the church and down a back street, then another. The crowd thins and we break into a trot. Under the awning of a beach souvenir shop, he turns to face me, breathless, hands on hips.

"Can we go now? Have you seen enough?"

I take deep gulps of air until my heart slows. I look longingly back toward the church. "But when are they carrying Sarah to the sea?"

Jean-Jacques throws his head up in despair.

11 AM: The beach of Stes-Maries looks like an armada has landed and charged to shore. There are thousands on thousands of people, more than I've ever seen together outside a football stadium. Security police swagger up and down the concrete walkway, sticks in their hands.

"You see? We can't get near the water."

"But don't you want to try to get some pictures?"

He gasps a laugh. "How can I shoot this? There will be an even bigger crowd with the procession. And they'll all be moving toward the water. If I shoot from the beach I'll have pictures of their backs. Do you want pictures of the back of a sculpture?"

"But there must be a way."

"I would have to wade out into the water and shoot toward shore. I can't do that."

I nod. "Okay. Fair enough. We tried."

He looks chagrined. "Mayg."

I hesitate. I look up sideways.

"I could hold your cameras."

Noon: The bells of the church peal frantically above the din of the crowd. I have Jean-Jacques' camera bags crisscrossed over my shoulders and am standing on the concrete walk above the beach. I scan the crowd. I can't make him out anywhere.

I hear singing coming from the direction of the church. The procession!

"Jean-Jacques?" I shout. "Jean-Jacques! They're coming!"

But of course he can't hear me. I don't even know where he is.

I shade my eyes and scan the beach, look out into the water. There he is: Jean-Jacques has waded out to a stone breakwater and is clambering onto the rocks. He did it! My hand rises to my mouth. I feel a surge in my chest. He really is doing this . . . for me. I wave, but he doesn't see me.

He pulls himself up carefully, holding something high over his head — the camera! — and stands. He pans the shoreline, spots me, and raises a hand to wave. He is grinning in triumph. I laugh and wave my hand like a semaphore. He braces his feet between the boulders. Then he leans back to shoot.

Now I can hear the procession coming. There is a rising murmur and a surge of movement as the crowd presses in, jockeying to see. I can feel the press and I brace my own feet. There is a tidal wave of pressure, jostling and pushing. Babies on shoulders sway precariously, screaming. I am pressed backward and I slip off the concrete step. I couldn't have fallen down if I'd wanted to. The crowd is so dense I am held upright, buoyed toward the beach.

I strain to see. Jean-Jacques is standing, shooting something high above my head. I turn. The statue of Sarah rises above the mob like something disembodied, floating and bobbing forward, her eyes crazed. Then I see men carrying the platform on their shoulders. They can barely move forward. I am pushed back and back. I turn toward the water so I can walk forward, not be carried, not be swept along. But I can barely control my feet. I am moved like a puppet, helpless.

I don't like this.

The cameras are crushed against me. I cling to them.

I can't see the statue anymore, but I can see the breakwater and the sea. Jean-Jacques is snapping away, crouching, aiming straight into the crowd. He doesn't see the man in a black vest who dives into the water and strokes angrily toward the boulders. He doesn't see the arms crawling out of the water. He doesn't see the hand grip his foot.

I scream. *"Jean-Jacques! Look out!"*

But it is of course too late. I stand frozen as he reels, arms flailing, ponytail bannering behind him, and topples into the sea.

2 PM: We leave the gendarmerie in silence and walk back toward the car. There is no crowd now. The mob is in the village and on the beach. I am still carrying the cameras. Jean-Jacques has his hands in his jeans pockets. His shoes squinch water when he walks.

I glance up at his face from time to time. It is impassive.

When we get to the car he reaches into the back seat, swipes up his Arabic scarf, and dries his hair.

A strangled sound bubbles out of me. Oh god, Meg, no. Don't laugh.

He looks at me, hair tangled across his eyes. His face is a mask.

I swallow hard. I grope for words. "I'm so sorry. I'm so . . . I mean, thank you for . . . It's all my fault. Are you angry?" It sounds incredibly lame. It *is* incredibly lame. He could have drowned. He could have hit his head on the rocks and died. He could have been torn limb from limb by angry . . . Oh god. I can't help myself. A snort escapes, why? I reach for his arm, stop myself. I look up at him, a little bit scared.

He digs for his cigarette pack. When he pulls it out of his pocket, he tips it and water pours out. His face is black and still.

"I'm so sorry about the camera. I'm so sorry."

He tosses the cigarettes into the reeds.

"I have insurance," he mutters.

"That's good!" Then I look at his face and swallow again. "Jean-Jacques, I shouldn't have—"

He turns to me. "*Écoute,* Mayg. I told you. I tried to warn you. Didier tried to warn you. It was no place for us."

"I know. You're right."

"There are places we shouldn't go. Even for stories. Even for books."

"I know. You're right. But it was so enormous. So epic. Just *spectacular.* The pictures would have been wonderful. Jean-Jacques, you have to admit the pictures would have been wonderful."

"Maybe. We'll see." His lips twist. He reaches into his breast pocket and pulls out a plastic film canister in a knotted sandwich bag.

My mouth gaps open.

"I'd just put a new film in when I fell. This one . . ." He holds it up into the salty air. "I guess it's been baptized."

He looks at me.

That laugh.

11 PM: Didier pokes up the fire and turns back to the kitchen, where Jean-Jacques is easing a cork from a bottle. "You got lucky. It could have been a lot worse. I haven't gone near the Pentecost pilgrimage in years."

"It was spectacular." His hand passes over a small smile.

I look at him. He meets my eyes. Complicity.

He has changed into dry khakis and a pullover. His hair is washed and hangs wet down his back. His scarf is draped on the mantle, steaming. He and Didier are cooking together, side by side. Jean-Jacques is quiet, intent. I sit with a glass of wine and watch his hands work. Coring baby artichokes. Shredding ham. Chopping shallots. Peeling garlic. Pestling salt cod under a trickling stream of olive oil. His fingers are long, sure, almost graceful when he cooks. I watch them. He feels me watching and looks up from time to time. His face is carefully empty now.

After we eat, he lies sprawled on the couch, barefoot, his arm cocked under his head, smoking. I am curled cross-legged under a quilted *boutis* in the deep armchair. There are two empty bottles on the table, three empty plates. I feel weak and warm all over. It has been a long day.

"I guess I'll turn in," Didier mumbles without looking at us. "Coffee's in the kitchen for morning. You can make your own way, you two."

He climbs the stone stairs and disappears.

Jean-Jacques smokes quietly.

I watch the fire quickening over the coals like distant lightning. His bare feet are so close I can almost feel their warmth. I could touch them if I dared. I think of his hand. How it felt in my fingers, on the small of my back. How it looked when he held the knife, the pestle, slick with oil and salt.

He sits up suddenly and tosses the cigarette into the fire. He rises to his feet and stands over me.

Oh god.

But he says "'Night, Mayg."

Then he climbs the stairs and I hear the click of his bedroom door.

Sunday, 8 AM: I stand at the base of the stairs, my bag and my laptop at my feet. "I really need to go. There's a train at eleven twenty from Orange. I could be home by eight. The kids might still be awake."

I haven't called them.

our mutual children

Jean-Jacques looks down into his coffee for a moment. Then at his watch. "*D'accord.* Okay."

He steps around me and climbs the stairs. When he comes back down he has his bags, too. "We can drive together. I'll turn in the car. There's a TGV at noon."

"Okay."

Didier slouches downstairs, yawning. "Everyone sleep well?" He glances at Jean-Jacques.

"Very well." Jean-Jacques strips his scarf from the mantelpiece and winds it around his neck.

10:30 AM: He drives very fast up the A9. The landscape streams past, marshlands dissolving into drylands dissolving into white rocky hills and olive groves. We pull up to the *gare*. He parks in the Europcar rental lot by a scarred date palm.

We lift our gear out of the Clio and stand beside it. I fumble in my purse for my ticket. I can't look up.

"I'll send you jpegs," he says.

"Good. Thank you. I can't wait to see them." I am looking deep into my purse. I take a brisk breath. "We need to plan the Mercantour trip."

"Yes."

"I'll send you the details. The background. The Bronze-Age carvings. The legend of the mountain gods. I have a lot of material on that."

"Yes."

I feel flustered. "But you don't want that. I'll just do the research."

"Yes, you'll do the research, Madame l'Historienne."

I look up, worried, expecting a smirk. But there is something else. He is standing very close.

"Well, bye." I say it in English.

"Bye." He says it in English.

I hesitate for a moment. He is leaning into me. I close my eyes, anticipating.

it is one of france's pleasanter customs

His lips graze one cheek. Then the other. Then they hover for a moment. Then they cover my mouth and stay.

My eyes fly open. Then they drift shut. Oh god.

There is a hunger to his kiss. He is tasting my lips, devouring my lips, my cheeks, the corners of my mouth. His hands wrap around my face, his fingers lace around my ears. He pulls my mouth into his, consuming me.

I respond. There is a very long moment where I am nothing but mouth.

Then a slow wave washes over the rest of me. Hunger. My fingers rise to his hair. I melt into him.

He pulls away abruptly. My heart is hammering. I can't look at him. We stand, catching breath, staring at our salty shoes.

"Mayg." He says it to his shoes. "*Écoute*, I . . . This train. Do you really
have to . . . If we . . ."

He raises his eyes.

Another wave washes over me. Panic. Terror.

It's my turn to bolt. I grab my bags and head for the quai.

1 PM: I am sitting upright, fully conscious, on the north-rolling day train,
watching the Rhône valley sweep by. The landscape is greening, ripen-
ing, swelling. My lips are pulsing, my skin scratched from Jean-Jacques'
stubble. I taste smoke on my tongue. I close my eyes.

I see Nigel.

Oh god. I stare out the window and finger the pink-scarred flesh
where my ring used to be.

7 ⚜ Blitz

Monday, June 9, 11 AM: I have a clean apron tied around my waist and I'm scrubbing the kitchen sink. I have stripped and waxed the flagstones. I have reorganized the silver drawers. I have laundered the children's school clothes, even the clean ones, and ironed everything, even their socks. I make *oeufs en meurette*. I make *anchoïade*. I make mocha *dacquoise*, whipping the egg whites hard. Gerald skulks around my ankles gratefully. He looks thin. I cook him pasta and mix in the leftover daube I simmered all day yesterday for Nigel.

I am a good wife.

I have not gone down the ladder since I got home. The laptop sits in the corner, untouched.

The hole in the barn wall gapes, uncovered.

I tackle the garden. My neck burns to dark red as I dig around the roses, clipping with secateurs. I claw the earth and rip weeds, plunge the spade deep into the soil and turn and turn and turn.

In the shower I wash my blackened hands and turn my face into the spray, letting it pound me. The water beats on my lips till they're red.

I remember to meet the school bus. When the children come home, there is juice and homemade pound cake. I play Duplos with Cloey and "walk" him on a leash to his pillow house. I drill Kate on English idiom and draw pictures with her and sing.

Sometimes I catch them staring at me.

is that woman me?

In bed with Nigel I try to tone down my intensity and keep it jolly, the way he likes it. He accepts my ministerings gratefully, waxes poetic, sleeps deeply. Last night I pushed things a little too far and left him briefly breathless. I rested my cheek on his belly, panting. He recovered his wind, chuckled, and patted my head.

"Well done, you," he murmured, settling into his pillow. Then he started to snore.

It's been two weeks now.

Monday, June 16, 2 PM: I am waxing the dining table when the phone rings.

"Mayg?"

I look desperately around as if someone might see or hear. I take a deep breath. "Hi."

"Are you okay? You haven't answered my e-mails."

"I've been busy. I haven't been keeping on top of work things."

There is a pause. I hear the click of a lighter. "I was worried."

I don't know what to say.

He goes on. "We have the Mercantour story coming up."

I take another deep breath. I am aware of this. I am aware of this. "I know. I—I haven't done anything about it yet."

He hesitates. "I can meet you in Nice. We can drive up together."

There is another pause.

"Mayg I—"

"Jean-Jacques. I can't—I just can't—I can't talk now. I'll check the e-mail and get back to you. Bye."

I hang up, shaking.

I rub the dining table so hard it shines like patent leather.

I eye the laptop.

Then I pick it up and carry it down the ladder.

4 PM: There are eight messages from Jean-Jacques. I can't help but feel a shiver.

I open the book shoot first, twelve jpegs, copied to Nikos. It is, of course, spectacular. The fervor and frenzy of the pilgrimage—golden babies on shoulders, a man on his knees weeping, the roiling mass of dark heads and jewel-bright clothing, the statue tipping precariously above the crowd, floating above the water.

I close them quickly.

There is another message, almost three weeks old, written the day I left him at the *gare*. There is text first, a jpeg below.

Meg. I love your mouth.

It is a picture of my lips. They are moist with juice and closing around a strawberry.

My breath catches. I stare.

The next he sent three days later.

Meg. I haven't heard back from you. Are you all right?

The next came a week later.

I'm sorry. I made a mistake. We can still go on with the book, no?

Then a whole week passed.

why don't you answer. please forgive me.

I scroll on. The next is brief.

My mistake. Won't happen again. Let's keep this professional. Send travel details please.

The next one, sent last Friday, is a jpeg. It is not copied to Nikos.

It is of me. I am sleeping under the trees, legs splayed loosely under my cotton skirt, eyelashes on my cheeks, lips parted. I swallow. There is something almost wanton about the pose. And something innocent, too, like Kate in her bed at night.

At the bottom there's text.

I can't stop myself thinking of you. Meet me in Nice for the Mercantour story. Stay a week. Please.

I stare. My heart is pounding.

There is one more, sent yesterday. It reads:

Forget this. I have made a terrible mistake. I am stupid. We can do Mercantour story in one day. Perhaps it would be smartest to rent two cars and meet at Tende.

jj

I read the messages over and over. Then I open one from Nikos.

Gypsy stuff looks good. Best theme yet. When can I expect text?

I can't do this book.

Tuesday, 4 PM: I have made enough bread dough for ten loaves, bristling with bran and fiber. Virtuous roughage chafes my hands as I knead. I play the Gipsy Kings so loudly they rattle the windows.

"*Maman!*" Do I hear something? Then louder: "*Maman!*"

I jerk my head up, glance around the kitchen. The children are cowering under the table, Gerald licking their faces.

3 AM: There's no use trying to sleep. I wrap the kimono around my nightgown and ease down the stairs, then down the ladder.

The laptop glows blue in the darkness, a watchful eye.

I scroll through Jean-Jacques' pictures, all of them.

i can't stop myself thinking about you

Am I really that woman?

I run my fingertips over my lips. I can feel his kiss. The scrape of stubble. The taste of tar. Urgent. Hungry. As if he would eat me alive.

I shiver. I type:

> *Yes, I will meet you in Nice.*
> *meg*

I stare at the screen a long time, hands twisting in my lap. Then I raise a finger and click Send.

Wednesday, 9 AM: Work. Work? I am hunched guiltily over the laptop when *The Storming of the Bastille* print begins to tremble.

Raimondo. No! Not this. Not now.

I hunker over the keyboard despite the roaring and crashing overhead. Nikos needs text. Gypsies, I think. Pilgrimage.

I type.

FERVOR FROM THE EAST
Returning their blessed virgin
to the waters that bore her hence

I type.

> *the fingers of babies caress a face worn smooth*
> *by the supplications of millions*

I type.

> *thousands on thousands, pressed shoulder to shoulder*
> *in shared passion*

I erase.

> *laying on of hands*

I erase.

> *Meg. I love your mouth.*

I erase.

It's hopeless.

A chunk of plaster falls onto my desk, missing the keyboard by inches.

4:30 PM: I hear the trucks pull away and rumble down the highway. The sound is very clear. And I can hear cows lowing. Have Mémé Mathilde's Charolais broken into the back garden again? It sounds like it's right over my head.

I climb up the ladder and lift the trapdoor. The barn is very bright, summer sunlight probing its deepest corners. I see thick whorls of dust in the light. The wall is half gone, a hole broken through it the size of three garage doors.

I step through. There is a massive pile of old stone — what used to be wall — heaped high above what used to be my rosebed.

The cows gaze over the barbed wire, curious but unperturbed.

6 PM: I call Nigel on his cell phone. He should be on his way home. There is a click, then the genial roar of the Hare and Hound.

"Nigel? The masons came."

"Hul-lo! The builders? Well, that's good news, isn't it?" He is extra jolly for his listening friends.

"Well, it's not. I mean, they bashed down half the wall. Then they left. Nigel, they didn't even tack a tarp over it."

I hear Nigel's hand muffling the mike. He is muttering something on the side.

"Nigel? Is MacGregor with you?"

"What's that, darling? Andrew? Oh, well, he's . . ." There is the sound of manly laughter. "Well, as a matter of fact he is. Would you like to speak to him?"

"No, I would not like to speak to him. I would like *you* to speak to him. This is your conservatory, isn't it? Ask him when Raimondo is going to cover the hole. And for that matter when he's going to — frame it or build it or whatever the . . . whatever he's going to do."

"Now Megs love, if you're worried about rats or mice getting in, Gerald will . . ."

"*Rats or mice?* There are *cows* trying to get in. An *elephant* could get in. Talk to him. Please."

I hang up in despair. Then I face Cloey and Kate who are wrapped in afghans on the daybed, peering up at me with their thumbs in their mouths.

"Elephants in the barn?" Cloey's lower lip is trembling. He stops it with his thumb.

"No, no, that's just . . . It's okay, honeys. It's okay." No, it's not. I pull a pan off the overhead rack and slam it onto the stove. I dump a bucket of soaking salt cod into the sink and refill it, the spray spattering the walls.

Midnight: I'm working in my bunker when the phone breets. I snatch it up midring. I know in advance it's not Nikos.

"Hi."

"Hi."

There is silence. Jean-Jacques speaks first.

"I've reserved the car for Nice, for Thursday."

"Good. That's good." I hesitate. Then I go on. "I guess I'd better book the four-wheel drive. If you're still willing to go all the way. To the refuge."

"Yes. I got permission. We don't need to use a guide. I'll bring as little gear as possible."

"Good. Me, too, I guess. No laptop this time. I barely touched it last time."

I cringe. I shouldn't have mentioned last time.

We swim for a moment in silence. Nothing is clear.

"Well." I swallow. "I'll confirm my night train. It usually gets in around eight forty. I'll let you know."

"Good. That's good."

"Well. Good night."

"Good night."

I hang up. I sit and stare at the phone for a while.

stay a week

It rings again. This time I pick up slowly.

"Mayg?"

My breath stops. "Yes?"

I can hear him lighting a cigarette.

"I just wanted to say I . . ." There is the sound of smoke blowing between his lips. "Never mind. I'll see you next Thursday."

He hangs up abruptly and I listen to the dial tone for a long time.

2 AM: I am in the kitchen tearing salt cod away from warm bones, filling the marble mortar. I sink my fingers into the soft flesh and flake and separate the shreds. I pour a thread of olive oil, long and slow, into the bowl, feeling the pestle in my oily hand, turning, grinding. I lick my fingers, eyes drifting.

Thursday, 10 AM: I open Google and enter Merveilles + Bégo + gravures. Three hundred and three links come onto the screen. I click on the first one.

> *High above the village of Tende at the edge of the Parc National du Mercantour in the Riviera Alps, the Vallée des **Merveilles**—Valley of Marvels—lies in the shadow of Mount **Bégo**, focus of both fear and worship by a Bronze-Age cult. The glacial stones that scatter at **Bégo**'s base are chiseled with some 30,000 drawings of weapons, tools and priapic bull-gods.*

I click on the next one.

> *The inspiration for the rock drawings in the Vallée des **Merveilles** will never be known. There are many interpretations. The most famous image . . .*

There is a photograph of a strange stick figure, hands raised above his head

> *. . . is often seen as having his hands raised in supplication or prayer. To whom were the artists praying? Some factors point to the legends of Mount **Bégo** and its angry gods. The Vallée des **Merveilles** is also a storm pocket, a focal point for intense electrical storms and heavy rains. Were the artists appeasing these gods? Importuning them for rain on their southern crops?*

I scroll down. There is a stick man kneeling with an alarming projection thrusting up between his legs, shaped like the blade of a dagger.

> *The pronounced phallic imagery (bull's horns, daggers, plows) seems to indicate a dual purpose to the supplication as well, whether toward sexual prowess or military strength will never be clear.*

I study this for a while, scrolling back to the dagger man from time to time. Then I close the file. Petroglyphs. Will Jean-Jacques think it's another nonstory? Will he care?

I select a few sites in French and forward them to him. I don't want any surprises this time. There is already too much that's ambiguous about this trip.

Friday, 9 AM: A rainstorm pounds in from the south and the barn is filling with water. I dial Andrew MacGregor and listen to Greensleeves for quite a while before his secretary puts him through.

"Meg? Lovely as always to hear from you. How are you, my dear?"

"Andrew, it's raining hard and the barn is flooding. When are the masons going to cover the hole?"

"Any day now. Nothing to worry about there."

"But I am worried. The barn is ankle deep. If it gets high enough it will flood my office."

"Ah, yes, well. That old fruit cellar. I've been meaning . . . right. Suppose I might give Raimondo a ring."

"Please do. Please. And do you think I could have his phone number myself, just in case something comes up and I can't reach you?"

There is a pause. "Well, I'm not sure that will be necessary —"

"Andrew, how much are we paying these guys?"

"We have a budget. Nigel is well aware —"

"Have they been paid in advance?"

"Just the first bit, really. Another bundle due soon enough."

"Andrew, please don't pay them until they've finished the hole. Until they've finished the work, in fact."

Silence. When he speaks again, his voice sounds pinched.

"Never you mind, Maggie dear. Love from Brenda."

He hangs up hastily.

Saturday, 6 AM: It can't be. The rumble of truck wheels in the driveway. Gerald scrambles off the bed, clawing me in his frenzy to get to the door first, barking so fast he can barely close his jaws between cries. I pull on a t-shirt and shorts and follow.

Gerald fires past me through the front door and runs on out to the garden after a cat, original mission forgotten. There is no one there but a gangly old man with a stray eye. He must be seventy. His curls are whiter than his mason's cap.

"Raimondo send me to close hole." He grins. I'm not sure which eye to talk to.

"At six on a Saturday morning?"

He shrugs and grins some more. I open the barn door and wade through the puddles. He stands looking at the hole. He whistles, impressed, and waggles his hand at his side. "This will not be easy," he says. "Does your husband have a hammer and drill?"

"Well, yes, we have a hammer and drill. Did you bring a plastic tarp or boards?"

"Do you have any boards? Old boards around?"

"I guess the scrap lumber out back would be okay. We were meaning to use it for a playhouse but . . ."

He sizes up the wood pile and nods. "This will do."

I watch, amazed, as he gathers our materials together. He carries the drill to the hole's edge, then dangles the short cord in the air. He grimaces ironically and shrugs.

"An extension cord maybe?" I venture. "The plug is by the door."

"Good. You have a saw?"

I slip back into the house and make a pot of coffee.

5 PM: The proportion of hacking, sawing, hammering, and drilling to actual hole surface covered is surprising. After I hear the tires squeal away at four forty-five, I peek into the barn. About a third of the hole has been concealed and only at the top. There is no protection against rain and nothing to discourage cows. They stand, chests pressing against the barbed wire, chewing their cud and regarding me blandly.

I climb into the loft and throw down three paint tarps. By five thirty I have pegged them over the hole and weighted the edges to the floor with paving stones.

Nigel pulls the Rover into the drive at six. "There you are, Megs," he says, patting my shoulder. "I told you Andrew would take care of everything."

When I close the barn door, I notice the drill is gone.

Wednesday, 9 AM: I am gathering all my notes and materials for the trip. I scroll through my e-mail one last time. There is nothing from Jean-Jacques or Nikos. Only junk.

I send one last message to Jean-Jacques.

Arriving Nice gare 8:20 AM Thursday.

As I am about to turn off the computer, a reply comes back.

I am ready.

A shiver goes up my neck. I am ready. What does that mean?

11 AM: "*Maman,* I don't understand what is the hole for."

Kate is studying my face. We are sorting socks into pairs on the bed. My suitcase lies open on the floor, half full already.

"Well, Papa wants to build a conservatory there, a big sunroom. You know that."

"But there is no sunroom."

I sigh. There is no sun either. "I know, honey, but there will be soon."

"You are packing again."

"Yes. I told you, I'm going to the mountains to write a story about the storm gods."

"Yes." She swallows. "My sroat is hurting."

I stroke her hair. "I know darling. It will get better soon. Mama will be gone a while this time."

stay a week

I keep my voice neutral. "Sophie will be here. And Papa."

"Papa is never here. Either."

I sit down on the bed and pull her into my arms. She feels so thin and fragile, and her hair smells of Nutella.

I lay the hiking socks into my bag. I roll my anorak and stuff it in the end. Jeans. Sweaters. I open my underwear drawer and paw through. I lift up a few underpants, some bras. Silky black. White cotton. I hurriedly push them back. I close the drawer and sit on the bed.

What am I thinking?

"Come here, you." I hug her hard to keep my arms from shaking.

Why am I shaking? I haven't done anything. Yet.

2 PM: I call Sophie one last time. "Just wanted to make sure you're all set for my trip."

"Yes. How many days this time?" She sounds underwhelmed.

I pause. I haven't admitted this to myself yet. "A week. I'm going very far into the backcountry, in the mountains, and . . . it will take some time."

"*D'accord.*" Do I hear a sigh? "And Monsieur Thorpe is *au courant* of the schedule?"

"Yes, Monsieur Thorpe is definitely *au courant.*"

"Because last time he . . . when he didn't come back, very late, I fell asleep on the couch." She hesitates.

"Go on, Sophie. He came back very late?"

"He didn't come back . . . until morning."

I take this in slowly. "I'm sorry, Sophie, I'll speak with him about that."

I hang up and stare at the telephone.

9 PM: I am waiting for him when he comes home. He kisses my cheek absently, heads for the freezer for ice.

"Nigel."

"Hmm?"

"Nigel, we need to talk." He glances up, eyebrows raised. "I talked with Sophie today. She said you didn't come home one night, when I was in the Camargue."

He studies his hands, flicks a dog hair from his cardigan. "Yes. Well, I'd had rather too much to drink at MacGregor's and Brenda — Brenda's a love, you know that, darling — well, she opened the couch and I stayed over. Didn't want to risk the drive, you know. It was too late to call Sophie, I thought."

I look at his face, expecting guile, guilt, defensiveness, anger. Feelings to match mine. But something in me melts a little. He looks so sheepish. I walk over to him. His arms hang at his sides. We face each other.

"You all right, honey? Everything all right?"

"There's my Meg, always probing around, looking for trouble where there is none." I hesitate, then lean into his woolly shoulder. He pats my back lightly. "All packed then? Where to this time?"

I pull back. My stomach squeezes. Looking for trouble. "The Mercantour. In the Alpes-Maritimes."

"Well then. Have a good trip."

He slouches up the stairs, ducking the beam. I stand for a while, thinking.

stay a week

Something shrivels inside me.

11 PM: I lie in the sleeper berth, rolling south, and stare at the padded ceiling.

meg i love your mouth
meg i was stupid i have made a terrible mistake
stay a week please
forget this

Looking for trouble.

Thursday, 8 AM: I'm alone in the *couchette* cabin. Everyone else got out at Avignon, at Marseille. The final kilometers I rolled alone, suspended.

I sidle, rocking, to the bathroom. There are palm trees scrolling past, flashes of indigo sea. I wash my face and look in the mirror. I brush my teeth and rub balm on my lips. I look at myself. I wipe it off. I flash on lips, whiskers.

i am ready

The train lurches violently and throws me to the wall.

9 AM: I stand, shrinking in place. I have been waiting on the quai of the Nice *gare* for forty minutes. A cold feeling is creeping through me. Another train rolls up where mine pulled away. More people climb down, more bags. They disperse. I stand.

Oh god. I take a shuddering breath. Did I misunderstand? Did I misinterpret?

My phone vibrates. I scramble for it frantically. It's a text message.

> *Sorry. better if we meet in st-dalmas gare. car reserved in your name.*

He's changed his mind.

10 AM: I barely see the landscape. I maneuver the Mégane through urban corridors, dodging tourists and businessmen and shoppers and dogs. The sun is intense, Matisse-bright. Italianate façades catch the light—yellow, cream, red. I fumble in my purse for sunglasses, one-handed. I never need them in Lorraine. I fight through clogged channels and aim for the sea. When I break free and turn onto the Promenade des Anglais, the waterfront is a parking lot of traffic. The sea crashes alongside, spilling white foam over the tide-polished *galets*. There are palm trees. Roller skaters. Lovers.

I grip the steering wheel very hard and point the car up the coast toward the mountains. By the time I break free of the outskirts to swing onto the A8 it is after eleven.

I don't know why I'm hurrying. There is no hurry. It's just a story now, isn't it?

work is work
forget this

12:30 PM: The landscape reels by me on the broad ribbon of the A8, cliffs and gullies and torrents emptying into the sea. I am climbing at 150 kph and there are sports cars screaming past me as if I were walking a dog. Trucks labor up the steep and steeper hills and I swing around them. The Mégane is a turbo diesel and I am grateful. I need all the power I can get just to survive.

I reach the Italian border, wheel off and corkscrew around a ribbon of bridge. Then the Mégane plunges deep into rock canyon and climbs.

I can't drive fast here. The roads twist like spaghetti. The Matisse light darkens to Cézanne, black pines and red rock towering above.

I don't even know when he's getting there. If he's getting there.

i am ready

He can't have changed his mind now. I've come too far. I've gone too far.

The switchbacks tighten, shoelace sharp. The mountains are green walls around me, toy trains chugging over spider-web trellises high above the road. I have crossed back into France but Fiats and Lancias and Alpha Romeos buzz past me, swarming like hornets toward the next Italian border and Turin. I sink my foot down and the diesel labors against the grade.

St-Dalmas, twelve kilometers. Almost there.

Then what?

2 PM: I wrench the car into the parking lot of the St-Dalmas *gare* and stop. My hands are clenched on the wheel. My legs are trembling. I look around me. The arched stone station is spectacular, overscaled beyond reason. It is also empty.

I step out of the car and uncurl my limbs. There is only the cool, broad background roar of a mountain torrent. The air is impossibly clear, moist, green. I push my hair back out of my eyes and breathe.

Then I dive for my phone. Surely there's a message.

There is no message. There is no signal in the mountains.

3 PM: I'm sitting at a lone table in front of a gas station that doubles as a coffee shop and bar. I left a note on the windshield of the Mégane back at the *gare*. I don't know what to do but wait. I rest my forehead on my hand and crumple empty sugar packs with the other.

6 PM: I have walked back to the car three times, but there's no sign.

I came for nothing.

He changed his mind.

What am I doing here? What was I thinking?

I have plenty of time to study my scarred ring finger. I'm *married*, for god's sake. Acting like a . . . like a . . .

looking for trouble

The kids are home by now. Will they notice I haven't called? No signal. I am cut off from the world.

I ask at the café about rooms. The waitress looks at me with pity. I have been here a long time. She tips her head and points north. "There is a hotel. The only one. Near the base of the Casterino road."

I settle my bill—three coffees, two mineral waters—and head for the car.

I should never have come.

7 PM: When I pull into the parking lot of the Hôtel Mont-Bégo, the terrace is full of diners. Early for a dinner in France. Late for *sportifs*. Everyone, at every table, wears hiking boots and Polartec. Lanterns are lit on the tables, blooming yellow against the darkening green. I can hear a mountain stream. Its cold, sharp clarity fills my nostrils.

If there hadn't been a room free, I'd have driven straight back down to Nice. I feel my mouth settling into a grim line. I heft my bag onto my shoulder and climb skimpy, pine-lined stairs.

"Mayg!"

I crumple.

"Mayg, what happened? Where have you been? I thought you'd . . ."

Jean-Jacques is standing barefoot in a wedge of light.

I turn on him. His hair is hanging loose. He is in a t-shirt and briefs, pale and thin. He ducks behind his room door and reappears, tugging on jeans.

"What . . . Where . . . ?" I sputter.

"I've been calling you since nine. I was working in Italy. I wanted to meet you here this morning. I sent messages. I called. You didn't answer. I was afraid you had changed your mind."

I pull out my phone. No signal.

I stare at him weakly. Relief is slow to flow through my veins. Too slow.

He steps toward me. I step back. This is too strange. What must he think? What was I thinking? I don't know *what* to think anymore.

Maybe I *have* changed my mind.

10 PM: I have showered and dressed and come to sit in the lonely fluorescent-lit dining room with Jean-Jacques. Everyone else has gone to bed. Even the kitchen staff, bringing a last carafe of wine, asked if we'd turn out the lights when we'd finished. This is mountain country. We'll be getting up early.

Two plates of lamb daube have gone half eaten. We have barely spoken. Jean-Jacques peeled his cheese and left it. It is covered with cigarette butts. He is smoking, smoking.

He breaks the silence. "Mayg, I guess I made a big mistake last time. I'm sorry."

I sigh shakily. "Me, too."

"We will work together, okay?"

"Okay."

We climb to our rooms. We fish for our keys. We open and close the doors.

3 AM: I hear the floorboards creaking in Jean-Jacques' room and smell smoke curling under the door. I remember the taste of smoke on his mouth. I pull the quilt over my head.

I am thinking about Nigel. In Cambridge. The first time. The scene plays through my head and plays again. I can't turn it off.

He is towering above me, still sweaty with greasepaint, the floorboards creaking under his stocking feet in his tatty red-carpeted flat. In college, in Indiana, I had made hot, fumbling love with boys. I have never gone to bed with a grown man before. He is talking, talking. His hands knead my breasts, slide over my bottom. My fingers and lips and skin are on fire. He is still talking.

"... 'by mine honour, in true English, I love thee Kate . . . by which honour I dare not swear thou lovest me . . . yet my blood begins to flatter me that thou dost' . . ."

I pull his head down and cover his moving lips with mine.

We are on his bed. I am everywhere, all over him until even he is rendered wordless. It is finished very quickly. I lie quiet, every inch of me burning still. He is already snoring.

you have witchcraft in your lips kate
meg i love your mouth

Now I pull the quilt from my head. I smell Jean-Jacques' smoke.

Friday, 5:30 AM: I am staring at the ceiling, still wide-eyed, when the alarm goes off.

I open the casement window and lean out. The roar of the stream fills my ears but there is a pristine stillness to the air, scented in pine. I can't see the sky, only massive slate-grey cliffs rearing on all sides, bearded with firs and wreathed with mist.

In the driveway below, there's a four-wheel-drive Jeep waiting.

I pull back in and dress quickly, yanking on jeans and tank top and sweater and anorak, thick socks and my hiking boots. They feel solid and sure on my feet. My fingers shake on the laces.

Downstairs on last night's table there are bowls and two thermos pitchers, a basket of bread. I quickly mix my coffee with milk and gulp it down. Jean-Jacques' bowl is clean but for three cigarette butts. The hotel managers have left a bag of sandwiches on the counter with a bill and the Jeep keys. I gather these up and head outside.

Jean-Jacques is standing on the terrace, bundled in down and khaki and the Arabic scarf. He points a long lens up at the mountaintop, still in shadow. "Too dark," he says simply. He keeps looking at the mountain, then he glances over at me. "Are you ready?"

i am ready

I nod and open the trunk. Jean-Jacques lifts in his camera bag. I throw in my backpack. "Notebook. Research materials," I explain. "Binoculars. Map. And two box lunches."

He nods. "Can you drive so I can shoot?"

"I guess. Sure. How bad can it be?"

7 AM: It is very bad. Heading up the Casterino road was easy, only switchbacks smoothly paved. But when I swing up the trail, it's a different game. The "road" is really two stony ruts riddled with gullies and mined with loose shale that sets the tires spinning. To one side the land drops away straight down. I switch into four-wheel drive with a lurch and the wheels bite. We rock and jostle up the grade, my hands gripping hard, Jean-Jacques hanging on the passenger loop.

I attempt a feeble joke. "I feel like the Seventh Army, rolling up from the coast." I dart my eyes over. "My grandfather was . . ."

Jean-Jacques slumps down and jerks his head away to stare out the side. I don't try again.

All around us the forest grows wilder, its floor a carpet of wildflowers. "Rhododendrons! Lilies! Columbine! And look, gentian!" I rubberneck to see but Jean-Jacques grabs the wheel and yanks us away from the edge.

"Can you do your botanical research when we're stopped please?"

I look at his face to see his expression but the Jeep veers again.

"Mayg!"

I stop the Jeep in midroad and set the brake. "Look, if you don't want to do this, say so."

He sighs and rubs his eyes. His fingers are yellow with nicotine stains and they shake slightly.

"I don't mind doing this story. I just want to survive."

"Okay."

I pull ahead.

We climb and climb, my eyes locked on the road. It is banked hard and there are times when the Jeep seems to cling to the road like a mountain goat, teetering over the void. The picnic slides to the right, then the left. Jean-Jacques aims his camera out the window but the lens bobbles up and down.

"Do you want me to stop? I'll stop."

"Okay."

I haul the Jeep over to what little side there is and we climb out. He begins photographing columbine then stops. The lens is still bobbling up and down. He fishes for a cigarette. The lighter flame has trouble finding the tip. He sucks deep.

"Did you eat any breakfast?"

"No, it's okay," he shakes his head. He bites the cigarette, squints against the smoke, and lifts the camera to shoot some more.

We ride on. I try to keep it light but my voice rings false. "Are we both clear on this story this time? No surprises? Anything you found on the Internet you want to tell me about? A McDonald's at the top, maybe?"

He laughs, but only politely. "No. I read the links you forwarded me." Then he looks out the window. "I will photograph the rocks. Another good story, rocks."

I look over at him sharply. "I think you'll find the gravures interesting. I hope so." But I feel a flicker of dread in my stomach. I'm feeling surer by the minute that I should have stayed home.

11 AM: We pull higher and higher and pass a stone shepherd's hut. At its corner a sign points right to "Valley of the Damned," left to "Valley of Marvels." I pull the wheel hard and cut left.

We pass hikers descending the trail with tall frame backpacks and high-tech walking sticks, first in groups of two or three, then in groups of ten or more. They are all hiking downhill. They peer at us and shake their heads as we pass. One wags a scolding finger.

"Guess they don't like to see motor vehicles up here," I say.

Jean-Jacques says nothing.

I keep my boot down and grind ahead. We break free of the forest at last and labor across an open meadow, then pull over a crest and stop.

All around us stretches a broad plateau ringed with high, dark mountains. There are no trees, only heaps of white boulders. Over our heads the sky is a vast bowl of lowering clouds.

At the bottom end we spot the refuge, a low, flat-roofed brick structure on the edge of a chalky turquoise pond. I aim the Jeep for it, following barely visible tire traces in the close-cropped tundra.

It is closed and shuttered.

"Well, it's a good thing we didn't plan on staying here," I say.

Jean-Jacques says nothing. I look at him and sigh. Then I haul my backpack out of the Jeep, stuff the picnic in, and start walking.

1 PM: The map shows symbols around here indicating engravings but I can't find a thing. It's so cloudy I can barely see the rocks at all. I have climbed up every path and compared every turning with the directions in the guidebook but find only pockmarks and scratches on the stones.

Oh god. Don't let this happen again. Not now.

Please let me find the pictographs. Please.

I scan the sky. The clouds have thickened, boiling and churning overhead. I look around for Jean-Jacques. He is high up a hillside, panning his wide-angle across the mountaintops.

Please let me find the pictographs. Please.

He is walking downhill now, scrambling down the rubble with his boots turned sideways. He heads my way.

There is a rumble of thunder.

Please god let me find the pictographs.

"Nice weather for a picnic. Shall we eat?" He isn't smiling.

I look at him imploringly and slide my backpack off. "I can't find them."

"I figured."

There is another rumble.

"I guess we should have hired a guide."

He grunts.

I pull out the picnic bag and sort out long baguette sandwiches, a patty of sheep cheese, a thermos, a plastic container of wild strawberries. I hand him a sandwich. He stands and tears into it absently. I unwrap mine and take a bite of the end, put my hand over my mouth and turn away. Butter and prosciutto melt in my mouthful of tears. Jean-Jacques has already turned his back.

Please let me find the gravures.

I am gathering up the picnic litter and stuffing it into my sack when I see the bill. It's not a bill, it's a note, scribbled on the Hôtel Mont-Bégo stationery.

Severe electrical storms predicted over Mount Bégo for afternoon. Mercantour park security evacuating hikers. Please leave valley by noon. Thank you.

Oh god. I pass it to Jean-Jacques.

He reads it and looks at me. Then he looks at the sky. "Which one is Mount Bégo?" he asks.

There is a deep rolling roar of thunder.

I study the map, turning it, and look up. "That one." I point to a blue-black mass looming high above the other mountains, its tip whorling with mushroom-colored clouds.

At that moment the gods of Mount Bégo choose to launch a trident of blue-white lightning. It forks through the sky and over the mountain face. An instant later a horrendous crack splits the air.

"*Putain!*"

"Oh god! We have to get back to the Jeep!"

Another bolt splays across the sky followed by an explosion that presses into my ears.

"Incredible!" Jean-Jacques says. He is standing up straight, his face to the sky.

He is reaching for his camera.

I turn on him and gape. "No, Jean-Jacques! Are you out of your mind?"

But he is already clambering up the stony face of Mount Bégo.

I cower in the hollow and huddle against a stone. There is another bolt. I crouch lower and hold onto the rock for dear life.

There is another crack. Another bolt laces across the sky, reveling lazily in its own magnificence. An eerie light crazes over the whole of the valley bowl.

And then for an instant I see it. It is the carved form of a horned warrior, its lines thrown into bright relief. Its hands are raised in supplication.

"Jean-Jacques!" I scream. "They're here!"

But he is a speck on the hillside, tightening the legs of his tripod and staring at the sky.

I huddle in terror through a series of bolts but they seem to be playing high in the air, weaving between mountaintops.

I crabwalk warily from stone to stone, watching the surfaces pop into relief with every flash. There are bull heads and spears, daggers and spikes. And everywhere there are hands, fingers splayed, importuning the gods.

"Jean-Jacques, you have to see this! You have to shoot this!" My voice floats into the rising wind.

I search around desperately. We can't miss these shots! I dig out the binoculars and focus them on Jean-Jacques. He has his lens mounted, pointed at the peak of Mount Bégo, and he's crouching, squinting through the viewfinder. He is holding an extension-cord shutter release and counting with his fingers. There is a crack. He presses the button and counts. There is another crack. He presses and counts again. His scarf has blown open. Is he *laughing?*

I cast around frantically. Then I see his bag. I zip it open with trembling fingers and pull out the digital camera. Then I, too, begin to count and click, count and click.

2 PM: The wind is howling now and the clouds are closing in, blacker by the minute. The electrical play is slowing and Jean-Jacques scrabbles down the hill.

"Hurry!" I call. "You have to see this!"

He trots up and watches where my finger is pointing. Lightning flares and reveals the dagger man.

"*Merde!* Wait, let me change my lens!" he sputters.

But by the time he fits it into the socket, the worst of the lightning has passed.

It has been replaced by rain. And not just rain. A freight-train wind drives the downpour sideways across the valley, roaring over the slopes, drenching us from every direction. There is no escape.

We throw the gear into our packs and sprint back toward the Jeep. It is a lot farther back than I remembered and my boots slip on the wet gravel. We leave the path and cut diagonally across the valley, slaloming around the sacred stones, pulling our hoods over our heads. The wind curls over the mountaintops and funnels around us, whipping rain into our faces. We run hard, slogging ahead.

The Jeep is locked and I can't find the keys. I fumble and dig, then dump my pack in the mud and paw through.

"Got them!" I scrape the wet mess back into the pack. Then we throw our gear into the seats and peel away, barely closing the doors.

The wipers slash but it's as if someone were throwing buckets of water at the windshield. I squint through the steaming glass and aim for the road. It is as steep and rocky as it was on the uphill climb, but now inertia pulls us down and the brakes are wet, the rocks are wet, my boots are slipping on the pedals.

"*Doucement.* Take it easy. We'll get back when we get back." Jean-Jacques wipes his scarf over my side of the windshield but it's wetter than the glass.

I feel the skid coming but there's nothing I can do. I jam my boot down on the brake. I shouldn't have. The rear of the Jeep fishtails right, then left, then wildly right again. There is a tremendous crunch and our heads snap back. Then everything is suddenly still.

We sit, staring ahead at the opaque windshield. Then I crack the door and look. The front end of the Jeep is wrapped around the trunk of a fir.

For minutes we sit, drawing breath. Then Jean-Jacques says, "We'll have to walk."

I look at him in horror. "In this rain? In this wind? There could be trees coming down."

"We can't stay in this hunk of metal all night. There could be more lightning."

"But we can't leave the Jeep. We'll drown!"

We reach for our cell phones. There is no signal.

We sit and steady our breath.

"We'll go back to the refuge."

"Jean-Jacques, it was padlocked. Chained."

"Where was that shepherd's hut?"

"I don't know. I don't know."

"It wasn't far from the edge of the forest. It must be nearby."

We grab our gear and head out into the forest. The rain is waiting for us, slashing down on our heads, into our eyes, down our necks. My boots grapple with the stones and gullies, ankles twisting, lug soles losing ground. Jean-Jacques grips my shoulder and we steady each other like ice-skaters.

We don't have far to go. The road sign with the double arrows looms into view and we run toward the hut. I land against the door. It's locked. Damn. I haul back a boot and kick it hard. It doesn't move. He kicks it hard. It doesn't move. Jean-Jacques squints at me from under his hood. "Together, with our shoulders maybe?"

"Okay."

We count down and lunge. The door gives way and we are out of the rain.

The hut is dark. Jean-Jacques flicks his lighter and shields it with his dripping hand.

It's just a hovel of piled dry stone, a circle of charred pebbles in the middle of the floor below a primitive toggled chimney. There is a stool and a broken basin and a heap of moldy straw. There is one dirty window jimmied into the stone.

I throw my gear on the ground and shake my head, raindrops flying. "Now what?" I try my phone again. No signal.

"We'll wait for the storm to pass. Then we'll walk down."

One hand holding the lighter high, Jean-Jacques digs for his cigarettes.

"*Merde,*" he says. They are as wet as the ones that fell in the sea.

3 PM: Our eyes have adjusted to the light that oozes dimly through the dusty glass. We have sat for a long time on the earth floor, our backs to stone. We're not looking at each other. The rain has not relented. Wind howls in every chink, the whole hut moaning and whistling like a thing alive.

"Maybe we should build a fire," I say. "We're soaked."

"There's no firewood."

"Maybe we should just make a run for it."

"And fall off the edge of the road? You can hardly see your hand in front of your face in this rain. Did you see that drop-off? You were too busy looking at the flowers."

There is a splitting noise, a crack. A branch crashes onto the roof over our heads.

"We're staying here," he says.

We stay.

We sit for a very long time in silence.

4 PM: Jean-Jacques stands, leaning his forearm on the wall, staring into nothingness out the window as if he could will himself away.

Silence.

This is all my fault, I think. Again.

I've got it all wrong. That's what I do best.

What am I doing here? What are we doing here?

I look at him. He feels my eyes, I know he does. He avoids them.

He has given up pacing and staring. He plops down across from me, resigned.

His long fingers fidget.

5 PM: Now I stand staring into nothingness out the window. The storm is deafening. The silence is thick. I can't stand it.

"Talk to me, please. Jean-Jacques . . ." I don't know where to begin. "Jean-Jacques, we have to talk about . . . about what happened."

"There's nothing to talk about. Forget it." His hand flies up to his pocket by reflex and he fishes out a cigarette, bent and soggy. He puts it in his lips anyway and lets it drip. He stares at his boots.

But after a while he raises his eyes and looks at me. I can't read his look. Even. Wary. Carefully empty. The way he looked at me in Didier's *mas.*

A chill runs over me.

My eyes drop.

5:30 PM: My stomach growls, breaking the silence again.

"We should eat something. We can't stay here all night without eating something."

He looks at me. "I'm not hungry."

"There's the Brebis. And some strawberries. We need to eat something. We have to walk back eventually."

I kneel and open the dripping backpack. Soggy baguette. Scraps of sodden ham. A waxed-paper square of sheep cheese. I unwrap it. "The Brebis is okay. I don't have a knife, though."

He lifts his haunches and digs out a pocketknife. He unfolds it and passes it to me. He is looking at me.

"Thanks."

I cut a wedge and bite it carefully off the blade. The skin is velvety and withered and there's a line of cream oozing underneath. "Oh god. It's good. It's ripe. Jean-Jacques, try this. Please. It's so good."

I cut a wedge for him. He leans forward and takes it from my hand. I feel the heat of his fingers. He is looking at me. He puts it in his mouth.

I feel a flush creeping up my cheeks. "Want a strawberry?" I try to sound bright, but my voice is husky. I clear my throat. "There are wild strawberries. They're a little bit crushed but . . ." I slip one in my mouth. Perfume. "Mm. Incredible. Try one." I hold out a strawberry. It hovers in the air between us. He is looking at me. My heart is pounding.

meg i love your mouth

He's still looking at me. Waiting.

Waiting for me to . . . what?

Decide.

i am to follow your lead

I take a deep breath.

"Jean-Jacques, I . . ."

I what?

"I . . ."

i am ready

I kneel forward. I am very close to him now. He's looking at me. Waiting. I raise the strawberry to his lips. They open. I slide the berry between them. Then I can't help myself. I cover his lips with my mouth.

Oh god. I remember his lips. Smoke. Stubble. Brebis. His mouth softens, opens under mine. I taste strawberry on my tongue.

His hands rise up and grip my head and pull me to him.

5:45 PM: Mouths. I pull my lips away and gasp for air. Something is flickering through me. Something electric. Lightning.

"Mayg." He's rising to his knees, spreading my anorak wide. I see steam rising from the wet clothes. Hands. Oh god. It's happening fast now. We're on the straw. I look down and see my breasts gleaming pale in the dim light.

is that woman me?

A beam of light slashes across them, then slides up to my face, then his. There is a pounding at the door. It pushes open. I sit bolt upright and pull my coat around me.

A silhouette and a voice. "Sorry to inconvenience you, monsieur, madam . . . oiselle. We found the Jeep. There's a whole team out looking for you. Hikers told us they tried to stop you, but you drove right on ahead. Who was driving?"

I raise my hand and give my best midwestern smile.

"Hope you've got insurance."

10 PM: The owners of the Hôtel Mont-Bégo are not very gracious about the Jeep. I give them my Crédit Mutuel papers and try to apologize, but I feel Jean-Jacques' hand on my wet shoulder and my knees are going weak. We leave them muttering at the front desk and climb the stairs.

"Mayg."

I fumble for my room key. My hands are shaking hard.

"Mayg. Wait." His hands are on both my shoulders now, turning me to him. His fingers lace around my ears. He kisses me so gently I shake harder. Tasting me slowly, surely. I melt into him.

I pull away and guide the chattering key into the lock. Then I lead him into my room and bolt the door. We look at each other in the soft light. His hands are on my shoulders again and he draws me to him. I am shivering. His mouth hovers over mine.

"Are you sure?" he says.

It's the last thing he says for a very long time.

Saturday, 6 AM: Stillness. I can hardly tell his skin from mine. Our bodies are tangled together, warm and limp and at peace. There's honey flowing in my veins. My face presses into the hollow of his neck and his hair tangles over my cheeks. He's finally fallen asleep.

The tiny fringed bedlamp stayed on all night, casting a golden light over the pine walls. I rest my hand on his ribs, prop up on one elbow and look down the length of his body, sprawled unselfconsciously over the jumble of quilts and sheets. He is so thin. The few tufts on his chest are as mixed with grey as his hair. I have never seen an uncircumcised penis before. Oh god. Strange, unreal, to be lying here with him, naked. I have ventured into new territory now.

I study him.

He stirs. I feel his hand on my hair.

"You okay?"

"I'm okay. You?"

"Mm."

He pulls me to him.

10 AM: "My cigarettes."

"Mm?"

"I'll just sneak quickly across the hall and get my cigarettes."

"Mm."

I feel his body pulling away and cold air bathes my skin. "No!"

"I'll be right back."

He paws through the pile of dripping anoraks and boots on the floor. He pulls on his wet jeans, wincing, unlocks the door with an echoing click and tiptoes into the hall. He returns with an armload of dry clothes and a fresh pack of cigarettes. He steps out of his jeans again, hopping, an unlit cigarette in his teeth.

I moan. "No."

He crawls back under the covers and wraps his cold hands around my back. I pull the cigarette from his lips and lay it on the side table.

11 AM: He reaches for the cigarette.

"No!"

He lights and drags deep, his eyes closing.

"Oh god." This time I slide out of the bed into the cold air. I open the shutters and squint in the sudden crystal light. Air is rushing through the fir branches and the gush of the stream has become a thundering roar. Yesterday's rain is draining off the slopes of Mount Bégo.

I rinse myself on the bidet. I feel his eyes on my back.

I come back to the bed and sit facing him on the foot of the mattress. His eyes flicker over me. I flush and slide under the covers. We lie end to end, looking at each other. He smokes.

"So."

"So."

We look at each other. There is no wariness now. His face is soft and calm, a trace of a smile on his lips.

"Hungry?" he says.

"I don't know. I guess so. Yes."

"We could go down for breakfast."

"I don't dare."

He smokes.

My stomach grumbles.

He smiles now, all the way.

I smile, too. I look at my backpack, lying in a puddle on the planks. "There's the rest of the Brebis. And the strawberries."

He looks at me.

12 PM: In the shower cabinet, under a driving hot spray, he washes the last of the strawberry juice from my lips with his thumbs.

4 PM: We sit on the edge of the bed, bare legs dangling, the down quilt wrapped over our shoulders. He is looking at the miniature screen on the back of his digital camera, clicking through the shots.

"These aren't bad," he says. "Four-square. Carefully framed. Good documentary work."

I shove his shoulder with mine. "Don't be mean."

"No, they're good."

"I used to shoot microfilm in the archives. Library work. Wren Library."

"Cambridge?"

"Mm."

"Very professional. I should have shot these."

"You were busy."

"Yes." He clicks through the images again. The dagger man. Horns. Fingers.

"Why couldn't we find them before?"

"I don't know. I searched and searched. They were right there. It was almost as if you could only see them in a storm."

He glances up at me, that look playing around his mouth. "Pretty superstitious for a Cambridge girl."

"Well, it was very cloudy and dark before. And the lightning was so intense."

"We could go back. I suppose I could get them with my flash."

"I don't want to go back."

He looks at me. "Why not?"

Why not. I want to stay here. I don't want to leave this room. Ever.

I shrug. I pull up my knees and wrap my arms around them.

"You okay?"

I nod. "I just want to stay here . . . with you."

Here. Now. After. It's as if I had switched on a harsh overhead light.

"Mayg." The hand, the cigarette, the lighter.

"I know." I lean my head on my knees.

He drags deep. The tip glows red. Then he says evenly, "When do you have to be back?"

"Wednesday. I said I'd be back Wednesday."

"What day is it today?"

"I don't know." I think hard. "Sunday, I think."

"No. Saturday."

I look up at him. "You said — you wrote 'Stay a week.'"

He brushes the hair out of my eyes and hooks it behind my ear. "A week is better than nothing. For the Bretagne story we'll need more, no?"

I feel a bubble rising in my chest. Happiness.

8 PM: When we climb down the stairs for dinner I avoid the proprietress' eyes. She brings menus and red wine, then stands by the table, her mouth tight. "Do you know when you will be checking out?"

I keep my eyes on the menu. Jean-Jacques glances up. "Wednesday," he says. He fills my glass.

There is lamb daube again. This time we eat it all. And the potato gratin. And the greens. And more sheep cheese, creamy and tart. We are ravenous, insatiable. When she brings the crème brûlée to the table he cracks the sugar with the tip of his spoon and carries a mound to my mouth. There are red currants on the saucer, miniature globes of tart, bright juice. We pick them off their tiny stems and bite.

11 PM: The window is open, cold green flooding in over warm pine. We're leaning out into the darkness, the quilt over our shoulders. He is smoking.

"Your parents, they were farmers?"

"Well, kind of. I mean, they tried to make a go of it. They weren't exactly born to it. It was an idea."

"Mm?" His smoke trails into the mist. The tobacco smells mellow, roasty. "An idea?"

"They were teachers, really. Latin. History."

"Ah."

"But they wanted to grow their own food. My grandmother—she was from the Isère—she filled my father's head with ideas of—dreams of—fresh stuff. Real food. She didn't approve of Birds Eye."

"Bird's eye?"

"*L'oeil d'oiseau.* A brand name. Frozen vegetables. Convenience food. Labor-saving."

"I would have liked your grandmother."

"You would. She was wonderful."

His warm bare shoulder is resting against mine. Wonderful. I watch the cigarette tip glow.

"I was named after her. She never spoke a word of English with me. I wouldn't answer in French, not for years. I just stared at her. Then when she died . . ." I look out at the mercury light. Soft vapor is rising from dark branches. "All of a sudden I had so many things to say to her. In French."

He smokes for a while. "What's 'Mayg' short for? Mégane, no?"

"Marguerite. Like the flower."

"Marguerite."

"And it's 'Meg.'"

"Mayg."

"No. *Meg*."

"That's what I said. *'Mayg.'*"

"No. Look at my lips." I say it again, slowly. "Meg."

His mouth is very close to mine. "Again."

Sunday, 11 AM: I wake up to the smell of coffee and warm rolls.

"I ordered it for two rooms. She brought it on one tray, to my door. She gave me a look like this." He rolls his eyes.

I giggle and sit up. The window is open and clean air cuts in.

"Maybe we should move into your room for a while so she can change the sheets."

Jean-Jacques lifts the coverlet and puts it back down quickly. "I think you're right."

The hotel is crowded with guests, but we migrate proudly across the hall in our bare feet, me wearing Jean-Jacques' scarf. We are beyond the laws of God and man.

1 PM: He is studying my body objectively. "You look different in here."

I start a little, flushing.

"I mean in this light."

"Photographer!"

He runs a finger gently over my side, along my hip. "What are these?"

I look down. "Stretchmarks."

He kisses them, tracing them with his lips. "Stretchmarks?"

"From having babies."

The words hang in the air. I fight down a sudden wave of feeling.

"Jean-Jacques, I have to call home. I have to. Even if there's no cell phone signal up here it doesn't mean . . . it doesn't mean . . ."

"I know. It just feels like it."

But he's warm under the clean sheets. I doze again on his chest. When I snap awake he is reading "The Mystery of the Marvels of Mount Bégo."

4 PM: He reaches for a cigarette.

I prop up on an elbow and block his way. I'm feeling braver now.

"You have a fixation," I say.

"A fixation?"

"An oral fixation. Didn't your mother breastfeed you?"

"*My* mother? No."

He reaches again for the cigarette. I stop his hand. He laughs.

I stop his laugh.

7 PM: I am dressed in jeans and climbing the hotel driveway to the phone booth on the corner. The roar of the stream is strong. The sun has already dipped behind the mountaintops. I limp a little. My clothes chafe against raw skin. I savor the pain. I am about to lie to my husband.

I slip my phone card into the slot and punch the stiff metal numbers. I have to do it twice because my fingers wobble so. I take a breath and prepare.

But Sophie answers. *"Allô?"*

"Sophie?"

There is the sound of the hood fan, a children's story tape turned up loud. Cloey and Gerald are barking.

"Oui. Oui. Bonsoir, Madame Thorpe."

The story tape reverberates, tinny, distorted.

. . . once upon a time

"Sophie, this is supposed to be . . . you aren't supposed to work until tomorrow morning . . . Are you?"

It is Sunday night, isn't it? I probe the depths of my brain.

. . . there was a beautiful princess

"Yes." Her voice is thin. "Yes. Monsieur Thorpe asked me—"

"He went out?"

. . . vain and proud and selfish

"Yes. He has gone out."

I digest this.

"Well, is everything all right? The children?"

. . . the suitor was lonely but brave

"Yes." But her voice doesn't convince me. "They are very wild today." There is a shriek and the barking duel redoubles intensity.

"Cloey, arrête! Je te dis, arrête!"

Sophie sounds ten years older. She sounds like me.

"I'm sorry. I will speak to Monsieur Thorpe."

. . . he answered the riddles one by one

"Yes." She sounds unconvinced. "You're coming back on . . . ?"

"Wednesday night. Or rather, very early Thursday. I'm taking the night train."

She sighs. "*D'accord.* I must go now. *Cloey!*"

"Wait a minute!" I grip the phone and call into the mouthpiece. "Can I talk to the children?"

I hear her hand, muffling. She is whispering urgently. She removes her hand and says, "They are playing. They won't come."

. . . the icy heart of the princess was warmed

My heart freezes.

"Oh. Okay. Um. Kiss them for me . . . Well. Good night."

. . . and she knew love for the first time

The phone clicks.

I step out of the phone booth and stand in the chill canyon roar. I don't dial Nigel's cell. I walk back to the hotel and my lover.

Monday, 7 AM: Jean-Jacques pulls the covers off, exposing me. It's freezing.

"Wake up."

I snatch at the covers. "Hey!"

"Wake up. We are going out of the front door. And we are going to walk." He is dressed. His camera bag is on his shoulder.

"Out? I want to stay here." I reach for him but he's covered in cloth. I scowl. "What about breakfast?"

"In the other room. But you can't get to it unless you get dressed."

I shower. My body stings. He's right: It's time to go out.

I dry quickly and dress, cross the hall to my room, and gulp a bowl of coffee. Then we climb down the stairs and push side by side through the front door.

The air is sharp as ice, metallic. We walk past the driveway and up the Casterino road, then we cut up a path and follow the hiker's trail. As hard as the four-wheel road was, this trail is easy, like walking over a carpet of fir needles and meadow flowers. The scent of fern and resin mingles with pristine damp. We climb steadily, short-cutting across switchbacks. There is a herd of sheep flowing up the hill. We fall in with them and flow, too. I feel immortal.

It takes three hours to reach the valley bowl. The sky is blue today with clouds like down quilts. Mount Bégo gleams, benevolent, in the sun-washed mist. We waste no time. We both walk toward the stones. The gravures are there, everywhere this time, clearly etched in shadowy relief.

"You see?"

I trace my fingers over the cool lines. They are rough with lichen and velvety with moss. The supplicating hands. The plow. The horns. The dagger man. I feel Jean-Jacques standing over me.

He sets up his lights with the battery pack and shoots away.

I smile a prayer of thanks to the gods of Mount Bégo.

9 PM: There is trout on the table tonight and a good bottle of Riesling. Even after the bowl of *ravioles,* we eat two fish each. I slip out buttery trout cheeks with the tines of my fork and slide them into Jean-Jacques' lips. He laughs. I kiss his cheeks, his lips. The hostess shakes her head.

He wipes his mouth with the napkin and studies the dessert menu. "So. Are we expensing this to Nikos?"

"Oh god, I don't . . . What do you think?"

"Maybe not."

"Think it's deductible?"

"Absolutely. Research, no?"

I glance up. Is he smirking? I don't care. I lay my napkin on the table. "Research! That's it. I mean, Jean-Jacques, I want to know about *you.* I know you're off working somewhere but you always just appear like you've clicked your heels together."

He furrows his brow. "My heels?"

"Wizard of Oz. *Le Magicien d'Oz.*"

"Got it." He closes the menu and faces me. "*D'accord.* So, what do you want to know about?"

"Um. Work?"

"Okay. Work. You've been very expensive. When I was in Turin I turned down a story on truffle oil to be here."

"Are you sorry?"

"No. Ask me another one."

"Your family?"

He pats for a cigarette. "Next question."

"Sorry." I look down at the trout bones and take a breath. "Other lovers?"

His laugh escapes like a gasp. "I couldn't. You exhaust me."

"I mean *before*."

"Well. Sure." He smiles and shakes his head. "Don't do this. Mayg, I have never met anyone like you. You are . . ."

I look at the trout bones. I hold my breath and wait.

"You are . . ."

I wait.

"Délicieuse."

3 AM: I wake up with a shudder, sweating, cold waves of horror rolling over my skin. The bubble of happiness has suddenly ruptured, like my water breaking when I gave birth to Kate. I sit up gasping for air.

What am I doing?

I have to lie to Nigel. I have to lie to the children.

I scramble out of the bed and stand in the dark. Jean-Jacques is sound asleep, his arm flung over the hollow where I lay.

I grope for clothes but only find my anorak. I wrap it around me and creep across the hall to my room. I sit on the toilet and hold my head.

What am I doing?

What am I going to do?

There is a tap at my room door and a whisper. "Mayg?" I sit and shake. He stands for a long time. He tests the door. I've locked it. He goes away.

Tuesday, 8 AM: He knocks again. I drag myself from the clean, starched sheets. I'm still in my anorak. I crack the door.

He is dressed and holding a breakfast tray. "Can I come in?"

I look at him imploringly. "Jean-Jacques, I can't do this."

He looks at me. "Do you want to go?"

I nod, mute.

"Okay. Eat something. We'll drive down together."

But there is a peach on the tray and he hands it to me. I bite. Before long he is probing me deep inside as if looking for an answer.

After, I squat on the bidet and quietly cry. He kneels behind me, dips his hand into the warm soapy water and washes my sins away.

8 ⚜ Absent without Leave

Thursday, July 3, 7:30 AM: "You're a bit pasty, darling. Thought you were in the south of France." He kisses my cheek absently with unfamiliar lips. Bowed. Smooth.

Nigel is having his breakfast before leaving for work. I have just dragged my bag in the door and stand shivering in the skirt I wore on the train from Nice.

"I was in the mountains. It was cold."

"Good trip?"

"Yes." I run my hand over his hair. The shape of his head is strange.

"Where are the kids?" There are no other places set on the table.

"They're at Fabienne's for breakfast. She's driving them to school. It's all right, love. She offered." He goes back to his Weetabix.

I am too numb to address this. With a twinge I think, I'm glad they're not here. I'm not ready.

There is a tornado of bucking fur at the kitchen door. I open it and Gerald explodes into the room. He churns around my legs barking joyously, then stops suddenly, pricks up one ear and plunges his nose between my knees.

With a silent gasp I seize his head and wrench it away. Nigel is reading the *Telegraph:* "Franco-American Fisticuffs."

He is chuckling and shaking his head.

"Been following this?"

9 AM: I carry my suitcase upstairs. I can barely cross the landing. There are wet towels and sheets on the floor, Duplos and puzzle pieces, miniature socks and overalls. There is the strong smell of urine.

Cloey's mattress is bare and soaked under a twist of sleeping bag. His quilt is soaked, in the bathtub. His potty stands unemptied.

I pick my way to Kate's room. Her floor is knee-deep. Her bed is so full of books, tapes, and stuffed animals, I can't find the dent where she slept.

I wilt. Then I sigh. My penance. I embrace it.

3 PM: I have scoured and stripped and laundered and swept with a fury. Bleach. Ammonia. Wax. Disinfectant. I open every window in the house. The wind whistles through.

I take a deep breath and look around me. My real life.

But then I pick my way through tassled hay to the back hedge and fill a bowl with currants. I carry them into the kitchen and roll them through my fingers, scoop sugar over them, crush them until they juice.

I lick my fingers and hold my breath at the feeling, remembering.

4 PM: In the barn, I see no change. The tarps flap in the sun. One rose, thrusting from under the stone pile, struggles to bloom.

My bunker has been shaken again and dust covers my books and files. Thank god I packed up the laptop while I was gone or it would have been preserved like a body at Pompeii.

I boot up and sip my coffee, my lips chafing against the chipped rim. They're still swollen and sore and tingling with memory. The Nice *gare*. Jean-Jacques wrapped his scarf around my neck in the rental lot and pulled me to him for a last devouring kiss. Now I bury my face in it. It smells like hair and sweat and brine and smoke, too raw and real for words.

I write:

> *i love your mouth.*

I tap Send.
There's a message from him waiting.

> *i still can taste you.*

A shiver runs through me. I wrap the scarf around my neck.

5 PM: I walk out to the bus stop and stand beside the other mothers. Fabienne is there. She looks me over in my long cotton skirt and scarf. The scarf.

"Chilly?" she says.

I smile.

"Did you have a good trip?" she presses.

"Yes. Too long. I haven't seen the kids since Wednesday."

"I know. I've seen a lot of them. Monsieur Thorpe's been very busy, no?"

I hesitate. "Busy? Yes. Thank you for taking them this morning."

"I thought it was better for them. Kate was having trouble locking the front door last week so I offered to help them in the morning."

My breath stops. "But Nigel . . ."

"He's been leaving very early some days." She looks at me, eyebrows raised. "You're both very busy these days."

The school bus rounds the last curve and pulls up to us. Through sanded glass I see Kate following the children down the aisle, herding Cloey before her. She spots me and freezes. She looks like a deer in headlights.

A week is a long time.

I gather them both, carefully, into my arms. They feel rigid and very small.

Inside, I present the currant tarts to them, holding them out like peace offerings. They stand staring, detached, Cloey scratching between his legs.

"You were taking pictures, *Maman?*" Kate is scraping her toes side to side across the flagstones.

"I did take pictures, yes. This time I did." I smile.

"Vacation!" Cloey looks at me. "All home together!"

I had forgotten. Tomorrow is the last day of school. "That's right, honey. We'll all be home together."

It takes most of the evening for them to seem real to me and me to them. By bedtime we have melted back together. I tuck them in and smell their necks until they giggle.

I remember this. I remember this.

9 PM: I am waiting at the dining table when Nigel comes home. He pets my shoulder with a small, soft hand. He heads for the fridge, then spots the last of the tarts. "Well well!" He turns and scans the room. The table

is waxed. The *Telegraph*s have been hauled away. There is a bouquet of lupines on the table.

"Trip's done you good, I see. Back in the spirit of things! Glad to be home?"

"Nigel, we have to talk."

There's something in my tone that makes him stop, still holding the refrigerator door. He hates this tone. He knows it well.

"I called on Sunday night, Nigel."

Sunday night. I flash on the hotel room. Knotty pine. Bare skin. I falter. Who am I to scold?

"You were out again. And Fabienne told me you've been leaving early. Leaving the kids alone."

My voice echoes back in my own ears. Leaving the kids alone.

He drops ice cubes into a glass. "Hardly seems to bother you, dear. Off having adventures."

I look up. His face is bland. I soften my tone. "We agreed. When I'm on the road, the children need you. Not just a nanny."

The children need you. Not just a nanny.

"Right then. No more pub nights for Papa. Home to the apron strings."

"You used to understand. Nigel, you used to be wonderful with the kids. You used to cook for them and—"

"How much longer will you be working on this 'book'?"

for bretagne we will need more

I duck my head, cheeks hot. Who am I to take the moral high ground? I'm the one leaving the children. I'm the one off having . . . adventures.

Friday, 11 AM: I set a Nutella jar of bloody urine on Dr. Arnaud's desk. He raises his eyebrows, impressed, carries it into his examining room and comes back clicking his tongue. "It's a good cystitis," he says. He pulls out a prescription sheet and begins to scribble. "You and Monsieur Thorpe been finding your second wind?" he chuckles.

I feel blood creeping up my face. "I guess so!" I laugh, shrugging.

But I hesitated a moment too long. His hand stops scribbling. Then it scribbles again. He leans back and, over his glasses, checks my dossier on the computer screen.

"How's that burned hand?"

I hold it up.

"Still haven't got the ring back on?"

He glances up and turns back to the computer. He scrolls.

"IUD? No. Pill. Good. Try urinating afterward. Clears the urethra." He looks up at me and pushes up his glasses. He seems to be reassessing me, PTA crêpe flipper, mother of two. "If you can tear yourself away."

This is a very small village.

11 PM: Oh god. I shouldn't have gone to bed first. Nigel comes up the stairs, humming exuberantly. "Hul-lo there!" he says. He rubs his hands together. His nose is red.

I squeeze my eyes shut and feign even breathing.

"'Thou art inclined to sleep,'" he sighs.

In the night I dream of lightning.

Monday, 10 AM: I face the blank screen and try to write.

SUPPLICATIONS TO THE MOUNTAIN GODS
Ancients in the Alps pray for potency and power
1800 BC

Gods, I kneel before ye on the mountaintop,
dagger thrust to the sky

I snicker. I erase.

The horns of the cuckold or the horn of Priapus?

I catch my breath. I erase.

Gods, I beseech you, make a man of me for woman

My gorge rises. I erase.

Oh help. I can't do this. I try to concentrate. Lightning, I think. Rain. Wet anoraks. Tongues.

Damn. I close the file. I check e-mail. There is a flood from Jean-Jacques, twenty jpegs. I smile hungrily.

His mind is in the same gutter. The carvings have been magnified and reframed. They throb with thrusting daggers and pikes. The priapic stick man glistens. He has interspersed them with his lightning pictures, so rawly charged they burn off the screen.

And there's one shot, close up and lustrous and trickling juice, of the box of wild strawberries, half crushed on the rumpled sheets. A wedge of oozing Brebis lies beside it. For a moment the taste and smell of them come back to me and the feel of his thumbs on my lips. My eyes close.

There's another message from Nikos.

> *Looking forward to your text. Layout running behind.*

Midnight: The office phone rings and I grab it.

"Hi."

"Hi."

"You okay?"

"I'm okay."

"You shouldn't call me here."

"I wanted to hear your voice."

There is the click of a lighter. Neither of us speaks.

Tuesday, 10 AM: The children are puttering in their *cabane,* a kind of shack-house they're "building" from piles of straw and paint buckets. I'm in the bunker, working on *La Vie en France, Level Two.*

> *The portable telephone has invaded French society in a way that has altered communications between families, colleagues, friends, and children.*

DIALOGUE

Francine: Salut.
   Hi.
Pascal: Salut.
   Hi.
Francine: Ça va?
   You okay?
Pascal: Ça va.
   I'm okay.

Francine: Il ne faut pas m'appeler ici.
　　You shouldn't call me here.
Pascal: Je voulais entendre ta voix.
　　I wanted to hear your voice.

4 PM: I am browning chunks of lamb in olive oil, rubbing tight leaves of thyme between my fingertips, peeling pods of garlic and crushing them with my knife blade, sliding the slippery flesh into the sizzling pot, my face over the steam, breathing to the bottom of my lungs.

Thursday, 10 PM: The children are asleep at last despite the light still pouring in their windows. I am back in my bunker trying to finish *La Vie en France, Level Two.* I have had a little too much wine.

Traditionally the men of France do not opt for circumcision unless practicing non-Christian faiths. Male newborns are left with fore-skins intact.

DIALOGUE

Francine: C'est quoi ça?
　　What is that?
Pascal: C'est mon pénis.
　　It's my penis.
Francine: Ça je sais, mais . . .
　　That I know. But . . .
Pascal: Tu veux dire ça? Ici?
　　You mean this? Here?
Francine: Oui. Comment . . . ?
　　Yes. How . . . ?
Pascal: Tu n'as qu'à . . .
　　All you have to do is . . .
Francine: Mm.
　　Mm.

I am holding my cheeks in my hands and giggling like a girl. I highlight the text in blue and backspace. It disappears.

Two weeks until Bretagne. I run my fingers over the scarf. I stand up and pull *Historic Brittany* off the shelf.

Sunday, 11 AM: We are all sitting around the kitchen table "reading" the weekend papers, the kids cutting out the animal pictures. I help Kate trim around a walrus tusk. Then I reach for the *Herald Tribune* and turn to the Op-Ed page.

> ### Food Fight
> *Despite a historic alliance dating back centuries, the French have once again given a great Gallic shrug in the face of global advancement . . .*

Nigel reads over my shoulder and crows. "Well done! Put the arrogant bastards in their place. Tiresome lot, the French. You'd never see them get worked up over this if it was about anything but food." He turns back to his *Telegraph.* "Don't give a damn about anything they can't eat. Or roger."

Cloey jerks his head up. "Roger who?"

I'm grateful for the newspaper that hides the color of my face.

Monday, 4 PM: We are out in the hills walking Gerald, Cloey and Kate taking two booted steps for my every stride. Even on Bastille Day we have to wear rubber boots and sink to our calves in mud. Gerald is in ecstasy, galloping over the pastures, tongue flying in the wind. Nigel is home watching a cricket match.

Two forms clear the crest. It's Sophie and Ahmad/Paul-Marie, holding hands. She is mincing around the mud tracks, careful to keep her combat boots clean.

"Sophie!" The children sprint to her and jump into her arms. I catch up, smiling away the pang in my chest.

"*Bonjour,* Madame Thorpe." She kisses my cheeks. Her nails are unpainted and broken. Her smile isn't as warm as last time I saw her.

I immediately begin to apologize again. "I have spoken with Monsieur Thorpe," I assure her. "He completely agrees with me. He will be spending more time with the children and will stick to the schedule. Now that the kids are free perhaps you can get out more. It'll be easier."

She looks unconvinced. "When do you leave?"

"I am going to Bretagne next week."

Next week!

"And for how long this time?"

for bretagne we will need more

"Um. A week or so."

She wilts a little. Ahmad reaches for her hand. "Okay. We'll discuss the schedule. And Monsieur Thorpe will be there in the evenings, no?"

"Yes."

9 PM: "Nigel, she looks so tired."

"It's just the makeup, darling. Those black circles she paints around her eyes."

"No, I mean it. She'll be dealing with the kids all day now. You promise to spend the evenings with them, right? And weekends?"

"Right, right, absolutely."

I study him across the table. "Maybe if you got back into cooking. Or grilling."

Nigel considers this. "Might do. Might do. Might have the lads round . . ."

"Nigel. The *children*."

"Quite right. Of course, they enjoy a good barbecue themselves. Do you remember that Guinness marinade?"

Thursday, 11 AM: The children are running in the backyard, playing in the barn. I have snuck down into my bunker—just for a minute or two—and am writing to Jean-Jacques, the scarf around my neck.

> *i dreamed about you last night. the way you taste. m.*

He writes back almost instantly.

> *Meg i can't wait much longer when is bretagne story not soon enough*

I am hovering over the pale-blue screen, running my fingers over the flickering letters, when there is a rumble overhead and a heavy thud. Cloey gives a piercing scream. I can't pull myself up the ladder fast enough, hands cold with horror.

Cloey and Kate are standing in front of the opening, the tarp pushed to the side. A chunk of stone the size of a watermelon has fallen from the jagged lip and lies in the rubble, dust swirling around it.

"Get out of there!" I hiss. "Come to me!"

They are frozen with fear. I dive for them and drag them to me. Cloey begins to whimper. I try to lighten my tone but my voice is hoarse. "It's okay, guys. Just don't go near that opening."

A shower of sand dumps just behind us, out of the widening crack.

Midnight: I can't do this. I stuff the scarf into a drawer. I *won't* do this.

The phone rings and I grab for it.

"Jean-Jacques?"

"Mayg."

His lighter clicks.

My hand slides into the drawer.

Saturday, 6 AM: There is a rumble in the driveway. I've never been so glad to hear it. I lift Gerald bodily out of the way and open the barn door to Raimondo's grin.

"I have brought the cement, Madame Thorpe. We will need it to frame in the opening."

"Thank god!" I say. "You can see what a state it's in."

He studies the hole — tarps sagging, boards dangling. "Rico did not use the braces?"

"The braces?"

He points at the floor. "The braces to support the opening." He shakes his head.

Midnight: I am writing again to Jean-Jacques.

> *i can come next thursday. where shall we meet*

He responds so quickly it's almost in real time.

> *we will pick up a car in versailles. i don't care where we go*

Sunday, 11 PM: I sit cross-legged on the bunker floor surrounded by open books. *La Belle Bretagne. The Legends of Brittany. The Prehistoric Stone Works of Brittany. Celtic Culture in Brittany. Arthurian Tales in Brittany.*

I have not even narrowed the subjects down to one. I am losing hold.

8 PM: ". . . and when Merlin opened his eyes he found himself gently shackled in a prison-bower of bliss, far above the world."

Kate snuggles into my neck. Cloey dropped off to sleep a while ago. The book is heavy in my hands.

"'Alas,' quoth he, 'my lady Viviane—'"

"The lake lady?"

"The Lady of the Lake. 'Rest with me here, for with mine own enchantment thou hast beguiled me: No one hath power to dissolve these bonds but thee.'"

Tuesday, 11 PM: Another e-mail from Nikos.

Meg, what's up? Still missing copy for Mercantour. Are you on top of Brittany?

I write back:

Swamped with Brittany research. Kids on vacation, full time job. Don't worry, you'll get text.

I have to write. I have to try.

We'll find a story in Bretagne. We always do, don't we?

Thursday, 6 AM: I pack carefully this time. Gauzy skirts. A thirties sundress. An old Saint James sailor's pullover I found at the Salvation Army, three buttons across one shoulder. Out of the drawer I lift out layers of tissue paper and unwrap the vintage silk underwear I bought at an auction last spring. Peach and pale rose, embroidery so fine I can hardly make out the stitches. A shoulder strap catches and draws out the Pooh-print flannel nightshirt Nigel bought me from Harrods for Christmas. I stuff that back down. I flash on Jean-Jacques' hands in the shepherd's hut, pushing my clothes out of the way.

i am ready

I peg the black-and-red schedule on the fridge, wind Jean-Jacques' scarf around my neck, and head for the door.

Then I stop cold. I forgot to kiss the children good-bye. I turn and tiptoe guiltily up the stairs.

1 PM: When the train rolls into the Versailles station I am waiting at its folding door, peering down through the glass. He's standing there on the quai in a t-shirt and baggy shorts, his hair bound into a messy knot at his neck. He has gained a little weight and there's some color to his skin. He looks younger than I remembered.

He is grinning.

The train hisses to a stop and I step down. We face each other for a second, people jostling past. Then he presses me back against a riveted pillar and dives for my mouth.

People stare. Somebody smiles. He unwinds the scarf and kisses my neck. I push him away self-consciously.

"You should wash this." He dandles the scarf over my shoulders.

"Never."

We stand facing each other, smiling so happily it hurts.

1:30 PM: He has rented a Peugeot 307 and, even in the Europcar parking lot, the back seat is full of market baskets. "I thought maybe lunch," he shrugs.

"That looks like a lot of lunch."

"We have big appetites." He spreads his hands. I laugh. The joy is irrepressible.

We load my bag and climb into the car.

"So where are we going?" he asks.

2:00 PM: We haven't gone far. We are still sitting in the car in the middle of the Europcar parking lot kissing like high school kids, wetness welling between my legs.

I pull my lips to the side for air. "Where are we going?"

He pulls my lips back. "I don't care. Here."

"We can't stay here."

"Why not?"

"Mm."

2:15 PM: "I know what," he murmurs against my mouth.

"Mm?"

"We'll go to France Miniature."

"What?"

"Just outside Versailles. The park with the tiny models of France. The Eiffel Tower. The Pont du Gard."

I pull back an inch and look at him. "Why?"

"I will photograph all the monuments of France and send them to Nikos, one week at a time. He'll never know the difference. And then we can stay in a Formule 1 motel all summer and . . ."

He kisses me again.

"Do they have anything from Brittany?" I mumble.

"Who?"

"This park. France Miniature."

"Mont-St-Michel, I bet."

"That's Normandy."

"Brittany."

"Normandy."

"Mm."

3:00 PM: We have driven west for a while. He turns the Peugeot off the highway and down a tractor road. "It's getting very late for lunch," he says. He drives until the tracks run out at a grove of poplars. We unload the baskets and spread this morning's *Le Monde* under the trees.

"First we eat," he says pointedly. I plop down on the grass and he follows. There is pâté and cheese and bread, cherries, apricots, and wine. We open the wax-paper packages and handle the food, hefting it.

"Just a *casse-croûte*. A snack."

"Some snack. Mmm. I am hungry after all."

He unwraps a newspaper bundle and shows me a withered pork sausage. He draws it under my nose for me to smell like a Havana cigar—musk and salt and a gaminess that makes my mouth water. With his pocketknife he cuts a paper-thin slice, peels off the powdery skin, and lays it on my tongue like a wafer. He cuts a piece for himself and eats it off the knife. He starts to peel another one, but I am already laughing and opening his shorts buttons and pulling him down.

4:30 PM: When my eyes drift open Jean-Jacques is nowhere in sight. My skirt is still up above my knees. My skin stings from nettles and spiking grass. I grope for my underpants. I can smell his cigarette smoke coming from beyond the car. A cloud is passing overhead. I don't feel so joyous anymore. I straighten myself and go to him.

His hands are on his hips and he is staring into space. I put my forehead on his chest and thread my arms around him.

He throws the cigarette down and scuffs it with his foot. "We'd better go."

"Where are we going?"

He laughs a smaller version of his laugh. "You tell me."

8 PM: We ride in silence. We get as far as Rennes and check into a Formule 1. In a shoebox room lined in wood-look plastic we lie on the polyester quilt in our clothes all night, staring at the ceiling, listening to trucks roar past over the highway.

Friday, 5 AM: He is undressing me with such slow tenderness, I feel tears roll into my ears. He cups my face and brushes them away with his thumbs.

10 AM: "Where are we going?" he asks. We are back on the road and I am squinting at the map. "Paimpont. Paimpont. Here it is. Forêt de Paimpont."

"Standing stones?"

"No. Brocéliande. Merlin's forest. Where he loved Viviane."

"You will have to brief me on her."

I do. He listens thoughtfully. "Fairies are hard to photograph." I push his shoulder and we swerve slightly.

"It's an ancient forest of massive trees. Very Druid. Mossy, dark, magical. Can't you evoke that?"

He unleashes the laugh. Then he looks at my face. "Sure I can 'evoke' that. But you have to get the photo rights from the wizards." He drives. "Wait a minute. Paimpont. By St-Cyr, the military school, right? Isn't that the one that burned down?"

I turn on him. "Burned *down?*"

His lips are twitching. "Biggest forest fire in the history of France. Back in the nineties."

I stare ahead. He drives.

10:30 AM: "So, where are we going?"

The Peugeot is streaking down the *autoroute,* vaguely westward. I am leaning on my hand and staring gloomily out the window.

"Jean-Jacques, I can't write this book."

"Don't, Mayg. We'll work something out. Maybe — maybe the history angle is going to have to change a little."

"But that's the whole point."

"I know. But it has posed some . . . euh . . . problems."

I sigh. "I know." I stare at the countryside streaming past, backroads lined with poplars arching over the hills. "France is just *saturated* in European history. Antiquity. Mythology. Prehistoric stuff."

"But not everyone can see it in their heads like you, Madame l'Historienne. Let alone capture it on film."

I look up. He is smirking just a little now. "*Alors.* What are the next stories to look forward to?"

"You still haven't read the story list, have you?"

He wipes the smirk off his lips with his hand. "Euh . . ."

"Well, there's the *débarquement,* D-Day."

He keeps his eyes on the road. His hand pats for a cigarette. "Do we have to?" he says levelly.

"And Agincourt!"

"Agincourt?"

"*Azincourt* in French. The great battle of the Hundred Years' War, 'this hungry war,' when Henry the Fifth of England — "

"Dead, right?" He lights.

"But there's a festival. With costumes."

"Ah." He drives. "Why not Verdun? Or Poitiers? The Saracens! We could use my Arabic scarf."

"They're not *all* about battles."

"No. Sometimes there are fairies."

12 PM: "Okay, think of all the sites in France where something important happened. Something historic. There's the Bastille in Paris."

"Are you kidding? It's a modern opera house."

"But still . . . Lascaux! The cave paintings!"

"It's closed to the public. There's a plastic reproduction. I photographed it for Geo. It's good, but it's plastic."

"What about Carcassonne?"

"It's a tourist trap, a medieval theme park."

"Versailles?"

"It's a museum."

"The papal palace at Avignon! There are still the frescoes in Clement the Sixth's chambers!"

"And you can visit them with those little radio things to your ear."

"Orléans?"

"Full of banks and gas stations like any other city."

"Varennes!"

"What's Varennes?"

"That's where Louis the Sixteenth was arrested trying to escape the Revolution. In his stagecoach, in the night, in the middle of the woods."

"Now that would make a good photo. Is he available?"

"You're so cynical."

"Mayg, there's no point. Life goes on. The world moves ahead. Historic moments don't just go on looping in time for your viewing pleasure."

"But I've gone to all those places. I've paid tribute. I've *felt the feeling*." I stare over the panning landscape.

"Mayg?"

"What?"

"We're getting very close to Lorient. Do you mind if I ask: Where are we going?"

"I don't know. I don't know. Lunch."

"Okay."

He exits and heads for the coast. When he pulls into the parking lot of a seafood diner, he kisses me.

My stomach growls.

1:30 PM: There is a mountain of langoustine shells dividing us and we are tearing into more. I am up to my elbows in salty juice and I lick my fingers. My wineglass is smeared and my napkin lies soaked in a ball. I pry the pink case off another one and slip the meat into my mouth.

Jean-Jacques passes his napkin over his mouth and shakes his head. "*Putain,* Mayg. You eat like you make love."

I look up. I flush a little. I wipe my lips with the napkin ball.

He watches. "You're *voracious.* Your mouth . . . When I saw you eat asparagus in Arles I had to keep my napkin in my lap."

I throw a shell at him. "Don't make it dirty."

"It's not dirty. It's *fabuleux.*"

"Americans don't fuss about table manners so much." I suck on a claw, licking the juice from my lips.

Jean-Jacques watches. Then he peels one himself and presses it into my mouth with his thumb.

2 PM: When I come out of the restroom scrubbed pink and smelling of pump soap, he is talking on his phone. "I'll ask her," I hear him say. "I will let you know."

He is wearing the scarf now and I dry my hands on it.

"Eh!" he says.

"They're clean. It can only help," I say. I kiss his matted hair. Langoustines. "Who was that?"

"Some friends. Listen, I am not trying to take away your lead. You decide the story, right? *Whatever* the story is. But we do need a place to sleep tonight and my friends live on the coast above the Baie d'Audierne."

I feel myself flushing again. "But friends . . ."

"It's okay for them to know. They're good friends. You would like them."

"Jean-Jacques, I don't even know what we're doing in Bretagne."

"Mayg. I do."

He looks at me. He lays a hand on the small of my back just under my shirt. I feel goose bumps on my arms.

3 PM: We ride along the coast west of Lorient, winding around tiny ports and crawling up the waterfront. The Atlantic ocean sparkles white-hot in the afternoon sun, spreading to an indigo band of horizon. There are fishing boats hauled up the shoreline and nets drying in the sun. I smell brine.

The road curves inland, wheeling over emerald flatlands. Every village begins with a *K*. Kérandoare. Kervagon. Kergabet. Then suddenly they all begin with a *P*. Plozévet. Plouhinec. Plogoff. There are cypress looming low over the ground, green-black branches sweeping wide. White cottages with pointed roofs float in masses of hollyhock and hydrangea.

"It looks like Peter Rabbit country," I say.

"Who?"

I explain Beatrix Potter. I wish I hadn't mentioned it. It makes me remember for a moment who I really am.

4:30 PM: We are driving almost straight into the sun, already halfway down the western sky. Tourists are pouring inland at the end of their beach days. Jean-Jacques parks in a lot that is rapidly emptying of trailers and caravans. He takes my hand and leads me west. We leave the pavement and break out over open rocks, the sun hard on us, our shadows sprawling east. I shade my eyes. I can see a towering lighthouse. "Why are we stopping at the Pointe du Raz?" I ask. "Idea for the book?"

"No. It's just beautiful."

"Oh," I say. He's right. For as far as I can see, the ocean spreads before me, waves seething and crashing below. To the north and south, mossy cliffs undulate to the horizon.

Jean-Jacques squints into the sun. "It's the farthest point west in France," he says. "Can you see home?"

"Home?"

"Inda . . . Indi-*a*-na."

"Oh." I smile a little and look over the gleaming whitecaps. "That's not home anymore."

Home. I pull away from him and wander to the cliff edge and dig the phone out of my bag.

The phone rings five times before Nigel picks up. There is a roar in the background of male voices and a television match turned up loud. I look at the screen of my phone to see if I've dialed his cell by mistake and have reached the Hare and Hound. It's the home number all right. I put it back to my ear.

"Nigel?"

"Sorry? Sorry? That you, darling?" He muffles the mouthpiece and the background noise dims. He comes back. "Hello, love, where you ringing from? Wilds of Brittany, is it?" His lads-are-listening voice.

"Yes. What's going on?"

"Well, you did suggest I spend more time with the children, didn't you? Simon and Geoffrey came round for the match and I'm stirring up a little something. In fact, I've just lit the grill."

I pause. "Where are the kids?"

He pauses. "Well, they're round here somewhere. Kate? Kate? She was out on the swing earlier." I hear footsteps. "And Cloey? Been a bugger all day but—*here's* Cloey! Watching the cricket with Andrew like a . . . like a . . . What's that, Cloey my lad? She's gone to Mémé Mathilde's? Right. Well then. I shall just go and fetch her. Call you back, Megs?"

"That's okay." I hold the phone and breathe. "Um. *Bon appétit.*" I punch No and hold it down with my thumb. The phone goes blank. I slip it back into my bag.

I turn back toward Jean-Jacques. He is holding his own phone to his ear. "Not before next week. Sorry. Okay. Sure. Next time."

I lay my hand on his back. "Work?"

"Sorry. I had a . . . I had to . . ."

"Are you missing *real* work for this?"

He shrugs. "There's always more."

He presses No, too, and holds it down.

5:30 PM: Jean-Jacques swings the car north along the Baie des Trépassés and follows a tiny road up over velvet cliffs. There is a painted arrow marked "Kereol." He turns and the Peugeot labors slowly up a lumpy trail. Then it nose-dives suddenly and I grab the loop. We crawl down a steep gravel drive and onto a green plateau high above the water.

"This is incredible."

I step out of the car. There is a cottage set back against the cliff-face, a neat whitewashed cube between twinned chimneys. Seagulls scissor and cry overhead. A patch of heather ripples with the breeze. Stone steps fall away over the edge and shoelace down, down to the churning sea.

The red door opens, fluttering the cutwork linen in its window.

"J-J, I'm so glad you came."

It is a very tall, very beautiful man with a rich, deep voice. He kisses Jean-Jacques on both cheeks, twice each, then wraps his arms around him and squeezes hard. Then he faces me. "This must be Meg. I am Benoît." He bows, his massive hand spread across his chest, and kisses my cheeks four times. Then he leads us into the cottage. "Watch out for your head," he pronounces, but only he has to duck.

We are in a tiny flagstoned kitchen, with a row of bubbled windows looking out toward the sea. A woman sways through the inner door. She is very small and very beautiful, too, with a rich, deep voice. She gathers a great mass of black curls on her head and jams a chopstick through.

"Hello, Meg. Annick." She kisses me warmly, fingers the Arabic scarf around my neck and raises a black eyebrow at Jean-Jacques. Then she kisses him and trails his ponytail through her open palm. "Never a haircut. Still a hippie." She ambles, flat-footed, into the inner room. "Come in. You're lucky you found us here. We're rehearsing in Bordeaux tomorrow."

Jean-Jacques whispers close into my ear. "Actors."

"Ah." Somehow this explains a lot.

The room is a bazaar of pillows and tapestries and rugs and throws, South American and Asian and Indian and African. The fireplace is full of candles. The walls are lined with vertical piles of yellowed paperbacks wrapped in wax paper. CDs and video cassettes, hand-labeled, fill the corners. Two scripts lie face down, open, on the floor. The ashtray is overflowing.

Annick sinks into a pillow. Benoît picks up ceramic plates and carries them to the kitchen. "So you are working on a book, you two?" he intones through the door.

"Yes." My French sounds thin and nasal. I smooth my skirt around my knees and sink into a pillow, too. "Well . . ."

Jean-Jacques looks at me. "Yes, we are. Its name is *Vive l'histoire*."

"*Vive l'histoire.* 'Long live history.'" Annick spreads it through the air before her, a cigarette dangling from her full lips. She lights it. "Sounds *very* dramatic."

"It's not," I say. "In fact it's not turning out the way I meant . . ."

"Mayg is a historian."

I shoot him a nervous look.

"Well, she's a writer who studied history. And we're pursuing historic moments in France. And I am photographing them."

I shake my head and sigh.

Annick's brow furrows slightly. "I can't quite picture—"

"Never mind," I say.

"It's for American readers, this book?"

"Well, yes."

"And with the current misunderstandings you're not afraid to represent our *belle France* to an audience that's less than receptive? Americans seem more interested in our eating habits these days than our culture."

"I haven't really been following all that. It seems so silly somehow."

"And here in Bretagne you are . . . ?"

"Annick! Let her breathe!" Benoît commands from the kitchen. He comes out with Japanese tea bowls steaming.

"In Bretagne we are . . ." I look desperately at Jean-Jacques. I flush.

He shrugs, settles onto the cushion beside me, and lays a light hand on the back of my neck.

"It's okay, Mayg."

Annick pulls smoke wisps up her nostrils and studies us. "I see." Then her mouth spreads into an affectionate smile. "I thought I recognized the scarf."

10 PM: The sun is lowering and the sea is flooded with neon. We are outside, seated around a wooden table among the heather and despite the steady salt breeze we are wrapped in a pocket of stillness. The plates are full of cheese scraps and the wine bottles are running low. Our chairs are turned toward the sea.

Benoît and Annick are telling stories. His long body slouches gracefully in the folding chair, a huge batik scarf wrapping his neck and shoulders. His hands are gesturing wide. The sound of his voice is magnificent and he is enjoying it as much as we are.

"So King Arthur returned to Camelot and found Lancelot there with his beloved Guinevere, sleeping in her arms."

Jean-Jacques is smoking and watching the sea. His hand rests over mine, his thumb tracing my palm.

"King Arthur's pain was great, but his wisdom was greater. Loving Guinevere as he did, he knew the passion his knight felt for her and respected him all the more. His wife was his gift to his closest friend."

Waves seethe over the cliffs below, then churn slowly away, hissing.

Annick speaks first. "I liked *my* story better. Viviane and Merlin trapped in eternal love, mutually bewitched, the glass tower . . . It's kind of a happy ending, at least."

Jean-Jacques' fingers separate mine and weave between them. Annick looks at our hands.

"So how long have you two . . . ?"

But Benoît interrupts. "One more bedtime story. Tristan and Isolde. Another good Breton tale. A true *histoire vivante*. Perhaps you can photograph it. Tristan was a prince of ancient Brittany . . ."

"No. This one's mine, *chéri*." Annick rises and stands against the sunset. She is barefoot, her skirt billowing, and her hair has come down from its stick.

"Tristan was a powerful prince whose kingdom commanded all the coast of Brittany," she declaims. "He was the nephew of Marke, King of Cornwall, and served as his most loyal soldier, faithful and true."

Benoît leans forward, searching his pockets for a lighter. "Why is it always the most loyal . . ."

"Hush, *espèce de con*. Let me tell it." She takes a deep breath and begins again.

"He was a passionate man, of quick temper and fierce devotion. His task: To sail to Ireland to escort the Princess Isolde to Cornwall to be married to his uncle, the King."

Her voice is voluptuous, thrilling. It rises up out of her and pours forth like singing. "In Cornwall, Tristan confronted Isolde's betrothed, the faithless Morold, cut off his head, and sent it back to Ireland. So loyal was he to Marke, his Cornish king."

Annick lowers her eyes. "But Isolde has learned of Tristan's deed.

Loathe to marry King Marke and despising Tristan, she vows to kill herself and take Tristan with her as final vengeance. Wise in the arts of her mother, a sorceress, she prepares a poison death potion.

"But Brangäne, her lady in waiting, panics. She hides the poison cup. She secretly replaces it with one of her lady's own love philters, more powerful than poison, as eternal in its reach as death.

"Isolde offers the cup to Tristan in a treacherous toast of 'friendship,' with none but the intent of murdering him and dying herself. He bows and drinks. Then she wrests the cup from his hands and drains it."

Annick's voice drops to a hoarse whisper. "The power of the philter is mighty. The cup falls to the floor. The two, once enemies, gaze into each other's eyes. They wait to die. They fall into one another's arms instead."

She bows her head, an aureole against the burnishing light. A breeze whirls around her ankles and flutters the hem of her skirt. Her feet are wide apart.

"Their love is stronger now than they themselves. But King Marke knows nothing. He places the royal mantle over her shoulders and marries Isolde."

My throat catches. A sound slips out. My fingers cover my mouth.

"Isolde longs to be in Tristan's arms. He remains in Cornwall living only for the moments when they can be together. When King Marke is off on a hunt she signals for him, waving her scarf from the ramparts. Tristan comes to her."

Jean-Jacques is sitting very still.

"They embrace in an ecstasy so powerful it is like pain. They cry for death so that they may be forever united beyond the reach of King Marke and the world. But King Marke strides in and finds them. Tristan shields her naked body with his cloak. The king's servant is unable to restrain himself. He raises his sword. Tristan faces him and lowers his own, willingly embracing the servant's blade."

No one breathes. Even Benoît listens.

"Mortally wounded, Tristan returns to his castle on the coast of Brittany. Isolde sails to him with healing potions and throws herself into his arms. But the wound is too advanced. He dies in her rapturous embrace.

"King Marke arrives. Brangäne has confessed her ruse and King Marke has forgiven the bewitched lovers. He comes to give Isolde to her beloved. Too late. He finds his loyal Tristan dead and Isolde weeping over his lifeless body. She expires of grief. The lovers are united in death at last."

There is a long silence. Annick stands, head down, arms hanging at her sides.

Then Benoît raises broad hands and slowly applauds. "Excellent. Wonderful," he says. "But I thought it was the *king* who wounded Tristan, not the loyal henchman . . ."

"Hush," she hisses.

Jean-Jacques is lighting a cigarette. I am grateful for the darkness because my face is bathed with tears.

2 AM: Jean-Jacques and I lie on the futon, whispering, me gulping back quiet sobs. Annick and Benoît are sleeping in the open loft upstairs. "Tomorrow we'll drive to the northern coast," he hushes in my ear. "Anywhere. It doesn't matter. Nowhere."

"Why? Why? I should go home to my family. I can't do this."

"We'll be together this week. *Écoute.* We'll figure it out."

"There's nothing to figure out. We know that."

Saturday, 9 AM: The mood at the breakfast table is subdued. Annick is packing in the next room. Benoît smokes thoughtfully. "I haven't played Bordeaux in ten years."

Jean-Jacques reaches for his cigarettes.

"You still on the outs with your family there?" Benoît asks.

"Of course," he says without looking up.

"Your mother? Your sister?" Benoît smokes. "You know what we're playing in the Grand-Théâtre? *Antigone.* Not the Greek one. The Anouilh, from the war years. I am, of course, King Creon." He expands his arms grandly. Then he leans forward and puts a broad hand on Jean-Jacques' shoulder. "I have been thinking about you a lot. It's strange you called. The play has so much of your story in it." His stage voice suddenly rolls forth like thunder.

"Don't judge me. Don't you judge me too."

Annick returns the cue through the doorway.

> *"That great force, that courage, this giant god who took me in his arms and saved me from monsters and shadows, that was you . . . ?"*

I look up at Jean-Jacques' face. It is carefully closed.

"J-J, *écoute*. You made your point, but there's no reason to cut yourself off, close yourself up in a tomb, *mon vieux*. It's ancient history. Your father has been dead for fifteen years."

Jean-Jacques' cigarette glows a deep-red ash. "My mother still sleeps in his bed." He gets up abruptly and carries the bowls to the sink.

"Now you sound like Hamlet. Come *on*, J-J. You want her to kill herself?"

Annick returns her cue again.

> *"O Hamlet, speak no more: Thou turn'st mine eyes into my very soul, and there I see such black and grained spots as will not leave their tinct."*

Jean-Jacques hovers over the sink. His shoulders sag a little.

Benoît looks at me and shrugs. I am privy to something I don't understand.

"So, how's Renée?" Benoît aims a fresh voice toward Jean-Jacques' back. "She happy in her new life?"

Jean-Jacques suddenly laughs so the windows rattle. "Yes. Yes, I think she is very happy. I don't know about Robert though."

Annick leans into the room, smoldering cigarette caught in her lips. "You kids on the road today or do you want to stay? The house is empty. We'll be in Bordeaux for weeks. Nothing in the fridge, I'm afraid. We planned to close up."

I sit up and glance around. My eyes still feel puffy from last night. "I really—I really need to get home."

"'Home'?"

Annick takes the cigarette out of her mouth. She peers into my face. Then her eyes move to the scar on my empty ring finger. *"Ah bon. Ah bon! . . . Madame?"*

Benoît looks sharply over at Jean-Jacques, who is screwing the coffeepot shut. Then he looks at Annick.

She shrugs one shoulder. "Come on, Bennie. We have to catch the train." She hauls her wool knapsack into the kitchen. Benoît unfolds himself and goes for his. She lifts a set of keys out of her bag.

"J-J, listen. Take the house keys. Stay here if you like. Lock it when you leave. But *sois prudent*." She stretches up and plants four kisses on his cheeks. Almost motherly.

She takes my shoulders and probes my eyes. "Be careful with our J-J," she says. Then she kisses me, too.

Their car pulls away and Jean-Jacques and I stand in the kitchen looking at the floor.

Be careful with our J-J.

It's the first time it has occurred to me that this could hurt Jean-Jacques, too. I am aware of his eyes on me.

"Stay the night with me," he says. "If you have to go home, you can go home tomorrow. Stay tonight."

I nod. He smiles a little, turns his back and puts the coffee on the stove.

11 AM: A clock ticks on the mantelpiece. We are alone. We drink our coffee. Then, strangely awkward, we wander the cottage, sorting curiously through the CDs and scripts and books, admiring exotic bibelots.

Jean-Jacques tugs out a homemade video. "I remember this. *Les liaisons dangereuses*. Comédie Française. I saw them in this. They were new together and they were incredible to see. Spit. Sweat. Sparks flying. I thought they would melt the stage."

"They *are* larger than life."

"They are. I've known Benoît since we were little and he's always been grandiose." He laughs. "I took pictures of him in Carnaval costumes. I wonder what happened to those photos?"

"In Pauillac maybe?" I nudge gently. "At home?"

He quickly shelves the video. "And here's *Henry V* from Avignon."

"Shakespeare doesn't work in French." I say it hastily, categorically, flushing.

"Well, I find it beautiful. But I'm not a scholar like you."

We look in the kitchen. He opens cupboards. "We'll have to eat something, you know. We have the picnic things from Thursday."

Barely touched. We pull them out of the fridge and sort. "Two days in a hot car didn't do the pâté any good." I toss it into the garbage.

Jean-Jacques smells the cheese. "*Époisses* okay."

"How can you tell? It always smells horrible."

"Chèvre fine. Sausages fine. Fruit fine. Wine fine. Bread long gone. We could make croutons maybe? Biscuits for breakfast. Butter . . ." He waggles his hand ambiguously. His head is deep in the fridge, echoing. "They left ham from last night. An onion. And eggs, good eggs. Omelette? I saw wild garlic on the cliff. And some fennel by the car. And I think this is the last of the cherries."

possibilities

I rest my hand on his back, my heart swelling.

12 PM: We fill a basket with food and carry it down the stone stairs to the sea. The descent is harrowing, the steps slippery from spray and carpeted with moss and heather. I grip the cable that serves as a railing and make my way slowly. The day is hot and bright but here the air is cold.

I packed only sundresses. I cuddle my pullover around me and climb on.

At the bottom of the cliff, the sea is seething around an endless jumble of black-gold stones. Kelp writhes in the washing waves.

Jean-Jacques is standing on a flat rock.

"Is the tide going in or out?" I ask.

"Don't know. We'll see."

We settle on the rock and spread out our picnic. The sun feels warm. He opens the wine and fills two jelly glasses.

" 'Me, I prefer my Romanée in a jelly glass,' " I quote. His ears flush.

"Okay, maybe I was a little grandiose myself there. But she . . . Renée . . . she gets to me."

"That's okay. You get to me."

Dumb. Lame. A cheap phrase for an inexpressible feeling. A feeling neither of us dares express.

He laughs, his eyes down.

We eat, side by side.

2 PM: I lie stretched on stone, basking. Jean-Jacques is climbing over the rocks, pant legs rolled up, his feet bare. "Look how the tide's dropping," he says. I sit up. The rocks are exposed all around us and the sea has retreated, leaving only pockets of crystal water in the hollows of barnacled stone. I tie my sweater around my waist and pick my way over to him. The tidal pools are alive with creatures — darting needlefish, miniature crabs, an eel. We climb out farther. My sandals slip on the kelp that slicks the bared stone. I crouch and move on all fours.

"Jean-Jacques, I'm too old for this!"

"No, you're not. Come on!"

Suddenly he stands straight upright and cheers like a schoolboy. *"Ouah!"* he whoops. "Look! *Moules!*"

I follow his pointing finger and squint at a pile of seaweed. "Those aren't mussels, that's kelp!"

"No, it's not." He pulls his knife out of his hip pocket. "Look!" He digs and pries until a handful of blue-black shells come free, clustered tight. "See?"

"You're right." I hold them up to the sky. "They're beautiful!" Light glows through banded amber brushed with purpling blue. They are dripping on my face.

He takes them back. "Here!" We squat together like toddlers and I watch while he twists one free then flicks away its top. He passes it to me. I slurp. He opens the others and we slurp them, too.

Then we clamber out toward the open sea, kicking and prying and tearing with our nails, with rocks, with shells. We're laughing.

"Dinner!" he shouts. He strips off his t-shirt and we fill it till it sags. I gather up the picnic. He stands there looking at me. I hold the baskets close. Then we climb up the steps to our cottage.

4 PM: I lie under him on the futon shaking, my eyes veiled. His arms spread weakly above my head, his fingers still gripping my hair. He shudders again. I feel him slipping out of me and close my thighs.

"Don't go." The words slipped out of me.

He gasps a laugh.

"Don't *you* go."

I take his face in my hands and kiss the sweat away.

8 PM: We are showered now and playing house. I have braided back his hair and tied my own in a knot. He stands in the kitchen in drawstring pants, chopping onions with long fingers. I am wrapped in his sweater, melting butter in a pot. My thighs drip. He blots it away with a tea towel. We cook. The windows are open and a steady breeze blows in.

"You said you watched me at Arles. Eating. What did you think of me then?"

"I thought you were *chiante*. A pain."

"I know *that*. But I mean . . ."

He studies the chopping board. His knife hovers a moment. "It was the way you tasted food. The way you drank wine. Your mouth. You were so . . . *aroused*. It made me wonder. I couldn't help but wonder."

I slip a buttery finger into his mouth. "And?"

"I was right."

"Still think I'm a *casse-couille?*"

He lays the knife on the cutting board and slides his hands into the sweater. Onion rises from warm wool. He doesn't speak.

I fight for words. "Nikos said I was okay when I got off my high horse."

"Mm . . . okay . . . yes . . . pretty good for an American . . . *Aïe! Arrête!*"

"Mm."

"And you thought I was . . . ?"

"Mm. I don't know the word for . . . 'jerk' in French."

"Mm."

"I meant to look it up."

"Mm."

". . . always . . . bolting . . ."

He comes up for air. "I'm not bolting now."

10 PM: The door is thrown open wide to clear away the burned-onion smell and the sunset slants in rosy gold. We have lit the candles in the fireplace and sit cross-legged on the futon eating the *moules* with our hands, one hinged shell pinching the flesh from another. They are exquisite. Sweet. Nutty. The croutons float in the fennel-scented broth and we slurp the flavor out and crunch.

Midnight: He is smoking beside me. I lie on my stomach, my arm flung over his chest. His profile is sketched in gilt relief by the candles. He is staring at the ceiling beams, thinking.

I am thinking, too.

I have to go home.

This isn't real.

Sunday, 6 AM: "Don't go." Now he is shaking, shuddering, holding on hard.

It's my turn to gasp.

"I'm not going anywhere. I'm staying here with you."

9 AM: "We can't stay here all day."

"Why not?"

"We need food," he says.

"Food."

"There's a market in Pont-Croix."

"How do you know?"

"I asked Benoît."

I prop up on my elbow and look hard into his face.

"Jean-Jacques. Tell me you didn't plan for us to come here. Don't laugh that *laugh!* I need to trust you. Please. Tell me you didn't plan this."

He drags a tangle of hair out of my eyes. "I didn't plan this."

I flop down, relieved, on his chest.

"I called Benoît before. I thought I might come here after you left."

"Left?"

"When . . . if you went home. I thought you might get scared."

I digest this. "I am scared."

He hooks my hair behind my ear. "Me, too."

11 AM: My vintage silk sundress slides pleasantly over my skin as I walk down the cobblestones of Pont-Croix. Everything slides pleasantly over my skin, the warm sea breeze, my loosened hair, Jean-Jacques' hand on the small of my back. I am brazenly happy.

The streets are lined with low granite storefronts, window frames painted bright. The tree-framed marketplace is crowded with stands. It is a small town market, far from the tourist-clogged coast, so there are no souvenir stands. The farmers are in their glory, folding tables heaped with their own greens and fruit. The season is peaking and everything is possible.

We hunch together over the stands, squeezing and smelling and tasting. We fill our baskets. Berries. Smoked fish. Milky summer oysters. Jean-Jacques takes pictures. At a *brocante* stand I buy a starched lace *coiffe*. Jean-Jacques buys me a yellowed copy of *Tristan et Iseult*. We drift down to the place de l'Eglise and settle into café chairs. We order the blackboard menu. There is *cotriade,* first the briny broth ladled into our crockery bowls, then the fish and shells heaped in after. We draw the flesh off the bones with our teeth and sop the dish with bread. We spoon raspberries and cream into each other's mouths. We drink too much Muscadet, we dip sugar cubes in our tiny black coffees and suck the flavor out. We kiss.

Jean-Jacques goes to the car for cigarettes. I feel charged with the power of love. Love. I say the word out loud in my head.

I am just finishing my coffee when the music rises. A droning, mournful, murmuring chant. Somewhere there are monotonous drums. People are scraping back their chairs and lining the *place.* I go, too.

There is a procession coming down the street. I see velvet banners raised high bobbing toward me. Rows of marchers come into focus. There are men in dark suits, women in chaste skirts and stiff-starched *coiffes.* Four boys in sailor middies. A cassock, draped in prayer beads. They are chanting softly, heads low. A tall brass crucifix sways precariously past.

"What is it?" I whisper to an old man beside me.

He looks up into my face. "The *pardon.*"

"What's that?" An old tradition—I know I read this somewhere. "I mean, what's it about?"

His wife leans between us. "It's the Pardon de Notre Dame. They come to ask Our Lady for protection, for forgiveness for their sins. It's been like this for a thousand years."

The chanting is very loud and very close. Jean-Jacques comes up beside me. He watches in silence. He raises his lens and shoots.

"Don't."

"It's beautiful."

"No."

"Yes."

I fall in behind the procession and follow them. Jean-Jacques follows me.

They are chanting and praying.

Our Lady, rich in pardon, forgive us our trespasses.

Others fall in with us. Grandmothers in blue-striped Sunday best, sons in tight acrylic suits, wives on their arms. Wives. Mothers.

Pardon us, protect us, give us grace, grant us peace.

They are pouring into the blackened granite church, anchored to the ground with thick buttresses of carved stone. Gargoyles arch leering from the eaves. I flow through the portal behind the supplicants.

Inside, the church is already packed, but soberly, regally. The people stand in silent rows and face the altar. The priest in a white soutane raises his hands.

I sink into a pew. I snatch for my sweater suddenly and pull it over my naked shoulders.

Our Lady, rich in pardon, forgive us our trespasses.

1 PM: The mass is over and the crowd has dispersed, their penitential mood dissolving away easily in the festive air. They are heading for the *kermesse,* the community festival.

I am still sitting in the pew.

Jean-Jacques comes up behind me. "Come on, let's go." He sounds chastened, too.

I don't move. He sits down beside me and reaches for my hand. I pull it away. "I have to go back."

"To the cottage?"

"Back home."

"Come on, Mayg. Come with me. Let's get a coffee. We can talk. We had too much wine. I'm sorry."

"Jean-Jacques, it's wrong. What we're doing."

He waits. Then he sighs heavily. "Come on, Mayg." He takes my arm and leads me to the church door.

Wincing in the daylight, I fumble for the cell phone. It's been off since . . . Friday? I hold down the Yes button and punch in the code. Jean-Jacques pivots away and lights a cigarette.

Nigel picks up. There is a roar of white noise—television, men's laughter, a woman's rowdy hoot. Gerald is barking, barking.

"Nigel? Can you hear me?"

"Hello love, how's the book coming along—bloody dog—?"

"Okay. Nigel, can I talk to the kids?"

"Sorry? Didn't quite catch."

"Can I talk to the children?"

"Darling, I'm sorry, I can't hear. Bugger. Ian, bloody hell, *would you turn that down?*"

The noise dims slightly.

"Can I talk to the kids."

"Right. Well, Kate's about somewhere. Kate? Been playing in the barn. Here she is, then."

I hear thick, wet breathing on the line.

"Kate? Honey, is that you? It's me, Mama."

"Maman?"

"Yes, sweetheart. I'm on a trip far away, but I'm still in France. Are you all right? What have you been doing?"

"Playin'."

"Playing?"

"In the barn."

I swallow. "Not near the hole, I hope, honey."

"Nope. The hole is always there. It's e-nor-mous." She breathes eagerly. I can hear her wipe her nose on her sleeve, the way she does when she recites a poem. "Bloody builder's done fuck-all."

"Kate!"

There is an explosion of male laughter. Nigel snatches the phone away. "Don't worry, darling, Geoffrey put her up to it. Just taking the piss out of you. Miss you, m'dear. Keep up the good work!"

There is a click and a dial tone.

I stand blinking at the phone.

Keep up the good work.

I turn and head back for the church door. My breath is short. I seesaw a little, right and left. Home. Him.

"Mayg." Jean-Jacques intercepts me and takes me by the elbows. Steadies me, like on the *haras* grounds. He kisses my forehead, my cheeks, my eyes. He lays his scarf over my shoulders and kisses my mouth. I calm a little. We walk back to the *place*.

The streets are full of people. The same people who walked so solemnly this morning, praying forgiveness, are red in the face now and laughing out loud. They are wolfing down crêpes and guzzling another bowl of cider. Mothers. Wives. Children. Husbands. Grandmothers. Nuns. An old man is dancing with a little girl. Two teenagers are kissing as if they could find the answer to life at the back of their partner's throat.

give us grace, grant us peace

I slip my arm through Jean-Jacques'. We walk to the car and drive back to the cottage. I leave the phone in the car.

6 PM: Side by side in the kitchen, we unpack our market goods.

"There's enough here for an army," I say.

"We're staying here. I don't want to go out again—you might run away. I've hidden the car keys."

"Besieged." I smile. I am beginning to feel happy again.

I fill a wooden bowl with cherries. Jean-Jacques counts the eggs into a wire basket and drapes the oysters with a wet towel. We open our waxed-paper packages like Christmas gifts. There are cheeses rolled in herbs, a scoop of butter sparkling with sea salt, smoked mackerel dappled bronze, shortbread galettes, a hand-lettered jar of blackberry jam. We carry the cherries down the stone steps and sit on the table-rock, throwing the pits into the sea.

Monday, 3 PM: "Where are all the pleasure boats? It's summer!" I stand on the far end of the rocks, looking across the clean horizon. Audierne was seething with tourist yachts and catamarands. No one cruises past our private inlet.

"Too many rocks. Bad tides, maybe."

It's too good to be true. I take off my sandals, lift my skirt, and wade in.

"Ouch! Oooh! Ouch!" I mince back onto the rock. I peer into the water. "Sea urchins! We can't swim here. We can't even wade."

Blood trickles off my feet. I dabble them in the tidal pool. Jean-Jacques picks his way back carefully, pries a few urchins out of a pool with his folding knife, and carries them to me. Then he cracks them open and spoons the coral jelly out with a mussel shell. It slips into my mouth. Intense. Insubstantial.

We climb back up the steps. We can hear nothing but the sea.

11 PM: Jean-Jacques stands in his drawstring pants, whisking an omelette. I am slicing bread, his scarf around my hips. I spread a chunk with butter and bring it to his mouth. I rest my ear on his bare shoulder and listen to him chew.

"You haven't been smoking so much lately."

"Mm." He presses buttery lips into my hair.

2 AM: I wake up with a start. He is propped on one elbow looking at me.

Tuesday, 10 AM: "Do you realize we haven't mentioned the book since Friday?"

I stir my coffee, standing by the window. Jean-Jacques is smearing blackberry jam on a galette.

"Book? What book?"

I narrow my eyes at him. "There must be a pile of messages from Nikos waiting for me. I haven't sent him a word in weeks."

He crunches thoughtfully.

"I don't even know what I'm going to write for Bretagne. Maybe we should go to Carnac after all. See the *menhirs,* the Druid standing stones."

"We have a lot of pictures of rocks already."

"I know, but at least they're still there. Not like the forest of Brocéliande."

Only a little smile. "And the *pardon* yesterday? I got some good stuff. That's the real thing. Been coming to that church for a thousand years."

I sigh. "Another one of your Vibrant Traditions."

"It could work."

"I'm losing this battle, aren't I?"

He pads to his camera bag and pulls out the digital. Then he comes up behind me and holds the viewer out. He advances through the pictures one by one, his cheek against mine. A grandmother in a stiff lace *coiffe,* her face somber and proud. A little boy in cadet blue pacing beside his father. Velvet banners, embroidered in gold, the Queen of Heaven's hands raised in blessing. A priest's hand fingering rosary beads. Feet treading even steps on grey cobblestones.

"They're gorgeous, Jean-Jacques, but they're so noble and sad."

"That's okay. It was." He clicks ahead. There are two old men in flat caps and stiff Sunday suits lifting bowls of cider to their lips, their faces furrowed with laughter. A rose-cheeked girl licking jam from her cake. A baby smashing a crêpe into its face, Nutella in its hair.

I laugh. "Okay. Okay. I'll write, I don't know, 'Forgiveness through Food.' Or something. I'll think of something when I get back."

"You're not going back." His lips on my shoulder.

I check my breath. I feel a chill. "Jean-Jacques, you know I . . ."

"I've lost the car keys."

That laugh.

2 PM: Now he's not laughing. We're walking along the clifftop in a steady sea wind. His hands are in his pockets. I have my hands up my sweater sleeves, braced against the blast.

"How long have you and Nigel been married?"

"Nine years. Ten."

"How did you meet?"

"Jean-Jacques, let's not . . . there's no point . . ."

"How did you meet?"

"He was at Cambridge. He bought me a drink in a pub."

"Just like that. And you married him."

"Well, there was stuff in between. My parents had just died and I was on my own."

"Why did you fall for him?"

"Jean-Jacques . . ."

"Why did you fall in love with him? Why do you love him? It's important."

That word. I walk, shivering. "He seemed so worldly, I guess. Seems silly now, he's anything but. And grown up. Courtly. That *accent*. He was smart. He made me laugh. And he quoted Shakespeare. He still quotes Shakespeare."

"I can quote Molière. Well, not really."

"*Don't.* Please. It's a kind of nervous tic, really. His mind is always searching for words, for phrases. He's like a little English island unto himself, in France. He does crossword puzzles too."

"So? What else? Does he love you?"

Love. I walk and think. "I think he *likes* me. He likes the *idea* of me . . . simple, wholesome. He likes my American *plainness*. I think it makes him feel superior."

"You said he patronizes you."

"Yes." I think. "It's almost as if he colonizes me. Like he does France."

We walk a while.

"Do you still love him?"

I start to walk faster.

"Jean-Jacques, don't."

He catches up and blocks my path.

"Do you love him now?"

My hair is blowing into my eyes. I can't see a thing. "I don't know, I don't know, we have children together, there's the house, there's Gerald, we're *married*."

"Gerald?"

"The dog."

"Ah."

He steps aside and we begin walking again.

9 PM: The candles in the fireplace are replaced with a driftwood fire. There are empty oyster shells scattered over the sheets. He is resting his cheek on my belly. I am shaking all over, still white hot.

"Are you always like this?" he asks.

I reach down and lay an electrified hand on his hair. I gasp a little. "What?"

"Like this. With Nigel."

"Don't." I turn my face away. He pulls himself up to my face and turns it back. He bites at my lips. His tongue tastes like the sea.

"No, I'm not."

"Too bad for Nigel."

"No." I breathe in and return to earth. "He'd be sick at the thought," I blurt. "And if I tried to—tried to—he'd die laughing." It just slips out. Then I wish it hadn't. Oh god. The windows rattle with Jean-Jacques' laugh.

"Don't laugh. Don't! It's just that he's . . . embarrassed. He likes to keep things kind of cozy and silly. And he doesn't like . . . oysters."

His long fingers are tracing circles around my breasts, down to my navel, around the triangle of hair. My knees part all by themselves.

"And the cherries? Where have they gone to?" He gropes for the wooden bowl. "Time for dessert."

It's my turn to laugh. "Don't *you* be silly. Please."

But he's suddenly, intently, serious.

Wednesday, 2 PM: We are climbing into the tidal pools wearing nothing but sneakers. The rocks are slick but the tide is rising. Jean-Jacques crawls carefully down the table-rock and slips into the water.

"Aïe! *Putain!* It's *freezing.*" He huddles, hops up and down. Then he reaches for me and drags me in, too.

"God! Oh! *Oh! I can't!*"

The ache rises up my legs and back until my head pounds.

"Only one way to do this. One . . . two . . . three!" He dives and emerges, spluttering, hair running rivulets across his face. "Now you!" he gasps.

I dive, too. The cold seizes me, wrenches me, pulls at my teeth and skull. I stroke ahead and under. The water flows over my skin and I kick hard. When I come up, I am laughing and shuddering and clean.

7 PM: We are washing dishes side by side at the sink. Jean-Jacques rinses and dries. I am bundled in his sweater and scarf. Water is spattering on the floor, mingling in onion scraps, shreds of greens, smudges of tidal mud.

"What was Benoît talking about? Your mother and sister? The Antigone stuff?"

"Forget it." He turns away and puts a crockery bowl in the cupboard.

"Why is it such a big secret?"

"I told you. I broke with my family. That's all."

"Why don't you want to talk about it?"

"Everybody wants to talk about it. I don't want to talk about it."

"Why not?"

He pats his drawstring pants for his cigarettes. There are no pockets. He goes into the salon by the fire and comes back lighting one.

"*Écoute,* Mayg. You and Benoît and Annick, you get all mixed up about *histoires* and *histoire.* Stories and history. You think everything can be told in a neat story. Like a movie. Beginning, middle, end. Happy ending. Tragic ending. Victory in battle. Loss in love. You like to think about that stuff a lot. I don't. I don't have a story for you to . . . research. To write. To dramatize."

He sucks the cigarette till it glows.

"Jean-Jacques, that's not fair."

He spreads his hands and shrugs.

"That's not fair. Everywhere we go, people talk to you about it. Your friends. People you hardly know. Waiters. Colleagues. Your 'story' seems to be practically famous. Why can't I know?"

"I closed a door. I don't want to open it. You wouldn't understand."

I wash two plates and rinse them. "Okay. But when you love somebody . . ."

The word floats out and hangs in the air, changing the subject abruptly. I wish I could reel it in. Jean-Jacques puts out his cigarette. He dries a plate, then another.

"It's true," he says quietly. "I do love somebody."

My breath catches slightly.

"But she's married."

That word hangs in the air too. *Married.* It's as if one word snuffs out the other.

He sets down the towel. "Mayg," he says. *"Je t'aime, tu sais."*

I love you, you know.

My eyes close.

I say it out loud, too. *"Moi aussi, je t'aime."*

Then I open my eyes. We stand there, looking at the dirty floor.

Thursday, 2 PM: We are reading on the cushions. Jean-Jacques is reading a wax-papered *Antigone,* frowning. I am reading *Tristan et Iseult.* I sigh.

"Isolde didn't have kids."

He looks up, shifting with effort from his story to mine. He fishes for a cigarette. He holds it unlit for a while.

"I love kids. Mayg. I've always . . . You know I could . . ."

"Don't. Please, don't."

He lights. He blows out a stream of smoke.

We go back to our stories.

8 PM: Jean-Jacques is sliding an enormous fish on a roasting pan, deep into the oven. "Where on earth did you get that?" I say. "Did you spear it in a tidal pool or what?" It is a sea bass as big as a cat. Its eye gleams, fresh and rounded.

"I went into town while you were sleeping this morning. The fishermen were just coming in."

"That's great! But . . ." I stop. My mind adjusts. Reality. I didn't want to know. "Then you hadn't really lost the car keys."

"No, I hadn't really lost the car keys."

He closes the oven door and faces me. "I will take you back when you want."

"I don't want."

"When you need."

"Okay."

Midnight: I'm dozing by the fire, sated. There is a roasting pan on the hearth with two forks, a skeleton picked clean. The wine bottle is empty.

"Leave him."

"Mm?"

"Just leave him."

I'm suddenly wide awake. Jean-Jacques is sitting on a pillow, look-ing into the flames and smoking. I sit up and wrap the quilt around me.

"You don't love him."

I look at him. His face is concentrated, intense, fixed on the fire-place.

My mouth feels dry. "Jean-Jacques, this isn't real."

"It feels pretty real to me." He throws his cigarette into the fire.

1 AM: He is feeding his intensity into me, concentrated, searing-hot, un-til I feel it, too.

an ecstasy so powerful it is like pain

Friday, 9 AM: Daylight. Reality.

I can hear the mantel clock ticking.

Jean-Jacques pulls the car keys out of a high kitchen cupboard and hands them to me. When I push through the red door he is standing, looking at his bare feet. I get my phone out of the front seat and tap 888 for messages.

> *Vous avez trois messages.*
> *Hello, love, just a quick ring to see how you are. Kids miss you. We all do, darling. Bye.(click)*

Then:

> *Hello, love, just a quick ring, hoping to hear from you. Children are well. Bye for now. (click)*

Then, in a gruffer voice:

> *Hello, love, was rather hoping to catch you. Bit of a problem here on the home front. Part of the barn wall has collapsed, I'm afraid. Nothing too serious really, roof is holding. Nobody hurt. Just wanted to . . . wanted to hear your voice. Well, do give a call. Please. Bye. (click)*

10 AM: I have washed the bedding and hung it on the line in the wind, where it flaps beside Jean-Jacques' scarf. He empties the refrigerator. I sweep the ashes from the fireplace and put the candles back. He mops the kitchen floor. We stretch the fresh-dried sheets onto the futon together. I pack the silken underwear I never wore. We carry our bags to the car.

We pull into the Versailles train station rental lot by three, in plenty of time for our trains. We kiss in the car, but it's not the same this time. We're not laughing anymore.

9 ⚜ Beachhead

Friday, August 1, 9 PM: I pull the Citroën slowly into the driveway. It's still light and the air is heavy with summer damp. The neighbor children are playing in the street. Cloey and Kate thread out the front door and wait shyly on the welcome mat. Cloey. Kate. I kneel and smell them, my lips against their smooth, sweaty necks, thin and strange to me.

Gerald tiptoes up to me, quivering, cowering, bathing my cheeks with his tongue. Then he sniffs hard once, his muzzle lowering. No! I am swatting his head away when Nigel comes out.

He looks very tall and very pale. I struggle to my feet, the children dragging awkwardly from my arms.

"Hello, love. Bad luck, eh?" He lays bud lips on my cheek. "Still, MacGregor's got everything under control." He leads me past my trapdoor and into the barn. Or rather into the back garden. There is no difference now. We are outdoors, sheltered only by the roof. There is a pile of rubble and stone where the wall used to be. A forest of metal trees has grown while I was away, bracing up every beam, every jagged edge.

"Oh, Nigel."

He rests his hand on my shoulder. "Good trip?"

"Yes."

We walk into the kitchen. Kate slides away and runs to fetch something. Cloey clings to me, his legs locked around my waist, his cheek on my neck. "Was it scary, my love? When the wall fell down?"

His head nods against me. "In the night! In bed!"

I kiss his rusty curls. They are so soft. Kate pads back into the room. "I *dessin*'d this for you."

"You drew me a picture? Thank you, sweetheart!" I draw her to me and we look together.

"That's the barn. That's the hole. And I *dessin*'d big poles in it to hold it up. Like in the *cathédrale*." There is a wide, grey box of a farmhouse with a red roof like ours. A black smear fills the middle of it. Two columns, drawn over the black with repeated coats of felt pen, bar the gap. "That's how the builder will fix it," she explains. "When he is coming back. He has done fuck-all—"

"That'll do Katharine, dear, enough of that. Had anything to eat, darling? Hair's nice like that. Done something different?"

It is tied at the nape of my neck with one of Jean-Jacques' elastics. I am wearing the scarf. "I had a sandwich." The last of the rillettes.

"Gin and tonic? Hot July night, just the ticket."

"Yes, thanks." I sink into a dining chair, pulling the children around me. Only now do I take in the room. There are four crates of empty bottles in the kitchen. Glasses are scattered everywhere. The stove is mounded with pots and pans two deep, dripping curry-yellow. Empty Sharwood's cans, shards of microwave puppadoms on the floor. Newspapers and socks and Duplos lie scattered. "Looks like a wall caved in here, too."

"Yes. Well. Been a bit distracted of late, what with the builders."

"We had lots of fun, *Maman*. There were loads of people and we had parties and Papa cooked."

"Yes, well, Ian was in town from London. And Geoffrey, you know. MacGregor."

The dining table is spread with architects' plans and spreadsheets. There is a heap of bills and a scratch pad. The copies of *Hill and Dale* have been kicked into a corner, face down.

He sets a glass in front of me, ice tinkling.

"Cheers."

"Cheers."

There is a silence. Kate lays her cheek on a spreadsheet. Cloey is curved, passively, into my neck.

"Cloey, how's my puppy dog? You haven't been barking at me! Lost your woof?"

He looks up at me with a shy smile. "Woof." But there's not much life in it.

"He's tired, darling. Had a rough night. Nightmare. Found him in the bed with me. He was asking for you, of course." He looks into his glass and takes a swallow. "Thanks for coming back so quickly. Hope you didn't interrupt anything. Story on track, is it?"

"Yes." I sip my drink, eyes down.

"Did try to reach you. Must have been out of range. Bloody antennas in France don't cover anything but Paris half the time." He takes another sip, looking at the tabletop. "Perhaps leave a fixed number, next time, from the hotel?"

"Yes, I should have. I—"

"*Maman!* Woof! WOOF!"

I am grateful for the interruption. I sweep Cloey into my arms and scratch his tummy until he screams. "Bedtime for puppies and little girls!" Then I take them both up to their baths.

I wash their bodies gently, warily, frightened by the softness of their hair, their skin. I kiss their foreheads and tuck them in. Then I stand under the shower rubbing baby oil onto my tender breasts, into the whisker scrapes on my neck and thighs. The water stings between my legs and I wince.

forgive us our trespasses
give us grace, grant us peace

I wrap myself in my kimono and go back downstairs. Nigel has the gin bottle on the table and is refilling his glass. He holds it up and cocks his head.

"Yes, please. Thanks."

I sit across from him. "What does MacGregor say? Raimondo's insurance will take care of this, right?" I look at the budget sheets. There are bold circles around some figures with lots of zeros. Too many zeros.

"Well, actually . . ."

I look up. He is shaking his head ruefully. "Afraid we'll have to absorb this, Megs love. The wall was old. Been doing a bit of juggling with the figures and if we just cut back on the finishing work, cut a few corners . . . been looking into cheaper flooring, that sort of thing."

He looks up brightly. "Good news, though. Raimondo's keen to take on the extra work. Should have it patched back together in no time!"

I stare at him. He catches my gaze, lowers his. He takes another sip. His cheeks are etched with ruby veins.

"Nigel." I drink, too.

"Hm?"

"Nigel, maybe . . . maybe we should call this whole thing off. The hole. The conservatory. We could build it back up like it was and . . . like it was before . . . we could . . ."

What am I saying? My eyes are burning with sudden tears. The gin. I blink them back.

He sits up. He lifts his chin, looks down his nose, with an effort sets his face along familiar lines. "Megs. Darling, if you'd only . . . You've got to get on *board*." He pats my hand. "It will be brilliant. You'll see. Brilliant."

Saturday, 7 AM: I sneak down the ladder while the children are still asleep. The rungs are thick with sand and I slip on them as I descend. All my collection has fallen from the walls and lies in a heap of dust and sand. There are fault lines jagging across the groin vault overhead. I brush the laptop lid carefully, wipe it, open it, and boot up.

There are three e-mails from Nikos.

> *how is bretagne coming?*

> *art ed needs mercantour text YESTERDAY.*

> *will call mon pm to talk through stories. hello? you and jj still on track?*

There are three jpegs from Jean-Jacques, only to me. I sit up, my heart surging. I open them slowly. The first is an oyster, open in the firelight, oozing with the milk of the summer spawn. The second is a close-up of the wooden bowl of cherries. One of them is bitten in half, the center a dark-traced slit in glistening flesh. The third is of me — Oh god. Oyster shells. Cherries. And . . . I stare. My hand rises to my mouth.

j'ai mordu dans le fruit de la vie

"Megs? Darling? You down there?"

I hit the Close button so hard the alarm signal beeps.

"Nigel?"

He never comes down here. His voice is coming from the top of the ladder.

"Megs, I meant to tell you last night. MacGregor thinks you really shouldn't go down there anymore. He thinks the ceiling might . . . he thinks it would be safer if you worked upstairs."

I freeze. I look desperately around me. My bunker.

"I could help you carry a few things up if you like."

"No! No, thanks, honey, that's all right. I—I don't think it's so bad down here."

I look at the cable snaking out the ventilation window. My lifeline.

"All right then, darling, but keep an eye on that ceiling."

His voice fades away.

8 AM: I am in the barn, dragging a metal brace across the floor toward my ladder.

4 PM: The children are at Mémé Mathilde's, sharing the plum tart we baked together. I am in my bunker, a metal column at my elbow bracing the ceiling over my head. I have cleaned up the dust and sand and set the *coiffe* on a shelf next to my képi. There's no room for the pith helmet now. I glance at the crumbling plaster above me. I put it on my head.

Thursday, 7 AM: *Tristan et Iseult* stands on the shelf next to *Légendes Bretonnes*. But I am not writing the Bretagne text. I am working on *La Vie en France.*

> *The verb* aimer *in French has many nuances for which there is no parallel in English. It can mean "to like" or "to love" and the listener must be attuned to the context.*
>
> *Il est très sympathique, mon collègue. Je l'aime bien.*
> He is very nice, my colleague. I like him.
> *Il aime nager en baskets, juste en baskets.*
> He likes to swim in sneakers, nothing but sneakers.
> *Je t'aime de tout mon coeur, de tout mon corps, je t'aime à la folie.*
> I love you with all my heart, with all my body, I love you madly.

9 PM: "I love you, sweetie. Sleep tight." I tuck the sheets over Cloey's tummy. He sighs, snuggles down, and kicks them off again. It's so hard for the kids to get to sleep when it stays light until ten.

I hang a sheet over Kate's curtains to block out the evening glow. "Better?"

"Mmph," she mumbles. "Better. *J't'aime, Maman.*"

"I love you, too."

Friday, 3 PM: "You don't love him."

"Jean-Jacques, *don't.* I can't talk to you now. The kids—"

"I want to talk to you. Nigel is at work, right?"

"Yes, but—"

"I want to talk to you in the daytime. I think about you. All the time. Not just . . ."

His lighter clicks. I shiver.

"I know. I think about you, too."

"You said 'this isn't real.'"

"I know."

"It's real, Mayg."

My eyes drift shut.

He smokes a while. "When can you meet me next?"

"Well the next story—"

"Which is—"

"You know, D-Day. The *débarquement.*"

There is a long pause. When he speaks again, his voice sounds like someone else. "Does it have to be?"

I sink into my chair. "Well, yes. I mean, Nikos agreed and we needed something more recent to balance out the other themes."

"Mayg, I don't want to do this."

"Why not?"

"I—I just don't. Let's find something else. Another story. Another battle. A different war. Verdun, maybe."

"They're not all about battles. There's Van Gogh."

I wince. There isn't Van Gogh anymore.

"Gypsies."

I am losing hold.

"*Écoute*," he says. "I don't care what we make the story into. I don't care about the book. Meet me somewhere. When?"

"Next week. Omaha Beach."

There is a heavy exhalation of smoke.

"Or Bayeux, next door," I offer.

"We've already been there. We met there, you remember."

"I remember."

"Why didn't we shoot the *débarquement* story then and get it over with?"

"Because—well, because you *bolted*, remember? Jean-Jacques, you hadn't even read the story list. Nikos said I needed to get your attention."

There is a pause. Then the pull on a cigarette. Then a soft exhalation.

I can hear a smile come back.

"You have my attention now."

Monday, 10 PM: I am drinking a gin and tonic with Nigel. The conservatory plans have been rolled up and put away. The table is waxed. There is a small vase at the center propping up a single rose from the one bush that survives at the edge of the rock pile.

"Been awfully quiet of late, Megs. Everything all right? Working hard?" Personal questions from Nigel. Unaccustomed. Oh dear.

"Mm. Just having trouble with the book. Wrenching it into shape. Sorting it out." I try to laugh lightly.

"Getting on all right with that photographer chap? Jean-Paul, is it?"

"Jean-Jacques."

"Right. Awful lot of time on the road. Thrown together a lot. He still being disagreeable about the—the history theme, is it? I know he was a bother at first, wasn't he?"

He is drinking his drink. He isn't looking at me. I brace myself for the lie.

"He's—still difficult. Pretty full of himself. Have to keep him on the subject, you know? Always off taking pictures of . . . of . . ."

Think, Meg, think.

". . . of food."

"Right. These fellows have their specialities, don't they?"

"Yes."

"How does his . . . wife? . . . feel about his being on the road so much? Has kids does he?"

"Yes, um, she's — she's fine, very supportive. They talk on the phone all the time, in fact, way too often. That's one of the problems with him, he's forever tapping out messages."

I am babbling falsehoods. I reach for my drink. The ice rattles on the way to my lips. I take a breath. "It's coming along fine. Everything's coming along. Fine."

"Good. That's good. Well, I'm off to bed. Coming up?"

"Later. I still have work to do."

He scrapes back his chair. His hand rests briefly on my shoulder. Then he heads upstairs.

I press my fingers to my eyes.

Lies.

I wait with my empty glass for a long time until I hear his snores. Then I head for my bunker.

Midnight: The new jpeg glows in the darkness. The futon, firelight, blackberry jam. Me, with galette crumbs. I gaze at it, shaking my head. How did he . . . ? When? There's only one word of text:

délicieuse

I shiver a little, remembering.

The phone rings and I reach for it. "Jean-Jacques?" I whisper.

"Nope. It's me, Nikos. Remember? The man who signs your paychecks."

"Oh! Hi, Nikos." I sit up sharp and click Close.

"You were expecting Jean-Jacques? Does that mean you are actually communicating with each other? Actually putting this book together?"

"We are, yes. We're . . . working on it."

"All I got from J-J last time was a bunch of stuff on a religious procession. We've already got a religious procession, with Gypsies. Don't you think it's a little redundant?"

"Well, the tone is very different."

"Okay, okay. If I had the text in front of me, maybe I'd *know* that. Maybe we can separate the stories in the front and back of the book. So where does that leave the Mercantour text? J-J's photos were in last month. Art department's climbing the walls."

"I'm working on it. I told you, lot of deadlines lately and the kids . . ."

"Deadlines? Deadlines. I've got deadlines too, Meg. Most of them are past already."

"Nikos, I'm really sorry. I'll get something to you before we go to Omaha Beach."

"Good. I'll be watching for it."

He clicks off.

Tuesday, 8 AM: World War II histories are piled around me. I mustn't get too bogged down in background this time. Still, D-Day doesn't make sense without understanding why France had to be liberated in the first place.

> *On June 17, 1940, the day Maréchal Pétain called for France to "cease combat" against the German onslaught, Charles de Gaulle evacuated to London. The next day he addressed the French people from a BBC radio studio, calling on them to rally and resist. "Must hope vanish? Is defeat definitive? No! France is not alone, she is not alone."*

> *France's humiliation was somewhat relieved by the creation of a "French" puppet regime, ostensibly self-ruled out of the capital city of Vichy. The northern territories, however, remained under the thumb of German occupation.*

> *Vichy Maréchal Pétain submitted to increasing manipulation by the Nazi conquerors. Anti-Semitic statutes were approved. Deportation of the Jews was practiced even more aggressively than under pure Nazi rule.*

D-Day, Meg. Get to D-Day.

> *Over four years the Germans had time to build up considerable fortifications along French shores. The Allies faced solid machine-gun nests and impenetrable bunkers armed with artillery.*

The element of surprise was key to Operation Overlord's success and despite foul weather the complex cooperative assault was launched. More than 150,000 American, British, and Canadian soldiers ferried across pitching waters, aiming for beaches dubbed Gold, Sword, Juno, Omaha and Utah.

I rub my eyes. I paste my notes into an e-mail to Jean-Jacques, but my finger hovers over Send. Maybe not. He doesn't seem that enthusiastic about the World War II stuff. But maybe this will help get him . . . on board.

Thursday, 6 PM: Nigel is paging through the day's mail. "What's this from Crédit Mutuel then? They've raised your premium, rather a lot."

Oh god. I managed to conceal the police papers, but I forgot about the car insurance for the Jeep. If I'd put it on my Visa card it would have been covered, no questions asked. I make a mental note for the future. The future?

"Rental car I scratched in Nice. Remember, I told you? They blew it all out of proportion. The parking garage . . ."

Lying is getting easier. False information pours out of me these days, the way text used to.

"I'll have a word with the agent. What's his name?"

"That's okay, honey, I'll take care of it."

"Right." He is looking at me. Is he looking at me?

Friday, 7 PM: *Tristan und Isolde* is playing, again, the love death, loud. The leg of lamb I bought at the butcher's lies on a cutting board. The children are in the apple tree outside the kitchen window. Nigel's watching Sky News in the back room. I fill my palm with olive oil and spread it on the red flesh. I sink the knife in along the bone and press whole peeled cloves of garlic deep inside and spear branches of rosemary after. I pestle black pepper slowly, my hand sliding on the wood, and rub it into folds of muscle. I push my hair out of my eyes with my forearm and wipe my hands on my apron. Then I sink the roasting pan deep into the Aga.

Saturday, 7 AM: The doorbell rings and Gerald lets fly. I pull shorts under my t-shirt and open the door to a cloud of Raimondo's smoke.

"*Bonjour,* Madame Thorpe! Everything is holding, you see?" He points at the roof. "I am sending you a team Monday, next week."

I don't say a word. I lead him into the barn.

He shakes his head and clicks his tongue. "These old barns. Why do you Anglo-Saxons love them so? I could have built you two houses brand new for less than you pay me to fix this heap of old stones." He shrugs and tosses his Gauloise aside. Then he turns the full force of his smile on me, embellished now with three shiny-new gold teeth.

I don't trust myself to speak.

11 PM: Heavy with menstrual cramps and curled around a couch pillow, I am watching *Casablanca* on France 3. I haven't seen it in years and now I see the French details, the Vichy water, the double-barred Lorraine cross—*la France libre!* The film is dubbed and the husky French baritone coming out of Bogart's twitching lips moves me to tears.

Maybe not today, maybe not tomorrow, but soon and for the rest of your life.

My eyes swim like Ilsa's.

Sunday, 11 AM: I am pushing Kate on the swing with one hand and holding out the other to guard Cloey on the slide.

"Sophie!" Kate cries. "Look at me! I am pumping with my feet like you taught me!"

Sophie is walking around the back of the house, smiling. The children jump off the swingset and cover her with kisses. She kisses my cheeks. She looks a little better this time, freckles showing through her makeup.

"The kids have told me how much fun they're having with you," I say. I feel almost shy.

"Eh! Watch out, Cloey! You'll break your neck, you little *casse-cou.*" He breaks out barking and starts bucking around her ankles, just like Gerald. She laughs and scratches his ears. Her nails are painted again.

"It went better this time, didn't it? I mean, with my husband?"

"Yes. I was here every day but he came home every night. There were a lot of friends sometimes."

"Well, I did encourage him to invite friends in so he could be with the children."

"It was a good idea. It worked." She smiles conspiratorily. "And you're leaving Tuesday?"

My knees feel a little weak. "Yes. But Monsieur Thorpe will be available every night."

"Okay. And I will be here every day."

I don't tell her I calculated the trip around my period so it would be over, clear for my next tryst. I am getting good at this. I am becoming shameless.

Tuesday, 2 PM: The Citroën is rolling down the *autoroute* at 150, the fastest I dare push it. Duke Ellington's "I Got It Bad (And That Ain't Good)" is cranked up loud on the CD player and my spirits are high. I have dressed carefully in a forties silk shirtwaist with padded shoulders and my lips are thick-painted fire-engine red. Under the embroidered teddy, my Lorraine cross—*la France libre!*—hangs on a long gold chain. The high-heeled sandals are hard to drive in, but make my legs feel . . . well . . . *I am ready.*

We agreed to meet at Caen and drive up the coast to St-Laurent. When I pull into the lot of the *gare,* he is standing out front in the sun. He's cut his heap of hair to shoulder length . . . nice . . . and it hangs loose over a faded Hawaiian shirt (can it be vintage? . . . not on purpose). His hands are in his pockets, and when he sees the car he grins and shakes his head. I pull up to the curb and before I can jump out he has thrown in his gear and climbed in. He doesn't kiss me at first. He looks at me, laughing.

"You look great like that. But the lipstick has got to go."

He smears it with his thumb, grimaces, then fishes out a tissue and wipes it away. Slowly. He takes his time, hovering, his lips just an inch from mine. I feel his breath. Then his fingers slide into my hair, his palms cover my ears. We look at each other. Then we kiss.

A taxi honks. I pull myself away from him, put the car in gear, and roll to the far end of the parking lot by the rental cars.

3 PM: "The Avis attendant walked by again. He was staring."

"I don't care."

We're not just kissing now. His hands are sliding over silk.

"Jean-Jacques, let's go."

"Mm?"

"Let's go."

"Mm. What have you got on under this? Nothing?"

"Mm. Don't. It's an old silk teddy."

" 'Teddy'?"

"Before they wore bras."

"Mm. How do I get in?"

"Sorry. Those are hooks and eyes. And there's a zipper on the dress. And . . . mm."

"Mm?"

"Let's go somewhere. Not here."

"Mm."

"Please."

Jean-Jacques sits up, blows out a breath, and runs his fingers through his hair. "Okay. Drive on."

The Citroën rolls through the center of Caen, drawing nostalgic smiles. I turn north and head for the coast. Duke Ellington swings softly from the dash speaker. Jean-Jacques is sitting very still next to me. His hand is around the back of my neck, fingers threading through the hair at the nape.

"How far is it to the hotel?" His thumb caresses my jaw. When it reaches my lower lip my eyes close. I force them open and grip the steering wheel.

His other hand is engaged now. My foot slips on the accelerator. His mouth is over my ear now.

"Mayg. How far is it to the hotel?"

I take a deep breath. His lips are under my hair. "Um. Well. I . . . I wanted to stop and look at some of the *débarquement* beaches before . . . before we . . ."

He pulls back.

"I mean, we'll be going right past Juno Beach. And Arromanches . . ."

He looks at me.

"Just a quick stop. Just to have a look. I've never been to . . ." I breathe. I focus. "Think of it! All the Allied forces, 150,000 of them, *amassed* in the middle of the channel. They called it Piccadilly Circus, the meeting point." I look at him. "You know, like in London. British humor."

He isn't laughing. He rifles for a cigarette. He slumps into his seat.

"Then the different forces sailed straight for the coast, all at once, together. A real unified blow. All five beaches."

His lighter clicks.

"The Germans were waiting for them, of course."

He blows out smoke. "Mayg."

I glance over at him. He is looking at me. His mouth, stained pink, has gone grim.

5 PM: At Luc-sur-Mer we see the channel and I turn west along the coast. Jean-Jacques has fallen silent, his hands on his knees. One village melts into another, resorts and villages blurring into one. Snack shacks. Row houses. Brasseries.

At Arromanches I pull onto the green clifftop and park in a lot full of tour buses. There are French voices and British and American, moving across the grass in earnest knots. I hear a Canadian "Eh?" and smile.

"Everybody comes here to pay homage!" I say over my shoulder. Jean-Jacques trails just behind me, his cameras hanging limp. He doesn't answer. He's looking at the bars of concrete in the churning tide below.

"They built that to protect the carriers coming in. Kind of an artificial harbor."

But there's no point. He's staring, elsewhere. I touch his arm and sigh. "I'm going to look around. Be right back." He nods without looking.

I walk along the clifftop. There are old men in windbreakers with somber faces. Veterans in black berets. Americans listening intently to tour guides who explain, interpret, in French accents. "The waters they were horribly rough that morning. The visibility it was poor. When the first boats arrived they were pitching so badly the men . . ."

I study the orientation table. Arrows point toward Cherbourg. The beaches. Southampton. There's a poster of a Lorraine cross, de Gaulle's BBC *cri du coeur: "La France n'est pas seule, elle n'est pas seule . . ."*

France is not alone. I feel goose bumps.

I buy a postcard of a Churchill tank and slip it into my bag for Cloey. Then I look around. I wish Jean-Jacques would try.

When I find him, he's at the far end of the parking lot, looking east. Toward Juno Beach. Gold Beach. Maybe he feels it, too, after all. His camera is up, long lens pointing down the waterfront.

I lay a hand between his shoulder blades. "What is it?" I whisper. "Casemates? Pillboxes?"

He lowers his camera. There's a trace of a smile on his lips. He turns and looks at me.

"Oysters. Oyster beds."

"*Oyster* beds? *Here?*"

His hands slide up my arms, his fingers slip under the silk cap sleeves, under the shoulder pads. "Mayg. How far is it to the hotel?"

4 PM: The Citroën is parked between hedgerows, deep in a field outside a grey stone village. We are in the back seat, Jean-Jacques braced beneath me on the cream-colored banquette, my silk skirt ballooning over us. His fingers are pulling at the side zipper impatiently, tearing at the hooks and eyes. He swoops for my breasts. The cross swings free.

He stops. He looks. He moans.

"*Merde.*"

He falls back on his elbows.

I fall forward and bite at his neck, drawing him to me. But he puts his arms around my back and pulls me down against him.

"*Merde.*" He is patting for a cigarette, but his hand connects with his own bare skin. He gropes for his shorts in the footwell, threads out a cigarette, and lights. His other hand is pressing hard on my back.

"Sorry." He pulls deep and blows out a thick smokestream. I lower my face into his neck.

"What's wrong?" I feel suddenly scared.

"Nothing. Just . . . *Putain.* Bad thoughts." I roll onto an elbow and look at him. I pet back his hair. Then he bites the cigarette, reaches between my breasts, and lifts out the cross.

"I don't want to do this story."

"Story?" I blink. "*Story?* How can you think about the story when we're . . . ?"

"I'm sorry. Maybe if you took this . . . get-up off we could . . ."

But we lie until he finishes the cigarette. Then we dress quietly, climb out separate doors, get back into the front seat, and drive west down the coast.

His silence is so intense, I don't try to break through.

8 PM: The hotel I booked in Vierville-sur-Mer is heavily furnished, the carpets thick and patterned, the wallpaper flocked. It is air-conditioned and the lobby is full of Americans in beltless slacks and Reeboks.

"We *specifically* asked for a *sea view*," a woman with stiff pink-blond hair is enunciating in very slow and very loud English to the reception clerk. There is a knot of men in baseball caps waiting at the elevator, so we carry our bags up the stairs.

The bay window in our room looks over Omaha Beach and an arsenal of concrete pillboxes. "I *specifically* asked for a *sea view*," I say, in my best Indiana accent.

He smiles oddly. "You sound funny when you speak English."

"I do it every day. Just not when I'm with you."

I throw my laptop on the king-size bed. The polyester coverlet is splashed with turquoise geometric flowers. I pull off the high-heeled sandals. They are hurting my feet. I sit on the bed.

"Do you want to tell me what's wrong?" I try to keep my voice neutral.

"It's stupid. This story is stupid. I don't want to be here."

"Did I do something?"

"It's not you. It's not you." He is patting his pockets again.

"It's a nonsmoking room. American clientele."

He nods, lights up, and breathes deep. "This history thing. It's got out of hand. I don't want to shoot this book."

I sit very still, listening. A chill.

"You come here all tarted up in your . . . costume . . . like you were in a play, like Benoît and Annick. It's a story to you. Wartime! Big-band music! Lipstick! That car."

I don't know what to say. I listen.

"These tourists come here like it's some sort of theme park."

"It's not a theme park. It's a memorial. A battlefield. A lot of men died here."

"Do you *know* how many men died here? Two thousand five hundred Allies, I don't know how many Germans. Do you know how many people died in the war? Fifty *million*. How many Jews? *Putain,* do you know *why?*"

"Jean-Jacques, why are you telling me this?" A month ago he'd barely heard of Agincourt.

"You want to make *that* into a pretty story? Put it in a silly picture book?"

"It's a part of history. It happened, just like Agincourt or Poitiers or Orléans or—"

"No. Those happened a long time ago. This is recent. This is *real.*"

"They're all real." But I know he knows that. I don't know what he means.

"I don't understand. I don't know why you're so upset."

He glances around for an ashtray, then crushes out his stub in the fruit plate. "I'll take your pictures for you. Then tomorrow let's go somewhere else."

"Okay."

He goes into the shower alone.

9:30 PM: The carpeted dining room is big as a ballroom but feels stuffy. It is nearly empty. Only a few stragglers are finishing their desserts and looking desperately at their watches.

"I can't *believe* the service. Unbe*liev*able," an American grandmother stage-whispers. "*Two hours* to eat dinner."

"And he refuses to bring my coffee. My dessert's almost gone."

Before long we are alone.

I brought nothing but vintage clothes with me—nothing but "getups"—but I cover my twin set with Jean-Jacques' scarf. We sit side by side on a banquette looking over the bare tables. The waiter doesn't seem happy to see us.

The food is stale and smothered in thickened sauce. "Canned mushrooms!" I say in nasal English. "Can you believe it?" But Jean-Jacques doesn't laugh. I can't make him laugh. I am getting scared.

But the Meursault is very good. He chose it carefully, winning over the waiter with questions. I hold it in my mouth, watching him. He's drinking it. He isn't really tasting it.

By the time the bottle is empty, he has covered my hand with his.

"So, your father was in the war?" he asks. He is making an effort.

"No. My grandfather."

"Of course. Sorry."

"My grandfather was in the Seventh Army. A captain under General Patch. He landed at St-Raphaël in '44. I still have his uniform jacket. I wear it in my bu — my office."

"You were very fond of him?" He looks at his scarf, draped over my twin set. Very fond. I look at him, feeling a little shy. He lights a cigarette. The waiter slips him an ashtray with a wink of complicity.

"Yes, I was. He was wonderful. We had a special . . . thing. He used to tell me about his war experiences. He taught me a lot of stories — history. He loved France. He stayed on after the war. He married my grandmother here."

"The one who taught you French."

"Yes. She died when I was nine. She seemed very . . . I don't know, exotic. Feminine. She wore scarves. She taught me how to chop onions."

"Ah."

"But my grandfather, too, he taught me so much. He cooked with me. Meat! The stuff my parents wouldn't eat."

"They were . . . ?"

"Vegetarians. It was our thing, between us, cooking sweetbreads. Kidneys. Brains. Tripe. Drove my dad crazy. Cholesterol! Bad karma!" I am smiling a little. "We used to watch old war movies together while he smoked his cigars. Then he would tell me what was wrong with the movie, historically speaking. And what it was really about."

"What it was *really* about?" He blows out a stream of smoke.

"Well, I guess. He took me to France once. I was ten. I guess he was still sad about Mamie. We drove up the Route Napoléon from where he landed in the war. I remember hill villages. Mountain gorges. We went back to the village where he met her. I never got over that trip. That was it for me. It was love."

His cigarette has burned to the filter. He stubs it. He says nothing.

"And your father?" I venture. "Er, grandfather?"

"Father. No. He was not involved in the fighting. So, do you want dessert?"

Abrupt. Something in his tone ties my stomach back in a knot. "No, thanks."

"Maybe we should go upstairs. We need to get up early to photograph the beaches before the tourists arrive."

But as we climb the carpeted stairs his hand has found the small of my back again. It makes me shiver.

Midnight: We leave the windows open to hear the sea. He leaves on the bedlamp. He takes off the scarf. He takes off the Lorraine cross. He takes off all my vintage clothes, nickel zippers, hooks and eyes and all, and lays them carefully aside. I lie very still, watching his hands. I love this man. I love him.

He is focused on me, attentive, serious. Moving over me, in me, slowly, looking into my eyes. Whatever was bothering him in the Citroën isn't bothering him now.

Wednesday, 7 AM: The beach below our window is still abandoned and the light is cool and soft. We walk down the road, past cottages and summer houses. Jean-Jacques stands looking up and down the cliffs, the sand, the water. There are concrete pillboxes above us, behind us. Flags flap in the wind. His hands are on his hips, his cameras hanging.

"Do you want to see the cemetery at Colleville?"

"No."

"I want to. And the museums."

"You go ahead. I want to shoot here for a while. Maybe you could meet me later?"

"Okay. When?"

"Noon?"

"Noon!" I blink. "Okay. Um, here?"

"Sure."

I walk back to the car and drive up to Colleville alone.

The American cemetery is vast and glossy, manicured, morning-inspection-slick. The holly oaks, trained and trimmed. The fountain, squared, smooth. And the graves. The graves. I wander through rows and rows of white crosses. Crosses and Stars of David stud the green as far as I can see.

There are no grave markers at Agincourt or Orléans. They've faded into legends of themselves, half-real. But this is real.

Jean-Jacques is right. It's not a story to him. "Do you know *why?*" he said. Why they did it. Why they had to in the first place. The history. That's what he wants to avoid.

Why? Why is he so troubled? Is he ashamed because his father didn't fight? But Frenchmen were in no position to . . .

Annick. Benoît.

and there i see such black and grained spots as will not leave their tinct

I walk quickly back to the car and head for the hotel.

10 AM: I lock the room door and hang out the *Ne pas déranger* sign. I set up the laptop on the desk and plug into the phone line.

I type in "www.google.fr."

I type in "brissac + chabrol."

My fingers are cold.

There are 7,852 results.

I click on the first one. It is all about wine.

> *Château* **Brissac-Chabrol.** *Bordeaux red wine. 3rd growth. France. Commune: Pauillac. Vineyard area: 150 acres. Average production: 10,000 cases. One of the oldest established vineyards in the Médoc peninsula, the* **Brissac-Chabrol** *properties produce an excellent wine universally considered to have been underrated in the classification of 1855. Its holdings, expanded considerably in the late 1940s, dominate some of the finest soil and placement in the Pauillac commune and yield a red of extraordinary suppleness and breadth.*

There is a photograph of a low-slung manor in pale-grey quarry stone, symmetrical behind an iron-grill gate. It is the same I saw etched on the label at the restaurant in Arles.

I click on the second one. It is all about wine, too.

. . . *Château* **Brissac-Chabrol** *being among the finest . . . the most under-classified of the Bordeaux reds . . .*

I click on and on. When I get to the bottom of the page I click on "next ten" and read on.

Then I reach *Philippe de Brissac-Chabrol, while influential and intimately allied with the Vichy government . . .*

I feel a chill. I click. An obituary from *Le Figaro* dated 1988 opens.

Philippe de **Brissac-Chabrol,** *while influential and intimately allied with the Vichy government throughout the occupation years, was never tried for war crimes . . .*

My mouth is dry. I scroll down.

. . . *actively encouraged a rising Fascist movement in France as early as 1934, when he entertained Nazi luminaries in his ancestral Médoc château . . . key to collaboration between SS and Vichy police . . .*

I fumble for the scroll button.

. . . *avowed anti-Semite making frequent public slurs against prominent Jewish colleagues in the Bordeaux wine world, some of whose vineyards he annexed and exploited after expediting the owners' deportation . . .*

The back of my neck is crawling.

I return to the list and search on. There is another obituary from the *International Herald Tribune.* I skim through it.

. . . *known for his extravagant entertainments that served, some believe, as rallying points for a growing fascist movement . . .*
. . . *embraced, and profited from, Nazi occupation . . . dubbed "Weinführer" by the conquerors who enjoyed the bottled spoils of war . . .*

At the bottom of the story there is a photo. I click on it. There is a thin man with a thick moustache under a bony nose. He is standing in a timbered

Bordeaux wine chai. He is laughing. And he is shaking the hand of Adolf Hitler.

It's a while before I can move my fingers again.

I scroll and click. There is a 1982 article, in English, from *Wine World* flagged *de Brissac-Chabrol, working closely with his son and heir, Jean-Jacques . . .*

I stop cold. I click.

> *. . . de Brissac-Chabrol, working closely with his son and heir, Jean-Jacques, has expanded production and greatly improved the quality of this earliest and most respected of 3ème crus. De Brissac-Chabrol "fils," known to his friends as J.J., is a promising adept in the mysteries of "assemblage," or blending, of Bordeaux varietals despite his age, a mere 20 years. Boyishly charming and with a winning enthusiasm for all things* oenologique *he led us through the process in halting English. "The most important thing to remember," he explained, "is the 'taste of the land,' le goût du terroir."*

I stare. There is a thin boy in the picture with short dark hair and a blazer. His long fingers hold a balloon glass to his bony nose.

11:30 AM: When I find him on the hillside above the waterfront, Jean-Jacques is sitting under a jagged cypress, smoking. His knees are pulled up. His cameras lie beside him. Omaha Beach stretches below and the waves are sweeping up high over the sand. I sit down next to him.

"Hi."

"Hi." He smokes.

"Did you get what you wanted?"

He laughs a little and shakes his head.

"I mean, the light, the tourists?"

"Yes."

The first tourists are straggling down the sand, loaded with umbrellas and beach bags and coolers. "It's a good thing we came early."

"Yes."

I sit. I don't know where to begin. I meant to put my arms around him, lighten his load. But there is a chill coming off him. Cold. Hard. I swallow.

"Jean-Jacques, I know, um, I know about your father."

His cigarette freezes in midair. "What?" Evenly.

"I know about the Vichy story."

He is quiet for a while. The cigarette returns to his lips. "How?" Neutrally.

I am suddenly embarrassed. "I . . . I looked it up on the Internet."

"You what?" Evenly.

"I looked it up on the Internet. I Googled you."

"You Googled me?"

"Your family name. De Brissac-Chabrol."

"I know my name." His voice is still level.

"I looked it up. I found your father's obituary."

The cigarette arcs through the air. He is still looking at the sea. Then he stands abruptly and walks away from me, down toward the sand.

"Jean-Jacques, I wanted to know."

"You wanted to know." His voice is rising. "You Googled me because you wanted to know."

I trot beside him, trying to catch up, to see his face. "You were so upset and I—"

"Madame l'Historienne does her research."

"No. Don't!"

"Madame l'Historienne wants the facts."

"No. Jean-Jacques, you—you seemed to be in such pain and I wanted—"

He stops. "So. What do you know?"

"I read about his . . . collaboration. The Occupation. The Vichy government. His taking the wine property from the—"

He throws his head back. "You know about the vineyards?"

"Well, yes."

Now he looks at me. "So, now you want to know more."

"No, I—"

"You know he went to Nuremberg in '35? A regular pilgrimage. The speeches he made? The rallies?"

His voice is rising, tightening strangely. "Or do you really want to know about the money and the land and the wine. You know what my family is worth? A lot. A lot. You know how it got that way?"

"I know. The vineyards he took from the Jews. But *you* didn't know."

"*Putain de merde!*" He swings away from me and walks back toward the road. I follow.

"Jean-Jacques, I know you didn't know. It wasn't you."

But when he looks at me, his face is contorted with anger. The bones on his cheeks and his nose stand out hard. "You love this, don't you? You are enjoying this. This is exciting for you. This is . . . *living history!*"

"No! No, I . . ." I reach out and try to take his hand. He throws mine away like a stone. I stand and breathe evenly. "I'm sorry. I thought you were . . . were . . . and I wanted to know."

His hands clench his hips. His lips work but he doesn't speak.

"It wasn't you." I am whispering. "You didn't know."

Now he speaks. I flinch. "*Merde!* Of *course* I didn't know! I grew up with . . . with . . . what? Porcelain and crystal and . . . on my dinner table and—cars and—You want to know why I know about horses? My father kept a dozen, more, whatever, all of them too good for him. He couldn't even *ride*. I drove all over France with him in his *putain de* Citroën—oh yes, just like yours—and sold his wines like a good little son. I *tended* those vines! I—we *nursed* those vines! We turned that place around, oh yes, I made it the . . . it was the best . . . the best . . . I didn't know! I didn't know till the story came out in *Le Monde!* And then when I found out I . . . left."

I touch his arm and he flings my hand off. He drags his hair out of his eyes, across the top of his head. His face is very red. "Did you see those cemeteries?"

"But Jean-Jacques, you can't blame your—"

"Did you see the graves?"

"Yes."

He stands, breathing hard. His face is frightening to see.

"Now you got your story. Very neat. Collaborators! Fallen heroes! Saving Europe from the evil—from the evil—Hey! *Why don't we put it in the book?* I can get archive stuff! The roundups! The camps! The—"

"Jean-Jacques, stop! Please! You're twisting this all . . . it's okay! It wasn't you. You weren't even born. It was your father. He's dead. It's . . . ancient history!"

His face is suddenly horrible. His laugh is uglier.

"*Ancient history!*" He stands there, fighting for breath. "Ancient *history. Fils de pute.*"

Now he is looking at me as if he'd never seen me before. "With all the 'stories' you've *foiré,* fucked up, got all wrong, missed the point, you had to go and—*merde*—dig up mine?"

"Jean-Jacques." My throat is tight. "You're overreacting. I didn't mean to make you angry or—I—I love you and I want to be with you and I—"

His mouth twists. His hands are back on his hips. He calms himself with an effort. Then he answers, too quietly.

"You don't want to 'be with me.' It isn't 'real.' It's just another story. Go back to your 'bunker.' Go back to your '*research.*'"

"Jean-Jacques, don't, please—"

"*Fous moi le camp.* Fuck off, get out of here. Go back to your husband and kids."

3 PM: I go back to the room and pack my things. The underwear. The cross. The lipstick. I wash my face with icy hands. I put on the silk dress. I close the laptop and strap it into the case. I can't work the zipper so I force it with a yank. I pull on the sandals and rise, teetering. I carry my things down the carpeted stairs.

"You wish to check out, Madame? But for the second night—"

"Monsieur is still here. I have to go."

"Ah. As you wish."

I roll out and across the blacktop to the Citroën. Where will he go? There's no train here. I load the bags into the trunk and look up and down the beach. There are bands of tourists in neon tracksuits. There are fat glazed buses in the parking lot. But I can't see him.

go back to your husband and kids

I start the Citroën engine, rise on air, and roll down the waterfront, craning, searching, one kilometer, two. I spot him.

He is walking along the shoulder, hands in his pockets, his head down. I pull over. He glances up. His face is as streaked as at Cluny. Sweat. Something else.

I roll down the window on his side. "I'm so sorry, Jean-Jacques. Please get in. Please talk with me."

He looks away. He looks at me. He opens the door and drops in beside me. I drive inland, away from the beaches.

5 PM: "Of course my mother knew. She married him after the war, but she knew. She never told me. She let me find out."

We are sitting in a truckstop bar, two glasses of cheap Calvados on the scarred wooden table in front of us, two more sitting empty at the edge. The ceramic ashtray is overflowing. We haven't eaten and the liquor gnaws at my stomach.

"How did you find out?"

"There were all these documentaries coming out in the late eighties. Nobody talked about 'collaboration' before. It wasn't in our history books. Only the Résistance, the noble heroes of the Résistance."

"I know. I remember when the real — I mean the other — story started coming out. The books. The documentaries. I was at Cambridge and I did — some research."

Mercifully, he doesn't laugh. He's not in a laughing mood.

"I saw it on television," he says. "Footage. There he was in black and white, shaking hands with Hitler."

"I saw the photograph on the net."

He grimaces. "It wasn't hard to dig it up. Even *before* the Internet. I went to the library, then I started calling friends. It's amazing how many people knew. He gave parties. He gave speeches. He even formed a little group — half Fascist society, half wine-tasting club." He laughs now, but it turns into a cough. He lights another cigarette.

"What was he like?"

"Oh, a real bon vivant. A storyteller. Big entertainer. Life of the party. Always opening another bottle. I thought he was *great*. He was old enough to be my grandfather but you'd never have known it — the force, the energy. He taught me all about wine. Amazing. His nose. His *palate*. Took me with him everywhere. The vineyards. The chais. He taught me to taste, to assemble, to blend. Everything. I was just a kid. I didn't know the wine we made was . . ."

He fades. I lay my hand over his. He resurfaces.

"If he'd just told me himself. It's not as if he didn't have a chance. We traveled all over the country together, father and son, in that damned car. Now I know why he wanted to sell the wine himself, instead of *négociants*. He wanted to be *seen*. In that Citroën. Just like de Gaulle. A real pureblood, true-blue Frenchman. Tastings. Wine fairs. *Concours*. I think I got to know every three-star restaurant in France."

"That explains it. 'J-J!'" I try to smile, but it wilts on my lips. He is shaking his head.

"I wish people wouldn't call me that."

"I don't call you that."

He looks up at me. "Mayg." He wipes his hands over his face.

I put my hand on his arm. "Have you ever . . . couldn't you give back the vineyards to the survivors?"

His mouth twists. "There weren't any survivors. He saw to that."

We sit for a while in silence.

At last I take a shaky breath. "Go on. What happened when you found out?"

"I wanted to kill him but he was already dying. Then I thought about killing myself. I was twenty-five, Renée—"

"You were already married then?"

"Yes. She didn't understand why I was so upset." He laughs and shakes his head. "I didn't go to the funeral. My mother was horrified. It *looked* bad, she said. I threw my stuff in my car and left. I drove to Paris and stayed. Renée came for a while, but when she saw I really meant to—"

"Cut yourself off? From the inheritance?"

"Yeh. She just didn't get it. She didn't like that at all." He is smiling a little bit. He takes a sip of Calvados and swallows, wincing.

"So she left you. And then she found Robert."

"Yeh. You saw. Paintings. Rugs."

"Fishbowls."

He does laugh now, then he coughs. He reaches for another cigarette. I stop his hand. "Don't. You'll make yourself sick." I pull his hand to my cheek instead.

He looks at me for a while. His eyes are traced with veins. "Everybody

282 ❖ Nancy Coons

else in France knows. I should have known a historian would figure it out."

His hand is cold on my cheek. I look at him. His face is drawn, his shoulders rounded. Something in me dissolves, delicate, ephemeral. A bridge, unreal to real. I don't mean to say it, it just slips out.

"Jean-Jacques, I meant what I said. I want to be with you."

But he only shudders.

8 PM: I have no business driving with three Calvados burning in my stomach, but I make our way slowly back to the hotel. "We should eat something," I say. "We haven't eaten all day."

The dining room is full tonight and the air is thick with American accents. "T-A-P W-A-T-E-R," someone is pronouncing slowly and loudly. "Eau doo roh-bee-nay." The waiter is pretending not to understand. He returns with a liter of Evian.

Jean-Jacques holds the vinyl-bound wine list with yellowed fingers. He is suddenly self-conscious. "What do you want to drink?"

I laugh. "I trust your judgment. 'The most important thing to remember is the taste of the land.'" He winces.

We are still pretty full of Calvados but he orders a Sancerre with the sole. We hardly touch the fish. Then he orders a Côte-Rôtie with the cheese. We hardly touch the cheese. The first mouthful of wine stops us short for a moment of appreciation. Then we drink it down like pitcher wine.

By then I've found more than enough courage. I sit up straight. "Jean-Jacques? There's something about *me* you should know. I haven't been totally honest with you."

Full disclosure, I think. It's only fair.

"*D'accord.*" He drains his glass and sets it down a little too hard. "I'm listening." He listens, but I don't speak. "So am I going to have to Google you?"

"No, It's just that . . . Jean-Jacques." I drain my glass, too. "I'm not really . . . a historian. I didn't really go to Cambridge. I mean, I did, I spent a year there, a school year, a junior year abroad. A couple of history courses. I volunteered at the library. And the Sorbonne thing . . . that was just summer classes. I really only have a degree from my college back home in Indiana."

I don't dare look at him. There's a prickling under my arms.

There is a long, long pause. Jean-Jacques casts around the room as if looking for an audience. Then he laughs. The other diners' heads snap up. I cover my ears.

"It's not funny!"

He laughs until he coughs. "You scared me for a minute!"

"It's not funny. I thought you'd be . . ."

"What? Did you think I checked your curriculum vita before I—"

"Curriculum vit-*ae*."

He coughs so hard I have to order water. He waves it away and orders another bottle. We drink. He smirks. I lean into him and lay my hand on his arm.

"Jean-Jacques. Tell me. When did you talk with your mother last?"

His smirk goes ugly. He folds his arms across his chest and his cigarette scorches his shirt. He rears back, brushing away ashes.

"Haven't."

"You haven't spoken with her since 1988?"

"No."

"But she's your *mother*."

"Got blood on her hands."

"Now you're being dramatic. You said she wasn't even married to him until after the war."

"Still, she knew. And now she's living in that *putain de* château with the family silver and the family . . . whatever . . . and old portraits and . . . and two Bentleys . . ."

"She has two Bentleys?"

"At least."

"How do you know?"

"I see her in *Paris Match* all the time. Party pages, gossip, 'people.'"

I take this in with a swallow of wine. "You read about your mother in the 'people' pages?"

"Not very often." He drinks deep.

I focus carefully. "Jean-Jacques, you should go to her. She gave birth to you. She's your family."

"Family."

"You need to get this out, purge this. I don't know, cauterize the wound or something."

"Sure."

"It's your birthright."

"Yeh."

"And your sister? What about your sister?"

"How'd you know about Justine? D'you Google her too?"

"Benoît."

"Oh. Right." He focuses carefully. "She's all right."

"All right?"

"She keeps her distance. From the house, the business. She moved to England when it all came out. But she keeps the money. She likes the money."

"Did you sign away your inheritance or just move out?"

His eyes narrow slightly. Then he reaches for a cigarette, lights it from the stub of the last, leans back, and looks at me.

Someone at the next table is gesturing broadly at the waiter and pointing at Jean-Jacques. "NO SMOKING!" he is saying very slowly. "This is a *no smo-king* section. *Pas de fumier.*" The waiter is shaking his head, uncomprehending. *Fumier* means manure.

I cover my mouth and smother a giggle. But then I see Jean-Jacques' face. "Why are you looking at me like that?"

But he is smoking and thinking. He orders two Calvados and the waiter sets up enormous snifters, pours an amber stream in each. Too much.

"Fishbowls!" Jean-Jacques snickers. He drinks. I drink. Then he looks at me. His fingers brace on the table, cigarette between his knuckles.

"So you want to 'be with me' now."

I am startled at the change of subject. Why has his mouth gone all twisted?

"Last week it was 'This isn't real.' 'There's Nigel.' Today you want to be with me?" He tips the glass back, deep.

I am staring at him. I've had too much to drink. I must be misunderstanding.

"We're drunk, Jean-Jacques. Let's go to bed."

" 'Go back to your mother,' you said. 'It's your birthright.' "

"Stop, please. You don't mean this. You don't think—"

"Renée thought it was my birthright too."

"Jean-Jacques, let's go to bed. We'll talk in the morning."

"Let's go to bed."

We sign the bill and push back our chairs. I rise, wobbling slightly. Jean-Jacques shakes the waiter's hand and claps his back like an old friend. He navigates across the thick carpet and heads for the stairs.

In the room I grope for the light, teeter over to the window, and open it. I have inhaled a lot of secondary smoke today. The wine and Calvados are turning in my stomach. The wallpaper print wheels slowly around me.

But Jean-Jacques flips the light back off and comes up behind me. His lips scratch the back of my neck. He smells like booze and tar.

"Let's not. Please, wait until morning."

He is sliding up the skirt and pressing me to the wall. My cheek is smashed against the stiff foam-lined curtains. I stumble and he catches me hard.

But suddenly I feel his face between my shoulder blades. Warm. Wet. He is crying.

Thursday, 8 AM: When I open my eyes, he is lying beside me on the vast jazz-print bed. He is still fully dressed and his face is ashen. The effort of moving my eyes to look at him sends a split of pain across my forehead. I am still in the dress. The window is wide open. The sea pounds ruthlessly in my ears.

The cell phone is ringing. That's what woke me up. Four rings. Five. I grope for it but it stops. Jean-Jacques opens his eyes and then shuts them very quickly, tight.

9 AM: I open my eyes again. Jean-Jacques is fumbling for a cigarette.

"Please, don't. I'll be sick."

He lies back. Then he sits up again, grasps the cigarette, and lurches over to the window. He hangs his head over the railing for a minute. Then he lights up.

The cell phone rings. I pick it up.

"Hello, darling?"

"Nigel!"

Jean-Jacques' head drops forward. I sit up straight.

"Hi. Everything all right?"

"Absolutely splendid, love. Hadn't heard from you. Forgot to leave your hotel number again."

"Oh. Well, the cell is working fine."

"Right. Work coming along?"

"Yes, thanks."

"D-Day, was it?"

"Yes, that's right. Are the kids okay?"

"Yes. Playing outside in the builders' sand pile."

Kate. Cloey. Oh god. My stomach lurches. I take a deep breath. "Nigel, I have to run. There's — there's — I have an interview."

"Veterans? Salute them for me. Still haven't forgotten what you lot did for us back in the Big One."

There is an edge to his tone. Or is there?

"Okay, Nigel. Bye."

I have to go home.

Jean-Jacques throws his cigarette into the parking lot and turns back into the room. His lips look pale green around the edges. There are purple circles under his eyes. "So is the roof holding up?"

I sink back on the bed and bury my face in my hands. "Let's get out of this hotel. It's poison here."

10 AM: Moving carefully, we shower and dress and check out of the hotel. I drive inland to a grey stone village and a 8 à Huit, buy a liter of apple juice and drink straight from the bottle. I feel the pain in my head recede. I offer some to Jean-Jacques and he drinks, too. We buy a baguette and stand on the sidewalk stuffing warm bread into our mouths. I buy another bottle of apple juice and we drink it more slowly. Then we sit on a stone memorial. I don't even know where we are.

A little color is coming back into his lips. "Coffee?"

I nod. There is a sandwich board shaped like a pig holding a menu. Bar-tabac. We walk in and order doubles from the bartender, then stand at the sheet-metal counter, sipping the scalding brew. He fumbles for another cigarette but I stop his hand. "Don't."

We go back to the memorial and sit. It is a sandstone obelisque ringed in artillery shells, plastic French flags propped in their detonator mouths. A man on a black bicycle pedals past, his hoe and spade bound to the back fender. A boy on a motor scooter raspberries by. A stray dog sniffles around our feet, lifts a leg on the stone beneath us, and saunters away.

There's nothing left to leave unsaid. I take a breath.

"Do you really think I'm after your money?"

He lays his head down into his palms and lurches forward. I think for a moment that he's finally going to throw up. "I'm sorry, I'm so sorry."

We sit for a while.

"I mean, I'd only known you had it for a few hours. And you *don't* have it."

"Oh *putain*." He tolds his head for a minute. Another. He shakes it back and forth. He makes an effort to breathe evenly, slowly. "I don't know what to say. I was drunk. Everything was so . . . bad. You were so out of focus. And I looked at you and—I don't know. Renée."

I rub my eyes. I look at him. "Was it Renée you pushed up against the curtains?"

He squints and reflects, confused. "*Merde*, I'm sorry. I didn't . . . Did I . . . ?"

"No."

We sit very still on the stone for a while. Then he says, "Will you stay with me? Tonight? Please?"

"Jean-Jacques, I have to go home."

He gropes for a cigarette.

"Don't." I stop his hand. "Don't."

He pushes the cigarette back into the pack and sighs. "Mayg. *Écoute.* We don't have to go to hotels, you know. It doesn't have to be for the book. You come to Paris. Stay with me. I'll cook for you."

I close my eyes. "I can't."

"Why can't you?"

"I just can't."

"You said you wanted to be with me."

"I do. I can't."

"Is that too 'real'? Does that make it too 'real'?"

"Don't."

"And when the book is done?"

"Don't. We have to be honest."

"Honest. *Putain*."

We sit. Two women roll baby carriages past, gossiping in flutey tones. I watch them pass. Then I take a slow, shaky breath. "Jean-Jacques, I have to go home. I'll . . . I'll drive you to the *gare*."

12 PM: We pull into the Europcar lot and the Citroën sinks with a sigh. Jean-Jacques stares at his hands on his knees. "Just tell him."

"Tell him what? What do I tell him?"

"About me. That you love me."

That word, out loud, again. I look at him.

"Jean-Jacques, you don't understand. He's . . . he's . . . *English*."

The short laugh, the bark. "What is that supposed to mean?"

"I mean, you can't confront him. He doesn't . . . confront. And it would hurt him, really hurt him, but he'd be all *noble* about it, 'stiff upper lip, that sort of thing.' And—I can't do that to him."

He looks up at me and shakes his head.

"Mayg, it's already done."

10 ⚜ The Greater Share of Honor

Thursday, August 21, 6 PM: Kate is in the front apple tree when I roll up the drive, and Cloey and Gerald are barking wildly at the roots. She is flinging green apples down and Gerald is diving for them. They are barefoot, their buttermilk skin a map of orange freckles. There are two piles of construction sand in the driveway. The Rover is parked beside them.

"Maman!" Cloey gallops over and wraps around my knees. Kate drops neatly out of the tree and runs to me. Gerald crouches, whining ecstatically. I flop on the ground in my crumpled silk skirt and hold them all.

"Sophie took us to the fireman's picnic! We ate roasted *porc!* I won a Barbie! Ahmad bought me six crêpes!"

"Moi aussi!"

I extricate myself. "Come on in. Let's find Papa." But instead they charge the sand piles like San Juan Hill and start scrambling to the top. I open the trunk and carry my bags to the house, my skirt billowing out. Gerald trots behind me, sniffing ardently. Oh god. Nigel is standing in the front door, a gin and tonic in his hand. He is looking at Gerald. I twist away, swatting. He stands very still. Then he takes a sip.

"Hello, Megs." He bends down and kisses my cheek. He holds his face there for a long time, breathing. "You smell like smoke." I feel blood creeping up my cheeks. "Good trip? Did we win this time round? Hold the beachheads?"

"Yes." I laugh a little.

We walk into the house. This time I am not surprised to see bottles and glasses everywhere and the counters covered in dirty dishes.

"Sorry about the mess." He looks passively around him. "Don't know why Sophie doesn't—"

"She isn't paid to clean." It comes out sharper than I meant.

He looks up. "No. She's paid to watch the children while you 'work.'"

I feel a prickle rising on my neck.

"Drink?"

I nod. "Please."

We carry our glasses to the barn. The hole is wide open again and a deep trough has been dug across the threshhold, lined with a trickle of cement.

"It's a beginning," Nigel says brightly.

We return to the kitchen and refill our drinks. There are *merguez* sausages in the refrigerator and two bloody-red steaks. I spin the salad. Nigel spreads the meat on a platter and pulls on an apron.

"'Oh pardon me, thou bleeding piece of earth,'" he intones, raising the platter, "'that I am meek and gentle with these butchers.'" He laughs edgily. "Right. I'll just light the fire."

Midnight: I have swept the rubble off my desk and I am writing frantically to Jean-Jacques.

> *Don't phone. I love you.*

But the phone rings before I send it.

"That for you, love?" Nigel, at the top of the ladder.

"I've got it."

It rings.

"All right then. Coming up?"

"In a minute."

It rings.

"All right then."

It rings. I reach for it. It has stopped.

I hit Send and head up the ladder.

Saturday, 6:30 AM: I hear the rumbling and meet Raimondo at the front door well before he has rung the bell. He is swinging shut the door on a shiny silver Audi.

"*Bonjour,* Madame Thorpe."

"*Bonjour.* Is the team coming?"

"Yes. Normally, yes. We have a *chantier* to finish this morning. Then I send you a few boys." He regards his fingernails. They are remarkably clean. "Has Monsieur Thorpe prepared me an envelope?"

I pull up short. "I thought MacGregor takes care of that."

"Yes. He has paid me for the contract work. But with Monsieur Thorpe there is a separate arrangement. Since the small surprise with the wall."

11 AM: I take the children to the farmer's market. Kate's in a sundress, Cloey in long shorts. We hold the basket handles between us. I heft melons and sniff them. They heft melons, two-handed, and sniff them, too. I thump and listen. They thump and listen. We buy a box of blackberries and eat them as we walk. There is a neon-green inchworm in the box and we let it walk up our hands. Kate "sets it free" in a patch of grass by a lamppost. I buy them *citron pressé* in a café and we stir sugar into the tall glasses of raw lemon juice, Kate pouring the water. Her glass spills, flooding the tabletop with lemon juice. Kate regards me with huge eyes. We clean it up together and order another. I let her pour again. On the way home, Cloey throws up blackberries on the cream-upholstered banquette. I clean it up with rags.

I am patient. I am removed. I view them, tenderly, through the wrong end of a telescope.

Sunday, 7 PM: Nigel went over to the MacGregors' this morning for drinks and hasn't come back. I am relieved. I spend the day shaking down mirabelles with the children and canning them in the steaming kitchen, one eye on the ticking clock.

Monday, 3 PM: I have not gone down to the bunker since Thursday. I am avoiding Nikos. I have nothing to write. The book? I can barely remember the theme. I climb down the ladder and boot up.

I make myself read Nikos' message first. There is only one.

> *Publisher not a happy camper. If we put off pub date any further it*
> *may come out of your final check.*
> nikos

I close it quickly.

Then I begin to open the messages from Jean-Jacques, one at a time, in order, my cheek on my hand.

From Saturday, a text message.

> *i want to call but i won't. just tell him.*

From Sunday, a string of jpegs. These are images of pillboxes, torn concrete on the beach. He wrote:

> *i googled my father. there were things even i didn't know. i am doing research. like a good historian.*

From Monday—today, this morning, a few minutes ago:

> *come to paris, we will figure it out.*

I write back.

> *First Agincourt. Thursday morning. Meet me at the Amiens gare.*

I am still online when his reply comes back.

> *Meg I love you. come be with me.*

Wednesday, 2 PM: "And the French army, they were led by King Charles the Sixth—that's you, Cloey!"

"*Moi?* Me? *Ouaah!*"

We have draped blankets over our shoulders and Kate and Cloey have crushed tinfoil crowns onto their heads. Gerald is barking under the daybed, ducking their cardboard swords.

"And they closed in on the English army—that's you, Kate, Henry the Fifth! You were starving, exhausted, you'd been marching for days in the rain."

"*Comme ça, Maman?*" Kate staggers theatrically.

"That's it! And the English were rallied, inspired by King Henry. He just filled their heads with this idea that God was on their side and that France was theirs by right. No! Wait! *Stop!*"

Cloey and Kate have turned their swords on me. We collapse, laughing, onto the daybed.

10 PM: The children are slow to settle in their beds. I kiss and cuddle them good night and say good-bye for the trip.

"How long this time?" Kate murmurs sleepily.

I slide a pink plastic pony from under her cheek. "Not long."

I curl around Cloey for a while until his thumb slips out of his mouth.

I am already packed and sitting at the dining table looking at the map of Pas-de-Calais when Nigel pulls up the driveway in the Rover. It's the first evening he's come home before eleven all week. His cheeks and nose glow.

"Not down in your bunker?" He bends low and kisses my forehead. Then he sees my bags by the door and his voice drops to a strangely gentle croon. "Off in the morning, are you?"

I shiver. "Yes. Early."

"Where to this time? Dunkerque? Verdun? Waterloo?"

"Agincourt."

"*Agincourt?* Brilliant. 'Cry "God for Harry, England and Saint George!"' Splendid. And Jean-Claude will be there? Shooting?"

"Jean-Jacques. Yes. There's a jousting festival. With costumes."

"Excellent! Just the thing for your book. Pageantry! Revelry!"

"I'm going to bed. I have to get up early."

"I'll come, too."

"I'm going to take a bath first."

"Right."

He turns toward the refrigerator. But as I move to get up, he hesitates and turns back to me. I can't hold his gaze. He lays his hand on my hair. I sit, still and small, under its weight. Then he lifts his hand and turns away.

As I creep up the stairs, I hear him murmur, sotto voce, "'O, I have bought the mansion of a love, but not possess'd it.'"

I stay in the bathtub until the water goes cold. He doesn't come upstairs for a very long time. He lies awake even longer. When I finally hear his snores I crawl, shivering, in beside him. My lamp is still on. I prop on my elbow and watch him sleep.

His head is thrown back, mouth gaping. There are tiny traces of broken veins spidering over his jowls. His hands lie across his chest, twitching in a dream. An angry dream. He is frowning. His butterscotch hair falls away from his high, pale forehead and spreads stiffly across the pillow.

It is Cloey's hair, and Kate's. The eyebrows, too.

I used to love him.

do you love him? it's important.

Thursday, 8 AM: I wheel west along the *autoroute* with no music in the player. It's dead hot and the windows are down. The air beats in like a furnace blast. I have bound the scarf around my hair to keep it out of my eyes and peer through my antique Ray-Bans. I don't care what I look like. I want to get to Jean-Jacques.

The book, Meg, the book.

Focus. After Agincourt, what? I was supposed to take the lead on this book and it's in shambles.

I've fallen in love instead.

I wheel past a brown tourism billboard marked "Verdun: Les Champs de Bataille." The battlefields. I have seen them many times. There is nothing for Jean-Jacques to photograph there. Churned earth. Trenches and bomb pits grown over with ivy and beech. The ossuary is frightening, its tower like an artillery shell, its basement full of bones.

I press on. Every exit sign is history. Reims. Joan of Arc brought the dauphin there to be crowned King Charles VII. I know there's a plaque by the cathedral. A plaque and a statue. I drive on.

I cut west off the *autoroute* onto the *route nationale*. Soissons. The bell tower of the great abbey church stands in ruins. Like Cluny. "I can't photograph ruins," he said. I drive on.

Compiègne. Joan of Arc fell there, wounded in battle, captured by the Burgundians, handed off to the English. A turning point. Epic. Significant. I look at the landscape around me. I see smokestacks and factories, a gas station, a Buffalo Grill, a Formule 1. I press on.

I don't know why I'm going to Agincourt. Jean-Jacques is right. You can't photograph history.

I do know why I'm going to Agincourt.

I press down the gas pedal.

10:30 AM: I drove too fast and I'm early for his train, so I steer the steaming Citroën to the old town center of Amiens, past gingerbread row houses in Picardy brick. The cathedral stands at the heart. I pull the scarf down around my shoulders, push my sunglasses up into my hair, and step inside.

I take in the vast echoing space, the impossible height and weight and span of it. My breath stills. I am quietly exalted. Humbled. I sink into a caned chair and try to empty my thoughts, to make room for this nobler feeling. But my ignoble thoughts crowd back in on me.

I have to make a decision.

There are doors opening in my mind and heart, doors I have kept firmly closed.

come be with me

The book won't last forever.

Cloey. Kate.

I sit and think. I don't know who I am anymore. What I am. What country I belong to. Who I belong with. Who belongs with me.

Cloey. Kate.

this isn't real

I close the doors.

I pull down my sunglasses. I go back to the station for Jean-Jacques. Is he real?

I stand on the quai waiting and the train rolls up at last. The cars strobe by, slow, slower, then stop with a hiss and a wheeze. The door folds open. First his bags and cameras swing down. Then him. I stand frozen, trying to objectify him. His ponytail, knotted. His shorts. The sweat patches on his t-shirt. His whiskers grown thick. But I can't be objective. His mouth is all over mine.

I break free, the taste of him on my tongue.

"You smoke too much."

He pulls me back. "Mm-hm."

12:30 PM: Heatwaves rise from the *gare* parking lot. "Let me drive?" Jean-Jacques asks. I look at him. He is appraising the Citroën, his hands on his hips. I hand him the keys and kiss his cheek.

Inside the car is an oven and we crank down the windows. He turns the key and puts the car in gear. It rises on a cushion of air and we ease onto the road.

He's quiet for a while, driving another DS, somewhere else. I lay my hand on the back of his neck and he comes back, smiling a little. "It's a beautiful car. It really is. Smells bad in the heat though."

"Oh. That's Cloey. Got sick in the back."

"Ah."

"Too many blackberries."

He winces. He steps on the pedal and the Citroën streams ahead.

1 PM: The landscape is flat. Picardy is pale and monotonous here, its red-brick houses low-slung, serpentine. We are both trickling sweat. I lay my hand on his arm and feel the sinew moving under his skin as he steers. He looks over at me and tucks my hair behind my ear.

"Mayg?"

"Mm?"

"How many stories are there left?"

I take a breath. "I don't know anymore. I haven't written anything and the stories haven't been working out lately."

A smile twitches around his mouth.

Fields roll past. A mill town sprawls over a valley, old factory housing in blackened brick crowding the hills.

"Well. There's the Route Napoléon, in Provence. The road from Cannes to Sisteron. Grenoble."

"A road."

I sigh. "It's the one my grandfather followed. I've always wanted to write about it."

"And to photograph?"

"There's still Joan of Arc. The siege of Orléans. Or Domrémy-la-Pucelle. Where she was born. Where she saw her visions."

"Very hard to shoot, visions."

The Citroën swerves, steams onward.

"Still. We could. Domrémy is right next door to my village. But I don't think you'd want to stay with . . . us."

"No, I would not."

He rifles for a cigarette and pushes the lighter knob in. When it springs out, he lights. He keeps his eyes on the road. "Though I would like to meet Kate and Cloey."

A door, opening. I don't close it. I don't say anything at all.

He drives on for a while, then tosses the cigarette out into the wind. "Orléans would be good. The Loire. I have friends near Blois with a château. I've stayed in the gamekeeper's cottage before."

"No friends."

"D'accord."

He rolls on. "And after Orléans?"

"I don't know."

I don't know.

He keeps his eyes on the road.

3:30 PM: "By the time Henry's army got to Azincourt they were half starved and they'd taken terrible losses at the siege of Harfleur."

"Honfleur?"

"Whatever. The French king challenged them and engaged them at Azincourt. You know the Shakespeare, right? Henry the Fifth? You said you saw Annick and Benoît in it. In Avignon. *Incredible* play. *Incredible* story. There were only a few thousand British, and there were three times as many French, some say even five times as many. They were mounted, armed, trained knights. The English were exhausted and sick. But they had *archers*. Really skilled archers, longbowmen from Wales, and the French were using crossbows. Very heavy, very hard to load. It was an incredibly bloody battle and there was so much mud and the French were slaughtered, just *slaughtered*, overwhelmed by—I don't know—the sheer will of the British army."

Jean-Jacques takes a curve hard, laughing and shaking his head.

3 PM: "No, wait. We should have gone left there at Blangy. Oops, sorry, that was a right."

We have slowed to a crawl. Jean-Jacques patiently throws the dashboard stick into reverse and turns around again in a tractor path. Sweat runs in rivulets down my back.

At last a small, hand-painted billboard announces "Azincourt, Centre Historique Médiéval. Jousting Festival Aug 28–29."

"This is it!"

There are camionnettes and motorcycles parked along a rain ditch, and a handful of farmhouses. Jean-Jacques pulls up behind a motorcycle and stops the engine. "Where's the town?" he asks.

"I know it's not very big, but there's a festival, I'm telling you."

He pulls on his camera bag and we walk up the road. The village comes into view, such as it is. There is a *tabac-presse,* a visitors' center. A bakery. A bar. There is one hotel-restaurant with neoclassic pillars in PVC: the Henri V. But the street down the middle is full of tourists, milling up and down the pavement with water bottles in their hands.

"There's horse dung. See, I told you there was a jousting festival."

"Could just be a horse."

He is getting that look again. I don't care. We walk through the village and come out the other end.

"Hah! You see?"

There are masses of people spread out over a field. Cardboard soldiers with crudely painted faces flank the hedges. Plastic banners painted with red lions and blue fleurs-de-lys stretch from telephone pole to pole.

Tourists surge past us speaking English.

"Mummy, where's the loo?"

The air is full of British accents. There are khaki sun hats and sandals with socks and startlingly short shorts, cropped white hair and A-line skirts, freckled foreheads broiling in the sun. I hear French, too, someone muttering about *les rosbifs*. Roast beefs. That's what the French call the English, or used to. With all the gory sunburns around me, I can see why.

I lead Jean-Jacques through the crowd to a ticket stand with an enormous banner: FÊTE MÉDIÉVALE D'AZINCOURT. A poster announces the schedule: "Archery contests 8 tonight. Jousting tomorrow at 3."

"There! I told you!"

"Good. Then I didn't come for nothing this time."

"*What?*"

He leans down and kisses away my sputtering. "You did book a hotel, didn't you? There are a lot of people here."

"I didn't." Suddenly I'm flustered. "I was hoping we could drive out into the country . . ."

"Maybe we'd better get one. It's too bright to shoot now and there's nothing going on anyway. We'll have to find something else to do until the archery show." His hand touches the small of my back and I feel honey in my veins.

We walk back through the town and stop at the *syndicat d'initiative*. I pick up a brochure for a farmhouse bed-and-breakfast. Red brick. Cows. Lace curtains. "Henry the Fifth slept here on the eve of battle!" I look hopefully at the clerk.

"I'm afraid there's nothing left," she says, running her finger down a photocopied sheet. "With the festival on."

I watch nervously. "A country auberge? A *chambre d'hôte?*"

"There's a double in the Bar des Anglais."

"In the bar?"

"Upstairs. It's not rated with the tourist office, no stars, but there's a shower. We only use it for overflow."

I look nervously at Jean-Jacques. But his hand is sliding up my sweaty back, under the tank top. He is looking at me.

"Okay."

She points the way.

The Bar des Anglais stands on the corner of the tiny main street. We push in a fly-specked glass door with our bags and are assaulted by juke-box pop music and smoke. There is a TV tuned to a soap opera, on loud. There are three pinball machines and a fooseball table. The chrome-front bar is backed by a dozen bottles, upside down with dosing spouts. Ricard. Whiskey. Something green. Laminate tables scatter over the Op Art cement-tile floor. They are full of boys under twenty and men over sixty.

"Nice place," Jean-Jacques says.

"What do you think?" I say.

He looks at me. "As long as there's a bed."

He asks at the bar, where a woman with eggplant-colored hair is rinsing glasses, unsoaped. He comes away with an enormous plastic keyring. "Room Two. Sounds promising."

We follow the jerk of the bartender's head to a stair behind the bar. It is dark and slanted and framed in false-wood paneling. The steps are covered with something that used to be all-weather carpet. It is getting hotter as we climb, dead dark in midafternoon. There's a glowing knob on the paneling. I press it. A light flickers on and ticks on a timer.

"There's Room One. This must be Room Two." Jean-Jacques forces it open with his shoulder and a wrench of the key. It is surprisingly large and bare, its green linoleum floor slanting precariously toward sealed windows. The walls are glued over with pinkish vinyl. There are greyed nylon sheers hanging askew, an ivory plastic armoire. The bed has orange chenille thrown over its lumps. A door cracks onto a bathroom tiled in enormous brown and yellow daisies. It is very, very hot and it smells of burnt chickpeas. Johnny Hallyday is pounding through the floorboards from the bar below.

"Oh god. Jean-Jacques, I'm sorry. Let's go somewhere else. Out in the country. Someplace with a little charm."

"I see all the charm I need right here." He is already pulling up my tank top.

Oh god. It's only been a week since we saw each other but he handles me as if we hadn't touched in a month. "Mayg, I missed you, *putain*."

It's so hot. Even naked it is almost too hot to touch. Sweat is trickling down his back, between my breasts.

"The shower."

"Mm-hm."

We pull each other across the creaking floor to the bathroom and let cold water spray over us. It is a tiny plastic pod of a shower, smaller than a phone booth. The blackening curtain smells of moldy rubber and clings to us. He swats it away, laughing. We tear open little foil packets of liquid soap and wash each other all over. He's not laughing now. He tries to lift me to the wall but the pod rocks precariously. We hurry dripping to the bed and the springs shriek, a cloud of dust puffing up from orange chenille. When he moves, the bed skids and the vinyl headboard slams against the wall. Again and the armoire doors fly open. Again and the picture of Charles VI slips off its slanting nail. His laugh rings out, and a gasp, and a laugh, and a gasp. The yellow August air is opaque with dust.

6 PM: I shake the chenille spread out the jimmied window and carry it back to the bed. Jean-Jacques is lying on the polyester sheets, a wet towel over his face.

"We should go out," he mumbles through the cloth. "Get some air."

"We could sleep in the car tonight. Except for the blackberries."

"No. We'll stay here tonight. Then tomorrow we'll drive to the beach. It's only an hour or so to Le Touquet."

I sit on the edge of the bed. "You don't happen to have any glamorous friends who . . ."

"You said no friends."

"Well, that was before I saw this hotel room."

"Okay. Friends . . ." He thinks. "There's Deauville, but that's a long way. Friends with a boat."

"A boat?" I trace a finger along the thin line of hair that spreads from his navel downward. "Could be nice."

"I'll call them. Can you sail?"

"Of course not. I'm from Indiana. I live in *la France profonde*."

"Doesn't matter. You can work in the galley. Wash dishes."

"No thanks. I'll lie on the deck and bronze myself."

"Mm. I'll bring my camera."

" 'Mm.' I think we should discuss photo rights." I am tracing the line above his navel now. "Jean-Jacques?"

"Mm?"

"You shouldn't send me those pictures. Maybe — maybe you shouldn't have taken them."

"Mm. A photographer has to capture the moment. You're easy to catch with your eyes closed."

"Still."

"I like you better in three dimensions." He reaches for me, the towel still over his face, his hands exploring my body. "Nobody has the right to feel this good."

"In a room like this? In this heat?"

"No. You."

8 PM: The sun is slanting lower and the heat has calmed to a sultry stillness. We walk through the crowds swigging from the mineral water bottles our bartender sold us for eight euros each. We hold fingertips. Our hair is knotted at our necks. He has a long-lensed camera hanging off his shoulder. His tripod swings from mine.

"Hungry?" Jean-Jacques asks.

"It's still too hot to think of food."

"I am always thinking of food."

"I've noticed."

"When you come to Paris, I will cook for you."

There's a tone in his voice that turns my knees to liquid. I raise his hand and kiss his long fingers. They smell like shower soap.

We walk.

"I called my friends. The boat isn't in Deauville."

"Too bad. We can find a hotel at Le Touquet."

"No. The boat is in Le Touquet. The little boat. They are down in St-Tropez with the yacht. We can have the little boat."

"*What?*"

He looks at me, grinning.

At the far end of town, the crowd is thickening and we can hear a loudspeaker squawking. Musette waltzes pump tender, lilting, wheezy threads over the oven-dense air. We worm our way through the throng.

At the edge of the mob there is a rail set up and, halfway across the field, a row of soldiers. Not real soldiers, but cardboard figures. Half represent the English, with lions painted thick on their chests. The other half wear fleurs-de-lys.

"*Mesdames et messieurs,*" the loudspeaker crackles. "The archery spectacle is about to begin."

The musette music stops short. Then there is the solo fluting of a fife. Drums pulse into the refrain. I feel them in my feet on the sod. There are shouts and clanking and the tramping of boots. The back of my neck crawls.

The crowd parts. Two dozen archers in chain mail and cone-shaped helmets take form against the lowering sun. They clank through the crowd, then halt, swivel, and splay neatly into symmetrical ranks. They reach gauntlet-hands over their backs, draw arrows from their quivers, raise the bows, and stretch. There is a drum roll. Then it stops.

My breath stops, too.

"Fire!" shouts the master. Two dozen arrows arc through the evening sky, whistling and spinning, then plunging through the hearts of the cardboard men, where they shiver to stillness.

The crowd surges, cheers. I can't help myself, I cheer, too.

"Oh! Kate and Cloey would *love* this! If only . . ." If only? My hand stops my mouth.

Jean-Jacques has his camera up. "Stay here. I'll be back." He scuttles away.

The archers pull their strings. Another two dozen arrows fly loose. We cheer. I cheer. Who cares if the figures are cardboard? I see it. I feel it. I feel the feeling. Cluny. Arles. Aigues-Mortes. They happened. I felt them. I saw them in my mind's eye. But this . . . I cheer and jump up and down. The fields of Agincourt! *Yes!*

The arrows are flying. I search the crowd for Jean-Jacques. He's nowhere in sight. I hope he's getting this.

Then I spot him. He is scaling a concrete power pole, rung by metal rung, the plastic banners fluttering around him. His lens is aimed at the archers, who are aiming just beyond him. They pull, point, and release. A shower of arrows sails overhead and Jean-Jacques shoots, his lens swinging in synch with the arrows' trajectory.

I stand with my hand over my mouth.

When he comes back to me he is smoking.

"You could have been killed!"

"I think I got some good pictures." He shrugs and presses into the crowd.

I follow, searching his face. "Did you see—I mean, did you *feel* . . . ?"

He looks at me. Then he nods and grins.

I stop in the hot press of bodies and wrap my arms around him. "You got it? You saw it? You *felt* it! You did!"

He looses his laugh. "Yes, Madame l'Historienne. I felt the feeling."

We head, hand in hand, for the food stands.

10 PM: We are standing by a glowing fire, chunks of bread in one hand, plastic cups of honey mead in the other. Our faces are smeared with the juice of the meat of the suckling pig that turns and crackles before us. Jean-Jacques holds out his bread for more. A man, sweating red in an open-neck smock, takes a knife and draws it two-handed through the crust of golden skin. He lays the meat on Jean-Jacques' bread and cuts another for mine. Jean-Jacques wipes the juice from my chin with his thumb and licks it. We back away from the fire and press through the darkness to the lady with the crockery pitcher of mead. We are getting to know her well.

"What's in this stuff?" Jean-Jacques asks.

"I don't know. Fermented honey, I think. It's very medieval."

He drains his glass and wipes his hands on his t-shirt. He has been taking pictures right and left, the tripod dangling from the camera as he moves through the crowd. There are madrigal singers, lutes and drums. Women in laced-up bodices and pointed hats, men in doublets and tights. A veil of mist floats low over the field and the moon breaks above the trees. There are torches thrust at angles all across the grounds, their yellow light flickering over our faces.

A folk band begins to play, pipes that pulse and weave like Celtic knotwork. He grabs my hand. "Okay, if you danced with that hand-kisser in Arles, you will dance with me."

I gulp down my mead and we head toward the music. A ring of dancers has formed, tourists in shorts and performers in costume. Hands break and regrasp and the ring broadens. The costumed ones know what they're doing. We try to do the same. Jean-Jacques is concentrating on his feet, camera and tripod banging on his hip, forehead glistening. He puts a hand around my waist and turns like the others, but the wrong way. We bump another couple and pull back, flustered. We try again. We try again. We try again.

"Jean-Jacques," I pant. "You're really bad at this." I pull him out of the ring, deep into the flickering darkness. "I am so relieved to find something you are bad at."

"I was not bad," he says, gasping, his hands on his ribs. "Maybe I'm not as good as Baptiste but I was not bad."

"You were bad."

"I did ballroom dancing. At the *rallyes*. The cotillion. Boarding school. Bordeaux. I am *not* bad." He reaches for my hand, slips an arm around my waist and dances me alone across the grass, goofily graceful in the darkness. His ponytail is slipping, his t-shirt soaked. His laugh echoes over the field.

He tips me back just like in the photograph, my hair flying. I laugh, too.

He is not bad.

He is too good to be true.

this isn't real

I don't care.

1 AM: We lie wrapped around each other on the mattress we have dragged to the open window of Room 2. The sheets are soaked with sweat. The moon is high, pouring into the room. A searing sweetness flows between us as if he were still inside me. Our faces are very close.

"I will shoot the jousting tomorrow," he murmurs sleepily. "Then we'll go to the Le Touquet market. We will fill the boat with food. We will leave the shore and I will not bring you back. You don't know anything about sailing. You will be helpless."

"Mm. I'm a good swimmer."

I drift off to sleep with his skin against mine, our lips almost touching.

Friday, 8 AM: I open my eyes. It's the phone. I don't know where it is. I jump up and paw through the sheets, chenille, the clothes scattered over the floor. The phone bleats on. There! I grab it and press Yes.

"Sorry, darling, did I wake you?"

"No, that's all right. I have to . . . get rolling."

"Not too early? Good. Well, I have a little surprise for you. I've taken the day off and am bringing the children up to join you. Agincourt! Thought it might be fun. Make a weekend of it. Haven't been anywhere this summer and here's poor you out on the road all the time. Won't that be fun? You don't mind, do you?"

My breath has gone out of me. I search for my tongue.

"Nigel, that's—that's—" I find it. "Good idea! Good idea! Wish I'd thought of it myself!" My voice is loud and emphatic. My knees are rattling.

I look desperately at Jean-Jacques. He sits up.

"When are you leaving?"

"Well, as a matter of fact, we're just passing Verdun now. Wanted to get a good start on the day, so I packed up last night and—well, there you are. Should be there by noon, one at the latest. Think you can squeeze us all into your room?"

I look around frantically—the empty bedframe, the open armoire, the shower, the mattress, and Jean-Jacques sitting naked on it with a worried look on his face.

"I—I think so. I'll just have to see about . . . cots for the kids."

"I've thrown some sleeping bags into the boot just in case. Jousting, did you say? I'm sure the children will love it. Then maybe we can drive over to the beach. Le Touquet's not far if I'm reading my map right."

"Nigel . . . this is . . . wonderful. Um, I'll meet you . . . meet you at the Bar des Anglais."

"Bar des Anglais? Easy to remember! I've never been to 'Azincourt.' Ian and Geoffrey have all made pilgrimages and they said . . ."

"Nigel? Nigel? You're breaking up on me. I can't hear you." I press No.

No. This cannot be happening. Jean-Jacques is on his feet. His hand is on my shoulder.

"He's on his way."

"Here?"

"Here. With the kids."

We stand a minute, looking at each other. Then we look around us.

"I'll go. You can take me to the *gare*. Any *gare*."

"No. He knows you're here. He expects us to be . . . working."

"Then we'll find you a hotel room."

"Okay, okay."

I stand, my hand hovering over my mouth. I am suddenly aware of my nakedness.

9 AM: The *syndicat* is closed until eleven, so we walk down to the hotel at the end of town. There are no rooms, of course, on the Friday night of a festival weekend in August. They call around the area for us and there is nothing within fifty miles. We trudge back to the Bar des Anglais. The eggplant-haired bartender brings us buttered bread and tosses some jam packets onto the counter. Blackberry.

"I don't suppose you have another room free tonight," I mumble, my head in my hands.

"*Benh,* there's always Room One. Not done up. Don't use it much. You need it?"

Jean-Jacques looks up and nods. I look around me and try to imagine my children here. I swallow and smile.

"Yes. Thanks."

10 AM: We have put Room 2 back together and moved my things into Room 1. It is a mirror image of Room 2, back to back, but even bigger, L-shaped with a thick plastic curtain that draws across the end with a fold-out couch. "The kids can sleep there," Jean-Jacques says. I blanch at the thought.

The bartender has given us a pile of soured linens and Jean-Jacques and I make up the bed. "Don't finish it," I say. I glance up, ashamed to be calculating so coolly. "I was supposed to have slept in it last night, remember?" I punch the pillow. I muss the sheets, but not too much.

I lay my toiletries on the sink. My toothbrush, my hairbrush. I take another shower. I can't get clean enough. I put oil on the scrape lines from Jean-Jacques' stubble, all over. I wrap his scarf around my neck to hide the marks. I take it off again. I look into my eyes in the mirror. I avert them.

Noon: "I can't do this."

"Just tell him. This is it. You'll come be with me."

"This is crazy. I don't know."

"What is it you don't know?"

"I don't know."

We are waiting in the Bar des Anglais. Jean-Jacques has finished a pack of cigarettes. The ashtray is full. We have no appetite or thirst.

"Maybe you shouldn't be here when they get here. You need to be here. But not be here, you know?"

"Okay. I should go—take pictures!"

He slings his camera bag over his shoulder, pushes through the door, and nearly collides with Nigel.

"Well! Hel-lo there! You must be Jean-Marie!" He presses Jean-Jacques back into the bar with the sheer force of his smile.

"Jean-Jacques."

"Sorry! Sorry!"

"Hello, Nigel. I am pleased to meet you." Jean-Jacques says it in careful English and I start at the sound. Then he extends his hand. Nigel clasps it and claps him on the shoulder, man to man. I feel myself sink deeper into my chair.

He swings round on me. "And hello, darling." He busses me hard on the cheek.

"The children?" I say faintly.

"Right!" Nigel claps his hands and rubs them. "Mustn't forget the children! They're just having a look next door at the pastry-shop window. Thought I might spoil them a bit, holiday and all."

I jump up and head for the door, my shoulder brushing past Jean-Jacques'. He stands with his hands at his sides. "Cloey! Kate!" They are ogling through a plate-glass window next door. They see me and run into my arms.

"I was sick! I was sick in the car! I may have an éclair?" Kate cries.

Jean-Jacques has stepped outside. He is looking at my children. They have orange hair. Orange eyebrows. Ice-blue eyes. High, pale foreheads. Freckles.

He drops to one knee. "*Bonjour,* Clovis. *Bonjour,* Katharine," he says. "*Je m'appelle* J-J."

They stop short and study him carefully. Then Kate steps forward. "*Bonjour, monsieur,*" she murmurs and kisses him on each cheek.

Cloey follows. "*Bonjour, monsieur. Vous piquez.*"

You prickle. I swallow.

Jean-Jacques looks at me. "They're beautiful."

"Right then!" Nigel crows from the bar. "Something to drink? Open a bottle? *Garçon?*"

2:30 PM: "Always been fascinated by the photographic arts. Used to dabble in it myself. Not at your level, mind you."

Nigel has not stopped talking since he arrived, all of it showered upon Jean-Jacques. He has drunk most of the bottle of *vin ordinaire,* though he offered to refill Jean-Jacques' glass several times. I hide behind the children, fussing over their Oranginas, cutting their toasted-cheese *croques-monsieurs.* The bar matron has been studying us curiously from behind her cigarette.

". . . traveling all over the world, always in the thick of things. A real gypsy life! Adventure!"

Jean-Jacques is smoking. I'm not sure how much of the English he understands. It isn't the words that count.

Nigel drains his glass. "Shall we? Poster said something about three o'clock, I believe?"

3 PM: Now we are heading, the five of us, for the festival. Jean-Jacques and Nigel walk ahead, side by side. I hang back holding Kate's and Cloey's hands. Nigel is a head taller than Jean-Jacques. Above the turned-up collar of his pink golf shirt, his hair glints orange in the sun. Jean-Jacques has his hands in his pockets. There is a patch of sweat soaking between his shoulders, below the ponytail.

". . . sports, rugby, football. Always see those chaps trotting about the field backward, shooting away, don't know how they manage without getting injured themselves."

Jean-Jacques walks quietly on.

"But then you're a food specialist, aren't you? Meg's told me all about you. The gastronomy of France! Gourmet stuff! But then again this book you're working on is about something else altogether, isn't it? Living history! Not a lot of 'haute cuisine' in that, is there?"

The tips of Jean-Jacques' ears are pink. "Mayg," he turns around. "I go . . . to find a place by the horses." His English is painful, raw. His eyes barely meet mine.

"Okay. I'll—"

"Would you mind terribly if I tagged along? See the action from the inside? Watch a pro at work?"

Jean-Jacques lights a cigarette and focuses on the glowing tip. "Okay." He turns away and heads for the barn. Nigel's hand is on his shoulder.

"You see, Jean-Claude, I've always been curious about how these things are done. All those overhead views, panoramas . . ." Nigel's voice fades, but I can still hear it long after they have melted into the crowd.

"Where they going, *Maman?*" Cloey asks.

"They're going to take pictures of the battle, honey. There's a big battle coming up."

3:30 PM: "*Mesdames et messieurs,* the *cavaliers* are ready. Let the spectacle begin!"

I lift Cloey onto my shoulders, his sandals tucked under my arms. At the far end of the field I see horses. "See them? Knights!"

"Soldiers!"

Kate cranes on tiptoe and I nudge her in front of me, between the press of bodies. We press forward and break through to the barrier ribbon and lean past.

The field is lined with horses draped in fluttering silks, and on their backs knights in plumed helmets ride out the restlessness of their horses' feet. They are holding long striped poles streaming banners.

"The horses have ribbons in their tresses! *Regarde, Maman!*" Kate is breathless, pointing. "And their tails!"

Two riders trot to the center, one head to toe in cobalt blue and gilt fleurs-de-lys, the other in red embroidered with golden lions. They face each other and bow. Then they spin their horses away and trot to opposite ends of the field.

A trumpet fanfare screeches over the speaker, then the hollow beat of a row of drums. "*Mesdames et messieurs,* the battle of Agincourt! Henry V, king of England, confronted by the armies of Charles VI of France! We all know the results of this fateful combat. France has never seen greater losses—ten thousand dead—and the blow was to resonate through the centuries.

"But this is not just a fight between two armies, it represents more. It is a fight for the future!"

The drumbeat accelerates. The horses shift and skitter in place, restless.

"*Mesdames et messieurs,* I present to you the kings' own henchmen: The Knight of the Lion versus the Knight of the Lily!" The crowd erupts in shouts and applause. The drum breaks into a roll.

"*Aux armes!*"

The horses recoil muscled thighs and spring forward, their hooves pounding the turf. The riders' heads are high, their lances aimed dead ahead. They charge onward and with a ringing clank of steel blur into one at the center of the field. The blue knight rears back and drops from the saddle, landing with a thud on the earth. His horse gallops off. The victor rears high in the air, waving his lance, his horse's hooves pawing the air. We cheer and clap.

Cloey's sandals dig into my shoulders. "*T'as vu, Maman?* Did you see? Is it *real, Maman?*"

"No, honey, it isn't real." I squeeze his tiny foot.

I glance nervously around for Jean-Jacques. He isn't near the lineup or at the edge of the field. He is crouching on the roof of the temporary horse shed, aiming his camera down the field.

I squint. Nigel is nowhere to be seen. Then I see an orange head pop above the eave. He pulls himself up, then crabwalks over to Jean-Jacques. He huddles over his shoulder, peering down the line of the lens. He is talking; I can see his jaw moving and moving and moving. Jean-Jacques sinks down and crosses his legs, Indian-style. Nigel is talking, squatting beside him. Jean-Jacques passes him the camera and Nigel levels it, peering through the lens. Jean-Jacques lifts it gently away from him and aims it at the riders. Nigel is talking, talking.

5:30 PM: The crowd is dispersing and heading for the drink stands. I pull the children with me toward the horse shed. Jean-Jacques is there, patting the muzzle of a pureblood in blue silks.

"Where's Nigel?"

"He went to get beer." He strokes the horse's nose. He doesn't look at me.

"If you want to go now, I understand," I say. "I'll drive you to the *gare*."

He looks up. He looks at the children and searches carefully for neutral words. "It's time to leave," he says. "He's not worth it. The boat—"

"Boat?" Cloey says.

There is no language we can speak the children don't understand.

Nigel trots up with two enormous plastic cups foaming over. He is speaking a language Jean-Jacques doesn't understand. But I do. Too well. I feel the hair on my neck crawling.

"'The fewer men, the greater share of honour,'" he spouts. "'God's will! I pray thee, wish not one man more.'"

He hands Jean-Jacques a beer. "Brilliant show. Absolutely brilliant. I especially liked the finale—the full-out charge, all of 'em at once. 'Once more unto the breach, dear friends, once more'—Thirsty, darling? Here, have this one. I'll just nip back and get another." Nigel trots off again.

"May I pet the horse, too?" Kate asks. Jean-Jacques sets the beer on a plank and lifts her up by her slender ribs.

7 PM: We are sitting, the five of us, at a café table outside the Hôtel Henri V. It is baking hot even under the overhanging roof. The tables are crowded with sunburned tourists. Nigel's forehead is the color of raw steak. There are three empty *pastis* glasses before us, all of them Nigel's. The children haven't drunk their juice. They are sagging in the heat.

"Such an amazing story! Extraordinary really! Altered the face of Europe. The French aristocracy virtually wiped out in a single blow! Better than the rugby cup, really!"

Jean-Jacques is smoking. He is looking at the tabletop. His coffee cup is empty and he turns the saucer. He frames his English carefully.

"You are interested in history, too. Like your wife."

"Like my wife! Yes! My wife. She's terribly preoccupied with all things historic, isn't she? Her office—she calls it her bunker, you know—lined with all sorts of paraphernalia. Old lace hats and artillery shells and such."

The lace *coiffe* is new, from the Bretagne market. He's been down there recently. I draw Cloey onto my lap with shaky hands.

10 PM: The dining room of the Henri V is clearing out gradually, but Nigel is in top form, two empty bottles of generic Bordeaux on the table—claret, he calls it—and another one, near-empty, in his hand. Jean-Jacques' ashtray is full.

"Fascinating profession, photography . . ."

I have led Kate to the bathroom twice, Cloey three times. I have cut their meat, which sits untouched, oozing red across the thick white plates. They ate their *frites* and their ice-cream scoop. They are nodding against me in the red velvet chairs. I draw Cloey into my arms and his head lolls against me.

"Fascinating. I mean, photographers just *take it all in.*"

Jean-Jacques avoids my eyes.

Nigel forges ahead. "It must be rather effective with women."

Jean-Jacques stubs out his cigarette.

Nigel smiles. "But then, you're married, aren't you?"

I look up sharply at Jean-Jacques.

His eyes are down. "No." He says it simply.

Nigel turns to me. He is smiling. His cheeks are scarlet patches. He turns back to Jean-Jacques. His profile is taut and his chin cuts a clean line against the velour-patch wallpaper.

His voice is lower now. "Lots of luck with the ladies, then, I should think. I mean, a photographer just has to say 'You're so *lovely,* may I take your picture' and they flip back onto the bed!"

I press Cloey's head to me, my hand over his ear. Jean-Jacques reaches for a cigarette but stops himself. His hands go back to his lap.

Nigel grasps the bottle and pours a short stream into Jean-Jacques' full glass, then a long one into his own. He drinks deep. "Mind if I have a look again at that camera? I must say it was *amazing* watching you work today!"

"You wish to look at my camera?"

"Yes, if you don't mind, I mean. It's not often I get to see professional equipment."

Jean-Jacques leans down and passes his camera to him two-handed.

"Telephoto lens there? Two hundred millimeter? *Four hundred?*

Extraordinary. Very impressive. Quite a range! And that rim—that a shade or filter?"

"Sun shade."

"Retractible?"

"Pardon?"

"Does it retract? Or does it screw off?"

Jean-Jacques' ears are pink. He looks at his hands.

"Mine, you see, is just for *dilettantes.*" He gives the word a posh French inflection. "Just a toy, really." He pulls his compact Nikon from his pants pocket. He pinches a button and a tiny lens whirs out. "Twenty-five to eighty, I think. Or is it thirty-five to ninety? Zoom is nice though. Comes in handy!"

Kate perks up. "May I see, too? The big one!"

She crawls into Nigel's lap. She peers through Jean-Jacques' lens. "I see *Maman!*"

"Do you, darling? Let's have a look." He raises the camera and points the long lens at me.

"There's Mummy. Click!" he says. "You're rather out of focus, darling, let me see here . . ."

His fingers grasp the ring.

"Not that one," Jean-Jacques leans forward. "That's the . . ."

But Nigel turns the attachment threads and the lens lurches down and drops onto the table, smashing a plate of half-eaten steak.

"Oh dear. Terribly sorry! Butterfingers . . ."

I have only seen that expression on Jean-Jacques' face on the D-Day beach. His hands clench. Then he reaches for the lens, wipes it with his napkin, and slides it into his bag. He pushes his chair back. But Nigel hasn't finished.

"I do hope you'll let me know about repairs. Cleaning. We have insurance, civil responsibility coverage, haven't we, Megs? *La responsabilité civile* is a very practical thing to have!"

"I must go to bed. I leave in the morning. Early." He looks at me significantly. He rises. He lifts the camera bag onto his shoulder.

Nigel rises, too. He looms tall, swaying.

"Back to Paris then? Well, I must say it's been a real pleasure. Love your work. Saw the pictures you took of my wife. Quite nice. Rather . . . provocative stuff sometimes. All in the *angle*. The *details*. Goes with the profession, doesn't it?"

Jean-Jacques looks at me. I feel no blood in my lips. He shoves his chair aside and heads out of the restaurant.

Nigel stands looking at me for a moment. I am holding Clovis very tight. "Right then. Shall we adjourn to the Bar des Anglais?"

11 PM: "'Once more'—no, that's Harfleur, isn't it? Always wondered, darling, is that really Honfleur? Did Shakespeare get it wrong?"

We walk down the sidewalk, Cloey asleep over my shoulder, Kate draped half-conscious in Nigel's arms. My mouth is shut tight, jaw squeezing. There is no room for my words. Nigel fills the sky with them, his voice haranguing through the night air.

"The Saint Crispin speech. Which is Saint Crispin? 'Cry God for Harry England and Saint George!' No, that's Harfleur too . . . Saint Crispin . . . 'And gentlemen in England now a-bed.' That's it! 'Shall think themselves accursed they were not here and hold their manhoods *cheap* whiles any speaks.' That's it! Got it. 'We few, we happy few . . .'"

In Room 1, we lay the children on the couch-bed and tuck the polyester sheet over them. "Beddy-byes, Fair Katharine. There you go now, Cloey. 'Gentlemen in England now abed . . .'"

Nigel has not lowered his volume. I am wordless.

He pulls the plastic curtain shut and turns to me with a manic smile on his face. His eyes are very red. He slides a hand around my waist, lifts my hand into the air, and waltzes me around the room like a rag doll. "Inspiring place, Agincourt! The sheer *will* of them! 'But when the blast of war blows in our ears then'—something something—'stiffen the sinews, summon up the blood'—something, something—No, that's Harfleur again!" he crows, slapping his forehead.

Both my hands are over my mouth. I think I'm going to throw up.

"What's wrong, Megs, you used to love my recitations."

Both his hands are around my waist. His forehead props against mine. His voice lowers. "'What is't to me, when you yourselves are cause, if your pure maidens fall into the hand of hot and forcing violation?' Always liked that bit."

316 ◆ Nancy Coons

"Nigel, will you . . . Nigel, we'll talk in the morning. You're drunk and I—"

"'Now set the teeth and' . . . and something . . . 'stretch the nostril wide!'" His hands are moving. He is pressing against me. "'Hold *hard* the breath, and bend up every spirit to his full height!'"

"Stop, Nigel, it's not funny. You're crazy, you—"

"'Once more unto the breach!'" he cries. It doesn't take long. He has me, quickly, on the orange chenille spread and the bed is banging, banging, banging against the wall.

"Nigel! Don't, you're hurting me, you're . . ."

The armoire doors fly open. Then everything is still.

He lies on me, his face against my neck, and a strangled sound wrenches out of his throat. A sob? I lay my hands over his pink shirt. His hands grasp my head, trembling. Then he rolls away, shudders once, opens his mouth and snores.

Beyond the head of the bed there is a scrape and a muffled thud. Very distinctly, through the thin plasterboard wall, I hear the click of a lighter.

I lie very, very still, watching the clouds of dust settle around me. Then I crawl into the shower pod and cry.

2 AM: I rinse myself, dry myself, dress. I pull the plastic curtain back. The children are spread-eagled over the top of the sheet. I pack my toiletries, my clothes, my laptop. I go back to the couch-bed and lay my lips on Cloey's forehead, Kate's neck. I breathe their sourdough smell. Then I carry my things past Nigel's sleeping form and time the lifting of the doorlatch to his snore.

The landing is dark. I feel for the stair rail.

Another latch lifts. "Mayg."

The hall light comes on and ticks on a timer. Jean-Jacques is standing at the door of Room 2 in a cloud of smoke.

"Are you hurt? Did he hurt you?" He is whispering.

I am shaking so hard I can barely control my teeth. "No, I'm not hurt. I was already . . . sore."

He reaches for me. I flinch away.

"The bastard. *Salaud*."

"No. I . . ." I take a shuddering breath. "I deserved that."

"*What?*"

"I deserved that. I've hurt him."

"He's an ass. He's a monster. He was hurting—I should have—"

"He was just . . . being Nigel. Only more so."

Jean-Jacques looks at me, incredulous. "You didn't deserve that."

My throat is swelling and my voice chokes. "Yes, I did. Yes, I did. He knew. He *knew*. I don't know how long he's known."

"How did he . . . ?"

"He's been in my bunker. He's been looking through my things. He's known." I am straining to keep the tears back. "I've been *lying* to him. He's known I've been lying while we—"

"You should have told him. I told you to tell him."

"Oh! Stop. *Stop*." My hands are over my ears. "You guys always know *everything*. I don't know a thing. I don't know anything anymore."

He reaches for me. I throw his arms off. The timer light clicks off and plunges us into darkness. He slams his hand over the button and it clicks back on and ticks.

He looks at my bags.

"I'll get my stuff."

"Jean-Jacques, no."

He turns toward his room. "I'll be right there."

"*No*."

He stops and turns back.

"I have to go. I have to go alone."

"What?" He steps toward me. I step back.

"I have to think."

There is a wrenching snore from Room 1. The pain in my throat tears loose. I grab my bags and drag them down the stairs.

But he follows me down to the bar. Chairs are on the tabletops. The Eskimo cooler clatters and hums. He lifts away my suitcase and shoulders it.

"Jean-Jacques, no!"

"I have your car keys," he says simply.

"Please. *Please.*"

He stands, looking at me. Tears are pouring down my cheeks and my nose is running. I am shivering like a child. He reaches for me.

"No!" It is almost a scream.

He stares at me. Then he shrugs and shakes his head.

We push through the glass bar door. The street is dark, bats diving in and out of the single streetlight. We walk down the middle of the blacktop to the Citroën. He lifts my bag into the trunk. He stands for a moment looking at me. I shudder and wipe my hand across my lips.

"Okay," he says. "Call me. Tell me where you go. I'll come to you. If you still want."

He cracks the door of the driver's seat and holds it. I slide past him and he presses toward me. He holds his face close to mine. I turn and duck into the car. He passes me the keys. I pull the door shut and start the engine and pull away.

I look back in the rearview mirror. He is standing with his hands in his pockets, a cigarette in his mouth, unlit. He's barefoot.

11 ⚜ Full Retreat

Saturday, August 30, 5 AM: I am driving, driving through the darkness. My lungs fight their way past squeezing sobs. I pull to the side and blow my nose, mop my melting face. I study the map and drive some more. I don't know where I'm driving. I point the Citroën south. I swing west of the *périphérique* and give Paris wide berth. I drive hard and fast until the sky glows from black to peach to blue. Then I drive some more.

My body is a battlefield. There's a burning pain between my legs. It's nothing to the pain in my chest. My heart is twisted in knots. It takes two hundred kilometers down the road before I can breathe in light shudders.

I drive. I breathe. By the time I stop to fill the gas tank, an icy calm is descending. I wash my face in the piss-splashed restroom. I crouch over the seatless toilet and wince at the burn. I force myself to drink a cup of coffee from the vending machine. I study the giant poster map by the candy bars. I am somewhere north of Orléans, it seems. Far away. I need to go far away. South. Southwest. I climb back into the car and point it toward Limoges.

The countryside wheels past anonymously, a blaze of fields and forests without profile, without meaning. The *autoroute* is a ribbon across blank landscape and if it weren't for the brown and white tourist signs, I would have no sense of where I am. Loire châteaux are reduced to cartoons. Limoges is nothing but a china plate. My legs cramp, my ankle cocked hard on the accelerator. The temperature gauge is rising and I lift my foot. The Citroën isn't good at marathon drives. I stop and refuel, add water to the radiator, add oil. I eat something out of a bag, I think it is potato chips. I press south.

4 PM: The freeway gives out on me below Souillac and I am suddenly dumped back into France. There are limestone cliffs and dark billowing forests and stone villages wedged into bedrock. The Périgord. I roll down the windows. It is cooler here. Soft, green. A great brown river flows beside the road. The Dordogne. I have driven a long way.

I swing west and follow a tiny road that winds along the riverbank. The lanes are crowded with trailers and camper vans and four-wheel-drives. Half of them have GB license plates and steering wheels on the right. I am in Aquitaine, once English territory, and English territory still, with hotels and restaurants and shops and summer houses seething with British invaders. They seem to feel entitled, as if Eleanor of Aquitaine had deeded it to them directly, castles and all.

Oh god. I feel as if the Hundred Years' War had been fought over every inch of my body. I do not want to hear British voices.

I don't want to hear any voices.

I am heading west toward Bergerac. There is a sign for Bordeaux. No, I do not want to go to Bordeaux. The Médoc. Pauillac. De Brissac-Chabrol. I turn around hard and head east instead.

I sink my foot but the Citroën is past pushing now. It is laboring, chugging, and the temperature gauge bobs near red. I ease back and wind slowly, slowly along the banks of the Dordogne. I do not want to stop. I don't know where to go. Cliffs and castles loom above me. Walnut groves stretch along the floodplain. The roads weave precariously. Cloey would have thrown up by now.

Cloey. Kate. A hot flash of clarity and pain. They woke up this morning to no mother and a hungover father with his pants around his knees. To a strange photographer smoking in the room next door.

Jean-Jacques. Stranded. Without a car.

Nigel. Without a wife.

I look at the cell phone on the seat beside me. It is charging in the chrome cigarette lighter. It is Off. There is something white in the footwell. The Arabic scarf.

we will fill the boat with food. we will leave the shore and i will not bring you back. you don't know anything about sailing. you will be helpless.

I press down the pedal and roll ahead.

It is almost dark when the Citroën lugs hollowly, sputters and dies, giving one last resigned shudder. I roll the last few meters onto the shoulder near a row of walnut trees. I lay my forehead down against the wheel. Headlights strobe past.

I lie slumped like that for a while. Then I pull my bags out of the trunk. I unplug the phone. I lift the scarf up and stare at it. Then I stuff it into the briefcase, lean into oncoming headlights, and stick out my thumb.

10 PM: I sink onto the bed under the deep-slanting eaves of a tiny room. It's a bed-and-breakfast up in the hills. A woman in an old truck stopped for me and brought me to her friend's house. I will deal with the car in the morning.

The owner is soft-spoken and kind. She made up a tray with tea and a jam-smeared tartine. She gave me a key to the house, then she pulled the bedroom door shut behind her.

My hands are still curled into the shape of the steering wheel. I pull off my sandals and look around me. Oak rafters. Polished planks. Rag rugs. Clean. Plain. Like a little girl's bedroom. I make myself drink the tea. I chew the tartine. It sticks in my throat.

In the bathroom I fill the toilet with red urine, wincing at the cramps. I crouch on the bidet and wash carefully. It stings. I flash on foil soap packets. Long fingers. Orange chenille. At the neat, round sink I wash my face and neck and arms and breasts. Soap stings there, too.

Get thee to a nunnery, I think. This doesn't make me smile.

I limp to my bag and forage through. I didn't pack much clothing. I didn't mean to *wear* much clothing. I pull on the tank top from Thursday. It smells like Jean-Jacques. My sweat. His sweat. Smoke. My eyes close. I take it off and stuff it back in the bag.

With the quilt drawn around me, I pick up the cell phone. I thumb 888 and put it to my ear.

Vous avez sept nouveau messages.

At 3:20 AM:
Mayg. I—Mayg, écoute, come back. Don't—we—merde. I love you.
(Click)

At 6:55 AM:
Mayg. I'm going to stay here until Nigel wakes up, or he'll think we've ... I want him to know we didn't leave together. He should know that you ... I don't know. Mayg, call me. (Click)

At 8:10 AM:
Mayg? Mayg, pick up, putain de merde. Don't do this. Maybe I should ... I ... merde. I think I hear the kids. Call me. (Click)

At 9:30 AM:
Meg? Megs, darling. I am sorry. (pause) Jean—thingie—Jean-Jacques told me you'd left in the night. I must admit I was surprised to find him still here when I saw you'd gone. With your things. I behaved... I behaved abominably last night and I don't blame—Sorry, no Cloey, don't touch that! (Click)

At 11:45 AM:
Meg? You there? Jean-Ja—your friend told me he doesn't know where you are and I must say I believe him. I've just dropped him off at the Amiens railway station. He had no car, you see, and—rather a decent chap, really, aside from ... aside from the fact that he's been ... shagging my wife. Bugger. BUGGER. Meg, where in god's name are you? Pick up the bloody phone I can't—Cloey stop that, don't—(Click)

At 2:30 PM:
Meg? I'm heading off now. For home. I'm rather hoping you might have decided... that you might have gone back. Well. Please, darling, give a call. (Click)

At 3:25 PM:
Mayg. I am back at my place. Paris. It's ... I don't know where you are. You have to call me. You are ... You are too ... Don't do this, Mayg. I love you and I want ... Putain. I ... (click of lighter, deep intake of breath) Mayg, listen. I love you. That's all that ... After all we've ... You can't just ... Merde. (Click)

I steady the phone with both hands. Then I tap out two SMSs with clumsy thumbs:

First to Jean-Jacques in French:

> *must think. need time. don't know.*

Then to Nigel in English:

> *must think. need time. don't know. please kiss kids for me.*

That's when the tears come.

Sunday, 10 AM: The cystitis is very bad this morning. I fill a drinking glass with a scarlet sample. I shiver with cramps and chills. Where am I going to find a doctor on a Sunday in the middle of . . . wherever it is I am? I shower and dress in the one clean tank top left. I climb down to the miniature dining room. I look out the casement windows onto greening flower beds and a card-castle of stone houses, their roofs steep-pitched as witches' hats. The blackened yellowstone seethes with ivy and flowering vines. There are cats on the eaves.

"Good morning. Did you sleep well?"

The hostess, in a cardigan, trousers, a pitcher of orange juice in her hands.

I nod. "I guess so. I'm very tired."

She brings me coffee, milk, warm rolls, yogurt. I haven't eaten anything but the tartine and potato chips since Friday night. I flash on a bloody steak on a broken plate. I shudder.

She looks out the window at the garden. "Your car is at the garage on the valley road. My brother spotted it and towed it in. He's rather fond of the old DS. Are you in a hurry to get on your way?"

I am not. I flush. "I'm afraid I need repairs myself. Do you have a doctor in the village?"

"Not here, but in town, yes. About five kilometers. Should be on weekend call. I'll check. I can drop you there, if you like, or I can lend you a bicycle."

I cringe at the thought of a bicycle seat. "If you're going that way."

5 PM: I have visited the doctor, and the *pharmacie-de-garde,* and the garage. It's Sunday but everyone seems to be the friend of Madame Durand. The Citroën is recovering from exhaustion. I am, too. The *garagiste* drops me back at the bed-and-breakfast. I take my antibiotics. I sleep in the little bed. Madame Durand knocks on the door with a tray at seven. Soup. Bread. I am grateful.

She stands and looks out the window again. Her arms are folded across her bosom. "You are traveling to . . . where?"

It's a good question. "Just finding my way, I guess."

Monday, 9 AM: My head is clearer today. The infection is clearing, too. I slept a deep, dark sleep, twelve hours.

"Madame Durand, do you know of any *gîtes* around here? A rental?" My hands are wrapped around a huge cup of coffee and my thoughts are focusing.

"There are several. For a few days or . . . ?"

"Longer." Suddenly I know. "A month. Maybe more."

She looks at me. "You are . . . ?"

"On my own. For a while."

2 PM: "It isn't rented very often because of the size. Her son used it."

I am standing on the threshhold of a stone house. Not a house, really, a cube skewed against a broad manorial *presbytère,* itself canted up against a chapel. The roofs slant, steep and mossy, to gables sharp as knives. Around them loom high limestone bluffs, blueing in their own deep shadow.

"It's perfect." My eyes adjust to the light inside. There is a whitewashed kitchen—a gas burner, a toaster oven—half swallowed by a stone stair. I climb it. There's a bathroom niche halfway up. At the top, a single bed, a desk, an armoire. A window looking over green.

"Yes. It's just right." I look at the desk and see clearer still. "I have a book to write."

4 PM: I carry my bag and briefcase in the front door, ducking under the chiseled frame. It's cool inside these stone walls. I set the basket of bread and eggs that Madame Durand gave me on the tiny kitchen table, look around me and reassess. I have no sweater, no jacket, no shoes but sandals. I have credit cards. The Citroën will be ready tomorrow. I will buy what I need. I don't need much.

I climb the stairs and set my bag on the bed, open the briefcase on the desk. Jean-Jacques' scarf is stuffed inside. I lay my hands on it and feel the cotton, start to raise it to my face, my nose, my lips. I stop. I fold it carefully into a neat square and slide it onto the armoire shelf.

I pull out the cell phone and turn it on. There is an SMS in English.

What shall I tell the children?

Oh god. What *shall* I tell the children?
There is an SMS in French.

Tell me where you are. I will come.

While I am holding it, the phone breets in my palm. I squeeze down No and hold it. The phone goes black.

Downstairs over the bottled-gas flame, I scramble two yellow eggs. I eat them with the bread. I drink tap water from a jelly glass. I swallow antibiotics. Then I climb the stairs, open the window, and crawl into bed as the sun sets. I lie under the cool sheets alone and listen to the frogs peep, their voices blinking like fireflies in the growing darkness.

Tuesday, 10 AM: I settle myself carefully onto Madame Durand's bicycle seat. Better. So far, so good. I tuck my skirt hem around my thighs, sling a laundry bag over my shoulder, and point the bike downhill toward the Dordogne.

The air is clean and fresh and smells of walnuts. The wind is cool on my bare arms. I will buy a sweater. I feel my face shifting oddly. It's a smile.

3 PM: The Citroën is rumbling again and its banquette is loaded with sacks. Apples. Plums. Pears. Greens. Some rice, beans, pasta, milk, coffee. Tampax. My period is gushing out of me as if purging something away. It feels right to bleed this way.

Now I drive up to the *gîte* and haul the bicycle out of the trunk. My new sweater feels good, a thick truck-driver's *camionneur* with a zipper at the neck. Cheap canvas sneakers. A pair of socks. Stiff jeans.

On the gas ring, I cook a cup of rice and eat it out of the pan. I carry

26 ✤ *Nancy Coons*

an apple to the front step and watch the light shifting over the oak-bearded cliffs.

11 PM: There's a dull ache in my uterus. Above it, too. I climb the stairs and turn on the phone.

There is an SMS in English from two o'clock this morning.

> *vvtold chidren you wer workin blody good one q4x-xx*

The phone breets in my hand. I hold No down hard.
I wait. Then I turn it back on and type an SMS.

> *Nigel. I'm sorry I hurt you. I am working. Alone. Tell C & K I love them. Tell them I am writing a book.*

I hit Send.
The phone beeps. A new SMS, in French.

> *c'est tout?*

Is that all?
I ache.

11:30 PM: I curl up on the bed and listen to the voice messages.

> *At 10:47 PM:*
> *Megs, darling, I do apologise for the . . . the text message. I'd had a few too many. I have been rather out of sorts, but I'm trying to—but I—(pause. clink of ice. a slurp and swallow.) Actually, I don't see why I should be the one to apologise, really, what you've done is unforgivable, it's unspeakable, vile, parading that scarf under my nose, the lies, the lies, filthy pictures, you've—(ice clink) oh bugger, I've gone and—bloody hell, I really meant to—(Click)*

> *At 11:05 PM:*
> *Meg, if you would please send me an address I will try to write to you properly. Something civil. Don't seem to be able to keep talking into this . . . this . . . without your answering. The children are getting on. Sophie is helping. So if you'd just consider letting me know where I*

might . . . But then you'd probably rather . . . (sigh. clink of ice.) Well then. Bye for now. (Click)

At 11:20 PM:
(sirens, roar of a bus, a taxi horn) Mayg, écoute. I want you to come to Paris. To live here. With me. You don't have to run away from me. If you won't let me come to . . . wherever you are then you come here. To me. Okay? Will you? D'accord? (Click)

2 AM: I am typing an SMS to Jean-Jacques. My thumbs tremble and I can't make the letters work.

I cant come to you it wasntreal

The phone breets in my hand and I nearly drop it, slapping the keyboard. I hear a voice.

"Mayg? Mayg!"

I hold the phone away from me. Then I bring it to my ear.

"Jean-Jacques."

"Don't hang up!"

"I won't."

There is a silence. "Are you okay? Where are you? When can I—?"

"Don't."

"What do you mean 'don't'? You can't just—"

"Jean-Jacques, I'm so . . . confused. Nothing is clear."

"Clear? After what Nigel did to you?"

"After what I did to him."

"You don't mean you'd . . . you still . . . after . . ."

"I don't know."

"What don't you know? You love me, don't you?"

"Yes. I don't know."

"Merde."

There is a long silence.

"Come to Paris."

"Jean-Jacques, I have *children*."

"I know this. They're beautiful. They're—"

"You—you can't just crop people out of the picture."

"You're trying to crop *me* out of the picture."

"No. I just need to get back to *reality*. I can't just float on a boat with you forever, without car keys, with the cell phone turned off, swimming in nothing but sneakers, just living like a baby in my bare skin with sheet burns and swollen lips and scratched breasts and . . . and your se-men running down my legs and your . . . your . . ."

There is the click of a lighter.

I have forgotten what I was saying. My eyes are closed.

I hear him smoking.

"Mayg." His voice is hoarse, quiet, intense. "Tell me where you are."

I punch No.

Friday, September 5, 8 AM: It's better every day. In the morning I tap out an SMS to the children, so Nigel gets it before he leaves for work.

> *I love you babies.*

or

> *Hugs and kisses Katie girl.*

or

> *Woof woof to Cloey XXXX*

Silliness. Letters on a cell-phone screen. All my love.

Today I walk to the tiny *boulangerie* by the bed-and-breakfast. On the steps of my *gîte,* I drink coffee and dip the bread. Cloey likes to suck the coffee out when I do that. The bread catches in my throat. There are market tables set out around the fountain. I buy walnut oil and cheese and butter and more apples. My hand wavers over the onion braids. Kate. I shiver. It's chillier now and there is woodsmoke drifting above the slanted roofs.

I am beginning to think of practical things. I must pay my credit-card bills. I must turn in *La Vie en France, Level Two.* I must finish my con-tract for Nikos. I must write a book.

Then I will go home to my children.

Vive l'Histoire. The thought of it makes me cover my eyes. It's in shambles, a random scramble for themes. It got to the point where the stories didn't matter, just the . . . trysts. I crowd the word out of my mind. Think, Meg. What will you write for Nikos.

I climb the stone stairs and open the laptop.

Wednesday, September 10, 10 AM: I have thrown the story list away. I must start from scratch. Now I am emptying my mind and spilling out what I remember. Images, memories, themes.

> *Arles:*
> *bulls paella dancing lamb ochre pastis shutters stelae chickpeas straw chairs asparagus horns blood red peppers scarves cockade rosé café stars*

> *Burgundy:*
> *wine candles mold key barrels jelly glasses jellied ham baccarat dogs noses taste tongue scent must musk vines wax-jacket hills roots renée*

Jean-Jacques on the bed. The overhead light flashing on.

> *Cluny:*
> *steeple stones pillars chocolate friezes barns stones stallions hand-maiden andouillettes eggs hurdles saddles whiskey moonlight beyond god and man peccata mundi*

I erase whiskey and moonlight. I think about Jean-Jacques' smudged face wheeling before me on the *haras* grounds and how close my mouth came to his. If the phone hadn't rung would we have . . .

List, Meg. The list.

> *Aigues-Mortes/Saintes-Maries:*
> *fortress salt flats fountain oysters mouth birds bullsteak anchoïade gypsies statue sea candles ex-votos air hand crowd police artichokes salt cod fingers pestle fire foot mouth*

Had I reached for his foot that night . . . Stop it. I erase.

> *Mercantour Vallée des Merveilles:*
> *mountains pines flowers stream daube jeans boots cigarettes lenses lightning gods rocks strawberries fingers daggers plows horns wind rain jeep hut brebis breasts*

I erase breasts. I will not yield. I am getting somewhere if I can just stay the course. Concentrate.

> *pine skin body whiskers mouth foreskin honey tongue fingers dagger mouth cigarettes*

I erase everything but pine.

Bretagne:
> *broceliande lancelot nettles merlin/viviane langoustines thumb*

I plunge on. I will erase later. Just get it out on the screen.

> *tristan/isolde love oysters cherries tongue love pardons crêpes cider chant church cotriade fishbones crucifix rocks tidal pools urchins mussels futon salt butter blackberry jam*

Normandy:
> *lipstick silk cross beaches pillbox sole canned mushrooms cemetery google vichy calvados cigarettes apple juice*

Agincourt:
> *arrows helmets soldiers banners dancing costumes drums suckling pig mead torches knights lens lances*

I stop. I don't want to go any further. I see orange chenille and I squeeze my eyes shut.

I close the laptop lid and head down to the kitchen. I dip bread in walnut oil and carry an apple to the front step.

4 PM: There's a tap on the door. Madame Durand is standing there with a bowl of eggs. I make her a cup of tea. She is kind, diffident.

"Your book is coming along well?"

"Well, I guess so."

"There is no mail for you. Does anyone know you are here?"

"I have my cell phone. I can stay in touch."

"And your work?"

"When I have something to send to my editors, I guess I'll take the laptop into St-Céré. Maybe at the post office I can find an Internet connection."

"And why not use the telephone here?"

I look at her.

"There is a phone plug. The owner's son was quite adept with computers and he had it installed before he married and moved away."

I blink.

We climb the stairs together and push the desk to the side.

8 PM: I have waded through an avalanche of spam, hundreds of ads and jokes and forwarded virus warnings. Then I begin to read my e-mail.

There are two from Scholar's Way asking for the last of *La Vie en France*. It was due September 1.

> *We discussed some of your unusual dialogues in our editorial meeting this morning and have decided to keep them if you will approve a few slight modifications . . .*

There is only one from Nikos.

> *JJ being mysterious. what's up? where's the x?*+!! book? Nigel says you're on the road. tried your cell, no go. hel-lo meg are you out there?*

There are so many from Jean-Jacques, I don't want to open them, but I do. The key phrases are always the same, in different order.

> *Tell me where you are*
> *Come to Paris*
> *Call me*
> *I love you*
> *It is real*

Most seem to have come in the first days. Then there are fewer. Then none.

But there are two from nigel.thorpe@francetel.fr. Nigel? On e-mail? A personal address? His grasp of the systems, even at Barclays, has always been minimal. Or so I thought, until he found the pictures on my laptop.

The first is not really an e-mail. It is a full-out letter, formally, carefully composed. Worthy of paper and ink.

September 8

My dear Meg,

As I seem to be incapable of expressing myself clearly to you on your mobile phone, I have invested in a computer for our home. Ahmad was kind enough to help me set it up and has shown me the basic manoeuvres necessary for writing to you and, I do hope, hearing back from you.

Your absence has given me a good deal of time to reflect and to study on the reasons for your looking elsewhere for happiness, for want of a better word. It is clear to me now that you had drifted away from me well before your entanglement with Chabrol. I take, in no small part, the blame for this.

I don't wish to go into the details of your relationship with Chabrol. You are, or were, clearly besotted with him and he with you. It is a fact of adult life and I am coping with it, given the circumstances that led to this affair. However, there are other details that matter a great deal more. Their names are Kate and Cloey and they miss you enormously. Their attachment to Sophie grows daily but they ask for you. They often migrate into my bed. Our bed. I feel their loss.

But before this letter disintegrates any further into tiresome sentiment I will say it simply: Please come home to your family and take your place with us, where you belong.

Your husband Nigel

I wipe my face on my sweater and hold my eyes in my hands. I read it again. Oh god. I will go back. I will go back. I will do the right thing. This time I will finally do the right thing.

I open the second message, written at twelve twenty-seven AM. Another drinking bout. It is brief and badly spelled but I recognize it.

what isshe but a foul contnding rebell and gracelss traitr to her lovin lord

It's from *Taming of the Shrew*.

My eyes are dry now.

I tap Reply. I type:

Dear Nigel, I understand your anger. I am very confused. I'm sorry.
I'm writing the book. Then I will come home.

I erase "Then I will come home."
I stare at the screen. I type it in again.

Then I will come home. Tell the children I love them and miss them.
Tell them I am writing stories.
　—Meg

Sunday, September 14, 11 PM: There is a new e-mail from Nigel, sloppily typed.

I an my bosm mus debate a whil

I know this one. *Henry V* again. "I and my bosom must debate a while."

I need to think, too.

Tuesday, 11 AM: The laptop glows.

La Vie en France, Chapter 14
There is a primal link between the small farmer and daily life in
France that has thinned elsewhere in the western world. Nurtured by
government subsidy, small-scale agriculture still flourishes through-
out the Hexagon. Farmers' markets are just that: open marketplaces
where the goods of the local paysans are sold in a sociable ambiance of
pure free-market competition. What's good today gets the best price.
The freshest produce draws the most customers. Quality counts on
an intimate scale. And taste . . . and texture . . . and tradition . . .
roots . . . history.

5 PM: There is a new e-mail from Nigel.

Dear Meg,
　Lately I find myself climbing down into your bunker and looking
about, as if you might appear behind the desk. It is, as you have told
me, dark and dreary down there, yet you spent most of your days and
nights in it. If I have indeed driven you underground it was through

*negligence and no active will of mine. I have perhaps underestimated
you and your importance in the life of this household. And, more
specifically, in my life.*

*I do admit I have been fairly shameless in my probings through
your things since you left us. Clearly you have made a life for yourself in your "bunker" that incorporates the Meg Parker you left
behind when you married me in Cambridge. And now you have be-
gun to make a life for yourself outside our home, with or without
Chabrol.*

*The children miss you acutely. Kate confronts me with her sore
throat day and night but Dr. Arnault has been unable to find symp-
toms. He asked after you. When I told him you were off writing a
book he seemed to hesitate, then suggested a psychologist for the children. You know how I feel about such practices. The children need
their mother.*

*Cloey's incontinence has got entirely out of hand. The maîtresse
sent a note recommending we keep him at home for a period. A four-
year-old at home without a mother to raise him?*

*Gerald has recently taken to running off. Madame Mathilde brought
him home last night. He had been sleeping on her compost pile. She
has caught him digging under the chicken coop and eating out of the
dustbin. He has lost weight and hovers about the stove and the bunker
ladder. It's as if he's hoping for you to materialise. We all are.*

*At the risk of slipping into maudlin sentiment, I beg you to recon-
sider. Your place is here with your family.*

Nigel

And centered, at the end, a quote:

> *. . . take mercy
> On the poor souls for whom this hungry war
> Opens his vasty jaws . . .
> the orphans' cries . . .
> the pining maidens' groans,
> For husbands, fathers and betrothed lovers,
> That shall be swallow'd in this controversy*
> *—Henry V*

I wipe my face and answer:

> *Give me time. I am working on my book. Then I will come home.*

Saturday, September 20, 2 PM: I roll the Citroën back into the gravel hollow in front of the stone doorway and carry in two baskets full of market goods from St-Céré. There is a duck carcass—just the legs and bones, stripped of breast and liver—and I lower it into a pot of water. I scrub mud from carrots. I rinse and crush herbs. I peel layers of skin from onions, mince garlic. The flame flickers blue. Slowly a scent rises. I hold my face over it. It seeps into me, soothing, real.

4 PM: I slip the hot meat off the bones and mince it on the tiny cutting board with a butter knife. White beans. Turnips. When it's blended and tender and sharpened with pepper, I fill a salad bowl and carry it onto the front step. It doesn't matter what time it is, I eat it because it's good. My sweater feels thin now but the soup is hot. Shadows darken the cliffs but the sky is deep blue. I empty my glass of Bergerac into the dregs of peppery soup. I swirl the wine and broth together. *Faire chabrol*, that's called. I smile a little. I wipe the bowl with bread.

8 PM: The laptop glows.

> *La Vie en France, Level Two*
> *There is a symbiosis between artisanal food production and France's culture, running deep roots into the past. The small farmer, the family baker, the lone fisherman play their role in a story that has unfolded throughout the country's history, weaving together feudal traditions and modern conquests, family life and politics.*

Taste. Texture. Tradition.
Roots.
History.

10 PM: There's a duck bone in my teeth and I'm gnawing, thinking. I've made another list, reduced from my stream-of-consciousness story list.
It's only the food.

> *paella lamb chickpeas asparagus peppers pastis rosé romanée jellied ham chocolate andouillettes eggs oysters bullsteak anchoïade*

artichokes salt cod daube trout brebis strawberries langoustines oysters cherries crêpes cider cotriade urchins mussels salt butter blackberry jam sole mushrooms calvados suckling pig mead duck soup

1 AM: There is text pouring out of my fingers into a new file, created tonight. *France: The Taste of History.*

Bretagne: a region late-won to catholicism, where Bretons cling still to Celtic traditions . . . the Pagan and the Christian mingle both in festival and a cuisine based on the earth and sea . . . the spawn of tidal pools . . . the catch of the fisherman's line . . . interwoven with folklore with deep ties to Celtic Britain . . .

("they embrace in an ecstasy so powerful it is like pain")

. . . tides of pagan and christian culture seething in and out in symbiotic rhythm . . .

("forgiveness through food")

Cluny: the natural wealth of Burgundian wine united extravagant Benedictines with Cistercian austerity . . . grafting roots planted a thousand years before as Roman culture pushed inexorably northward . . .

("it's the roots that count")

The Camargue: fanning between the Spanish-scented Languedoc and the Latin lilt of Provence . . . once a launching point for the Holy Crusades, now a windswept backwater . . . bullfights and bull steaks . . . olives pressed to oil the feet of early believers from the shores of Egypt and Africa . . .

("tastes like Spain")

The Alps of Haute Provence: in storm-riddled heights, shepherds have prayed for shelter for their flocks for 4,000 years, raising hands to the mountaintops in supplication . . . cheese and meat made sweet by the flowers of alpine meadows . . . wild strawberries nestled in windswept tundra . . .

("taste it, it's ripe")

Normandy: beneath bunkers and barbed wire, oysters flushed clean along once-war-torn shores, the blood of battles purged and purified . . .

("oyster beds? here?")

*Agincourt: the pageantry of medieval history brought to life on an-
cient battlefields . . . fluttering silks and raining arrows . . . the victors
feasting, exuberant, on roast suckling pig, quaffing honey mead . . .
dances as they've been danced for a thousand years . . .*

("if you danced with that hand-kisser you will dance with me")

3 AM: I have a map of France spread wide on the kitchen table and, in
the dim light of the single overhead bulb, I am laying beans on the regions covered. Burgundy. Provence. Brittany. Normandy. The North.
The Alps. There is a gaping void where a bean should be.

The Southwest.

Of course.

I laugh out loud.

Duck soup.

I plug in the modem and write to Nikos.

*Sometimes you have to feel your way with a new project, you said.
Rewriting the book. Give me a month. Trust me.*

Friday, September 26, 11 AM: My words are calm and sure. The text
pours out of me. There is no silliness this time, no Whore Art or Fervor
from the East. No battles. No ghosts. The history is in the food. The
food is the history. There is a synthesis here.

*. . . medieval ships carried Camargue salt to the shores of Brittany
and returned bearing cargos of cod . . .*

And the recipes. The recipes!

*Soak salt cod, changing the water frequently, over two days or until
the smell of quicklime has passed. Poach the chunks with three pods
of peeled garlic, a handful of black peppercorns, two bay leaves, and
a branch of thyme . . .*

*. . . drizzle a thin stream of olive oil over the flesh as you move the
pestle steadily, steadily, increasing speed as the brandade approaches
the key emulsion point . . .*

I push my hair out of my eyes with my forearm. I open the next file
and write.

. . . The Camargue's culture seethes with Spanish blood . . . the fight of the bull still running like sap in its flesh that sizzles over grape clippings after the arenas empty . . .

. . . rub the meat with sea salt and olive oil . . . turn the steak twice to capture the running juices . . .

. . . Normandy's thorny hedgerows that defined the feudal patchwork of private lands, of crops shared and tithed . . . the berry bushes that bramble along the footpaths belonged to no one and so to everyone . . .

. . . Tie the steamed blackberries in a cheescloth and suspend them over a large bowl. Their own weight draws the juice, slow, from deep within, oozing through the fabric in a spreading stain . . .

Saturday, 9 AM: I have driven early into Sarlat-la-Canéda to the great market on the place de la Liberté. Tents stand pitched at the foot of grand yellowstone houses, Renaissance arcades. I buy salsify, sorrel, bundles of thyme tied in string. I fill my baskets with sweet squashes, apples, hard brown pears. I fill the laundry bag with carcasses of duck and goose, a tub of goose fat. I can barely walk back to the car. I shove aside the rock salt and shrink-wrapped mason jars and pile the booty onto the back seat. Then I head back to my kitchen.

Monday, 5 PM: "But marriage and passion have very little to do with one another, no?"

Madame Durand is sitting at the kitchen table nibbling on the *grattons* of goose skin I have sizzled in the skillet. We are waiting for the giant pot she lent me to come to a boil. The table is crowded with bowls full of herb-brined meat.

I have told her everything. She is a good listener. Her arms are folded across her bosom and she chews the *gratton* contemplatively.

"I don't know." I wipe my forehead with a tea towel. "I've only been married to Nigel and I always thought that's all there was. And now if I go back—when I go back—will I . . . what will I . . . ?"

"Things will remain as they were. He will be the man you left. He will not be your Jean . . . ?"

"Jean-Jacques."

"Your Jean-Jacques. You'll return to the home you share, to the children you made together. You will take up your family life. Your *aventure* will be over. You've renounced him, haven't you?"

Renounced him. "I guess so. I have to. I *have* to go home. I think and think about Jean-Jacques, how we could live together, how he would be with Kate and Cloey. He's so easy with them, so natural. *He's* so natural. And the way he handles food . . . and me . . ." My eyes well up for a second with tears and I fight them back. I put a *gratton* in my mouth and chew.

"Nigel treats me like a little girl. His Yankee Girl. He pats me. Like Gerald."

"Gerald?"

"Our dog."

She shrugs. *C'est normal.* "In our day we didn't dissolve marriages."

"No."

"We lived with the choices we made."

"Yes."

I turn to the pot, wiping my sleeve across my eyes. "I guess the water's ready."

She rises. "Your husband is very lucky to have married such a good cook. A cook who *feels* what she's cooking. *Primordiale.*"

"He doesn't really notice."

I look up at her face. It is suddenly a mask of consternation and pity.

11 PM: The kitchen table is crowded with jars of confit, the golden goose grease slowly thickening to creamy white, herbs and peppercorns a mosaic against the glass. I am writing an e-mail to Jean-Jacques. I have read and reread his. I never wrote back.

> *I think about you all the time. Of course. What I felt with you. What I feel for you. But I know now that I have to live with a choice I made a long time ago. I am Kate's and Cloey's mother and I am Nigel's wife. It would be selfish of me to tear their lives apart even for . . .*

My fingers waver. I can't find the keys.

. . . even for you. Please understand. I hope . . .

I wipe my face with my hands.

. . . I hope you will be willing to finish the book with me.

I can see his face when he reads this last. The twist of his mouth. The hardening.

I am so sorry.

1 AM: The cell phone is bleating, bleating. I sit up and grope for it. I know who it is.

"Mayg?"

"Jean-Jacques."

"You don't mean it."

I pull the quilt around me. "I do. When I finish this book I'm going home."

"*Putain.*"

"Jean-Jacques, I've been *acting* like a *putain,* like a whore."

"Are you crazy? You think it's only like that?"

"No! I mean . . . I just mean I married Nigel. I made a bargain."

"Now you do sound like a *putain.*"

"No. Don't."

His lighter clicks and we sit in silence while he smokes.

"You have to understand, Nigel came to Agincourt and he put the children in my arms. He's right. They're ours."

"Your children are beautiful. They're wonderful. They could learn to like me. He barely looked at them."

"You saw them. They're part of his blood."

"*You're* not part of his blood."

"*They* are."

He smokes.

"We could have kids."

I hold the phone away from my ear and close my eyes. My mind reels. "Don't."

"I don't need to live in Paris. I want to get a place in the country. Even back in the Médoc. Get a horse. I want to grow my own vegetables. Plant a few grapevines. I've always wanted . . ."

Oh god. "Jean-Jacques, don't. I can't. We can't."

". . . to get back to the vines. We could . . ."

"I'm sorry. I'm so sorry."

But he can't hear me. I've punched No and am holding it down hard.

Wednesday, October 1, 11 PM: There is an e-mail from Nigel. Another letter, painstakingly and soberly composed.

> *Dear Meg,*
>
> *The children are well. I have taken two weeks' holiday to care for them, as Sophie has accepted work as a replacement teacher in a maternelle in Toul. She was most apologetic but one can hardly blame her. She is not their mother. You are.*
>
> *I am hoping, of course, that you will be coming home soon. I've only two weeks' leave. Then I should be obliged to find another sitter which would be rather hard on the children.*
>
> *The longer you are away the more I realise how isolated I have become from the world we share. Sophie and Ahmad have been very sweet, as has the Mémé Mathilde. Nicolas Lapeyre came over yesterday and helped me move the sandpile out of the driveway. I think he was most impressed to see me with a shovel in my hand. He told me something that shocked me: He was surprised to know that I do indeed speak French. Perhaps I have been too wrapped up in my work and my friends. We got to talking about rugby—it does come up, you know—and it seems there is a team forming in the village. I thought I might have a go at it. Picture me wearing the French colours!*
>
> *The builders have been coming regularly and we are beginning to see real progress. The wall has been rebuilt and framed and the kit for the conservatory arrived on Monday. All this hasn't come cheap. I'm afraid I've had to sell the Rover—far too big for commuting anyway—and have bought a sensible used Xsara. Another Citroën to keep the DS company. Not a goddess, perhaps, but worthy of a humbled*

mortal. Steering wheel on the left, of course. You'll see it when you come home. I am hoping this will not be long from now.

The children send hugs and kisses. I might, too, if I thought you would accept them.

Nigel

I sit, suspended in a bubble of feeling. He hasn't written to me so tenderly since Cambridge.

I scroll down. There is a jpeg attached—a jpeg from Nigel? It is a photograph of the children. Kate, pale with tousled hair in her eyes and a vaguely baleful stare. Cloey looking off toward the side, his thumb halfway to his mouth.

Kate. Cloey. Oh god.

I *will* go home. I will go home to my family. I will go home to reality.

Midnight: I can't sleep. I am twisting and turning in the bed.

Two weeks.

I have to finish the book.

I will go home.

There's only the Dordogne left.

I pull the pillow over my head.

Will Jean-Jacques photograph it? Or will he refuse to finish the book now that I've 'renounced' him?

I could call Nikos.

No.

I throw off the pillow. I pull up the covers.

I will send Jean-Jacques the text, and he can come down and shoot it on his own. After I've gone home.

i too would prefer to work separately

He said it first, last spring. Work is work.

He has to understand. He has to.

I'll wait until I've finished, then I'll call him.

Thursday, October 9, 5 PM: I hunch over the desk, the quilt over my shoulders, typing.

... Talleyrand wooed England and Austria and America too with the foie gras and truffles of his native Perigord, gastronomic diplomacy more seductive than treaties ...

My fingers are cold. I never even got dressed this morning. I type.

... the hills and cliffs shaggy with forests of chestnut and black-green oak, at their roots the truffles and golden cèpes treasured by the peasants who dug them from the fertile mulch ... the English aristocrats who took them as booty, precious as the lands of Aquitaine ...

Friday, 6 AM: "Jean-Jacques?"

I am holding the cell phone to my ear. I am pacing under the fading stars, shivering, the quilt around my shoulders. I have worked all night. I am almost finished. I need to know he'll do this for me.

"Jean-Jacques?"

He didn't answer his home phone. I have dialed his cell.

There is a fumbling clatter.

"Mmmph."

"Jean-Jacques!"

"Mayg?"

"Yes. Yes!"

"Mayg?" There is a rustling of sheets. "Mayg, what time is it? Where are you?"

"Jean-Jacques, we have to talk about the book."

"What?"

"We have to talk about the book. The book."

"The book?"

There is a fumbling again, the flick of a lamp switch.

"Jean-Jacques?"

The click of a lighter. A stream of smoke. *"Merde.* It's six in the morning. Where are you?"

"There's a part of the book that still needs doing. Photographs. I've added a section on the Dordogne. I'll send it to you. And you can shoot it when you like."

"The Dordogne? Why the Dordogne? Are you in the Dordogne, Mayg?"

Oh god.

"No! We just needed something in the Southwest and I—"

"Where are you? Are you in the Périgord? Sarlat? Bergerac?"

"*No,* I just thought you could photograph this section, duck and foie gras and English castles, and I wanted to tell you where I've set it."

"Souillac? Domme? St-Cyprien? Are you there? *Putain,* Mayg. *Tell me where you are.*"

I take a deep breath. I look at the waning stars. "I'm in Autoire. Near St-Céré. But I'm *leaving.* I'm going *home.* I told you. You can take the pictures afterward. You can come down at the end of the month, maybe, for the walnut harvest. Fall colors. There might even be early truffles. And you can send me the jpegs so we're sure to be on the right . . . Jean-Jacques? Okay?"

But he's hung up.

He's angrier than I thought.

I should have sent an e-mail.

11 AM: The kitchen table is covered with papers and maps, the tiny sink full of pots and pans. I have dragged my laptop to the front step and am hammering away on my knees in the chill golden light. I haven't slept or brushed my teeth or showered. I can't remember when I last did. I can live with my own ripe smell. I need to finish this last recipe, clean up the *gîte,* and go home.

I look around me at the mess. I'd better get to work. I type:

> . . . *brush the moss and earth from the thick cèpe roots . . . leave the skin or peel back as necessary . . . melt a mound of goose fat in an iron skillet until it shimmers with heat . . . slip the mushrooms gently into the hot liquid, moving them steadily over the flame until the flesh swells then tightens and browns to glowing gold . . .*

I push my hair back with my forearm and look up, startled. A Clio is lumbering up the gravel. It's not Madame Durand. She drives a 205.

The shadow of a sycamore falls across the windshield and I can see inside. It's him. Impossible. Oh god. I am dreaming.

He climbs out of the car. My mind takes him in through a lens. Thinner than I've ever seen him. Thicker whiskers. Hair matted long, unwashed. Bundled in coarse wool, an Indian scarf I've never seen.

Jean-Jacques is standing in my driveway in three dimensions, looking at me.

I jump to my feet but catch the laptop before it falls. I lay it carefully on the step and stand.

He has the same wary look on his face he had when he first stepped out of the spotlights in Bayeux.

I breathe. "You weren't supposed to come. How did you . . . ?"

"I stopped at the Citroën garage below. They knew you."

"You got here fast."

"I was in Bordeaux. I drove fast. I'd have been here . . . I had to wait for the Europcar office to open."

He was in Bordeaux. Next door.

He stands, looking at me. Waiting.

I breathe again. "You've lost weight."

He shrugs. "I guess I lost my appetite."

We hover, rooted, for a while. Too long. His hands have found his hips now and he is looking at his shoes. "Do you want to tell me what this is about?"

I try to regroup. "Did you bring your cameras?"

He laughs at his shoes, his old laugh inverted, an ugly bark.

Oh god. Just when I finally get things right, I get everything wrong.

I step toward him and he turns away to open the trunk.

"So what is it you want me to shoot, Madame l'Historienne?"

"Please, just talk to me. I'll explain."

He lifts out his camera bags and carries them into the kitchen, ducking under the stone frame. He sets them on the floor and stands. The kitchen is immediately full. His head nearly touches the ceiling beams. I cower against the burner, then edge my way to the table and set down the laptop. He isn't looking at it or at me. He is looking around the kitchen, at the stairs, at the jars of confit, at the squash, at the butter, at the bundles of herbs. He is looking at my life. He is shaking his head.

"So this is your monastic retreat."

"Well. Yes."

"And you're working on the book."

"Well. Yes."

"And Nigel? And the kids?"

"They're . . . okay. I have to go back right away. The babysitter left."

"You're going back."

"Yes."

"For good?"

"Yes. For good."

He reaches for a cigarette and I flinch. The air smells like herbs and stone and soap. I'm not ready to smell his smoke now. He looks at my face and shakes his head. He ducks back outside. His lighter clicks. He raises his voice so I'll hear him in the kitchen, pitches it to the heavens.

"You're going back for *good*."

"Please."

He smokes.

"So I'm here for . . . ?"

He's here for . . . what?

I go to the door. "To finish the book?"

His cigarette sizzles in the fallen walnut leaves.

1 PM: "So I thought, why do we have to *separate* all this? The history categories. Why do we have to narrow it down? The stories. The historic events. The traditions. The festivals. It's the food, Jean-Jacques, the *food*."

He is sitting at the kitchen table, his body turned to the side, his legs splayed across the floor. I wish he'd say something. He hasn't said anything since he came back inside. He leans forward abruptly and rises.

"Is there a toilet here?"

I start a little. "Well, yes, of course. Upstairs."

"*D'accord*. Excuse me."

He climbs the stairs carefully, bent in half. I hear the plastic seat lift. I hear an echoing stream. Strange noises. Male noises in my haven. Familiar. A flush. His steps continue up the stairs to the bedroom. He comes back down, ducking.

"There's a twin bed here. So you weren't expecting me."

My face goes hot. "Of course not. I thought you could shoot this after I left. I *never* thought . . ."

"You never thought. That's what I thought."

He is picking up his camera bags. He is carrying them to the car. "*Écoute,* I'll shoot what you want me to shoot tomorrow morning. Nikos will be very glad. Then I'll go back home."

He heaves the bags into the trunk. "And your idea for the book, it's a good one. It's very good. It's what the book has been about all along, no? It just took you a while to figure it out."

My breath sucks in, cuts out sharp.

you guys always know everything

"No!" My voice is rising. I am standing in the door frame. "No, it's not! There's more to it. You'll see, there's a relationship between . . . if you'd just read the . . ."

"*Bon.* You can show me tomorrow."

He is reaching for the driver's door. He looks in the back seat. "Oh. Here, I brought you some things. There was a roadside stand."

He brings out a basket heaping with sueded cèpes. Stems mossy. Caps so firm they're bursting through their skin. For a second his face softens.

"I thought you might be hungry."

2 PM: Ravenous.

Camembert. Salt cod. Yeast. Brine. Our unwashed smells and flavors mingle in the narrow bed.

Devouring, consuming, swallowing each other whole.

3 PM: Earthquake. I'm shaking. He lies on me, exhausted, his face in my neck.

"*Merde,* Mayg."

"Oh god."

We lie still like that for a while. Our breath slows. His hands begin to move softly over my hair, his thumb tracing my lips.

I stare at the ceiling beams.

I have to leave. I have to go home. I will leave this afternoon. That was the last time. Ever. I am resolved.

3:30 PM: *"Putain."*

Oh god. I sink onto his chest, heart hammering. I sweep my hair from his eyes.

My stomach growls. His hand slides down the sweat between my breasts and rests over my navel.

"I was right," he whispers weakly. "I thought you might be hungry."

5 PM: We are standing in the kitchen side by side slicing cèpes, mincing shallots. Our hair is wet from the shower. He has opened a bottle of Cahors he brought and we are drinking it out of jelly glasses, the only two glasses in the *gîte*.

His face is soft and calm, a trace of a smile on his lips.

I am not smiling. I stare at the cutting board and mince.

Now I've done it.

His hand runs down my back and rests in the hollow.

My eyes close.

Saturday, 7 AM: A rooster is crowing in the darkness. When I open the front door, his sweater bundled around me, I see a bowl of eggs and two baguettes on the step, next to the saucer of cigarette butts. The Clio is a ghostly form beside the Citroën. I carry the bowl into the kitchen. There is a note, written on blue-grid paper in Madame Durand's looping scrawl. It says: *Bon appétit.*

9 AM: The Citroën is rolling along the banks of the Dordogne toward Sarlat and the market. We have stopped seven times already for Jean-Jacques to photograph looming castles, waddling geese, misty nut groves, their branches heavy with green-black fruit. I pull to the side again and again. A hand-painted FOIE GRAS sign. Ruins set deep in a cliffside, wheeling with rooks.

"See? I *like* ruins," I say. "They're *part* of the story. The big picture. It's not just about ghosts."

He is smiling. He is shooting. My hand rests on his back. I can't help myself.

At the market he is everywhere at once, climbing steps to shoot over the tent tops, ducking behind butcher wagons, squatting to focus across the necks of a dozen bottles of walnut oil. Merchants grin and hold out their wares for him.

My basket is filling, heavy with food. For what? I am going home. Today. Tonight. As soon as we finish the shoot.

5 PM: The sun has sunk behind the blue bluffs again. The lamp glows beside the bed. My fingers follow the curve of his lips.

He is still here. I am still here.

"I had lunch with my mother, Jacqueline, in Bordeaux."

I prop up and look at his face. He is staring at the ceiling.

"She came to the restaurant with this poodle thing in a Vuitton bag. It matched her hair. She's had stuff done to her face. Stretched. Her lips are kind of square."

I giggle. He has a half-smile on his lips. "I don't think she was very impressed with my looks either. She suggested I get a haircut. That it might help me *get* somewhere in life."

I run my fingers through the mats of grey and brown. "Maybe just a trim."

He smiles. He's still looking at the ceiling.

"She was pretty nervous, I think, when I started to talk about the money. She's used to the idea of having my share, even if the law in France says it's split between Justine and me."

"Why did you talk about money?"

"I've been reading a lot, about the Vichy story. Been to the library. *Tu t'imagines*, me in a library?"

His profile is soft in the lamplight.

"I can just picture it."

"There are photographs of everything. The rallies. The roundups. The detention camps. There are a lot more but they—no one has ever organized the archives, I mean really tackled it. It was hushed up for so long. There was no motivation. A lot was lost. I talked to some people. If there was funding they could maybe dig the photos up, save them, get them out there, even on the Internet."

"And you're thinking of . . . ?"

"I mentioned it to my mother. Her face . . . I don't think she'd want that expression to appear in *Paris Match*."

He reaches for my hair, tucks a strand behind my ear, and looks at me. "You could . . ."

My breath sucks in. Don't say it.

"You could help me, you know, Madame l'Historienne." He is looking at me. "You would know how to . . . I don't know, it's your kind of project."

I lie back down and bury my face in the pillow.

7 PM: He's over me, quaking, his intensity breaking up into shards and shudders.

an ecstasy so powerful it is like pain

I swim weakly in feeling. Oh god. I didn't mean for this to happen.

no one hath power to dissolve these bonds but thee

I have to be strong.

10 PM: The kitchen looks like a mine blew up in it. Pots and pans and carcasses, plates and bones and waxed-paper wrappings smeared with white fat and pâté and rillettes, dripping bottles of oil and half-drunk bottles of wine. Two slabs of raw foie gras quiver in the skillet, sputtering to mink brown. A halogen spotlight glares from a tripod. His laugh is back and it fills the kitchen and stairway and echoes off the timbers upstairs. I cover his mouth with my fingers.

"Jean-Jacques, don't. Don't. We have to talk."

He stops laughing. He looks at me with a defiant smile. "No." He dips up a mound of rillettes with his finger and slides it into my mouth. "We don't have to talk. Let's eat."

I swallow. My eyes drift shut. I force them open. "I have to go home. I am *going home*."

"You're not still—"

"Yes, I am. Still." I sink into a chair.

He turns the burner off, unplugs the spotlight. The room fades. He sinks into the other chair, heavy again. The smile has disappeared.

be careful with our j-j

"I've been here for a long time. Thinking. Thinking hard. And I made my decision. I told you, I never meant to . . . I didn't *mean* for you to come . . . I thought I wasn't going to see you again. You shouldn't have . . . we shouldn't have . . ."

"Yes we should. You know it."

"No."

"Mayg. Are you telling me you don't love me?" He looks at me.

je t'aime de tout mon coeur, de tout mon corps, je t'aime à la folie

I will my knees not to shake. I straighten my shoulders.

"Jean-Jacques, the book is done now. We have to go back to our real lives."

Sunday, 7 AM: Last night I was a good historian, the best I've ever been. I memorized him, cataloged him for posterity, inch by inch, with my lips, my tongue.

meg i love your mouth

Eyelids. Bony nose. Ears, turning pink. Adam's apple. The nape of his neck under his hair. The goose bumps. The skin between his long fingers. The arch of his bony foot. The base of his spine, the small of his back. The sparse whorls of grey on his chest. The line running down from his navel. The foreskin I know so well now and that I will never see again.

The lamp stayed on all night.

He comes out of the shower, dressed. His jaw is set hard. I wrap the scarf around his neck. He sets it harder.

The Clio backs out of the driveway, the windshield blanking over with the reflected sky.

9 AM: I have hung the sheets and tea towels and rags on the line to dry. I have scoured the pots and pans, put the jelly glasses and plates back in the cupboard. The laptop is packed. The armoire is empty.

Madame Durand embraces me, kissing both cheeks. I wrap my arms around her. She hands me a linen handkerchief. I give her half the jars of confit. The others I put in the Citroën trunk.

I point the car northeast. The forests of the Corrèze melt into the arid rock of the Auvergne. When I reach Clermont-Ferrand, I refill the hollow tank. My eyes are dry now. I tap out an SMS.

I'm on my way home.

12 ⚜ Armistice

Sunday, October 12, 4 PM: It is raining, of course, in Lorraine. By the time I roll into the gravel driveway, the Citroën is gasping and sputtering, its needle on red. I turn the key and the engine heaves and dies. There is steam rising from the hood, rain hissing off in rivulets. I sit for a moment and compose myself. I wish I'd stopped for the night somewhere so I could arrive fresh, focused, ready for this new life. My old life. I can still taste Jean-Jacques. I am about to kiss my children.

The car door opens with a groan and I duck out into the downpour. I draw the *camionneur* sweater around me. My neck is cold. I am scarfless. I am soaked by the time the front door opens. It's Nigel.

There's a strange white glow behind him. He is very, very tall. Thinner. He's cut his hair short. His face is pinched and his profile taut. He looks scared. I must look the same.

"Hi."

"Hello." He steps aside. "Come in, darling. I'm so . . . glad to see you. We got your message. Didn't know quite when to expect you but, well, here you are."

I drip, studying my shoes. The floor has changed. Now I look up. I see the source of the strange glow. The dining room is in the barn now, or the barn is in the dining room. Most of the wall that divided the barn from the house has disappeared and a raked partition of white plasterboard angles toward a broad bubble of glass.

"The conservatory!"

I stand staring, disoriented. Grey light fills the room. It throws the furniture into gothic relief, shadowing with sheeting rain. The blueish false-slate flagstone under my feet dovetails abruptly into the old polished stones. There are halogen bulbs. Plastic mouldings edge the opening, masking the joints and scars.

He is watching my face.

I lie. "It's beautiful."

"I must say I'm relieved to hear you say it. Was a bit worried, what with the angled wall and all. Andrew thought a contemporary touch . . ."

"Yes." I am still dripping on the artificial flagstones. "Where are the kids?"

"They're in the back room. I let them watch a film. Didn't know when you'd . . . if you'd . . . I'll just go and fetch them."

"That's okay. Give me a minute. Please." I need to steady my hands. I walk to the Aga and grab Gerald's rag. It's clean. I dry my hair in it. I flash on the scarf. Nigel is hovering. Watching. Waiting.

I take a deep breath and open the door to the back room. The children are sitting on the couch staring at the television screen. I am behind them and they don't see me. The Little Mermaid is singing. She is surging through the bubbling water. The music swells. I have a moment, frozen in time, to look at my children. They are so much bigger than I thought, their limbs flung every which way, their faces suspended, sucked into the screen. Kate's thumb is in her mouth. Cloey is twiddling his crotch absently.

Nigel steps forward and takes the remote. The mermaid pauses.

"Eh! Pourquoi tu . . ."

Kate reanimates, turns on him. She sees me. She stares. Cloey sees her face and turns, too. His mouth pops open.

I speak first. I mean to sound chirpy. It comes out hoarse.

"Hi, sweeties! I'm home!"

5 PM: We are sitting at the dining table drinking tea and chocolate. Cloey is in my lap, thumb in his mouth, petting my cheek and staring at me. Kate fidgets across the table. She can't take me in yet. I am trying to digest her.

"We walked *partout* and asked all the neighbors. He has been *disparu*'d for three days now and it rains. Do you think he was hit by a car, *Maman?*"

Gerald, gone. I am trying to control my face. "I bet he's just wandered off," I lie. "Give him time."

"He misses me. We must find him." Kate looks at me as if expecting me to conjure him. I have conjured myself back, haven't I?

"Well then, shall we have the grand tour?" Nigel unfolds himself and rests a hand on my shoulder. Then takes it away. "We have a surprise for you."

The conservatory. It can't be put off any longer.

I rise and heft Cloey onto my hip. He weighs nothing. I take Kate's hand. It is so small and fragile it is almost not there.

Nigel is walking toward the glass bubble. We follow. *"Et voi-LÀ!"* He gestures grandly, then quickly retires his hands. We enter the bowl of glass. It is faceted from floor to ceiling with white plastic. The floor is false slate. At the center of the great open space there is a desk. My desk. The picture of my grandfather is reframed in green PVC and stands beside the new computer. There are bookcases, laminated in white, and they are full of my books, my history books. The army jacket hangs in a plastic dry-cleaning bag. There are plastic cartons on the floor. I see the chasuble, the képi in them. The framed prints. A great white radiator steams the panes, where rain is draping down like wine in a swirled glass.

Nigel flicks a switch. A fluorescent tube light blinks, stutters on and washes the space in greenish pallor. "You like it, darling? A little light and heat for a change?"

I am standing very still. I will my breathing to even out. "And my bunker?"

"I'm afraid Andrew's wall—the partition—falls directly across the opening. We had quite a time getting all your things up the ladder but we cleaned it out down to the last piece of barbed wire." He is standing beside me now. He leans down to my face and rests his lips briefly, bravely, on my forehead. "The war's over, Yankee girl. Welcome to your new office!"

He is looking at me, his smile wary, vulnerable. It is his gift to me. His peace offering.

"Thank you, Nigel. It's wonderful."

8 PM: I have opened one of the confit jars and fried the salty duck legs with potatoes. I roll greens in nut oil. There is a fire in the fireplace and Kate has lit candles on the waxed table. A cleaning woman has come twice a week since I left and the house is tidier than I ever kept it. I wonder how we can afford it with the masons to pay. With Sophie, full time, for six weeks. It will take a lot of *La Vie en France* to catch up.

Kate tastes the confit and closes her eyes. *"C'est si bon, Maman!"*

Cloey watches his sister, tastes, and closes his eyes, too. "Mm. You kill the goose yourself, *Maman?*"

"Of course she did, Cloey. You've seen her wield that meat cleaver!"

Everyone is feeling braver. Nigel refills my glass with the Cahors I brought. That Jean-Jacques left for me.

"I've been doing a bit of cooking myself these days. Question of survival, really!" I glance up at him. He is looking at his plate. "Brenda and Andrew gave me that new Jamie Oliver cookbook. The one for 'blokes.' Easy recipes. Trifle, toad-in-the-hole, sort of thing. Been having a go at it. Haven't been doing badly, have I now children?"

"He made us fish fingers, not from a box!"

"Not like fish fingers at *all!*"

"Like *fish!*"

I smile. My hand wants to reach for Gerald's head but it's not there. So many things are not there. But the children are seated across from me and their faces glow pale and pure and beautiful in the candlelight.

11 PM: I am lying beside Nigel in the four-poster bed. He is awake. I am wearing the Pooh nightshirt. He is bundled in flannel. We are staring at the ceiling, nervous as teenagers.

"It's all right, darling. We have to give ourselves time. After the last time, when I behaved so . . ."

"Don't. Don't. You don't have anything to apologize for."

He turns over and faces me. "I'm very glad you've come home, Meg. I've missed you."

My face crumples. I lie again. "I've missed you, too."

Monday, 11 AM: The Citroën rolls slowly along the tractor roads around Dampierre. I steer with the door open, looking down into ditches for

Gerald's body. The rain drives down like arrows, stabbing, stinging my neck. The ditches seethe with yellow water. I call for him and honk the horn. Then I pull into a field and turn the engine off. I rest my forehead on the steering wheel and I cry. And cry. And cry.

I permit myself this once. It will be the last time.

Thursday, 10 AM: I am sitting in my new office in a bubble of glass. There is no wall at my back. I can't wear my grandfather's jacket; it's too hot in here.

I am trying to polish the last of the text. I drift from time to time into the kitchen. I'm already *in* the kitchen, after all.

I've been testing the recipes all week. The children are eager, grateful. Nigel anxiously seconds their praise. Sole in Normandy cream with mushrooms. Lamb daube. *Cotriade.* Artichokes *barigoule.* Mustard sauce for andouillettes.

> *... the crisp skin of the sausage splits and bursts with rough-chopped filling, coarse and raw and elemental. This is the offal the peasants kept while Cluny's wealthy abbots claimed the tenderloin and hams ...*
>
> *... a social revolution ... the cream reclaimed ... like the stones of a religious monarchy torn down to build shelter for the people themselves ...*

Synthesis.

I paste each chapter into an e-mail. I send them to Nikos and copy them to Jean-Jacques without a message of my own. He copies me the Dordogne shoot without a message of his own. Twenty jpegs. I scroll through them tenderly. Castles and ruins wreathed in mist and swirling rooks. My jars of confit lined on the *gîte* shelf. Two slabs of foie gras sizzling in the skillet. Walnuts splitting, gleaming, out of oily green shucks. Chipped crockery terrines mounded with rillettes, a wooden paddle thrust deep into the cream. And a farmer grinning and gesticulating, holding up a duck by its feet, its wings a blur. His cheeks are red, his fingers dirty. His blue jacket could be a medieval smock.

I rest my chin in my hand.

Friday, 11 PM: I am curled up in front of EuroNews. A story has been looping all evening and I watch it again: "Private enterprises in the United States and France have pooled resources to found the Institute for the Advancement of Organic Food Development, dedicated to research into new sources of *biologique* or all-natural alimentation for the world. While research is based at present on French territory, sponsors on the U.S. side include McDonald's and Birds Eye."

The camera pans across fields of corn and wheat waving in the breeze. There is a stone farmhouse in the background and row on row of plastic tents, lab technicians counting leaves and making notes on clipboards. There are turnips and cabbages and lettuce and tomatoes. There are cages of rabbits and chickens, pens full of sheep and cows. The camera pulls back and back, taking in the whole farm, the greenhouses, the barns, the fields, the hills beyond. And, behind them all, the four gargantuan cooling towers of a nuclear power station.

Monday, 6 PM: "I know they're here somewhere."

We are rummaging through boxes in the attic, searching in the trunk I keep of my parents' things.

"What's this?" Cloey is pulling a dashiki over his head. It hangs to his toes.

"My daddy used to wear that."

"For pajamas?"

"Well, kind of."

There are old books—Kahlil Gibran, Carlos Castaneda, Hermann Hesse. The article about my parents from *Mother Earth*, when they were going through the goat-cheese phase. Framed baby pictures of me, the blue tints faded to yellow-green.

Kate holds up a curled Polaroid. "*Maman,* what are you wearing?"

I look over her shoulder, my lips in her hair. "Don't you recognize it? That's Great-grandpa Parker's jacket."

"It's smaller now!"

I dig deeper. There they are! I fish out a brown felt-wrapped bundle and loosen the grosgrain ribbon that binds it. Grandma Marguerite's cooking knives, the ones she brought from France.

7 PM: Kate pinches the onion firmly on the cutting board, her tongue between her teeth.

"*Comme ça, Maman?*"

"Like that. Yes."

She brings down the blade. It slices through clean.

Tuesday, 3 PM: Contracts for *La Vie en France, Level Three* lie on my desk. This one will be easy to write. I know so much more.

I finger my history books on the white plastic shelves. Lytton Strachey. Maybe someday I'll write *The Comeback Kid*. Grandfather Parker. The Route Napoléon.

Maybe someday I'll write *Vive l'Histoire*. Tell the stories. Without photographs.

I reach into the desk drawer for a pen to sign with. There is a jewelry box. I open it. My wedding ring is in the velvet slot.

Nigel must have put it there.

I look at my scar. I take out the ring and stare at it.

Sunday, October 26, 6 AM: A rooster is crowing. I am roused from my sleep by a prodding presence against my thighs. Nigel has spooned behind me and is whispering warmly against my ear.

"'The cock is the trumpet to the morn . . .'"

His body scissors around me, gently urgent. He murmurs in my hair, nuzzles between my shoulder blades. He tugs up the nightgown. My breasts fill his hands. Vague electrical signals flicker through me, echoes, memories of feeling rising from the deep. I arch back into his sleepy probing.

Married love.

6:15 AM: There is a scratching and thumping on the kitchen door. I creep down the stairs shivering, a towel between my legs. Gerald! I wrench open the door. He cowers and churns skulking circles around my ankles, his tail between his legs. He is thin as a ferret, his ribs bulging. The smell of garbage rises off him. One eye oozes yellow pus. A cut on his neck drains freely.

He butts his head between my thighs. His tail wags once. Then he empties his bladder on the kitchen floor.

I wrap my arms around him and weep for joy.

5 PM: It is a good Sunday. We are a family again. Nigel makes French toast. I cook *pintade* with cabbage. We have bathed Gerald and dressed his wounds and are feeding him with a spoon. Eggs. Rice. Broth from the guinea fowl. Cloey lies on the daybed with him, arms wrapped around his bandaged fur. Kate reads them stories.

At lunch Nigel leans toward Kate and says, "Go ahead, a word, any word."

Her eyes light up. She raises an eyebrow and studies the ceiling beam. "Dog!"

"Easy-peasy. Piece of cake. 'Let slip the dogs of war.' Julius Caesar. Emperor of Rome. Or almost was. That one was yours, wasn't it, darling?" He remembers. His hand finds my shoulder.

Cloey scrambles down from his chair. "Toilet time!" he announces.

"Mind you put the seat back down," Nigel calls after him. "Remember what I've shown you now!"

Later Sophie drops by with Ahmad. When she sees Gerald, she falls on her knees and kisses him on his black lips. She wipes her eyes with her fingertips.

We flip crêpes together. She is wearing a turtleneck and knee-length skirt with her combat boots, and her eyebrows have grown back. A working woman now. A teacher.

"It's not so easy coping with twenty-five children." She tosses a crêpe in the air and catches it in the pan. "Two children and a dog are already too much! But this work is only temporary. I've registered to go back to the *faculté*."

"What will you study?" I am holding Cloey on my hip. His hand lies on the nape of my neck and strokes. His thumb is in his mouth.

She flips a crêpe and smiles. "Child psychology."

Friday, November 7, 11 AM: The children are home for the Toussaints vacation and I am trying to write *La Vie en France, Level Three*. Gerald and Cloey are barking under the dining table. Kate is whooping and beating them back with a broom. There is no door, no curtain to pull, no ladder to descend. I am in a bubble. I write.

The French set great store by family life, much of it focused around the dinner table. Every Sunday families gather for a midday meal of several courses, sharing home-cooked food and discussing the week's events. These meals can last for hours, providing food for the soul as well as the body.

Pascal: Qu'est-ce qu'on mange aujourd'hui, chérie?
    What are we having to eat today, dear?
Francine: J'ai fait de l'agneau en daube.
    I made lamb stew.
Pascal: J'adore l'agneau en daube.
    I love lamb stew.
Francine: D'abord il y a des huîtres.
    First there are oysters.
Pascal: Mm. Tu te rappelles?
    Mm. You remember?
Francine: Mm. Arrête! Tu peux aller me chercher des carottes du potager?
    Mm. Stop! Could you get me some carrots from the vegetable patch?
Pascal: Oui, chérie. J'emmenerai les gosses avec moi. Ils aiment bien patauger dans le jardin.
    Yes, dear. I'll bring the kids with me. They love to slog around in the garden.
Francine: Et donne quelques carottes aux chevaux en passant!
    And give some carrots to the horses on your way!
Pascal: D'accord, mon amour. Et je vais aller chercher une des nouvelles bouteilles à la cave pour qu'on la déguste. Un '06, celui des vignes qu'on a plantées.
    Okay, my love. And then I'll bring up one of our new wines from the cellar to taste. An '06, from the vines we planted.
Francine: Pas trop pour moi! Tu sais que ce n'est pas bon de boire quand on attend un enfant.

> Not too much for me! You know it's not good to drink when you're expecting a baby.
>
> *Pascal: Tu as raison. Mais il apprendra à apprécier le bon vin plus tard.*
>
> You're right. But he'll learn to appreciate a good wine later.
>
> *Francine: Tiens, j'avais oublié. On a reçu de nouvelles photos pour les archives de Vichy. Je les ai toutes scannées hier.*
>
> Say, I forgot. We got some new photos for the Vichy archives. I scanned them all yesterday.

I select and highlight the whole story in blue. It shimmers and flickers on the screen, ethereal. I gaze at it a while, my heart squeezing and swelling. I take a deep breath. Then I tap Backspace and it's gone forever.

Tuesday, November 11, 11 AM: Even Nigel comes to the Armistice Day ceremony this year. We walk as a family with the citizens of Dampierre, a somber procession from the dank Baroque church to the memorial, an obelisk of blackened sandstone. Thierry and Nadine kiss our cheeks, and Hervé and Giselle, and Nicolas and Fabienne. The children break free and run to join their schoolmates. The mayor lays a tricolor wreath at the base of the nameplate that runs long with names of the dead. The firemen salute with white gloves. When the children sing the Marseillaise, tears bathe my cheeks. They're good tears.

Nigel lays his hand on my shoulder and pats. I blow my nose and smile at him.

Midnight: I am working in the faceted bubble, my hunched form reflected in multiples all around me. It's the only time I can concentrate in here, when the darkness closes in on me as it used to down in my bunker. Rain sluices over the glass, the panes misted with steam. Nigel's snores drift down the stairwell. He stumbled in late tonight. Watching rugby with Nicolas, he said, then a "glass" or two at the café with *les gars.* The boys.

There is an e-mail from Nikos. I haven't heard back from him about the new text. He has been terse with me lately. I don't blame him. Still, he was happy to get copy, any copy, even if it was three months late.

I click on it.

re: Taste of History
à: meg parker à: jjchabrol

Great stuff. you guys have got something here. worth the wait (!)
Recipes great idea. didn't know food could be so sexy. may have to run
that oyster shot as a centerfold ;-) history tie-ins good, much more or-
ganic. Saved my derriere with publisher. Just doubled first print run.
Pretty sure there'll be more.
Now, are you ready for this? we're talking rematch/sequel! Taste of
History II. More food, more recipes, more history. include paris for
sure. plus bordeaux? alsace? loire? riviera? maybe that route napo-
leon you didn't work into the first one? I can pay you what you're
worth this time.
So, you two. Are you ready for another round?
    —nikos

I stare. My heart is pounding.
are you ready for another round
The new phone rings. My hand is on the white plastic curve before the
first breet ends. I lift it slowly to my ear.
"Mayg."
My breath pulls in despite myself. My fingers cover my mouth.
"Hi." I am whispering.
"You got Nikos' e-mail?"
"Yes." I have forgotten how to breathe.
There is a long silence.
are you ready
I hear the click of a lighter.
My eyes close.
i am ready

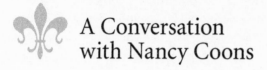

A Conversation
with Nancy Coons

The book opens with the novel's heroine, Meg, writing in her "bunker," which is described in such affectionate detail. Do you write in a similar space in your house in France?

Meg's office is an uncomfortable hole-in-the-ground where she surrounds herself with beloved, resonant objects. My own home office is relatively luxurious but serves the same purpose. It is a place off the back of the house where I "escape" my turbulent family life and listen to the voices in my head. There are a few story seeds around me—a pith helmet from the Belgian Congo, some scraps of barbed wire from the Maginot Line, a tinfoil crown from when I read Katharine in a *Henry V* scene for a British Embassy soirée—but my bunker lies comfortably above ground and my windows look out over old fruit trees and a boxwood-lined rose garden. I work in here every day, though I occasionally tuck a printed manuscript under my arm and drive into town to read and revise in a sidewalk café, watching all the J-Js smoke.

When I am really in the heat of creation—a few chapters rolling, a story that will not be paused—I go on the road and rent a *gîte* or borrow a friend's house in even deeper country. There, I go on a writing rampage—middle-of-the-night reworks, dawn walks, so tuned in to my characters that they take over the story completely and there's nothing left for me but to transcribe their dictation. Sometimes I can't wait to hear what happens next.

Have you been to the places you write about?

I got to know most of the places while researching travel/guide books. I always ended up digging up ten times more information than ever made it into print, and it all came bubbling out in these pages. Then, as I worked on the novel, I went back and dug some more. I have hiked and ridden a Jeep up to the Vallée des Merveilles pictographs, winced through Arles bullfights, observed horse shows (and horse sex) at the *haras* in Cluny, walked Pardon processions in Brittany, brooded on Omaha Beach, "felt the feeling" on the fields of Agincourt. I kept a safe distance from the Gypsies at Stes-Maries-de-la-Mer, as a seasoned local warned me away from penetrating the mob, and my photographer/ colleague didn't want to shoot from the seething waterfront. And there really is a stone hut at the crossroads of the Valley of Marvels and the Valley of the Damned in the Mercantour National Park... I never would have dared make that up!

The only fictional site in the book is Dampierre-lès-Vaucouleurs, Meg's village, just up the pollard-lined road from the very real market town of Vaucouleurs. I thought Meg needed a space of her own, and that she would have chosen to live near the birthplace of Joan of Arc.

Meg is an American living in France, her husband is British, and you've created a French romantic partner for her in Jean-Jacques. What's behind this assignation of nationalities? Could Nigel have been American? Could J-J have been anything other than French?

Neither Nigel nor J-J carry the flag for their countries (despite their confrontation at Agincourt!). Still, an ancient rivalry between the British and the French does exist, and because I have close friends in both circles I witness the love/hate firsthand. Much about Nigel grows from old cultural hang-ups one still finds dragging about the ankles of some hard-core Brits, and there is a tight-knit Brit bubble of expatriate "colonials" that frequent one anothers' French homes in the Dordogne and Perigord, Brittany and Burgundy, sipping G & Ts and dissing the tiresome French. (My own inner circle of Brits are multilingual Francophiles, I hasten to add.) There are American expat pockets in this vein, too: an American Nigel might have quoted old movies and had Louis XV armoires sawed apart to conceal plasma televisions.

It's hard to imagine J-J as another nationality; his culture is so deeply allied with Meg's longings, and he, too, carries baggage—a comfortable contempt for Americans, a sad discomfort with twentieth-century history, and a shameless obsession with food and wine. If we tossed American stereotypes into the salad, say, Meg's wistful repression, insecurity, overcompensation, and—dare I?—militarism, I thought it made a multicultural mix that, seasoned with the characters' individual and varied quirks, catalyzed a love triangle.

Next time around maybe I'll write an insipid, imperious, patronizing Frenchman and a smoldering, earthy Brit! I know plenty of both.

Speaking of an obsession with food and wine, reading your book makes me hungry! What would you consider the best thing to nibble on while reading *The Feasting Season*?

Hmm. Oysters would drip on the pages, and *brandade* would smear. Prop up the book with an *omelette aux cèpes* and a glass of Cahors, maybe? Believe it or not, I lost twenty pounds while writing this book!

Which brings me to the title, *The Feasting Season*. Was that your original title for your novel?

Actually, the original title was *Histoires,* but there was a fear that it wouldn't mean anything to American readers. *Histoire* is a French word for "story," and it can mean many things; it can refer to history, lies, hassles, and even sexual affairs—deliciously multifaceted for a title but not easy to pronounce. Stories are what the book is all about, both the legends and battles that Meg pursues, and the dark and all-too-recent story of Jean-Jacques' family. It seems that each time Meg gets near pinning down the history of France she loves so much, the true story gets in the way—whether it's the vibrant traditions that define J-J's world or the ugliness that colors his past.

There are lies, too. Not only does Meg learn to lie to her husband, but she lies to herself when she thinks she can live parallel lives—a home life, a lover—and then keep the door closed on her heart when J-J begins to want more.

Where did the character of J-J come from? All imagination, or . . .

Writers and photographers are always thrown together, and I have spent a lot of road time one-on-one with some very strong personalities behind the lens. There's a natural buddy-movie ambiance in careening down European highways with a trunk full of photo equipment heading for castles and wine caves and olive pressings and whale watches, all while trying to navigate and decide when to stop for lunch. Photographers are always making me pull the rental car over to take pictures of something that has nothing to do with the story, they are always talking on their cell phone when the real shot comes along, and they always try to get me to carry their equipment. They also patiently (or not) put up with my amateur "suggestions" for angles, styling, and subject, then (quite rightly) take another picture altogether.

J-J also comes from the world of food and wine, and there's just something about a Frenchman in those fields—a natural, masculine sensuality and grace, an earthy poetry, at ease with the physical, with men and women—that lends itself to a romantic theme. And J-J's upper-crust childhood combines with his bohemian rebellion to make him straddle two of the most colorful, folkloric aspects of French society.

So, in answer to your question: all imagination . . . alas.

[Spoiler Alert: The next question and answer reveal a turning point in the plot of the novel.] **For a long time Meg doesn't believe that J-J really loves her, but finally—at the *gîte*—she seems to know that their love is real. And yet she chooses to return to Nigel anyway. Why does Meg go home at this point?**

I never meant for Meg and J-J to fall in love. In early sketches for the novel, they had an intense affair and learned a lot about themselves, but they snapped out of it and Meg returned, chastened, to her also-chastened husband. With this in mind, I held the narrator's reins tightly until they got to Brittany, when the lovers jumped the traces and bolted off into a reality of their own.

Still, I do think Meg tried to compartmentalize her growing feelings for J-J as an *histoire*—just a romantic story or affair—and, like most of her historical pursuits, she got it wrong. When she acknowledges just how "real" it is, she's faced with an agonizing choice. Clearly, she believes in Home, Marriage, and Family. (I suspect Meg of being something of a closet Catholic . . . her grandmother Marguerite's influence? Notre Dame U.?) Her lopsided relationship with Nigel still had some foundation in affection and charm, and any strength she was trying to muster to unmake the marriage responsibly—as opposed to simply running away—was continually undermined by Nigel's eloquent remorse and efforts at reform. Right up to the last pages, when she writes her last dreamy *La Vie en France* fantasy, Meg is trying to erase her own Happy Ending in order to do the right thing.

Do you have a favorite character in the book?

Gerald. He is Meg's kindred spirit and counterpart. Like Meg, he confuses food and sex; like Meg, he tries too hard and gets it wrong. He is so acutely, adoringly tuned in to her that he ultimately betrays her with his sensitive nose.

This is your first novel. Was the process of writing it different from your travel and food writing?

I found my first experiments in fiction writing to be a surprisingly silent experience. As a journalist, you surround yourself with a lot of "noise"—notes, interviews, photographs, phone calls, research materials—and scramble from fact to fact, transcribing reality. Facing the screen with a story in my head, there was nothing to do but listen. I sat unnervingly still, staring out the window, then hammered away. Kind of spooky, like channeling voices from another world.

Then it gets noisy again: sharing the results with others is an agonizing next step. You want nobody to see it, and everybody to see it. Accepting feedback—on continuity, credibility, motivation, subtext, form—was an important part of the learning process. In fact, I became obsessed, and found I could think and talk of little else, exhausting friends and colleagues. This obsession finally found relief in writing again. A new *histoire*.

370 ✿ A Conversation with Nancy Coons

A new *histoire*?

This time, Jean-Jacques tells his own story. For better or for worse, there's a new woman in his life—his mother, Jacqueline. Jean-Jacques returns to winemaking in the Médoc and finds himself shadowboxing with the past, coming to terms with the complexities of righteous hate and reluctant love. If the first book was all about food, this one is all about wine. I did a lot of pleasant research.

And Meg?

Stay tuned!